BEYOND
THE
POINT

ALSO BY DAMIEN BOYD

BEYOND THE POINT

DAMIEN BOYD

THOMAS & MERCER

Published by Thomas & Mercer, Seattle

www.apub.com

Amazon, the Amazon logo, and Thomas & Mercer are trademarks of Amazon.com, Inc., or its affiliates.

ISBN-13: 9781542093293
ISBN-10: 1542093295

Cover design by @blacksheep-uk.com

Printed in the United States of America

For David and Clare

Prologue

Half the bottle. Then attach the hose.

Better switch the engine off too. He frowned. *Maybe he should have filled up with petrol on the way just to be on the safe side. Still, it shouldn't take long.* He checked the fuel gauge as the engine died, the needle dropping back from the right side of empty. *Yes, there'd be more than enough to do the job.*

He glanced down at the hosepipe coiled up on the green leather passenger seat.

Where's the bloody tape gone?

He leaned forward and felt around the passenger footwell in the darkness. Nothing. *It must have rolled under the seat.*

Sod it.

Leaning across the gear stick now, his right arm thrust under the passenger seat.

There it is!

The last of the masking tape, left over from when he decorated her bedroom. He smiled. *Pink paint and Barbie wallpaper behind her cot. She'll love it. Shame he won't be there when she arrives.*

He always said he'd never miss the birth of his child.

And she hadn't even got a name yet.

Gripping the steering wheel tight now, his chest heaving as he gasped for air between the sobs, the waves lapping at the base of the sea wall by the time his breathing slowed.

He wondered if she would ever forgive him.

Maybe one day. When she was a bit older, she might understand.

He wiped away the tears with the palm of his hand, twisted the cap off the bottle and took a swig. He grimaced, swallowing hard.

Why rum? You don't even like the bloody stuff.

'I thought it might make a nice change,' he said, aloud and to himself, watching the rain running down the windscreen.

Another swig; another grimace.

The lights on the old bridge twinkled in the distance away to his right, a few miles upstream: streetlights along the road; red lights on the towers marking them out for low flying aircraft. Lighting on the suspension cables too.

Movement in the yard behind his car – craning his neck to watch in the passenger wing mirror – a shaft of light from a hut door, then it was gone. He leaned forward and followed the hi-vis jacket across the compound to the Portaloos.

Then back again. Running this time. Must be watching the football.

They'd never hear his engine. Not tonight.

He looked up at the lights on the underside of the concrete viaduct above the compound and followed them as they stretched away into the distance, bright spot lamps on a platform illuminating workers fixing the monorail track, the best part of a mile away. And not even halfway across.

Months behind schedule too; the bridge was due to open in six weeks.

The streetlights were already in place right the way across to Wales, with red lights marking out the tops of the towers here too. Nobody knew about the monorail anyway and the crossing could open to traffic on time. He wondered if anyone would tell the Prince he was opening an unfinished bridge.

'*I won't be around for that either,*' *he muttered, letting out a long sigh – almost relieved it was not going to be his problem anymore.*

The tide was in, just as it had been the day his world had come crashing down around him.

'*It wasn't my fault!*' *he screamed, his fists pummelling the steering wheel in a flurry of punches, the blows slowing as the tears began to fall. Again.*

He leaned back in the driver's seat and closed his eyes, feeling the warm glow of the alcohol pumping through his veins. Strong stuff, rum, particularly when you're not used to it.

His head was tipped right back, and it was starting to spin. It felt heavy and that was just the alcohol.

Wait until the carbon monoxide kicks in.

Shame there were no headrests. Still, it was a nice car. Beautifully restored too and she'd loved it – the wedding anniversary present he'd always promised her. A 1969 British racing green MGB Roadster with chrome bumpers and wire wheels. The polished walnut steering wheel was a highlight too.

He unhooked the air freshener from the rear view mirror, wound down the window and threw it out into the darkness.

'*Won't be needing that.*'

Then he slid an envelope out of his jacket pocket and placed it gently on the dashboard.

'*I'm sorry, darling. I just can't stay.*'

He waited for the tears to dry on his cheeks. Another swig; then fix the hose. He'd fail a breathalyser if it came to it – there was no going back now.

'*I wonder if the soft top is airtight?*'

Only one way to find out.

He climbed out into the rain, steadying himself on the driver's door. Then he leaned back in and picked up the hose and masking tape.

Push the hose up the exhaust pipe and tape it in place. Simple.

'*I wonder if she'll keep the car after this?*'

The streetlights on the viaduct glinted on the stainless steel exhaust; an expensive upgrade, that one, but worth it.

No catalytic converter too. It should be over in seconds; a few breaths and he'd be unconscious. Asleep before he finished the rum. Now, that would be a relief.

Hosepipe through the window and taped in place, he sat down in the driver's seat and closed the door. Then he put on his seatbelt.

'What did you do that for? You're not going anywhere.' He shook his head.

'Some music too, I think.' He pushed the cassette into the machine and turned up the volume.

'A little Pink Floyd. "Wish You Were Here".'

Maybe not.

Then he turned the key.

Chapter One

Agony. That was the right word. Pain didn't come close to describing it.

'This may sting a bit,' the nurse had said.

Bollocks.

Detective Inspector Nick Dixon leaned back in his chair, his eyes clamped tight shut, the tears streaming down his cheeks.

'Don't be so wet.'

'Whatever happened to tea and sympathy?' he mumbled.

'Don't look at me. I'm just the chauffeur.' Detective Sergeant Jane Winter was sitting next to him in the diabetic centre at Musgrove Park Hospital, leafing through a copy of *Somerset Life*. She'd checked the society pages for anyone on the wanted list and was now looking at country houses they couldn't afford.

Dixon tried to open his eyes and focus on the BBC News, the TV mounted on the wall on the other side of the waiting area. The spelling mistakes in the automated subtitles had been keeping him amused while he waited for his retinal screening appointment. Being diabetic was a pain sometimes – in the eyes and the arse.

'I can't see a bloody thing.' He shook his head, sending a mixture of tears and eye drops on to Jane's magazine. 'I really haven't got time—'

'Make the time. Besides, you're here now.'

'Being stabbed wasn't as bad as this.' He rubbed his left shoulder with the palm of his right hand. He still felt the occasional twinge, but then it had been only six months ago. A fish filleting knife. Nice.

Jane closed the magazine and dropped it on to the pile on the table next to her, casually picking up another. 'What about your burns?'

Dixon squinted at the palms of his hands. 'You're right, that was grim.'

'Is it like this every year?'

'I had it done at Kingston last time. They must use a local anaesthetic or something.'

'If you ask, they might give you a general.'

'Are you taking the piss?'

'Yes.' Jane smiled as she fumbled in her handbag for a packet of tissues. 'Here,' she said, pressing a couple into Dixon's hand. 'Use these.'

'Thanks.'

'Hang on a minute.' She sat bolt upright, dropping the magazine on to Dixon's lap. 'It's on the news.'

He tried to focus on the television opposite, the glare from the strip lights on the ceiling proving too much for him now that the drops were taking effect. 'What does it say?' he asked, burying his face in the bundle of tissues.

'There's someone outside Express Park, standing under a brolly – must've been this morning, it wasn't raining when we left,' replied Jane. 'Er, "the massive manhunt goes into its forty-second delay".' She frowned. 'I think they mean "day".'

'Are you sure?'

'I'm reading the subtitles.'

'Anything else?'

'"Wanted in connection with four murders and the recent abduction of two children . . ."' Jane paused, waiting for the subtitles to catch up. '"Hijacked a police patrol car at knifepoint and fled the scene of" – they keep mentioning it was a police car and it makes us look a right bunch of idiots – "last seen in the Chippenham area . . . believed to be armed and dangerous . . . not to be approached" etcetera, etcetera. They're using the photofit you had done with the beard and hair. It's switched to the weather now.'

'He's gone to ground somewhere. The whole thing was meticulously planned, remember.' Dixon shifted in his seat, the tissues still clamped across his eyes. 'How long's it been?'

'Forty-two days.'

'Since they put the drops in.'

'Oh.' Jane looked at her watch. 'About twenty minutes, which means you can't drive until after six o'clock.'

Dixon sighed. 'The stinging's eased off a bit, but it's the glare.'

'Let me see.'

He opened his eyes and turned to face Jane, blinking furiously. 'I did bring my sunglasses, didn't I?'

'I've got them in my handbag.' Jane winced. 'Your pupils are all dilated, like you've been smoking cannabis.'

'I wish I had.'

'What are they looking for anyway?'

'Bulges in the tiny blood vessels at the back of the eye. If one bursts, you get a retinal bleed and go blind. Diabetic retinopathy they call it.'

'And if they find one?'

'They zap it with a laser.'

'Sounds horrible. Have you had it done?'

'Always been lucky up to now,' he replied, rubbing his eyes.

'Nicholas Dixon.' He looked up to find a nurse standing over him with a clipboard. 'How are they?'

'Fine.'

Jane coughed. Loudly.

'Like that, is it?' said the nurse, smirking. 'You're driving, I take it?' she asked, smiling at Jane.

'Yes.' She rattled a set of keys on a Land Rover keyring.

'Good, well, follow me, Nicholas. Or are you Nick?'

'Nick's fine,' replied Dixon, following her blurred outline along the brightly lit corridor, more strip lights overhead and sun streaming in through the windows.

'You've had this done before?'

'Several times. I moved down from London last year. They use anaesthetic eye drops up there,' he muttered.

'Do they?' The nurse stopped by an open door. 'That's nice.'

It had seemed like a good idea at the time. A chance to shine.

'A chance to get yourself killed, more like,' Lee had said, watching her wriggle into the red fleece top, holding the cuffs on her shirt to stop the sleeves riding up.

She peered into the darkness, hoping her eyes would adjust to the gloom, although taking her sunglasses off might help. She glanced down at the Royal Mail logo on the fleece as she slid her fake Ray-Bans into the pocket.

What were you thinking of?

Police Community Support Officer Sharon Cox looked over her shoulder at the patrol car blocking the narrow lane, and behind that a Royal Mail van, with the postie in his shirtsleeves sheltering from the wind, peering at her from behind the steering wheel.

Cold on Exmoor, even in mid-May.

Then she heard the central locking on the van. Locked himself in – nice touch, that.

An elderly lady, not seen for a few weeks. Sharon frowned. The old bird had probably had a fall, or a stroke or something. There'd be a sensible explanation for it, there always was. It was a lot of fuss about nothing and that wasn't about to change just because some hotshot detective inspector thought a serial killer was holed up in the area.

West Somerset is a big place . . .

Isn't it?

'Are you going down there or not?' asked PCSO Lee Morgan, standing behind the patrol car. Hiding actually, thought Sharon.

'You could come with me.'

'I said we should call it in, remember? We were told to call in anything unusual and wait for Armed Response.'

'It's hardly unusual. And you don't call Armed Response for a welfare check,' replied Sharon. 'Anyway, I'm just going to have a look, that's all.' She held up a piece of junk mail the intended recipient wouldn't miss. 'Delivering this.'

'She collects her post from Withypool. You heard what he said,' replied Lee, gesturing to the Royal Mail van, the postie watching them intently from the safety of the driver's seat; belt on, engine idling, ready for a quick getaway.

'If anyone sees me, I'll leg it, all right?' Sharon turned back to the rutted track, which shelved away steeply from the lane, with high banks on either side and overgrown willow hedges on top that met in the middle, bent almost flat by the prevailing wind. The odd shaft of light penetrated the darkness through the canopy. If she'd been driving, she'd have flicked her headlights to full beam, not that you'd get a vehicle down it. A tank, perhaps, but not a car.

She followed the track down, stepping over the ruts, the only sound the crunching of the gravel beneath her feet – in the few places it hadn't been washed away by the winter rains – and the occasional jet high overhead, the vapour trails just visible through the hedge above her.

I wish I was on it. Even if I do end up at bloody Gatwick.

The shaft of light at the bottom of the track grew larger as she approached, avoiding what little gravel there was, moving silently in the shadows when she could, every now and then stopping to listen: the wind rustling the fresh green leaves, another jet high in the sky. And buzzing.

What the hell was that buzzing? And why was it getting louder?

She stopped at the bottom of the track, still in the shadows, and watched the old farm cottage. No smoke coming from the chimney; no lights on; upstairs curtains drawn.

The large wisteria was in flower; holding the cottage up too, by the looks of things.

Two stables on the right were empty, the doors standing open; a barn to the left, the doors closed.

Sharon slid on her sunglasses as she walked across the yard to the front door of the cottage, past a water pump covered in cobwebs. Then she pushed the envelope through the letterbox. A quick glance through the windows on either side. Nothing.

A deep breath, then she followed the path around to the back.

'Mrs Boswell?'

The lawn hadn't been mowed for a while. The kitchen was deserted too; the back door locked.

'Mrs Boswell?' Louder this time.

Silence.

Apart from the buzzing.

The few bees on the wisteria couldn't account for that, could they?

She continued along the path around the back of the cottage, towards the barn. Several bird seed feeders were hanging in the apple trees, all of them empty. The chicken coop was empty too, but there was still food on the ground. Maybe a fox had got them?

The buzzing grew louder as she approached the barn. Red brick, the slate roof full of holes, the hayloft open; the buzzing definitely louder.

Sharon recognised the smell. It was a bit early for rapeseed, surely?

That smells like death too.

Then she opened the barn door.

Dixon peered into the darkness, the only light coming from the far corner of the room, where a figure was hunched over in front of a computer screen.

'You missed your retinal screening last year,' said the technician, frowning at him over a pair of reading glasses perched on the end of his nose.

'Did I?'

'My name's Arnie.' The technician spun round on his swivel chair. 'When did you last have your eyes looked at?'

'Must be two years ago then, if I missed last year.'

'No problems?'

'None.'

'Well, we've got a new optical coherence tomography machine, so we'll soon see, if you'll pardon the pun.' He pushed himself across the floor on his swivel chair until he was behind the machine. Then he reached round and tapped the chin rest. 'Usual drill. Sit down and put your chin on here; look straight ahead and try not to blink.'

Dixon did as he was told.

'There'll be a flash when the cam—'

'Sorry,' said Dixon, leaning back in his chair. 'I've got to take this.' His phone was buzzing as he slid it out of his jacket pocket.

'That's supposed to be switched off,' muttered Arnie.

'What is it, Louise?' asked Dixon, his phone pressed to his ear.

'We've got something over at Billingford, Sir. It's on Exmoor, just west of Withypool – remote with a capital "R". One of the local PCSOs went in on foot, dressed as a postie. It's not a pretty sight, apparently. IC1 female, approximately eighty years of age.'

'What about the ears?'

'Knitting needles. He left them in this time.'

'How long?'

'At least a couple of weeks, according to uniform.'

Dixon gritted his teeth. 'Any sign of Steiner?'

'No, Sir.'

'Where are you?'

'Express Park. Dave and Mark are on their way up there now. Scientific are en route too.'

'What about Roger Poland?'

'He said he was conflicted – personal involvement and all that – so he's sent the junior pathologist, somebody Davidson.'

'All right. See what you can find out about the victim,' replied Dixon. 'I'm leaving now.' He rang off and slid his phone back into his pocket.

'You're a police officer?' asked Arnie.

'Afraid so.'

'On the team looking for Steiner?'

'Leading the team looking for Steiner.' Dixon stood up. 'The Somerset end of it anyway.'

'Is there a Somerset end? It said on the news he was in Wiltshire.'

'I really can't—'

'Of course you can't. Sorry. I hope you get him.'

'We will.'

'Look, this'll only take two minutes,' said Arnie, gesturing to the OCT machine and shrugging his shoulders. 'Either that or you can come back some other time. It'll mean having the eye drops again though.'

Chapter Two

'How was it?' asked Jane, handing Dixon his sunglasses.

'I haven't had so much fun since I had my wisdom teeth out,' he muttered.

'Where to now? I've got the afternoon off.'

'Louise rang.' Dixon threw the bundle of tissues into a bin by the door. 'Looks like Steiner's been holed up on Exmoor. We've got another body.'

'That makes five then.'

'That we know about.'

A large white Staffordshire terrier was standing on the driver's seat of Dixon's Land Rover with his front paws up on the steering wheel. 'What shall we do with *him*?' asked Jane, as they walked across the car park.

'Monty can come. We haven't got time to drop him home anyway.'

Jane pushed the dog into the back of the Land Rover, then leaned across and opened the passenger door.

'Take the Wiveliscombe road, then head for Dulverton,' said Dixon. 'It's somewhere west of Withypool, but I'll ring Louise and get directions when we get there.'

'You were right then?' asked Jane, turning out of the car park. 'Last seen in Chippenham forty-two days ago and he's been here all the time.'

'We don't know that.'

'Stands to reason, if you ask me. Especially after you found his half-sister living in Cannington. And to think Charlesworth wanted to stop the surveillance on her.' Jane sneered. 'Dickhead.'

Harsh, perhaps. But Jane was right all the same. It had been a battle with the Assistant Chief Constable to keep the surveillance going this long, let alone to get the search focused on West Somerset in the first place. 'He'll be in Wiltshire somewhere' had been a favourite, or better still 'let the Wiltshire force pick up the sodding bill. After all, it was their fault he got away.' That was a belter, that one. Charlesworth had been on top form that day.

The Major Investigation Team had gradually shrunk in the days since the hunt for the missing girls had wound down. Detective Chief Superintendent Potter and her team had returned to Portishead three weeks ago, and the Bristol lot before that, leaving Dixon in charge of a much reduced MIT.

'It's a manhunt, which is uniform's job, not CID.' That gem had come from Detective Chief Inspector Chard, a thorn in Dixon's side since the investigation in the school in Taunton. Still, he was back at Portishead now too; safely out of the way and, more importantly, out of Dixon's hair.

Twat.

'How d'you reckon Steiner got here?' asked Jane.

'Back of his sister's car, I expect. It was a week before we found her and put the surveillance in place.'

'You'd think she'd be turning him in, not helping him stay on the run.' Jane accelerated past a set of temporary traffic lights, catching up with the back of the queue filing through the roadworks. 'He's murdered five people and kidnapped two children.'

'We don't know she is helping him,' replied Dixon.

'She must be.'

Steiner was smart, Dixon knew that. He'd had plenty of time to prepare before he'd snatched the girls, and his plan would have included his escape; vehicles, cash, mobile phones. 'If she did pick him up from Chippenham, it would've been before she knew what he'd been up to. There was a news blackout, don't forget.'

'And when she finds out, she abandons him. Is that what you're saying?'

'It might explain why the surveillance has drawn a blank.'

'Maybe they know we're watching?'

They spent the rest of the drive in silence, Dixon occasionally holding his phone up and moving it from side to side, looking for a signal. They were climbing west out of Dulverton, open moorland stretching away in the distance, before he spoke again.

'Here we go. Pull in here and I'll ring Louise.'

'We should've turned left at the bottom of the hill,' said Dixon. He plugged his phone into the charging cable that was dangling in the passenger footwell. 'The easiest way in is via Hawkridge, apparently.'

Jane restarted the engine and began to turn the Land Rover in a field gateway.

'There's a roadblock just beyond the village and they can give us directions from there.'

The Hawkridge roadblock consisted of a patrol car sideways across the lane. 'Stay on this road for about a mile, Sir,' the uniformed officer said. 'There's a patrol car blocking the lane to the cottage. Parking's in the field opposite. Well, I say field – there's a gap in the drystone wall and you'll be on the moor. You'll be fine in this old bus though. You can't miss it.'

Jane sped off before Dixon could draw breath.

The road beyond was narrow, the wing mirrors flicking leaves in the willow hedges on either side. A vibrant lime green, just like the highlighter pen on Jane's desk, he thought. That was one advantage of the Safeguarding Unit: there was no 'hot-desking' in an open plan office for her.

His eyes were beginning to calm down a bit too. Sunglasses were still a must, although the shade from the high hedges was helping.

'He called this a road,' said Jane.

'Maybe he's an optimist?'

'Can't have been on the job long then.'

The lane opened out on the climb up to Halscombe Allotment, Dixon squinting at the view across to Withypool Common: drystone walls, lush green fields, a herd of ponies sheltering under a solitary tree. And heather, lots of heather.

'There's the helicopter,' said Jane, pointing up to the right.

'Who the bloody hell—?' Dixon snatched his phone off the dashboard. 'The helicopter's here, Louise. Who authorised that?'

'The Assistant Chief Constable, Sir.'

'Well, get rid of it.'

Silence.

'This was supposed to be low profile, Lou. We might just as well put up a neon sign telling Steiner we've found the body.'

'Yes, Sir.'

'And get on to the press officer and make sure there's a news blackout.'

'Anything else?'

'Get Control to put out an All Units – no bloody sirens.'

'Yes, Sir.'

'What is wrong with people?' muttered Dixon, jabbing the red button to disconnect the call.

'Just following protocol,' replied Jane.

'She's been dead for weeks, which means Steiner could be miles away by now anyway. But if he's not, do we really want to tell him we know he's here?'

'I suppose not.'

'Of course not,' continued Dixon. 'As soon as he knows we're on to him, he'll figure out we've found his sister.'

'Yes, but he knows we'll find this body, surely?'

'Eventually, yes. But there's no need to tell him we've found it just yet, if we can avoid it. With a bit of luck, he still thinks we're looking in and around Chippenham.'

Jane slowed as a police officer walked out into the lane in front of them with his arm raised. A wave of their warrant cards and the officer directed them through a gap in the drystone wall opposite, the Land Rover bouncing over the stones lying between the tufts of marsh grass.

'Roger couldn't help himself, I see,' said Dixon.

Jane parked next to Poland's Volvo estate. An ambulance, three dog vans and two Scientific Services vans completed the car park.

'Inspector Dixon?' asked the uniformed officer.

'And this is Detective Sergeant Winter.'

'Mark Pearce told me to tell you they were dropping down into Withypool to see what they could find out.'

'What've we got then?'

'It's a small cottage, about half a mile down the track. Nice old bird. Mrs Boswell.'

'Did you know her?'

'Yes, Sir. She's lived here all her life. Eighty-two I think she is . . . was, and she still cycled everywhere.' The uniformed officer stepped back out into the lane at the sound of an engine revving. 'When the weather was nice she'd go up and over Porchester's Post and down into Withypool that way. Fit as a fiddle she was.'

'Who raised the alarm?'

'Mr Bales from the shop in Withy. She'd not been in for a few weeks and when he popped up here to check on her there was no sign. Just her dog barking.'

'Where is it now?'

'Mr Bales has got him.'

'Keep an eye on mine, will you?' asked Dixon, squeezing past the patrol car blocking the track down to the cottage.

'Yes, Sir.'

'Where's the PCSO who found her?'

'Gone home, Sir. She was in a bit of a state. Ex-army and she's never seen anything like it.'

'And where's Mrs Boswell?'

'In the barn.' The officer grimaced. 'Why would somebody do that to another human being? I've been on the job twenty years and I've never . . .' His voice tailed off.

'They live sheltered lives, these rural beat coppers,' muttered Dixon.

'You haven't seen her yet,' replied Jane, jumping from one rut to the next.

Dixon stepped to one side to allow an ashen faced uniformed officer to pass. He was heading up the track, his eyes glazed over. His top button was undone and he was carrying his tie, which was dragging in the stinging nettles beside him.

'Are you all right, Constable?'

'I just need some fresh air, Sir.'

'You went in the barn?'

The officer nodded. 'You'll need to watch where you're treading at the bottom, on the left by the gate, I'm afraid I puked up.'

Dixon watched the officer stumble on up the track.

'He looked like death warmed up,' said Jane.

The wind dropped as they followed the track down off the open moorland, the willow hedges above their heads standing upright by the time they reached the bottom, in the shelter of the combe. Dixon winced as the smell of death hit him, the fetid air drifting up the track, released from the barn now the doors were standing open.

Jane turned away and retched.

'Here,' he said, handing her a bundle of scented dog poo bags, before clamping another handful over his own nose and mouth.

'What's that buzzing?' she mumbled.

'Flies.'

They stepped to one side to allow two Scientific Services officers to pass, each carrying two large metal cases. A uniformed officer was following them carrying two spotlights. All of them were wearing masks.

Dixon frowned. 'Are you sure you want to see this?'

'Not really, no,' replied Jane. 'It's not even my case anymore.'

'You could take Monty for a walk?'

'I'll wait outside. It'll be nice to see Roger anyway. Are you sure you want to? You could just read the report.'

'I need to see it. Her. After all, it's my fault she's dead.'

'No, it isn't,' snapped Jane, moving the dog bags away from her mouth before hastily clamping them back in place. 'The Wiltshire lot let him get away. And what was the alternative? Let Hatty drown?'

'I keep thinking—'

'Well, don't.'

Dixon paused in the shadows at the bottom of the track and looked up at the cottage, the render crumbling beneath the windows. The front door was standing open, the light on in the hall illuminating a flagstone floor and a grandfather clock at the bottom of the stairs.

No straw on the floor in the stables on the right – empty hay nets hanging on the bars – the horses long gone, replaced by an old petrol lawn mower and a bicycle in one, bags of chicken feed in the other, the corners torn open by mice. Or rats.

Shafts of light burst from the barn door and the hayloft as the spot lamps were switched on inside. Then the unmistakable figure of Roger Poland appeared, striding across to the pile of metal cases flattening the grass growing between the cobbles in front of the cottage.

'Do you think that pump works?' asked Jane.

'Must do. Where else would she get her water from?'

Dixon watched Poland take a camera from one of the cases and walk back towards the barn. White overalls in size XL – a special order just for Roger, and the legs were still too short; blue latex overshoes and gloves; a white mask over his nose and mouth.

'Got any spare masks, Roger?' shouted Jane, stepping out into the sunlight at the bottom of the track.

'Ah, there you are,' he said, turning around. 'Yes, of course. They're not scented though.'

Was he smiling behind that mask? Dixon couldn't tell.

'I'd skip this one if I were you,' continued Poland. 'It's going to take a while too. We're having to carry everything in from the road.'

'I need to see her,' said Dixon.

'I'll sort you out a set of overalls then, if you must. Don't say I didn't warn you.'

'I thought you were conflicted.'

'I'm here in an advisory capacity. It's Davidson's case and the reports will have his name on them.'

'What about the cottage?' asked Dixon.

'Uniform have checked it's clear and there's another SOCO team on the way to go in. No sign of Steiner. The smell probably got too much for him.'

'Or he ran out of food.'

Poland opened a blue plastic crate and took out a bag. 'Masks in there. I'll get you a set of overalls.'

'Thanks.'

Mask safely on and Dixon had both hands free to put on the overalls. He still had to lean on the water pump though, Jane having followed the track behind the cottage that climbed out of the combe on the far side and up to Porchester's Post. The path had already been checked by uniform but she insisted on doing it again. He knew the real reason though, and could have done with some fresh air himself.

'Give us a few minutes,' Roger had said. 'To do the preliminaries, you know.'

Cottage first then.

Dixon pushed open the front door with his elbow and peered in. Low ceilings, small windows; it was dark even with the light on. The drinks cabinet was open in the dining room on the left; empty apart from an unopened bottle of Croft Original. Otherwise the room was untouched. Still, Steiner was unlikely to have been entertaining.

The living room on the right would be a useful source of DNA. Empty bottles had replaced the wood in the log basket by the fire and the coffee table was covered in dirty plates, knives and forks lying in amongst the chicken bones. The odd empty glass too.

No television explained the copy of *Pride and Prejudice* open on the arm of the sofa. Left in a hurry, perhaps?

Dixon looked at the photographs on the sideboard. A young family somewhere, the child holding a Koala bear; Australia then, or at a zoo possibly, although the postcard on the mantelpiece of the Great Barrier Reef confirmed it. Another of an older lady at a dinner table. He doubted Mrs Boswell would look much like that now.

The smell in the kitchen tested his mask to its limit. It failed, which didn't bode well for the barn.

Chicken feathers on the floor and an empty coop outside the back window – doesn't like sherry and not a vegetarian; an open bag of dog biscuits in the pantry with several bags of bird seed and nuts on the shelf; the fridge empty – solar panels at the bottom of the garden just visible over the long grass explained the power supply.

The stairs creaked beneath the highly patterned red carpet, reminding him there would be an understairs cupboard to check on the way out.

An old enamel bath, heavily stained. No taps – water from the pump it is then.

Steiner had at least had the decency to use the spare bedroom, Mrs Boswell's identifiable only by the clothes in the wardrobe. Spartan, or minimalist they called it these days: an old wooden bed, a dark oak bedside table with an empty jug, a glass and well-thumbed bible. Bare floorboards that creaked, a wardrobe and a dressing table with a mirror and a hairbrush sitting on a piece of old lace stained brown at the edges. The framed etchings on the walls were covered in mould spots too.

There was a rug on the floor in the spare room, in front of a small fireplace still littered with ash. Hospital corners on the bed, just like you learn in prison. Or boarding school. Steiner had done time in both.

Dixon reached up and opened the curtains.

Oh shit.

Chapter Three

Dixon ran out of the front door of the cottage to find another Scientific Services team piling up their equipment by the water pump.

'We need to get that shifted,' he said. 'And shut those doors.'

'Why?' asked Poland, emerging from the barn. 'What's going on?'

'Upstairs window, bottom right hand corner, on the windowsill.' Dixon grimaced. 'There's a webcam.'

'The satellite dish on the back of the stable block,' said Donald Watson. 'I wondered what that was for, seeing as there's no telly.' Dixon recognised the senior Scientific Services officer's frown behind the face mask.

'Sir!' The shout came from a uniformed officer running down the track and out into the sunshine at the bottom.

'What is it?'

'The sister is on the move. She left her house and got in a taxi about ten minutes ago. The surveillance team are following her towards Bridgwater now.'

'Tell them to keep us posted.'

'I'll need to go back up to the road for that. There's no radio signal down here, let alone mobile phone.' The uniformed officer was breathing hard, sweat dripping off the end of his nose.

'Let's get someone from High Tech out here as well.'

'Yes, Sir.'

Dixon turned back to stare up at the webcam.

'That's it then,' said Poland. 'Steiner knows we're here.'

'Looks like it.'

'How often d'you think the picture refreshes?' asked Watson.

'No idea,' replied Dixon. 'The one on Burnham seafront used to update every twenty seconds. Now it's a live feed.'

'Either way, he's seen us then, you're right.' Watson turned towards the front door of the cottage. 'I'll go and cover it with something. Better not switch it off until High Tech get here.'

'Ready for me in the barn?' asked Dixon, turning to Poland.

'Are you sure?'

'Yes, I'm sure.'

'Well, don't say I didn't warn you.'

'So you keep saying.'

Poland handed Dixon a small pot of Vicks VapoRub. 'Here, put a blob of that under your nose.'

'I'll be fine.'

'If I'm not, you won't be,' snapped Poland.

Dixon did as he was told.

'Whatever you're expecting, it's worse. Far worse,' said Poland. 'Brace yourself.'

'Let's just get it over with, shall we?' replied Dixon, replacing his mask over the large blob of Vicks plastered across his face.

The buzzing was louder behind him now, coming from the bees on the wisteria, most of the flies having dispersed across Exmoor when the barn doors had been opened. Some still lingered, flitting about in the light from the spot lamps. A Scientific Services officer was at work

24

photographing the scene, each camera flash preceded by a swat of the hand.

'Bloody flies!'

Dixon took off his sunglasses – no pain despite the glare from the spot lamps; the eye drops must have worn off.

He noticed the rope first, tied to the steering wheel of a ride on mower, and followed it up over the beam and down to Mrs Boswell. Or what had once been Mrs Boswell. He tipped his head, trying to make sense of what he was looking at.

'Five weeks, maybe longer,' said Davidson, recognisable only by his horn-rimmed spectacles.

A summer dress and a cardigan – bits of the dress light blue with small flowers and the cardigan cream possibly, it was difficult to tell – made a stark contrast with her skin. Purple, yellow, black, and all shades in between.

The noose had cut through the flesh of her neck to the bone, tipping her head forward, a small wooden knitting needle sticking out of her left ear. The cable tie binding her hands behind her back was through to the bone too.

'As the body decomposes, the flesh swells and—'

'I know.'

'I'll shut up then,' said Poland.

Dixon looked down at the floor beneath her, a thin layer of straw on the bare earth stained dark red and black.

'The internal organs liquefy and then gravity takes over,' said Davidson, raising his eyebrows. 'The legs swell, the skin ruptures, and you get this on the floor.'

The Scientific Services officer was squatting down, taking photographs. Dixon wasn't quite sure what he was taking photographs of though. It looked like a raspberry jelly that hadn't set properly. Or blackcurrant, perhaps. And it was moving.

25

'You wouldn't want to put one of these maggots under your tongue if you were out fishing on a cold morning,' said the Scientific Services officer, his broad grin visible even behind his mask.

'Get out!' snapped Dixon.

'But—'

'Out.'

The officer turned to Donald Watson, who was behind them, picking up cigarette butts and dropping them in an evidence bag.

'Better do as he says.' Watson shook his head. 'Make a start on the cottage and send Sal in here.'

'What's his name?' asked Dixon when the officer had trudged out of the barn.

'I'll speak to him,' replied Watson.

Dixon turned back to Mrs Boswell.

'Are you all right?' asked Poland.

'Cause of death hanging, I suppose?'

'We won't know for sure until we get her down.'

'What about the knitting needles?'

'Before or after, you mean?'

Dixon nodded.

'We won't know that until we get her down either.'

'Sixteen fag butts,' said Watson, behind them. 'Looks like he sat on this straw bale and watched. Probably came back several times too. You're not going to smoke sixteen cigarettes one after the other, are you?'

Dixon sat down on the bale of straw and looked around the barn. A few bales of dusty hay piled up against the wall behind him; a small tractor that wouldn't have looked out of place in a museum; various garden tools leaning up against a cart, the wheels rotten; mouldy leather tack hanging on nails on the wall and a leather saddle on a rack; all of it covered in a thick layer of dust and bird droppings.

The hayloft was empty, a shiny aluminium ladder leaning up against it, next to a wooden one – rotten, with several slats missing.

He looked up at the body hanging motionless on the end of the rope, the only movement the seething mass of maggots beneath her feet. And a swallow flitting about in the rafters above her head, several nests tucked under the beams.

'Seen enough?' asked Poland.

Dixon stood up. 'I suppose we should be grateful he fed her dog.'

'We should.'

'When you've finished, leave the hayloft open.'

'Why?' asked Watson.

'So the birds can get in and out,' replied Dixon, walking over to the door. 'It's what she would've wanted.'

Dixon stepped out into the sunlight and looked up at the front of the cottage, the webcam now safely covered by an upside down jug. Blue and white. It would end up at a house clearance sale along with the rest of the contents, probably, the cottage sold off by her estate to be turned into a holiday rental. He'd seen enough probate cases before he'd left the legal profession to know the way these things usually went.

A uniformed officer was standing by the water pump with her hands in her pockets, watching the Scientific Services officer photographing the stables.

'What's your name, Constable?' asked Dixon.

'Sarah Paulson, Sir.'

'Do me a favour, will you, Sarah? When SOCO have finished in the cottage, fill the bird feeders. The stuff's in the pantry.'

'Of course, Sir.'

'And I want to know what's happening to her dog.'

'Now, Sir?'

'Yes, now. I'll be in the cottage.'

An old Ewbank floor sweeper and a vacuum cleaner straight out of *Downton Abbey*; an ironing board; shelves along the wall to his right covered in jars full of screws and nails of varying sizes; a tool box on the floor; and an old mangle at the back. It was like going back in time in the cupboard under the stairs, not that Dixon should have expected anything else. He spun round when he heard Jane's voice in the court-yard outside.

'Where's Inspector Dixon?'

'In there.' Constable Paulson's voice, still leaning against the water pump with her hands in her pockets, probably.

'Nick?'

'What's up?' replied Dixon, closing the cupboard door.

'Louise rang. I got a signal on the hill behind the cottage.' Jane was standing in the doorway, her mask around her neck. 'Steiner's sister just walked into reception at Express Park. And she's asking for you.'

Chapter Four

One bar. It would have to do. Dixon stopped near the top of the track and put his phone to his ear.

'Yes, Sir.'

'Where is she?'

'Still sitting in reception,' replied Louise.

'Is there anyone with her?'

'Not that I know of. Hang on.' A clunk as the handset was dropped on to the desk. Footsteps, then the handset snatched up again. 'She's on her own. I can see her from the balcony.'

'Stick her in an interview room and give her a cup of coffee or something. I'm on my way.' Dixon was craning his neck, watching a vapour trail through the willow canopy above his head.

'DCI Lewis is on the prowl.'

'What now?'

'He wants to know what's going on.'

'I spend my entire life wanting to know what's going on. He'll get used to it.'

'And Mark rang from the post office in Withypool. No one's seen anything down there, apparently.'

Dixon sighed. 'Let's go public now, Lou. Get on to the press officer. And I want the helicopter back. House to house in Withypool, Hawkridge, Dulverton and anywhere else you can think of. Arm them with the photofit. Maximum noise, alerting the public, not to be approached, highly dangerous. You know the drill.'

'Yes, Sir.'

'See if you can get hold of Mark again. I want him down at the cottage. Dave can organise the house to house. All right?'

'It may be difficult if they've left the post office. They had no mobile signal.'

Dixon stopped in the shade at the top of the track, his phone still clamped to his left ear. He watched Jane open the back of the Land Rover to let Monty out into the field. 'We'll drop down there on the way back and see if we can see them.'

'What do I tell Lewis?'

'Tell him it's going to get expensive.'

'That's a stroke of luck,' said Jane, screeching to a halt in the middle of the narrow lane. She switched off the engine while Dixon got out to speak to Detective Constables Dave Harding and Mark Pearce, who had pulled into a passing place on the bend.

'House to house coordinator, please, Dave,' said Dixon, before Pearce had finished winding down the window. 'We can drop you back down in Withypool.'

'Yes, Sir.' Harding unclipped his seatbelt and got out of the passenger seat, knocking the door on a tree trunk sticking out of the bank on the nearside.

Pearce glared at him.

'I want you down at the cottage, Mark,' continued Dixon. 'Make sure you wear a mask and Roger's got some Vicks for under your nose.'

'Is it that bad?'

'It is.'

'Are they going to be much longer?'

'Rest of the day, at least. Another SOCO team was arriving when we left.' Dixon was watching Harding climb in the back seat of the Land Rover. 'I want to know immediately if they find anything to indicate anyone else was there. All right?'

'The sister, you mean?'

'Anyone.'

'Yes, Sir.'

Dixon glanced into the back of the Land Rover as he climbed in the passenger seat.

'I think he can smell my cat,' muttered Harding, watching Monty sniffing his trouser leg.

'You should be fine,' said Dixon, winking at Jane. 'Just don't move.'

'Oh.'

'What did the bloke in the post office say?'

'Not a lot, really,' replied Harding, nervously. 'There's a niece in Christchurch.'

'Dorset?'

'New Zealand. They used to Skype each other from time to time and she rang the post office when she couldn't get hold of Mrs Boswell.'

Slate roofs and limewashed walls, some painted cream, some peach, the cottages in the centre of Withypool had a picture postcard feel to them; even the post office and general stores.

'I'll wait here,' said Jane, parking directly outside the shop. 'How long will you be?'

'Five minutes, at most,' replied Dixon.

He went first to the cold cabinet, although the choice of sandwiches was limited. Egg and cress it would have to be. Diet Coke for them and a bottle of water for Monty. He dropped them on the newspapers laid out on the counter. Then he took his warrant card and the photofit of Steiner out of his pocket.

'This is Mr Bales, Sir,' said Harding.

'Have you seen this man?' Dixon asked.

'He just asked me the same thing,' came the reply, with a finger pointed at Harding.

'And what did you say?'

'No, sorry. Not seen him at all.'

'When did Mrs Boswell's niece get in touch with you?'

'Yesterday. Late it was. So, I went straight up there this morning. Her dog was shut in one of the stables, but there was no sign of her. The house was all quiet and locked up. Funny smell too. That's when I rang you lot.'

'What sort of dog is it?'

'He's a retired greyhound. Murphy, he's called. He's asleep in the back. Is she all right, Mrs Boswell?'

'When did she last come in for her post?'

'A while ago. I've got it here,' replied Bales. He reached under the counter and picked up a pile of letters. 'The oldest one's postmark is . . .' – flicking to the bottom of the pile – '. . . five weeks ago.'

'And you didn't think it odd you'd not seen her for all that time?'

'Not really. She gets very little post. Junk mostly, as you can see.' Bales handed the letters to Dixon.

'What about food?'

'She used to go to Dulverton sometimes. Is she all right then?' asked Bales.

'What are you going to do?' asked Dixon, when Jane pulled up outside Express Park.

'I thought I'd take Monty to the beach.'

'Lucky sod.'

'What time d'you want picking up?'

'I'll make my own way home, don't worry,' he replied, leaning across to kiss her.

'No fear.' She recoiled. 'You stink of Vicks.'

'And death.'

'And I don't know how you could eat that sandwich.'

'I had to do my jab.' He shrugged his shoulders. 'Don't you want yours?'

'No,' muttered Jane.

'Well, I'll see you later.' Dixon snatched her sandwich off the dashboard and climbed out of the Land Rover.

He ignored the receptionist's barbed comment about using the staff entrance, but couldn't get past DCI Lewis, who was waiting for him when he stepped out of the lift on the first floor.

'Is it him?'

Dixon nodded.

'There are going to be questions to answer about why we kept his presence here quiet.' Lewis had his hands thrust deep into his pockets. 'You do know that.'

'Firstly, we didn't know for sure he was here.'

'You suspected.'

'And, secondly, she was dead before we made the connection with the sister in Cannington anyway.'

Lewis puffed out his cheeks. 'That's confirmed?' he asked, raising his eyebrows.

'As near as they can at this stage.'

'Thank God for that.' Lewis looked down at his feet. 'You know what I mean,' he mumbled. 'It's my job to make sure your arse is covered.'

'You missed your vocation.'

'Eh?'

'You should've been a proctologist,' replied Dixon, setting off along the landing.

'And what about the overtime budget?' Lewis shouted after him.

'What overtime budget?'

'Ah, there you are, Sir.' Louise was standing in the doorway of the canteen. 'Vicky Thomas is here and she's lined up the Assistant Chief Constable for the press conference. She wants to know if you'll be avail—'

'Tell her to ask DCI Lewis. It needs to be someone more senior anyway.'

'Dave rang. There are teams out in Withypool and Hawkridge so far. More on the way too.'

'Where's the sister?'

'Interview room one.'

Hair dyed purple – interesting; a tattoo on her right shoulder, revealed by a sleeveless T-shirt. Dixon couldn't see what it was a tattoo of though, not on the monitor. Denim dungarees as well.

'What are those on her feet?'

'High-top trainers,' replied Louise. 'Not my cup of tea.'

'Did she say anything when she arrived?'

'No. She just asked to speak to you.'

'Me personally?'

'She asked for you by name.'

'Well, let's see what she wants.'

Once in the interview room, Dixon waited while Louise closed the door before sitting down opposite Steiner's half-sister. She was hunched over, her arms folded tightly across her chest.

'Monique?'

She looked up. Pale skin and dark, sunken eyes; her hair straggly on closer inspection, the purple dye fading to bleached blonde at the roots. Either she had a cold or she'd been snorting something.

'Are you Dixon?' she whispered.

'Detective Inspector Dixon, yes. You've met Detective Constable Willmott, I believe?'

Monique nodded.

'Louise will be taking notes. You're not under arrest and are free to leave at any time. D'you understand?'

'Yes.'

'Now, what can I do for you?'

'I need to tell you about my brother.'

'And what's his name?' Matter of fact.

Monique stared at Dixon, her head tipped to one side. 'You know.'

'Do I?'

'Tony Steiner.'

'So, let me make sure I'm understanding you correctly, Monique. You're saying that you are Tony Steiner's sister.'

'Half-sister.'

'The same Tony Steiner who is wanted for multiple murder and child abduction?'

She nodded.

'All right then.' Dixon leaned back in his chair and folded his arms. 'What d'you want to tell me?'

Monique drained the water from the plastic cup on the table in front of her and began picking at the edge of it with her fingernail. 'He rang me.'

'When?'

'Six weeks ago. He was in money trouble. Someone was after him for a gambling debt – trying to kill him, he said – and could I pick him up from Chippenham? He didn't even have the train fare.'

'Go on.'

'He was hiding in a commercial waste bin behind the Premier Inn.'

'You didn't think that a bit odd?'

'Not really. Tony's had gambling problems before. Anyway, he hid in the boot and I drove home.'

'Which way?'

'He told me to stick to the lanes and we ended up in Wotton-under-Edge. And Badminton, I remember that. Then I got on the M5 somewhere up north and came home. When I stopped on the edge of Cannington he said he needed to find somewhere to hide and told me to drive up to Exmoor. Anyway, when I stopped for petrol at Wheddon Cross he'd gone. He must've got out when I was paying for the fuel.'

'And you've not seen him since?'

'No.'

'When did you find out he was wanted for murder?'

'A couple of days later. I saw his photo on the front page of a newspaper.'

'What was he wearing when you picked him up?'

'A red baseball cap. Black jeans and green coat.'

Dixon reached over and slid Louise's notebook across the table. Then he took his pen out of his jacket pocket and wrote down one word, before sliding it back. He watched her look down.

Rehearsed

Louise nodded.

'When you found out what he'd done – was alleged to have done, I should say – why didn't you contact us then?' continued Dixon.

'He's my brother.'

'Half-brother.'

'That's still family.'

'You share the same father, is that right?'

'His mother died. Well, he was adopted. You do know that, don't you?'

Dixon didn't, but he wasn't going to tell her that. Best poker face. 'Go on.'

'They couldn't have kids, so they adopted him. Then his mum died, his father married my mother and I was born. Actually, I had an older brother, Paul, but he died in his cot.'

'How old was Tony at the time?'

'Eight, ten maybe, something like that.'

'Tell me about Tony's friends.'

'He doesn't have any.'

'He's never mentioned anyone?'

'Not to me. I don't see him much these days though.' Monique looked up.

Time to make her squirm, just a little.

'He stabs his victims in the ears with knitting needles, perforating their eardrums, sometimes through to the bone.'

Monique winced.

'D'you know why that might be?' continued Dixon.

'After Paul died, my father beat him up really badly. I only found out about it years later, but it happened more than once and left him with ear problems. He had to have grommets in for a while. And he's had tinnitus ever since. He's even tried suicide several times. It drives him mad.' Monique's shoulders drooped, her voice tailing off. 'Really loud tinnitus . . .'

Chapter Five

'You let her go?'

'Louise got a detailed statement from her and on the face of it she's done nothing wrong, Sir,' replied Dixon.

'What about assisting an offender?' snapped the Assistant Chief Constable, David Charlesworth – dressed in civvies this time; Dixon wondered whether he'd finished his round of golf before coming in.

Charlesworth was sitting at the head of the table in meeting room 2, with the press officer, Vicky Thomas – blonde bob framing a sharp face, to match the sharp pinstripe suit – to his left, and DCI Lewis to his right.

'She didn't know what he'd done when she picked him up from Chippenham and we can't prove she did.'

'Bollocks.'

'She thought he was running from gambling debts, Sir. And there was a news blackout in place at the time.'

Pennies dropping rarely make a sound, but Dixon could have sworn he heard that one.

'Yes, of course,' muttered Charlesworth. 'I'd forgotten that.'

'What about the surveillance?' asked Lewis.

'It needs to continue, Sir,' replied Dixon. 'Her story was clearly rehearsed, so she may well still be in touch with Steiner.'

Lewis looked at Charlesworth, whose shake of the head morphed into a nod. 'You've got a week, Dixon,' he said.

'Yes, Sir.'

'Find him. And if you can get Armed Response to finish the job, so much the better.'

◆ ◆ ◆

'What'd he say?'

'A week.' Dixon was sucking his teeth.

'A week?' Louise frowned. 'Is that it?'

'For now.'

The CID Area on the first floor was deserted, the printers quiet. Not even the kettle was boiling.

'They're all up on Exmoor, Sir,' said Louise, glancing around at the vacant workstations. 'DCI Lewis has lined up a team of PCSOs to take the calls when the press conference goes out on the evening news. The Incident Room upstairs hasn't been dismantled yet, so they're up there, getting ready.'

'Let's start checking the holiday cottages again,' said Dixon. 'Steiner's moved on, so he's going to be holed up somewhere else, isn't he?'

'Yes, Sir.'

'Uniform can check the empty cottages. And get the agencies to speak to the owners. We're looking for anything out of the ordinary. Start with Exmoor and then expand the area. He'll have been on foot, moving at night, probably, so it's hard to imagine him getting too far.'

'Anything else?'

'Get on to the council and see if they can give us a list of furnished holiday lets registered for business rates. That should bring up those not let through an agency.' Maybe that time spent in the property department when he had been training as a solicitor hadn't been wasted, after all?

'What do we do about second homes that aren't let out?'

Dixon shook his head. 'There's nothing we can do, unless they can tell us which properties have no occupier on the electoral roll. Second homes pay council tax at the full rate these days.'

'I'll try that.'

'And I'll make sure Lewis covers it in the press conference.'

Dixon hated press conferences, watching from a safe distance behind the cameras. Charlesworth had swapped the Pringle sweater for his uniform. At least he hadn't been wearing plus-fours. Lewis seemed to be enjoying the moment though.

They both emphasised the point, although 'laboured' was probably a better word, that Steiner was highly dangerous and should not be approached under any circumstances. And they managed to duck the question about why the public had not been informed that Steiner was at large in the area. Davidson would need to hurry up with that post mortem.

Lewis even remembered the bit about the holiday cottages.

Dixon headed for the door when Charlesworth called for one final question from the gathered journalists, ignoring the iPhone that was thrust under his nose and the whispered question that went with it – something about letting him get away in the first place. Tempting, but now was not the time.

Dave Harding and Mark Pearce were back from Exmoor by the time Dixon made it up to the CID Area, both leaning against Louise's workstation, waiting for the kettle to boil.

Harding had hung his grey suit jacket over a chair, although it would take months for the creases to drop out. He had taken his brown suede shoes off and was stretching his toes out on the carpet, still enclosed in black socks, mercifully.

Louise looked at Dixon and rolled her eyes.

'Put those away, will you, Dave?'

'Yes, Sir.'

'I think I've caught the sun.' Pearce was peering at the back of his right bicep, just below the short sleeve, the white shirt making a stark contrast with the pink skin. His tie was hanging around his neck undone.

'Did you find anything?'

'No, Sir,' replied Harding, stamping his foot into his shoe. 'I think my foot must've swollen up or something.'

'It's your age.'

'Shut up, Mark.'

'Yes, Sir.'

'How much longer are you here for?' asked Dixon, looking at his watch.

'As long as you need us.' Harding had his foot up on the desk and was tying his shoelace.

'Take over from Louise with the holiday cottages then. You can go, Lou, you've been here since the crack of dawn.'

'I wanted to come to the post mortem, Sir,' said Louise, standing up.

'Wanted to?'

'Think I ought to.'

'If you insist,' said Dixon, shaking his head. 'You can drive then. Jane's buggered off with my car.'

'He should've been a mime artist.' Dixon was watching Poland tapping on the window of the anteroom and jabbing his finger at a box on the shelf behind them. Then at the top drawer of the desk, at the same time opening and closing an imaginary drawer with his right hand.

Masks in the box and a large pot of VapoRub in the top drawer.

'Better had,' said Dixon, handing the pot to Louise.

She grimaced. 'Is it that bad?'

'Worse.'

Poland again, tapping on the glass, this time pointing at lab coats hanging on the back of the anteroom door.

White coats and masks on, top lips plastered with Vicks VapoRub, Dixon opened the door to the lab.

'Are you sure you want to do this?' asked Poland, looking up from the body of Mrs Boswell lying on the slab.

'Yes,' replied Dixon and Louise in unison.

Davidson was sitting on a chrome stool staring at something under a microscope. Each was wearing identical standard issue dark green trousers and smock, with a mask and hat. Only Davidson's glasses enabled Dixon to tell them apart. That, and Poland being a good six inches taller.

'Definitely a heart attack,' said Davidson, sitting back on the stool.

Poland covered Mrs Boswell with a sheet and walked over to the microscope on the steel workbench.

'Be my guest.' Davidson slid off the stool and stepped to one side.

'You're right.' Poland nodded. 'Myocardial infarction. You can see the scarring.'

'Is this it?' Dixon was looking down at a shrivelled human heart in a glass bowl on the workbench. It had been cut open, revealing the chambers, the various arteries and veins also opened in cross section.

'The blood's long gone,' said Poland. 'That was on the floor of the barn. What was left of it anyway.'

'Definitely a heart attack though,' said Davidson. 'That was what killed her.'

'So, the hanging and the knitting needles . . .' Dixon's voice tailed off.

'She was already dead.' Poland adjusted his face mask. 'Mercifully.'

'When?'

'Our best estimate is six weeks,' replied Davidson. 'We're going to get a forensic entomologist to see if they can get anything from the insects we found. We've collected lots of samples of maggots, pupae and dead flies at various stages, so they may be able to add something. Want to see?'

'No.'

'There's a Doctor Francine somebody up at Bristol University.' Poland had walked back over to the body and was standing behind her head, looking down at her skull.

'Could it be less than six weeks?' asked Dixon.

'A day or two either way, but that's it,' replied Poland.

'Probably the same day he got away from Chippenham, Sir,' said Louise.

'Certainly within a day or two of that.' Davidson picked up a piece of paper. 'The night time temperature was down to only two or three degrees above freezing on Exmoor until a couple of weeks or so ago, don't forget. Daytime temperatures were much higher though, and the barn was sheltered from the wind. It's a bit of a sun trap down there from what I can gather.'

'It was a week later we found the sister in Cannington.'

'She was long dead by then,' said Poland.

Dixon nodded. 'Let's hope he hasn't killed anyone else.'

'Quite.'

'Can I see her?' asked Louise.

'Er, yes, of course,' replied Poland. He folded back the sheet to Mrs Boswell's neck, revealing her facial features. What was left of them.

'Partially skeletonised, we call that,' said Davidson.

'Where are the knitting needles?' asked Dixon.

'Bagged up,' replied Poland. 'They hadn't gone right in. Just as far as the inner ear.'

'She was already dead, remember.' Davidson shrugged his shoulders. 'We've spoken to the sister and she's confirmed he suffers from tinnitus.'

'Well, that explains that then.' Poland replaced the sheet. 'He's making his victims suffer the same fate.'

'Would they?'

'If they were still alive when he did it, yes. Otherwise, it's symbolic, I suppose. But then I'm not a psychiatrist, am I?'

'There's nothing in his medical records?' asked Davidson.

'No. Not that we've been able to find anyway,' replied Dixon. 'But we've only got them starting when he joined the RAF.'

'How old was he then?'

'Seventeen. He went straight in when he was expelled from school.'

'Why wouldn't it be in his medical records?' asked Louise.

'He probably never mentioned it.' Poland had lifted his mask and was applying another blob of VapoRub under his nose. 'There's not a lot of point because they can't do anything about it anyway. Except help you learn to get used to it.'

'And he clearly hasn't done that,' muttered Dixon.

Davidson held up the edge of the sheet covering Mrs Boswell. 'More?' he asked, turning to Louise.

Dixon turned away when Louise nodded.

'What are those marks?'

The conversation was going on behind him and Dixon couldn't see what Louise was looking at.

'Teeth.' Davidson's voice. 'A fox, most likely. The flesh on the ankle and heel is quite well preserved, compared to the rest of her. Hanging her in the way he did has helped from that point of view. There's very little damage from animals. Otherwise, she'd have been—'

'I think they get the picture, James,' interrupted Poland.

'Seen enough?' asked Davidson.

'I think so,' replied Louise.

'He tied a rope around her neck and hoisted her up using the ride on mower. Why the bloody hell would he do that if she was already dead?' asked Dixon, spinning round when he heard the sheet being replaced over the body.

'Ah, we were coming to that,' said Poland, raising his eyebrows. 'We think that was for your benefit.'

'Mine?'

'We found this in the pocket of her cardigan.' Poland handed Dixon a sealed plastic envelope. 'Just be careful. That's all I'm saying. Be very careful.'

'A business card?'

Poland nodded.

'Mine, I suppose?' Dixon held the clear plastic envelope up to the light, the small card in the bottom corner, the Avon and Somerset Police crest visible on the back. He turned it around. 'I always did want letters after my name,' he said, a wry smile the best he could muster. Blue biro, block capitals, the handwriting neat.

Davidson stifled a small chuckle behind his face mask. 'Maybe not those, eh?'

'Maybe not.'

'What does it say?' asked Louise.

'Detective Inspector Nicholas Dixon.' He took a deep breath. 'R.I.P.'

Chapter Six

Louise floored the accelerator as they raced up the slip road on to the northbound M5.

'I've already spoken to her and she's gone to her parents' place in Worle,' Poland had said. 'And, yes, of course she's got Monty with her.'

'Step on it, Lou,' snapped Dixon, tapping out a text message to Jane with his thumbs.

Stay where you are. On way. Nx

Louise waited until he slid his phone back into his jacket pocket. 'So, he's after you then?'

'Let's just focus on the fact that we're after him. All right?'

'Yes, Sir.'

'We're police officers and he's a fugitive.'

'He could always pay someone to—'

Dixon's loud sigh was enough to stop Louise mid-sentence. But not for long.

'Where did he get your business card, I wonder?'

'I gave enough of them out when we were looking for Alesha and Hatty.'

They spent the rest of the journey in silence, Dixon busying himself checking his emails on his phone – mainly junk, but Louise hadn't needed to know that. She had flicked her headlights and windscreen wipers on by the time they reached Worle.

'You go home,' he said, opening the passenger door. 'I'll take my Land Rover.'

'Are you going back to Express Park?'

'Just go home, Lou. Put your daughter to bed and make sure you still have a life.'

'Thank you, Sir.'

He turned to look up at the grey stone terraced house as Louise sped off. Jane was standing in the downstairs bay window, with Monty sitting on the window seat. Then the barking started, followed by a thud against the inside of the front door as Dixon walked up the short tiled path.

Jane had the fingers of her right hand hooked in Monty's collar when she opened the door with her left and was strong enough to avoid being pulled out into the rain, but only just.

'Roger says you're going to rest in peace,' she said, frowning.

Dixon rolled his eyes. 'As if.'

'So we can go home then?'

'No, we can't.'

Jane's loud sigh was lost in the slamming of the front door.

Dixon raised his eyebrows. 'D'you want to take the chance?'

'I suppose not.'

'Hello, Nick.'

Jane's adoptive father, Rod, was small in stature with closely cropped grey hair – a number three with the clippers, two even – and a big grin. He was carrying a hammer in one hand and a screwdriver in the other; always tinkering with something.

'What is it this time?' asked Dixon.

'The downstairs loo.' Rod shrugged his shoulders.

'How was your holiday?'

'We've seen you since then.' Sue was standing behind Rod in the kitchen doorway, a tea cloth draped over her shoulder.

Jane frowned. 'They've only been back a week,' she said, turning to Dixon. 'When have you seen them?'

He scowled at Sue.

'No, you're right,' she said, hastily. 'It was before. That time you both came over. Sorry.'

'We need somewhere to stay for a few days, Rod.'

'Here's fine,' he said, with a smile and no hesitation. 'You can help me with the tiling.'

'I'll be a bit—'

'Of course you will. What about his lordship?' asked Rod, gesturing to Monty.

'If you don't mind?'

'Not at all. Corky's got used to him now.'

'They were curled up together on the sofa earlier.' Sue was shouting from the kitchen. 'I was going to take a photo and put it on Facebook. A ginger cat and a Staffie.' She appeared in the doorway, drying a plate with the teacloth. 'They looked cute.'

'Best not, if you don't mind. We don't want anything that might lead—'

'Leave it with me.' Rod winked at him.

Dixon was watching Jane out of the corner of his eye. She was staring at each of them in turn, her frown getting larger by the second.

'Well, I'd better be going,' he said. 'I'll bring some of his food back with me.'

'We've got some left over from last time he was here, so he's had supper.'

'Thank you.' Dixon turned towards the door, closely followed by Jane. Once out on the front step, she closed the door behind them.

'How long?' she asked.

'As long as it takes.' He put his arms around her waist. 'I'll call in at the cottage on the way back later and pick up some stuff.'

'You've been over here since they got back from holiday, haven't you?'

Dixon could feel her eyes burning into his.

'You have.' Jane leaned back, folding her arms. 'I knew it. You came to ask my father's permission to marry me.'

'It's something you do, isn't it?'

'Did.' Jane sighed. 'A hundred years ago.'

'They appreciated the gesture. All the more seeing as you're adopted.'

'Really?'

'That's what they said. Well, Rod said. Sue couldn't stop crying.' Dixon kissed her and then turned towards his Land Rover parked on the other side of the road. 'Actually, I was hoping they might say no.'

'Piss off.'

The TV vans had gone by the time Dixon parked in the visitors' car park in front of the Police Centre at Express Park. Most had descended on Withypool, according to the text from Mark Pearce.

Various sightings moving east possibly. BBC and ITN broadcasting live from Withypool

Must be the *News at Ten*, he thought, his finger on the Entryphone buzzer.

'You're supposed to use the staff entrance.'

Dixon pressed the buzzer again.

'I give up.' Followed by a loud sigh over the intercom, then the click of the door unlocking.

'Thanks, Reg,' said Dixon.

'The phones have been jumping all evening, apparently.' Reg paused, listening for the click of the front door lock. 'And Lewis was looking for you.'

'Anything else?'

'Nope. Shall I let him know you're—?'

Dixon was halfway up the stairs when the security door at the bottom slammed behind him, cutting Reg off mid-sentence.

Reg needn't have worried though; Lewis was waiting for him at the top.

'You're supposed to use the staff entrance. Then I can see when you've swiped in.'

Dixon didn't take the bait.

'Is it true?' continued Lewis. 'You're going to rest in peace?'

'We all do. In the end.'

'Just be careful. That's all.'

'Always am.'

'How many times have you been in hospital since you got here?'

'Three.'

'Four,' said Lewis, his hands on his hips. 'There was the bang on the head you got up at Priddy.'

'I didn't go to hospital for that.'

'Don't split hairs. And it's five if we include Jane.' Lewis was following Dixon along the landing. 'You don't go anywhere on your own. Is that clear?'

'Yes, Sir.'

'Take Louise with you. Armed Response will be on close stand-by at all times, and you're both to wear body armour.'

'Oh, for—'

'It's not optional. It's either that or you're off the case. Charlesworth's orders. There's a shoplifting case that needs looking at.' Lewis smiled. 'Tesco's at Burnham. Your choice.'

'What did they take?'

'A bottle of vodka.'

Dixon stopped. 'I never liked vodka,' he muttered.

'I'll take that as a "yes" then,' said Lewis. 'Looks like he's moving east. There are several sightings, and it ties in with a call they took over at Minehead a couple of weeks ago. A farmer this side of Monksilver had a couple of lambs pinched.'

'And we weren't notified because . . . ?'

'They thought it was probably a fox and he was just after a crime number for an insurance claim.'

The *News at Ten* had sparked off the phones again, by the sounds of things, the Incident Room on the second floor resembling a call centre. Dixon stopped at the top of the stairs and counted seventeen officers, including Dave Harding, sitting at workstations, each of them with a phone to their ear, the voices merging into a low murmur.

Harding spotted him, leaned across and tapped the PCSO sitting next to him on the shoulder. She looked up.

Dixon was clearly getting better at lip-reading.

'Yes, thank you for your call, Mrs Smith. Goodbye.' Then she snatched a piece of paper off the desk in front of her and followed Harding.

'This is Sharon Cox, Sir. It was Sharon who found Mrs Boswell.'

'You were supposed to call it in,' said Dixon. 'Not go charging in there on your own.' He glared at Harding. 'Stop grinning, Dave.'

'Yes, Sir.'

'Are you all right?' he asked, turning back to Sharon.

'Yes, thank you, Sir.'

'They gave you the rest of the day off, surely?'

'I came in when I got the shout about the phones.'

Dixon smiled. 'What've you got?'

'A woman over at Bicknoller rang.' Sharon glanced down at the note. 'A Mrs Windeatt. She's got a bit of land on the side of the Quantocks there and some stables. The horses are out at the moment, but she's got the farrier coming tomorrow so she went in the stables to muck them out and it looks like somebody's been sleeping in one of them.'

'Where's Bicknoller?' asked Dixon.

'East of Monksilver,' replied Harding. 'About five miles, maybe.'

'Someone had had a crap in the straw too,' said Sharon.

Dixon winced. 'She's sure it's human?'

'She's a geriatric nurse at Musgrove Park.'

'Please tell me she left everything as it was.'

'Er, no, Sir. I'm afraid not. She only saw the news when she got home. It's on the muck heap, though, so I rang Scientific Services anyway and they're sending a team over there now.'

'Good.'

'The search teams are on the way over there now as well, Sir,' said Harding. 'And the helicopter's up with its thermal imaging camera checking the woods at West Quantoxhead.'

'When did she last go in the stables?' asked Dixon, turning back to Sharon.

'A couple of weeks ago,' she replied, handing him the note. 'Longer maybe. The weather's been fine so the horses have been living out.'

'Definitely going east then. Let's get house to house going in Cannington first thing in the morning, Dave.'

'You think he's heading for his sister's?' asked Harding.

'Not now he knows we know about her.'

'And does he?'

'Oh, yes.'

Chapter Seven

'What are you doing down here?' Jane was standing over him with a mug in each hand.

Dixon yawned. 'What time is it?'

'Seven.'

'It was late and I didn't want to wake you.'

His diesel engine had done the trick, the front door opening before he had summoned up the courage to ring the bell. It had been nearly 1 a.m., after all. 'We were waiting up for you,' Rod had said, hanging on to Monty by the collar. 'And besides, *Brighton Rock* is on TCM.'

Two holdalls full of clothes were on the floor next to the armchair; Monty's bed on the rug in front of the fire, although the dog was curled up on the sofa by Dixon's feet.

'Did Dad watch the end of the film?' asked Jane.

'No, he'd seen it before. And I've—'

'Got it on DVD.' She rolled her eyes. 'I know.'

'Have you told them what's going on?'

'They're fine with it, don't worry. They also wouldn't have minded if you came up to my room.'

Dixon blushed.

'You're like a little old man of ninety sometimes,' she said, perching next to him on the edge of the sofa, before leaning over and kissing him on the lips.

'That was a big sigh.'

'Your phone's buzzing.'

Dixon reached down and picked it up off the floor. 'What is it, Lou?' he asked, holding it to his ear.

'I'm not interrupting anything, am I, Sir?'

Twenty minutes later they were speeding south on the M5, the morning rush hour just getting going, Jane brushing her hair. Dixon rubbed his chin. A shave would have been nice, but needs must.

'D'you want to pick up your car?' he asked.

'I'll wait for you, don't worry.'

'Rod does know not to let him off the lead, doesn't he?'

Louise was waiting for them when they turned into the car park in front of the Police Centre.

'Have they stopped him?' asked Dixon, winding down the window of his Land Rover.

'Not yet, Sir.'

'What's going on?' Lewis had been in the queue for the staff car park and jumped out leaving his engine running, his car blocking the entrance.

'We had a call this morning from a Mrs Smart, Sir,' replied Louise. 'They live in London, but they've got a holiday cottage they let out at Kilve. Her husband logged into their Eurosat account last night and somebody's been using the satellite broadband. And their first guests don't arrive until this Saturday.'

'The bloody idiot's on his way down to check on the cottage,' said Dixon, leaning across Jane in the passenger seat.

Lewis grimaced. 'We've got to stop him.'

'I've got traffic working on it, Sir,' replied Louise. 'They're liaising with Berkshire and Wiltshire. Apparently, he comes down the M4 from Kensington, then south on the M5.'

'Which bit of "dial 999" does he not understand?'

'All of it, I think, Sir,' said Louise.

'What time did he leave?'

'Six, so he'll still be out on the M4. His wife's trying him on his phone, but he never answers when he's driving.'

'And you're going out to Kilve now, I suppose?' asked Lewis, turning to Dixon.

'Yes, Sir.'

'Armed Response are on the way, Sir,' said Louise.

'Good. And remember what I said about body armour.'

A ride on mower abandoned in the outfield – at square leg if the batsman was at the pavilion end; an old fashioned Atco lawn mower sitting on the wicket, the petrol engine still running, a small puff of smoke coming from the exhaust. There must be a match this weekend, or maybe an evening T20; still, it was that time of year and the cricket season was just getting going.

Dixon watched an Armed Response officer appear in the doorway of the pavilion and give the thumbs-up signal. Clear. Another, crouching down behind the roller, peered over at the small cottage beyond the trees; four more creeping along the hedge line off to the right.

The chug of the two-stroke petrol engine, blackbirds in the trees and the smell of the sea. Dixon grimaced. It was a bit ripe – the smell of the mud then; the tide must be out.

He was peering over the wall of the beach car park, across the tree lined cricket pitch, at Groom's Cottage on the far side of the cornfield.

White with a slate roof and red roses in flower beds either side of the front door. He wondered how much it was to rent for a week. Maybe he'd ask the owner when he arrived, although he was enjoying morning coffee at Gordano Services on the M5, a pursuit vehicle having finally caught up with him.

'I think I've done this up too tight.' Louise was tugging at her body armour. 'It keeps catching me under the arms.'

'Better than a bullet catching you,' said Chief Inspector Bateman, crouching down to her left.

Lewis had got to him before Dixon had arrived at Kilve and the beach car park was as close as they were going to get. Until it was all over.

A dog barking in the distance, skylarks having their say. Then the lawn mower engine coughed and died.

'My mower's run out of petrol.' A head popped up behind the drystone wall on the far side of the car park.

'Get down, Tom!' The voice came from behind the wall, Tom unceremoniously dragged back out of sight.

Dixon glanced across at the estate car under the trees at the end of the car park, an empty cage in the back. There was even a uniformed officer holding dog walkers out on the beach. Some people have all the luck.

Then Bateman's radio crackled into life.

'AR14 ready.'

'AR15 ready.'

One word was all that was needed from Bateman, and there was no hesitation: 'Go!'

A loud crash. That was the doors, front and back.

'Armed Police!' The shout drifted across the cricket pitch, more used to cries of 'Howzat!'

Dixon waited for the shots, but they never came. The seconds ticked by. And not many at that.

'Clear!'

'Fuck it,' muttered Bateman.

'He's long gone,' said Dixon, standing up. 'Better get house to house going in the surrounding villages, all the same. Where's next going east?'

'Kilton and Stringston. We'll do Holford too.'

They walked behind the Scientific Services van as it trundled along the track down the side of the cricket pitch that led to the cottage; flat and no ruts this time, which made a change.

'Well?' asked Bateman.

'Looks like he's been here, Sir,' replied the Armed Response officer, his firearm hanging down by his side. 'Or someone has anyway. There's a broken window in the kitchen and the sitting room one's been left open. That's both ends of the ground floor covered. He knows what he's doing, that's for sure.'

'Eh?'

'Escape routes, Lou.' Dixon was peering in the sitting room window. 'Once a burglar's in, their first concern is getting out.'

Four stars, according to the Visit Britain plaque on the wall by the front door, the helicopter appearing overhead just as Dixon stepped into the cottage. An open plan kitchen-diner – he could live with open plan in a cottage, just not an office – the kitchen clean and tidy, apart from broken glass in the Belfast sink and a footprint on the draining board.

'Open the fridge, will you, Lou,' said Dixon. 'You've got gloves on.'

Empty, apart from a bottle of wine. The dishwasher was empty too.

'He hasn't touched a thing.' Bateman was standing behind them, looking over Dixon's shoulder. 'None of the beds have been slept in either.'

The sitting room window lock had been levered off the wooden frame with a kitchen knife, both left lying on the windowsill.

'The key's there,' said Louise, pointing to the corner of the sideboard.

'It was probably dark when he broke in,' replied Bateman.

The television had been left on stand-by. But nothing appeared to have been taken, although the owner could confirm that when he arrived. And the leather sofa had been sat on by someone; either that or the cleaner had forgotten to plump up the cushions.

'Looks like Steiner sat here,' said Dixon. 'SOCO may get something off the back to confirm it's him.'

'Otherwise, we can't prove he's even been here,' muttered Bateman.

Dixon was standing by a leather topped desk in the corner, leafing through the cottage handbook. 'We hope you enjoy your stay at Groom's Cottage,' he said, reading aloud. 'There's even the instruction book for the kettle.' Then he picked up a pen and flicked open the guest book, turning the pages one by one.

'What did he break in for if he didn't take anything?' asked Louise.

'The satellite broadband password,' replied Dixon. 'Get on to Eurosat for a list of the websites he visited.'

'Yes, Sir.'

'We still don't know it's him, though, do we?' said Bateman.

'Yes, we do.' Dixon dropped the pen on to the desk in front of him, his wry smile hidden from Bateman. 'He's signed the guest book.'

Chapter Eight

It seemed odd somehow, being on a beach without his dog, even if it was shingle and mud. Dixon was standing at the top of Kilve Beach, looking down at a fossil in the base of the short cliff – an ammonite; he remembered that much from a school trip.

He could just about hear the petrol mower again, on the cricket pitch behind the trees, the helicopter having moved off when the area had been declared safe. The birds too, not quite drowning out the buzzing of his phone in his pocket.

'Tell me exactly what it said.'

Bateman hadn't taken long to ring Lewis.

'"Hope to see you again soon." Then in the name and address column he put "Nick Dixon, Brent Knoll".'

'He knows where you live then. Did he date it?'

'Ten days ago. We're staying with Jane's parents over at Worle. For now anyway.'

'Good. You'd better get back to Express Park too. You can run the investigation from here.'

'Yes, Sir.'

'I know that tone.'

'Sorry, Sir, you're breaking up—' Dixon rang off. Give it ten minutes and Jane would be on the phone, Lewis sitting on the corner of her desk. Crafty sod.

'We've got a sighting, Sir.' Louise was standing on the top of the cliff, only fifteen feet or so above his head.

'Where?'

'Lilstock. It's just over the headland there,' with a wave of the hand east along the clifftops.

Shame; he'd liked Kilve. And so would Monty.

A couple of houses and a church – house to house wouldn't have taken long, thought Dixon when they sped down into Lilstock ten minutes later. He parked across the entrance to the church and walked back to the small group of uniformed officers standing on the corner.

PCSO Sharon Cox stepped forward. Again. 'It's Mr Plemons, Sir. He's got a mobile home just behind the farm. It's down that lane,' she said.

The sign on the corner – 'To the Beach' – had already caught Dixon's eye.

An old light green corrugated mobile home was rusting away in the corner of a farmyard that was more junkyard.

'That surely can't be it,' said Louise.

'Yes, it can,' replied Dixon when the door opened and a dog jumped down the steps. Some sort of terrier, by the looks of things, but it seemed more interested in rats behind the rotting silage bales. 'Mr Plemons?' he asked, peering in.

'Come in.'

Must we?

'You've got something for us?' asked Dixon, his eyes adjusting slowly to the darkness. It looked like blankets pinned up at the windows.

'Couple of weeks ago, it were. Late. I'd been down the Hood.' White hair. Hunched over in the corner. Blue overalls and an old pair of army boots. Arms folded. That was about all Dixon could make out.

'And what did you see?'

'I walks down the pub, along the clifftop over yonder. Then down the lane past the cricket club. Anyway, I sees a light at Groom's Cottage.'

'A torch?'

'No. There was no beam. Weird it was.'

Dixon took out his phone and clicked the 'Home' button, lighting up the screen. 'Like this?'

'That's it.'

'What did you do?'

'Nothin'. The light went out after a bit and that was that.'

'What time was it?'

'I'd been booted out at closing time, so 'bout harf eleven. I just thought it was one of them hippies from the Great Plantation. I saw no one, see, so reckoned he must've gone across the fields.'

'Hippies?'

'They calls 'emselves anti-nuclear protestors. I suppose it's better 'an working for a living. They started out in East Wood, but they's kicked out of there and his flamin' lordship over at Kilverton 'ouse lets 'em live in the Great Plantation now.'

'How many are there?'

'Ten or twelve, maybe.'

Dixon thanked the old man and left a business card on the side, wondering if he'd get it back at some point with more letters after his name.

'Surely the helicopter would've picked them up in the woods?' asked Louise, as they stepped back out into the sunlight.

'Well, if they are who they say they are, they should be out protesting, shouldn't they?'

'I suppose so.'

Two missed calls from Jane – she was probably just keeping Lewis happy; if it had been urgent she'd have left a message or sent a text.

'Where to now?'

'The beach,' replied Dixon.

They followed the lane, past the farm, leaving the trees behind them as they walked out to the coast path, a high hedge on their right screening the view along the coast to the east. In front of them Wales was visible on the horizon, across the Severn Estuary.

Large boulders acted as rudimentary sea defences, protecting the coast path from the high tides, and beyond them a shingle beach shelved away to the water's edge, the mud covered by the rising tide.

Louise gasped. 'Look at the size of that.'

Dixon spun round. 'Oh, that. Haven't you seen it before?'

'Only from Burnham.'

'A has been decommissioned, so B is the only one generating power. For now anyway. The cranes are what the protestors are protesting against – that's the building site that will become Hinkley Point C.'

'On the left just beyond Stringston,' he said.' Dixon parked in a field gateway and looked at the map on his phone. 'That's Kilverton House over there, which makes that the Great Plantation. And there's a public footpath across that field.'

Louise peered over the gate. 'Is there?'

'There must be, there's a stile.'

Kilverton House was screened from them by a stand of pine trees as they crossed the field; either that or they were screened from Kilverton House, several sets of chimney pots all that was visible. And two flagpoles, a Union Jack and the Cross of St George fluttering in the breeze.

'If that's Lewis, don't answer it.'

'Are you sure?' asked Louise, fumbling in her pocket.

A plume of smoke was rising from somewhere near the middle of the wood. A mixture of trees, mostly in leaf, the canopy differing shades of fresh green; it had looked circular on the map.

'Someone's at home anyway,' said Dixon.

'It was Dave,' said Louise, looking at her phone. 'Shall I ring him back?'

'Later.'

The path skirted around the edge of the wood, so Dixon followed it away from the house in the hope of finding a gate. It was either that or take on the barbed wire fence.

'There's a path there.' Louise was pointing into the trees. 'So there may be a gate up ahead.'

It was locked – a padlock and chain – but far easier to climb over than four strands of barbed wire, and with less chance of ripping your trousers, despite the strand wrapped around the top bar of the gate.

The forest floor was carpeted in ivy, the odd sapling shooting where sufficient light made it through. Dixon listened for voices; birdsong and the crunching of twigs and dead leaves beneath their feet were the only sounds, the volume amplified by the deathly quiet.

'See the washing line?' he whispered, pointing through the trees.

Louise nodded.

'Just make sure you don't put your foot in the latrine,' muttered Dixon.

Three tents had been pitched in a small clearing, the guy ropes tied to trees. Green and blue tarpaulins had been draped across timber shelters too; one even had corrugated iron walls. In the centre of the camp stood a round house, the roof partially thatched; beyond that a kitchen area with pots and pans hanging from wooden pallets used for walls on three sides.

A homemade stove was the source of the smoke, a kettle sitting on top of it, a wisp of steam coming from the spout.

'Hello?'

'Who is it?' The voice came from one of the tents, although Dixon wasn't sure which one.

'Police.'

Then a head appeared from the middle tent – goatee beard, straggly dark hair held back by a pair of cheap sunglasses clamped to the top of his head.

'Give me a minute.'

The sides of the tent bulged – arms being thrust into sleeves – then he stumbled forward out into the open, doing up a pair of blue jeans, his red sweatshirt still hooked over his head.

'What d'you want?' he asked, straightening up and pulling his shirt down.

'What's your name?'

'Ed.'

'We're looking for this man, Ed.' Dixon was holding the photofits of Steiner, with beard and without. 'Have you seen him?'

Ed's eyes widened. Not a lot, but enough.

Yes, you have.

'No, he hasn't.' The voice came from behind them, on the path, which explained why Dixon hadn't heard her approach.

Dreadlocks, nose stud, wooden beads and a hand knitted purple sweater. Was that a cobweb tattooed on her temple?

'And you are?'

'We've done nothing wrong.' Arms folded as she circled Dixon, taking up position next to Ed.

'I didn't say you had. I'm just looking for this man.'

'We haven't seen him.'

'You might like to try looking at the photograph.'

'We've got permission to be here. And we're exercising our right to peaceful protest.'

'How many are there of you?' asked Dixon.

'Twelve,' replied Ed, before the woman's elbow connected with his ribs.

'What's your name?'

'She won't tell you.' Dixon spun round at the sound of a new voice. 'None of them will. And arresting them does them a favour. It'll be all over the internet before you can say Hinkley Point.'

Tall, shoulder length straggly blonde hair, jeans and a flowery shirt. Dixon was sure it was a Rolex glinting in the shaft of sunlight. Clean too, so not of the camp.

'"Police Arrest Peaceful Nuclear Protestors".' He marked out the newspaper headline with his right hand. '"Avon and Somerset Police Brutality".'

Dixon forced his best disarming smile. 'You'll be their landlord?'

'After a fashion.' He grinned. 'Hugh Manners.'

Older than he looked too.

'Come up to the house,' continued Manners. 'I'm afraid I was out when your lot called round earlier. They left a card with a number for me to ring, but you're here now.'

Dixon looked back to the camp. Steiner had been there, that much was clear from Ed's reaction. But when, and where was he now?

He needed to speak to Ed, but that was going to be impossible in the camp surrounded by his fellow protestors. And plucking him out of the line at the gates to Hinkley Point, placard in hand, was not going to work either.

Heavy handed. No one had ever called him that before. Still, there was a first time for everything. He looked at his watch. Give it a couple of hours and they'd all be back in camp.

'I know what you're thinking, Inspector.' Manners was ten paces ahead as they followed him back to the house, but Dixon still heard the sigh, a field of solar panels just visible through the trees as the Great Plantation thinned out. Dixon had always enjoyed a good vested interest.

'I suppose you think nuclear power is a technological marvel?' Manners stopped and turned round, his hands in his pockets.

'I'm just a police officer, Sir,' replied Dixon. 'I'm not paid to think.'

Manners smiled. 'Ah, a fan of *Inspector Morse*.'

'Isn't everyone?'

'Sadly not,' replied Manners. Then he ducked through a gate into the walled garden. 'There's more than enough for us this time of year,' he said, with a wave of the arm, 'so we let them help themselves.'

Half a football pitch, with a wooden framed greenhouse against the side wall. Dixon had never been blessed with green fingers, but he recognised runner beans from the lines of canes, and lettuces, of course. The rest would need to be bagged up and labelled for him to identify it.

The house towered over the walled garden: old worn red brick with black painted timber framing and an octagonal tower in each corner with mullioned windows, all of them leaded. Dixon could smell chlorine – a swimming pool somewhere – and that must be a tennis court behind the garden.

'The original bit is sixteenth century, with later additions, of course. We do open days in summer for the local hospice, that sort of thing. You must come back,' continued Manners. 'We've got a few pigs, on the other side of the house, and some llamas. Even tried ostriches at one point. We produce a bit of gin from the spring water too. It all helps to keep the coffers topped up.'

Dixon could have driven his Land Rover through the kitchen door. It swung open and a small child burst out into the courtyard, her blonde hair wet.

'Cressida, you get back in here now!'

'That's my wife, Diana.' Manners raised his eyebrows. 'She's from Texas. They do a lot of shouting in Texas.' He caught hold of Cressida and turned her back to the door. 'Do as your mother says.'

A small foot lashed out at his shin and missed. 'She has her mother's temper,' he said, picking up the child and carrying her inside under his arm, despite the wriggling, her flailing legs knocking boxes of breakfast cereal off the kitchen table. 'Her brother's away at school. Francis goes to St Dunstan's in Taunton. Boards during the week and comes home at weekends. Maybe you've heard of it?'

Dixon had. But he decided to keep his old school tie to himself.

'Would you like some tea?' asked Manners. He put Cressida out in the passageway and closed the kitchen door behind her, then pulled out three chairs from under the table.

'No, thank you, Sir.'

'Have a seat,' he said, clearing piles of post off the chairs. 'So, you reckon Steiner came this way? That's why you're here, I suppose.'

'We have a sighting of him at Kilve ten days ago.'

'You've got a bit of catching up to do then, haven't you?'

'Have you seen him?' asked Dixon, handing him both photofits. Then he turned to look at the photographs on the mantelpiece, at the same time watching Manners in the mirror on the wall above.

Manners paused, staring at the photofits. 'No, 'fraid not.'

'Have you noticed anything missing?'

'Bit difficult to tell with everybody helping themselves in the garden.'

'Livestock, perhaps?'

'Definitely not.' Manners sat down at the head of the table. 'We haven't got many and they've all got names. Cressida would notice straightaway.'

Dixon had never quite understood why parents displayed their children's drawings with such obvious pride, even when they were – what was the right word – 'modern'. The tiles either side of the fireplace were covered in them. Maybe he'd find out one day.

'What about Mrs Manners?'

'She's just back from her parents in Houston, so you're wasting your time there.'

'And staff?'

'Ha!' Manners shook his head. 'We can't afford staff.'

Dixon had guessed as much from his hands: large, heavily calloused, with grime under the fingernails.

'Do you know how much a place this size costs to run?' Manners leaned over and picked up a box of cornflakes off the floor.

'No, Sir.'

'The heating bill is more than you earn in a year. And if you don't heat it, it gets damp.' He leaned back in his chair. 'Let's just say it's something of a burden, 'specially when you haven't got the proverbial pot to piss in.'

'How many acres do you have?'

'Three hundred, but it's all let to local farmers, apart from a couple.'

Dixon gave him the standard advice about not approaching Steiner, left another of his business cards and squeezed past the new Land Rover Discovery parked across the side gate.

'Follow the path round the side, then the drive back to the road. It'll be quicker,' Manners had said before showing them out of the kitchen door.

'We must remember to use the tradesman's entrance, if we come back,' whispered Louise, doffing an imaginary cap as she ducked under the wing mirror.

'When, Lou.' Dixon smiled. 'It's *when* we come back.'

Chapter Nine

Ten steps behind. Dixon could live with one, two even, but ten? He'd never felt that far behind anyone and it was enough to put him off his cheese sandwich. It had been the last one in the village shop at Stringston and Louise had very kindly said he could have it, seeing as he was diabetic, although he suspected it was more to do with yesterday's sell-by date. Still, needs must and he'd done his jab.

They were back in the beach car park at Kilve, parked in the shade of the mobile command unit, Dixon listening to Louise eating a packet of crisps. It had taken no more than five minutes to set up the search of the camp in the Great Plantation. The Hinkley beat officers at the main gate would let them know when the protestors had cleared off for the day, then all they had to do was wait for them to get home. Thirty officers, followed by two Scientific Services teams.

Bateman had wanted to nick the lot for assisting an offender, until Dixon had reminded him that news of Steiner's presence in the area had been released only yesterday, so it was not unreasonable for them to have had no idea who he was. And even then, there was no TV in the camp, so unless they had mobile phones they still may not have known. No, they would be helping with enquiries, unless and until they refused to cooperate, of course.

Unusual that – Dixon giving anyone the benefit of the doubt. Expect the worst at all times, then you are never disappointed and, sometimes, pleasantly surprised. It had served him well up to now.

'It's a lot of trouble to go to for a broadband password,' mumbled Louise, spraying crisps across his dashboard. She was staring at Groom's Cottage, a Jaguar parked outside with the boot up.

'What sort of data allowance do you get on a pay-as-you-go SIM card?' asked Dixon, still chewing on the last of his sandwich.

'Some can be quite generous, I think.'

'He'll have been checking the webcam from time to time, I suppose, but that's hardly likely to account for it, is it?'

'Whatever he was doing, it must have been using a lot of data then.' Louise scrunched up the bag of crisps and dropped it into the passenger footwell. 'I'll chase up Eurosat.'

Lunch in the Hood Arms at Kilve would have been nice, but it had been full of journalists, the car park outside crammed with vans, their satellite dishes extended skywards on long poles. Still, at least Withypool would be back to normal, the media circus moved on.

Dixon winced. Bateman had the look of someone about to break bad news – rubbing his hands together and shifting from one foot to the other in front of the Land Rover, careful to avoid eye contact.

'I think he wants a word,' said Louise, frowning.

'Either that or a leak.'

The seconds ticked by until Bateman could wait no longer. He tapped on the driver's window.

'Yes, Sir,' said Dixon, winding down the window.

'The search of the camp is off. Charlesworth's orders. And you're wanted back at Express Park.'

Expect the worst – it applied to senior officers too, and usually bore a direct relation to the level of seniority. The more senior the officer, the deeper the shit. 'Did he give a reason?'

'I'm sure you can guess. He's got the press officer with him, and she's—'

'Frightened of a bit of bad publicity.'

Bateman shrugged his shoulders. 'Can we find him without?'

'It's just a question of how many more people are going to die along the way,' Dixon said, starting the engine. 'And I'd ask Charlesworth to confirm his order in writing, if I were you. Unless you want to be the last man standing when the music stops.'

'Charlesworth's not like that.'

'It's only the depth that varies.'

'Eh?'

'Are you really going to ask the Assistant Chief Constable to confirm his order in writing?' asked Louise, when Dixon screeched to a halt outside Express Park.

'I am.'

'I'd love to be a fly on the wall.'

'Be my guest,' replied Dixon. 'The more people who witness the conversation, the better.'

'Looks like meeting room two,' said Louise, when they stepped out of the lift on the first floor.

Charlesworth would know they were in the building by now, but Dixon didn't blame Reg. He was only following orders, after all.

'There's Lewis.' Dixon nodded towards the CID Area on the opposite side of the atrium. 'Get him and catch me up.'

'Ah, Dixon, there you are.'

'Yes, Sir.'

'Have you got a minute?' Charlesworth was wearing a short sleeved white shirt, his top button undone; no tie either, which was a first. Sweaty armpits too. 'I'm in here with Vicky Thomas.'

Charlesworth's cap was upside down on the table, being used as a paper weight, the fan in the corner blowing the corners of the pages. It wasn't that hot, surely?

'You know DC Willmott, I think, Sir?' asked Dixon, waiting by the door for Louise to run along the landing.

'He's right behind me,' whispered Louise, slowing to a walk as she reached the door.

'And I've asked DCI Lewis to join us as well.'

Charlesworth watched them file in and sit down around the glass table.

Vicky Thomas shifted in her seat.

'Well, I—'

'Excuse me a moment, Sir,' interrupted Dixon, sliding his phone out of his pocket. He clicked on Voice Memos, then pressed 'Record', setting his phone down in the middle of the table. 'I'm sure you won't mind me recording this meeting, Sir.'

'Er—'

'I think it's in everyone's interests that there's an accurate record, don't you?'

'Well, yes, Dixon. Of course.' Charlesworth's face was flushed now, matching the press officer's crimson trouser suit. 'You don't trust me, is that it?'

'I can count the number of people I trust on one finger, Sir,' replied Dixon. 'And I'm guessing you didn't rise to the dizzy heights of Assistant Chief Constable by trusting people, let alone senior colleagues.'

Charlesworth grunted. 'Perhaps not.'

'My understanding is that you've cancelled the search of the camp in the Great Plantation. Is that right, Sir?'

'Yes. We . . . er . . . I was concerned that it might do more harm than good.'

'Who to?'

'Well, us obviously.'

Dixon scowled. 'It's not obvious to me. And it won't be obvious to the general public when they find out we had a lead and failed to follow it up because we were worried about a bit of bad press.'

A sharp intake of breath from Vicky Thomas. Her eyes narrowed. 'It's—'

'Leave this to me, Vicky,' snapped Charlesworth. 'It's my decision, Dixon, and that's an end to it. Do you understand?'

'I'd like it in writing, if it's all the same to you, Sir. An email will suffice.'

Lewis's eyes widened, a smile stifled.

'I see,' said Charlesworth, an impatient edge to his voice.

'Experience tells me this is very unlikely to be the end of it, Sir,' continued Dixon. 'And it may help investigators from the Independent Office for Police Conduct if the decision-making is clearly documented.'

'An email it is then.'

'And when can I expect to receive it?'

'I'll try to get to it tomorrow.'

'The search is set for five o'clock today, Sir, so I'll need it before then, please.'

Charlesworth's glare was something to behold. He sighed, then leaned over and picked up a laptop off the floor. 'I'll do it now.'

'Thank you, Sir.'

Dixon sat down on the corner of Jane's desk in the Safeguarding Unit – an office with walls and a door, even if she did have to share it with three other people – and closed his eyes.

Ten paces behind with one arm tied behind his back and a quarry making it personal. Things could only get better, although the likelihood was they would get worse first. That was the usual way of it.

'Did you get your email?' asked Jane, putting the phone down.

'My get out of jail free card.' Dixon smiled, tapping the breast pocket of his jacket. 'I've printed off a copy.'

'You made an enemy of the Assistant Chief Constable just for that?'

'People have been hung out to dry for a lot less.' Dixon took a swig of her coffee. 'And besides, I think he respected my directness.'

'I doubt that.' Jane leaned back in her chair and folded her arms. 'Lewis told me about the cottage at Kilve and the guest book. And Steiner didn't take a thing?'

'Just the broadband password.'

'Needs access to the dark net, then,' said Jane.

'Eh?'

'Most mobile data providers block it, so if he's on pay-as-you-go SIM cards he's buggered. Which broadband company is it?'

'Eurosat.'

'I'd check and see if they block the dark net. They might do if it's satellite broadband. If not, there's your reason.'

'We're waiting for a list of the websites he visited.'

'That won't help much if he's using the TOR app for iOS and Android – The Onion Router. The traffic is routed through umpteen different servers in the network, all of them random. The layers of an onion, remember? It's encrypted and re-encrypted loads of times.'

'What will we get then?' asked Dixon.

'Dark net website addresses are just random strings of letters and numbers. A list of IP addresses, possibly. Internet Protocol, each one's a computer somewhere in the world connected to the web. Let me have a look at it when you get it though. You never know.' Her smile accompanied a shrug of the shoulders, intended to sweeten the pill.

It didn't.

'What time are you going home?' she asked.

'God knows,' muttered Dixon. 'Here, you'd better have these.' He dropped his car keys into her outstretched hand. 'Remember, no walking on the beach. Not until Steiner's—'

'I know.'

An hour spent reading call logs, witness statements, updating the Investigation Plan and Policy Log, and Dixon's eyes were closing when a piece of paper fluttered down on to his keyboard. He was sitting at a workstation facing the floor to ceiling windows in the CID Area. It had become his preferred spot, the reflection normally offering some sort of early warning system, although Lewis had wised up to it of late, creeping up on him from the side.

'What is it?' asked Dixon.

'A press release. Vicky Thomas wants it out for the early evening news.'

Dixon glanced through it, phrases such as 'closing in' and 'search radius narrowing' leaping out at him. As did 'an arrest is expected shortly'.

'Great comedy.' He screwed up the piece of paper and launched it in the direction of the bin.

'Basketball not your thing?' said Lewis, watching the press release bouncing along the floor.

'They'll say what they want anyway, so I don't know why she's bothering.'

'It's her job.'

'Ask her who she's trying to convince.'

'I thought you'd say that,' said Lewis, turning away. 'Oh, and one other thing. Charlesworth has asked Deborah Potter to come down tomorrow and review progress. I'm assuming you'll be out?'

Dixon stared at Lewis in the reflection in the window, letting his silence hang.

'I thought you'd appreciate the warning.'

He watched Lewis sidestep Louise, who was running towards him. She took hold of the office chair at the vacant workstation behind Dixon, spun it around and slumped down on to it. 'We've got the Eurosat stuff, Sir,' she said. 'I've emailed it to you.'

He turned back to his computer and opened the only new email, then the attachment.

'This is the list from Groom's Cottage, Sir. It's mostly just a list of numbers and IP addresses,' said Louise. She leaned forward, pointing at the third one from the top. 'That's the webcam at Mrs Boswell's cottage he's looking at. He's using a normal web browser for that. Always after dark too, if you look at the times.'

Dixon checked the date – yesterday.

'Any proper websites?'

'Scroll down,' replied Louise. 'There are a few news sites and that one, Sir,' her finger jabbed at the screen. 'Bitfly.com. It's an online bit-coin wallet.'

'What about the satellite broadband at Mrs Boswell's cottage?'

'He didn't access the internet at all there, Sir. There's just the web-cam on it. We've got the server logs and there's the daily Eurosat visit, of course, plus a Vodafone IP address was accessing it regularly until yesterday. It must be him as well. We've got the number but it's dead. No trace.'

Dixon took a deep breath, letting it out slowly through his nose. Forty-three days it had taken.

'His first mistake, Lou,' he said, solemnly. 'We know he's accessed the broadband at Groom's Cottage as recently as last night and he's on foot, which narrows down the search radius.' Dixon frowned. Maybe Vicky Thomas had been right?

'Shall I tell Bateman?'

'Yes.'

'And let's get on to the mobile providers too. When did the Vodafone number go offline?'

'Yesterday.'

'Then we need to know if and when Bitfly.com is accessed from another mobile device using the base stations nearest to the area. If they can tell us that then they should be able to give us his new mobile phone number too, then we've got him. And let's get on to Bitfly, whoever the hell they are.'

Louise grimaced. 'They're based in the Cayman Islands, Sir, so we might struggle there.'

'I'll be up in the Safeguarding Unit,' said Dixon, getting up and walking over to the printer.

'It's just as I thought,' said Jane. 'This one's in the Ukraine.' She had selected an IP address at random and googled it, ending up on an IP lookup website. 'Although the reality is it could be anywhere.'

'Tell me about bitcoin,' said Dixon, sitting down at the vacant office chair next to her.

'How long have you got?'

Dixon raised his eyebrows.

'It's a digital currency. "Cryptocurrency" is the fashionable term. There are several, but bitcoin is the biggest.' She sighed. 'Central banks issue coins, right?'

'I get that bit.'

'So, bitcoin is a currency issued by a decentralised computer system, meaning it's not controlled by any one bank or country even. You can earn bitcoin online, running a complex computer program, and then use it to pay for goods and services.'

'What computer program?'

'Does it matter? Steiner's not going to be doing that, is he? He'd need a warehouse full of computers.'

'And this is all on the dark net?'

'That's where it started out, but you can use it in a lot more places these days.'

'And you can buy and sell it?'

'Just like you can with any currency.' Jane leaned forward, her head in her hands. 'If I knew then what I know now . . . One bitcoin's worth about five grand now.'

'So, if he's got an online bitcoin wallet, then it's reasonable to assume he has some bitcoin?'

'Right.'

'And he's going to have to sell them?'

'No reputable bitcoin exchange would touch him,' said Jane. 'You need to provide identification and all sorts. It's like opening a bank account now.'

'What about on the dark net?' asked Dixon.

'That could be it. He'd have to use a peer-to-peer exchange on the dark net. No questions asked.'

'Peer-to-peer?'

'Person to person. It could be a forum, or an exchange where buyers and sellers bid. Wouldn't do you much good without his username and password, though.'

'And what does the buyer get?' Dixon's brow furrowed. 'What does a bitcoin look like?'

'It's just a string of random numbers and letters, upper and lower case. It's a code, really. Encrypted too.'

'So, the buyer will need to send the money somewhere before he gets his line of code. We just have to find where.'

Chapter Ten

Waiting. He hated it.

He lobbed a chip on to the beach below and watched the seagulls swoop down. Others landed on the seawall in front of him, squawking, their beady eyes fixed on his supper. A wave of the hand failed to get rid of them, so he tried another chip, which just made it worse.

He had never been very good at waiting, preferring to make things happen when he could. But it was out of his hands now. Everything that could be done was being done, either by his team or by Chief Inspector Bateman.

Roadblocks, house to house, searches of fields and barns. Even the helicopter was up with its thermal imaging camera. And the Great Plantation was under surveillance. Charlesworth had agreed to that at Bateman's insistence.

Anywhere and everywhere that Steiner might be holed up within ten miles of Groom's Cottage was being checked.

Or was it? Dixon's eyes narrowed.

Several kites were dancing about in the evening breeze on Burnham beach: a shark, a dragon with a long tail, even one that looked like Paddington Bear, all of them being flown by children down on the beach, the occasional shriek of delight rising above the noise of the seagulls.

And beyond them, across the Parrett Estuary, the instantly recognisable square blocks that were Hinkley Point A and B nuclear power stations, both of them dwarfed by the construction site that would become Hinkley Point C.

He picked up a chip and scraped it around the inside of the bag, sweeping up the last of the salt and vinegar as he stared through the haze; the tide out now, a fisherman digging lugworm on the flats below the lighthouse.

The backdrop to his daily walks with Monty, Hinkley Point C had become a familiar landmark, the odd article in the local paper heralding some milestone or other reached in the construction.

The temporary jetty was complete now, all five hundred metres of it. He could see that much from Burnham, ships arriving on the high tides. You could even see it from space, apparently. And what were those things that looked like the NASA space shuttle on the launch pad? Something to do with concrete, possibly?

A workforce of 5,800 people working in shifts day and night. He remembered that from the briefing note he had glanced through before despatching it to the Trash folder in his email a few weeks ago. Maybe he'd move it back to his Inbox later?

There was even a dedicated Hinkley Point police beat team. Four officers, in addition to EDF Energy's own on site security, which was tight to say the least.

Dixon dropped the last of his chips into a bin.

Could Steiner really have got in there? Not without help, surely? Perhaps he was paying for that help with bitcoin?

Oh shit.

Dixon slid his phone out of his pocket.

'What is it?' snapped Chief Inspector Bateman, just before his voicemail cut in.

'He's inside Hinkley Point, Sir. He must be. Track his movements east and he's been heading straight for it. My guess is he's paid for his passage on a ship leaving from the jetty. That's what the bitcoin is for.'

'D'you have any evidence?'

'No, Sir.'

'That'll be Charlesworth's first question.' Bateman's sigh was exaggerated for Dixon's benefit. 'And what d'you think EDF are going to say when you ask them to shut down the largest construction site in Europe?'

'Yes, but—'

'There are no buts. You need evidence. You know that.'

'By the time we get that, he could be long gone.'

'Look, I'll get the beat team sergeant to make some enquiries. That's the best we can do unless and until you get some evidence he's actually in there. All right?'

'Not really.'

'It'll bloody well have to be.' Bateman rang off, leaving Dixon staring at the seagulls still sitting on the seawall in front of him, two ships moored at the end of the jetty in the distance, their outlines just visible through the evening haze.

He would have to content himself with a text message to Louise for the time being.

Are there any mobile phone masts inside the HPC site?

And then another.

Find out about WiFi too

Then it was back to waiting. Or was it?

◆ ◆ ◆

Dixon spotted the number plate recognition cameras as he drove west out of Bridgwater towards Hinkley Point. The delivery management system. He remembered that. At the same time wondering whether EDF's security team had access to it.

A stream of minibuses passed by travelling in the opposite direction, delivering shift workers back to their cars at the park and ride. Finished at nine, probably, given that it was twenty past. He wondered whether one of them was Steiner. Or whether he was staying on site in one of the accommodation blocks. That's if he was still there at all. He may have already got away on a ship leaving the jetty.

The streetlights were on when Dixon turned into the visitors' car park at the main entrance to HPC; deserted apart from two empty minibuses and several bicycles chained up in a bike rack on the left. A camera in each corner too, CCTV this time, one of them turning to focus on his Land Rover as he parked against the high steel fence. He glanced up at the spikes along the top – sharp and splayed, like the barb on a fish hook. Still, climbing over had never been the plan.

He was going to knock on the front door.

Two burly security guards greeted him at the entrance to the car park. 'The site's closed to visitors now, Sir.'

Warrant card at the ready. 'Detective Inspector Dixon, Avon and Somerset Police. We're searching for a fugitive we believe may be on the site. Can I speak to your head of security?'

'He's gone home.' The taller of the two.

Dixon pushed past them, heading for the main entrance. 'What about the beat team?'

'They're not here either.'

It looked like the entrance to Wembley Stadium, apart from the Visitors' Reception to the right of the turnstiles. Steiner must have a fake ID if he was getting in and out.

'I thought this place was twenty-four hours?'

'Not yet. That doesn't start until next year.'

'So, how many people are on site?'

'Four thousand or so, during the day anyway.'

'What's going on at night then?' Dixon was waiting by the security door.

'The jetty runs with the tide, so there'll be boats in, unloading aggregate. And the tunnelling's started. That's twenty-four hours a day, but then it's underground, so it doesn't make any odds.'

'Tunnelling?'

'Water. Two intake, one outfall. They go out about two miles. It's the same machines they used for the Crossrail tunnel. Huge things. And they're going to concrete them in and leave them there, would you believe it?'

'Yes, I would.' Dixon turned to the other security guard, who had remained silent up to now. 'What about your supervisor?'

'I'll go and get her, if you wouldn't mind waiting in here?' he replied, opening the security door and gesturing to the reception area.

The taller of the two guards stayed with Dixon, watching his every move. 'There was a five-a-side match earlier. Does that count?'

'Not really.' *A comedian.* 'What's that place there?' asked Dixon, pointing to a large block of units behind the entrance.

'That's one of the welfare blocks. Offices, changing rooms and a canteen on the ground floor.'

'I could do with a—'

'It closed at nine.'

'What shift d'you work?'

'Nights at the moment. Eight till eight. I was on earlies last week though.'

Worth a try then, thought Dixon, reaching into his pocket for the photofits. 'Have you seen this man?'

'On the telly.'

'Not coming through the turnstiles?'

'Here?' The security guard laughed. 'He'd never get in here. You're pissing in the wind, mate. There are security checks, background checks, an induction programme. He's on the run, for fuck's sake. Pardon my French.'

Dixon was staring at a map of the site on the wall when the door opened behind him.

'What's the . . . ?' The rest of the question was lost in her yawn, the back of her hand covering her mouth. 'Sorry,' she mumbled, running her fingers through her hair. 'What can we do for you?'

'And you are?'

'The duty manager. Paula Smart.' She yawned again.

'We're looking for this man,' said Dixon, handing her the photofits. 'And we have reason to believe he's here.'

'What reason?'

The honest answer was none. Just a hunch, based on the fact that there was nowhere else he could be, although 'fact' was pushing it a bit.

'Do you have a database of all staff?' asked Dixon, ignoring Paula's question.

'Yes.'

'And can you produce a list of new staff employed within the last month?'

'You'd need a warrant.'

'This is a murder investigation.'

'We've all seen it on the TV. And I can assure you we'd have seen him. He'd never have got past the security checks for a start.'

'Can you check with your—?'

'Of course I will. First thing in the morning.'

Dixon sighed. 'What time does the first shift start in the morning?'

'Six.'

'And how many workers are accommodated on site?'

'Five hundred. The rest are bussed in from the park and rides.'

'What about a list of those staying on site?'

'Again, you'd need—'

'A warrant. I know.'

'Speak to Martha. She'll be here at eight. Martha's the beat team sergeant.'

Dixon looked up at the camera in the corner of the reception area. 'How long d'you keep the footage from all these cameras?'

'Twenty-eight days.'

The floodlights were still on at the Astroturf football pitch in front of the accommodation block as Dixon drove back towards Bridgwater, a few lads kicking a ball around. He pulled over and looked back at the site, lights marking out the cranes and the temporary jetty. Several cabins were lit up, vehicles moving about on access roads and what looked like another welfare block on the far side, maybe two miles away.

The accommodation block consisted of two lines of timber clad prefabricated units, with streetlights outside and even grassed areas. It looked like a small housing estate, all of it to be dismantled when the construction of the nuclear power station was complete.

Dixon wondered whether Steiner was in one of them; or was he just barking up the wrong tree? It wouldn't be the first time.

'Yes, Sir,' he said, putting his phone to his ear.

'What the hell are you doing?' demanded Lewis. 'Charlesworth has had the head of security at Hinkley Point bending his ear.'

'It's the one place we haven't looked.'

'The beat team are keeping an eye out for him. What more d'you want?'

'A warrant. We need access to their personnel files and CCTV footage.'

'Based on what?'

'Are you saying we shouldn't check, Sir?' Ducking the question. Again.

'Well, you'll have to get it past Charlesworth. He'll be at Express Park first thing in the morning.' Lewis rang off, leaving Dixon staring at the lights on the jetty. The space shuttles were lit up too.

He kicked the gravel, sending a spray of small stones clattering into the steel fence.

Steiner was probably miles away by now anyway. It was thirty-six hours since Mrs Boswell had been found and twelve since the broadband had been shut down at Groom's Cottage – enough of a head start for anyone.

'Not quite the same, is it, old son?' muttered Dixon, watching Monty sniffing the lamp post on the street corner. A clear sky, a full moon; it would have been perfect out on the beach.

'He's already been out,' Rod had said.

'It's for my benefit, not his,' Dixon had replied, although it was more about escaping what was on the television – some reality thing with lots of people shouting at each other; even Jane's eyes had glazed over.

'I'll come,' she'd said, jumping up off the sofa.

They turned right, then right again, heading round the block, although it felt more like round in circles, which is precisely where Dixon had been going for weeks.

'Any news?' asked Jane.

'Not really. I've got a feeling he's inside Hinkley Point. I went over there, but can't do much until I get a warrant, and without any evidence I'll never get that past Charlesworth.'

'He's still sticking his oar in, is he?'

'Sadly.'

'What about the beat team?'

'I'll catch up with them in the morning.' Dixon was rummaging in his pocket for a dog bag. 'There are boats coming and going from the jetty now, so he may have got away on one of those.'

'It was on the news again this evening,' said Jane. 'No stone left unturned, they said.'

'Just the one,' muttered Dixon. 'Just the one.'

Dixon woke early. A single bed would have been a struggle just for the two of them, but with Monty asleep on the end as well it had made for a broken night's sleep.

He looked around the room, light starting to filter in around the sides of the curtains. Neither of them had bothered to unpack, clothes draped over still-full holdalls, a clean blouse on a coat hanger on the corner of the mantelpiece, where several swimming trophies were still proudly displayed, much to Jane's embarrassment. At least the posters had gone from the walls, although it had taken Rod ages to get rid of the last traces of Blu-Tack.

Dixon reached down, picked up his phone and checked the time. The early shift would've already started at Hinkley. Then the screen lit up and the phone started buzzing.

'You're in early, Lou,' he whispered, in a feeble attempt not to wake Jane, although she had already rolled over, dragging the duvet with her.

'We've got a body, Sir. IC1 female. Approximately twenty-five years of age.'

'Eardrums?'

'Sounds like it.'

Dixon sat up. 'Where is she?'

'Hang on.' Paper rustling. 'The ground granular blast furnace slag silo.'

Asking questions he already knew the answer to was oddly satisfying sometimes. This was not one of them. He closed his eyes and let out a long sigh through his nose.

'Where's that?'

'Hinkley Point C.'

Chapter Eleven

'Detective Inspector Dixon is it?'

The man was walking alongside Dixon's Land Rover as he turned into the parking space in the visitors' car park at Hinkley Point. Smartly dressed in a tweed jacket and tie, with short greying hair, he appeared agitated, shifting from one foot to the other while he waited for Dixon to switch the engine off and wind down the driver's window.

'Yes, Sir.'

'My name's David Pickles. Director of Communications with EDF.'

'You're here early, Sir,' replied Dixon.

'I got the call at six this morning. I can't believe it.'

Dixon turned to Louise sitting in the passenger seat. 'What time did we get the call?'

'0626, Sir.'

Pickles hesitated. 'I got a call from our head of security. I told him to call the police. What else could we do?'

'What else indeed?' Dixon picked his words carefully as he opened the driver's door, forcing Pickles to step back behind it. 'We'll need the visitors' car park for the mobile command unit,' he continued. 'Can we get those cars shifted?'

'But we need the car park for visitors.'

'There won't be any today, I'm afraid, Sir. And possibly tomorrow.'

'I can get the visits cancelled,' said Pickles, 'but do we really have to have the command unit right outside?'

'Can we take it on to the site?'

'Either that or we can give you some office space in the welfare block. That's where the beat team office is.'

'That would be very helpful, Sir,' said Dixon. 'It may avoid any awkward photographs appearing in the press too.'

Pickles blushed. 'Quite,' he mumbled.

Dixon winked at Louise. 'Stand the mobile command unit down, please, Constable.'

'Yes, Sir.'

'Look, I want to assure you, Inspector, that EDF will be doing everything we can to cooperate with you. Amy was a—'

'Amy?'

'I was told it was Amy Crook,' replied Pickles. 'She's something of a celebrity around here. Drives one of the hundred-ton dumper trucks. The batching plant manager recognised her. She's in the ground granular blast furnace slag silo over at the concrete batching plant. They were due to start filling it today.'

'Let's make sure that doesn't get out, Mr Pickles,' said Dixon, slamming the door of his Land Rover. 'At least not until her family have been informed.'

Pickles nodded. 'I'll see to it. We've cancelled the rest of the shifts for today and staff are being turned away at the park and rides. I hope that was the right thing to do?'

'How many does that leave on site?'

'The early shift would've come from the five hundred or so in the accommodation blocks and there'll be a few stragglers. They've been told to stay put. We can let you have a complete list easily enough. Everyone goes through the turnstiles.'

'What about the boat crews at the jetty?'

'They don't leave the boats. The aggregate, or blast furnace slag, or whatever it is they're delivering, is unloaded on to a conveyor belt on the jetty. Then off they go.'

'What about getting out along the jetty?'

'There are staff out there, yes. They use a walkway. Why?'

'No particular reason, Sir,' replied Dixon, watching Roger Poland parking his Volvo on the other side of the car park, next to a Scientific Services van that had just arrived. 'How do we get out there?'

'I can lay on a couple of minibuses when everyone's been through security.'

'The Scientific Services team will need their equipment.'

'They can take their van in, that's fine.'

Dixon followed Pickles in to reception and stared at the burly security guards who had been on duty the night before as he queued to sign the visitors' book, his identification documents at the ready: police warrant card and driving licence.

'Put my name where it asks who you're visiting,' said Pickles, looking over Dixon's shoulder.

He already had.

'Lewis said you'd been out here last night?' whispered Poland, a metal briefcase in each hand. 'You knew Steiner was here?'

'There was nowhere else he could be, unless he'd already got clean away. Maybe on one of the boats from the jetty?' Dixon was watching Pickles lead Donald Watson back to the Scientific Services van while Louise signed in, Poland and James Davidson behind her in the queue. 'It was a long shot.'

'That hit the target.'

'Some do.' He shrugged his shoulders.

'The buses are on the far side of the welfare block, so if you'll follow me.' The taller of the two security guards, not cracking jokes this morning.

'Sir,' said Louise, holding up a newspaper. 'I picked up one of these.' She handed Dixon a copy of *The Point*. 'Have a look at page two.'

The Essential Read for Team HPC, according to the strapline, issue number 32. He opened it and looked at the news item, 'Encouraging more women into the industry', and beneath it a photograph of a young woman in a hi-vis jacket standing by the wheel of a dumper truck. She looked remarkably like Jane, a blonde ponytail under the hard hat and a big smile for the camera.

Dixon read the caption out loud. '"Amy Crook to spearhead campaign to recruit more women."' He folded the paper open at page 2 and then handed it to Poland. 'Here,' he said. 'Meet Amy.'

The canteen was closed when they walked through the welfare block, the staff turned away at the park and ride. A few lights were on upstairs; Dixon looked up at the sound of footsteps on the ceiling above.

'Offices this end,' said the security guard. 'There are a couple of people in. Their names'll be on the list.'

Once outside they spotted the Scientific Services van at the far end of the bus stop, behind a minibus, David Pickles waiting by the side door.

In front of them the construction site sprawled away into the distance behind a red and white crash barrier, the space shuttles pointing skyward in the far distance, beyond another welfare block, the new sea wall marking the boundary off to the right.

Cranes, diggers, steel and concrete, miles of yellow railings, the site that would usually see thousands of workers swarming all over it like ants, quiet. Only one white van was moving along a road near the middle, a red flag on a long pole mounted on the roof.

'They've nearly finished the earthworks for the second reactor,' said the security guard. 'Six million cubic metres of earth they've moved. You see those diggers?'

Dixon grunted.

'They can fill a hundred-ton dumper truck in three scoops. They arrive in bits and are assembled on site.'

'Fascinating,' mumbled Dixon, wondering whether his old Tonka toy was still in the loft at home.

'This way,' shouted Pickles, pointing at the larger of the space shuttles. 'That's the blast furnace slag silo over there; it's for making concrete. Recycling at its best.'

Dixon listened patiently while Pickles gave them the guided tour on the way out to the concrete batching plant, figures going in one ear and out the other. Seventeen different sorts of concrete, a contract worth two billion pounds alone, foundations thirty-five metres deep, one hundred thousand tons of aggregate, fifty-two tower cranes, pressurised water reactors . . .

Then came the question Dixon had known would be coming sooner or later.

Pickles leaned over from the front passenger seat. 'I suppose you think nuclear power should be banned, Inspector?'

'I'm just a police officer, Sir.' He smiled. 'I'm not paid to think.'

'That bodes well for the investigation, doesn't it?'

Pickles had obviously never watched *Inspector Morse*.

It was almost impossible to get a sense of scale of the earthworks behind the site, were it not for the digger on the top of one of the new hills.

'It'll all be levelled off and landscaped,' said Pickles, noticing Poland's frown. 'And that's the foundations for the first reactor.'

They spun round in unison to look at a circular concrete plinth, hundreds of yards across, with a deep trench all around it.

'We call it the nuclear island. That trench is the stressing gallery for the steel cables. You can see the second one taking shape over there. But don't worry.' Pickles smiled. 'The nuclear fuel doesn't arrive for another five years.'

'Comforting to know,' said Poland.

'You get a good view of the new sea defences from here too; designed to withstand a tsunami. Even though we never get them.'

'Haven't had one since 1607,' said Dixon.

'I stand corrected.'

'How the hell d'you know that?' asked Poland.

'It said so on the Stop Hinkley! website.'

The minibus arrived at a set of traffic lights on a bridge. 'You can ignore them,' said Pickles, tapping the driver on the shoulder. 'There's no one else moving around on site today.'

'Except for that van down there,' said Dixon, pointing to the vehicle with the flag on the roof below them on a track deep in the earthworks.

Pickles leaned over and looked out of the window. 'That must be the ground survey team, I think. The flag is to warn the dumper trucks they're there, otherwise they'll go straight over them.'

The van turned right at the T-junction and headed towards another welfare block just behind the sea wall.

'That's the north block,' said Pickles. 'Contractors' offices and a canteen. And this is the concrete batching plant.'

The minibus forked left and parked directly below the silos next to a police van, the ladders at the base of the larger silo sealed off with blue and white tape, a uniformed officer standing guard.

'Looks like the beat team beat you to it,' said Pickles.

'That's what they're here for, Sir,' replied Dixon.

The silo was empty, the circular steel wall magnifying every sound: footsteps on the walkway, the catch of Poland's briefcase, the shutter on Donald Watson's camera, and their voices, of course, echoing around the chamber.

Thirty-five metres high according to Pickles, it had been due to be filled with five thousand tons of ground granular blast furnace slag that morning.

'I just thought I'd poke my head round the door to check and found her,' said Fred, the batching plant manager. He was leaning on the railings of the walkway opposite the body.

'What time was this?' asked Dixon, adjusting his hard hat.

'Just before six. We were due to start loading it up at seven. The boat's still out there. They said it might be later on today?'

'We'll see.'

'Anyway, the slag comes in the top on a conveyor belt straight off the jetty, and then out the bottom there when it's needed.' Fred was pointing to a grill in the bottom section of the silo. 'There's another conveyor belt under there.'

The bottom section of the silo funnelled down to the grill, the body lying on a walkway that followed the circular wall just above the funnel. Orange overalls, a hi-vis jacket, the hard hat gone. Dixon hadn't got any closer. Yet.

'When was the last time anyone checked in here?'

'A week ago, maybe,' said Fred. 'But I saw her yesterday in the canteen and she was fine then.'

'What time was that?'

'Lunchtime. I had a late lunch. Say, two o'clock.'

'She was a dumper truck driver, so what was she doing here?'

'No idea, sorry.'

'Is there any CCTV?'

Fred was rolling a cigarette. 'Lots on the way in, but once you're on site it's just the service roads.'

'If you hadn't checked and the silo had been filled, how long would it have been before she'd have been found?'

'Years, unless there was a problem of some sort. The batching plant will be dismantled in about four years. Probably wouldn't have been much left of her by then.'

'Thank you.'

Fred turned and left via the door behind them, Dixon listening to his boots on the steel steps down the outside of the silo, the flash of Watson's camera lighting up the inside, reflecting off the wall like bolts of lightning. Then the spot lamps were switched on. Poland and Davidson squatted down over the body, leaning back a little to avoid casting a shadow. He could hear their every word.

'Bruising at C3 and C4. Can you see it, Roger?'

'Roll her over and pass me the otoscope, will you?'

'Is it both ears?'

'It is.'

'Is it him?' asked Dixon.

Poland nodded. 'Her neck's broken. Then he did the ears. There's very little blood loss.'

'Looks like she was killed elsewhere and carried up here,' said Watson, standing over them, camera in hand.

'Probably thought he'd be long gone if and when the body was ever found,' muttered Dixon. 'Can you give me a time of death?'

'We may be able to narrow it down when we get her back to the lab,' replied Poland. 'But it looks like sometime between eight and ten last night.'

Chapter Twelve

Dixon stepped out on to the metal steps clinging to the outside of the silo. He hesitated, staring out across the construction site, the significance of what Poland had just said still rampaging around inside his head, leaving a trail of destruction in its wake. He gripped the rails with both hands, his knuckles whitening the harder he squeezed.

Between eight and ten last night. He'd been no more than a mile away while Amy's life had been snuffed out, her neck snapped, her body carried up this same flight of steel steps and dumped in the silo, ready to be buried in blast furnace slag.

A mile – maybe a bit more; the main entrance and reception hidden from view behind Welfare Block East.

Dixon looked at his watch. The two security guards would have gone home now, oblivious to the part they had played in her death. Albeit a minor one. After all, what could he have done even if they had let him in?

On a construction site the size of a small town? He shook his head. Nothing.

That might offer a small crumb of comfort to some.

He looked down at the vehicles parked in front of the concrete batching plant, Pickles now standing with a group of people that included two uniformed police officers. Several were shaking their heads, while others stared at their feet; all had their arms folded. They looked like they were standing outside a crematorium, waiting for the funeral to start.

Time enough for that.

Dixon slid his phone out of his pocket and answered it, if only to stop the buzzing.

'Yes, Sir.'

'I want you back at Express Park now,' demanded Lewis.

'Yes, but—'

'Look, I know the way this usually works.' Lewis sighed. 'You get an order, ignore it, and I get you out of trouble. The difference this time is that I'm the one giving you the order. Is that clear?'

'Yes, Sir.'

'Deborah Potter is on her way down from Bristol with thirty officers from the Major Investigation Team. They'll be taking over inside HPC. Steiner is in there, which means you can't be. It's as simple as that.'

'Yes, Sir.'

'This has come from the top.'

'Charlesworth again?'

'Higher. EDF have agreed a seventy-two hour shutdown of the site and—'

'What am I supposed to do? Sit at home twiddling my thumbs?'

'You and your team will be taking the investigation outside HPC.'

'What about the boats?'

'Any ship leaving the site within the last twenty-four hours is being recalled. And those on the way are being sent back to their port of departure. Potter knows what she's doing and she has the full cooperation of EDF. All right?'

'I'll need to speak to the victim's work colleagues.'

'That can be arranged. Now, get yourself back here. Potter will be here for a briefing at nine.'

Lewis rang off, just as Poland stepped out of the silo on to the landing.

'Any sign of a struggle?' asked Dixon.

'No.'

'What about her phone?'

'He must have taken it.'

Dixon lashed out at the railings with his foot. 'I've been ordered out. Potter's on the way to take over.'

'Probably for the best,' replied Poland.

'I was here, Roger,' said Dixon. 'Last night. And I never got past reception.'

'What could you have done if you did? Look at the size of this place.'

Pickles was waiting for them at the bottom of the steps. 'I gather you've been recalled to Express Park, Inspector,' he said. 'The minibus can drop you back to reception.'

'Thank you.'

'This is our head of security, Jim Crew. Jim made the call this morning.'

A white shirt that was too tight with a T-shirt underneath; hiding tattoos, probably. Dixon felt sure he could make out one on the right forearm, the hand outstretched. Top button undone, his clip on tie hanging off the top pocket. Cropped dark hair, thinning on top, and sunglasses.

'Shocking,' said Crew, shaking Dixon's hand. 'We've had the odd protestor trying to get in, but this . . .' His voice tailed off.

'How much longer will you be?' asked Pickles, turning to Poland.

'The rest of the day,' he replied. 'We'll need to get the mortuary van in here too.'

'I can organise that,' said Crew.

'Where's my colleague?' asked Dixon, looking around. 'She was taking a statement from Fred.'

'Got it, Sir,' shouted Louise, running towards them. She was looking at her phone in her hand. 'That was DCI Lewis. He wanted to know we were on the way.' She stopped in front of Dixon. 'So, I told him we were.'

Thirty officers and more than five hundred staff to eliminate; Dixon didn't envy them that one.

He had left the beat team sealing off the concrete batching plant, the sergeant, Martha Sparks, definitely in charge, and by the time he cleared reception on the way out an Incident Room had been set up in Welfare Block East; the furniture in the lounge on the ground floor of the accommodation block being rearranged to provide a venue for the interviews.

He had recognised some of the officers milling about in reception as he dropped his visitor's pass into the box and squeezed out through a turnstile, but not many.

He recognised Lewis and Potter though, sitting in meeting room 2 at Express Park with Charlesworth.

'Ah, there you are,' said Lewis, leaning across from his chair and opening the door. 'If you've got a minute?'

'Well done, Nick,' said Potter, smiling at him as he sat down opposite her; pinstripe trouser suit this time, grey to match the streaks in her short dark hair.

'I was too late for Amy Crook.'

'That wasn't your fault. And besides, we've got him cornered now. There's no way in or out of there.'

'I've authorised DNA testing,' said Charlesworth. 'Everybody on site yesterday. No exceptions.'

'What I need you and your team to do is find out how he got in there,' continued Potter. 'Someone helped him and we need to know who and why. All right?'

'He'll be in there on a false ID,' replied Dixon. 'When we have that we should have more of an idea. In the meantime, I'll start with Amy Crook. Either she recognised him and had to be silenced, or she was deliberately targeted.'

'How d'you know that?' asked Charlesworth.

'What other motive could there be?' Dixon frowned. 'There's no sexual element to it, no sign of a struggle.'

'The body armour stays on,' said Lewis.

'Even if he's stuck inside HPC?'

'And you can go on site if you need to, but no further than the Incident Room. Is that clear?'

Dixon sighed. 'Yes, Sir.'

He ripped the Velcro open and slid his body armour over his head, dropping it on the floor next to a vacant workstation.

Mark Pearce looked up from behind the computer on the other side of the partition. 'Dave said they've got him trapped inside HPC.'

'He can't get out,' said Louise. 'The site's on total lockdown.'

'I suppose we should be grateful it's not on total meltdown.'

'Shut up, Mark.'

'Yes, Sir.'

'We need to notify her next of kin. There should be a record on her personnel file at HPC. I'm going back over there in a minute anyway, so I'll pick it up. In the meantime, let's find out everything we can about her. You know the drill.'

'Yes, Sir,' replied Harding, sitting down at the workstation next to Pearce.

'She may have a car somewhere that Steiner's now got the keys to. Find it,' continued Dixon. 'There's more to this than just his parting shot.'

'She may have recognised him, Sir,' said Pearce. 'And he—'

'Maybe . . .' replied Dixon, his voice tailing off when he spotted Jane in the reflection of the floor to ceiling windows in front of him. She was walking up behind him waving a small black plastic wallet. He felt his jacket pockets. Empty.

Sod it.

'You forgot this,' said Jane, dropping his insulin pen on to the keyboard in front of him.

'Thanks.'

'You'd better check your blood.'

'I'm fine. Really.'

'What did you have for breakfast?'

'A banana.'

'That's a fat lot of good.'

'I'll pick something up on the way out, don't worry.'

'You've got him cornered inside Hinkley Point, I hear. Does that mean we can go home?'

'Not yet.'

'How did I know you were going to say that?' muttered Jane, as she turned on her heels and walked back towards the lift.

Ten minutes later, Dixon was sitting in the passenger seat of his Land Rover eating a bacon and egg sandwich, as Louise drove out towards HPC.

'Quiet, isn't it?'

'All the lorries have been sent back to the freight depot,' replied Dixon.

'Gives the drivers a few days off, I suppose.'

The visitors' car park was full, even the grass verge on the access road taken by TV news vans parked nose to tail.

'Park behind Roger's car. He won't be going anywhere today.'

The reception area was quiet, a wave of their warrant cards sufficient to get them through the turnstiles this time; different security guards on duty too. 'Incident Room's through that door and up the stairs, Sir,' said one.

It looked much like the top floor of the Police Centre at Express Park: open plan, vacant workstations outnumbering the occupied ones; phones ringing – some answered, some ignored. Deborah Potter was standing on the far side of the room, staring at a map of the site that had been pinned on the wall, following Jim Crew's finger as he traced the route over to the concrete batching plant. Then she followed him to the window and looked out at the same route in the distance.

'What are you doing here?' she asked, when Dixon and Louise approached the map.

'I need Amy Crook's personnel file. Her next of kin need to be notified. And I'd like to see her room in the accommodation block.'

'We've got a security file,' replied Crew, 'but she worked for Agard, so they'll have her main file.'

'Who are Agard?'

'They're a Tier 2 contractor on the earthworks.' Crew took a deep breath. 'Let me explain. Each part of the construction is contracted to a Tier 1 contractor. So, take hospitality, for example. EDF give it to a Tier 1 contractor, who will then subcontract out bits of it, such as the canteen, cleaning and stuff like that to Tier 2 companies. There are even Tier 3 in some cases.' He leaned back against the windowsill. 'No one company could do all this. So, with the earthworks, the Tier 1 is Manton, and Agard are Tier 2 supplying and operating the dumper trucks. Another Tier 2 contractor is supplying and operating the diggers. Does that make sense?'

Dixon nodded. 'So, the people in the accommodation block work for all sorts of different companies?'

'Yes.'

Definitely not the short straw, after all. 'Can you get her file?' asked Dixon, stifling his sigh of relief. 'I'd like to speak to her line manager too, if he or she is here.'

'Give me a couple of minutes, I think I saw him in the canteen.'

'We had to open it, for obvious reasons,' said Potter. 'And you're not going over to the accommodation block. You heard what DCI Lewis said.'

'What about Louise?'

'No, and that's final. I'll get it photographed today and you can go through her stuff with Scientific. There won't be much.' Potter shrugged her shoulders. 'And I shouldn't imagine it will be terribly enlightening.'

Dixon was still staring at the map on the wall when he felt a tap on his shoulder. 'This is Terry Pickford, Inspector,' said Crew, standing with a man in blue overalls and an orange hi-vis jacket. He was carrying a white hard hat in one hand and an electric cigarette in the other.

'Tell me about Amy,' said Dixon, gesturing to a vacant office chair.

'A hard worker.' Pickford sniffed. 'Been with us from the start. Sailed through her HGV and then moved on to the dumper trucks. I just can't believe it . . .'

'Where did she go at weekends?'

'Home, like the rest of us. She lived up Yatton way, I think.'

'How did she get on with the rest of your team?'

'Fine. There was no crap from anyone. She mucked in with the lads and they all got on with the job together.'

'Was she in a relationship?'

'Not that I know of.'

Crew reappeared and dropped two files on to the desk in front of Dixon: a thin one with 'Security' written across the top, and a thicker one with the Agard logo.

'What shift was she working yesterday?' asked Dixon, turning back to Pickford.

'She was on lates this week, so she would've finished at nine.'

'And when did you last see her?'

'Just before I finished at six, I suppose. She was taking a load up to the dump. We're excavating the second nuclear island at the moment, digging out the galleries around it.'

Dixon tried the photofits, more in hope than expectation.

'They've already asked me that.' Pickford shook his head. 'No. Sorry.'

'Did she say anything to you, about being nervous, feeling threatened perhaps, anything like that?'

'No, I don't think so.' Pickford curled his lip. 'She'd just had a couple of weeks off, but that was compassionate leave, so she was a bit down, as you'd expect, I suppose.'

'Compassionate leave?'

'Yeah, I can't believe it. I really can't. 'Specially after what happened to her mother.'

Chapter Thirteen

'Does the name Stella Hayward mean anything to you?'

Potter looked up to find Dixon standing in the doorway of the small office at the far end of the temporary Incident Room. She closed the file on the desk in front of her and leaned back in her chair.

'Yes. Why?'

'She's Amy Crook's mother.'

'Oh, for . . .' Potter puffed out her cheeks. '*Was* Amy Crook's mother.'

'Have you found a body?'

'Not yet. The house in Yatton looked like an abattoir under a UV light though, so the chances of her still being alive are pretty much zero. And, yes, before you ask, she was on the civilian staff at Portishead.'

'Her mother works at Avon and Somerset Police Headquarters and disappears, probably murdered, then, less than three weeks later, Amy is found dead with her neck broken.'

'Don't say it.' Potter folded her arms. 'Of course they're connected.'

'Who did you give it to?'

'You're not going to like it.'

Dixon sneered. 'Chard.'

''Fraid so.'

He turned for the door. 'You'd better ring him.'

'That's a complete copy of the file,' said Detective Chief Inspector Simon Chard, sitting behind a pile of paper on the desk in his office at Avon and Somerset Police Headquarters, Portishead.

It had taken Dixon just over an hour from HPC, much of the journey spent in a conference call with Dave and Mark, Louise holding the phone in the passenger seat. Not easy over the noise of a diesel engine on the motorway, even with the speakerphone on maximum volume.

A text from Jane had been the only moment of light relief on the way.

Try not to strangle him! Jx

Lewis had rung too, with a similar message.

Their paths had crossed three times in the months since Dixon had joined Avon and Somerset Police, and each time Chard's animosity towards him had become all the more apparent.

Yes, Dixon should have disclosed his personal involvement when he had gone undercover at the boarding school in Taunton. But he got the right result, albeit in spite of Chard and his mishandling of the investigation. And although Dixon had been the one hauled up in front of Professional Standards on a disciplinary, Chard still came out of it looking like a twat. More so when Dixon got off with 'management advice' – the lowest sanction available.

Then there was Manchester, when Chard hadn't taken kindly to being kept in the dark about Dixon's plans. All of it paling into insignificance though, when Chard's shambolic investigation into an earlier disappearance came to light during the hunt for the missing girls. He had been a detective constable based at Bath police station then, but it really had been the icing on the cake.

And now, here he was, investigating the disappearance of Amy Crook's mother. It really didn't bode well.

Louise was sitting out the meeting with Chard, preferring to wait in the canteen; a shame, thought Dixon, on reflection – a witness might've been useful.

'What am I supposed to do with that?' he asked, gesturing to the pile on the desk.

'You can shove it up your arse, for all I care.' Chard smirked.

'What about forensics?'

'The report's there.' Arms folded now.

Take a deep breath and count to ten.

It usually worked. Chard looked away when Dixon made eye contact.

'I'd like to see the original file, please,' he said, the politeness forced.

'Don't you trust me, is that it?'

Dixon recognised a question to be ignored when he heard one, tempting though it was. 'I'll need access to the scene too,' he said, calmly.

'It's sealed off.'

'I'm sure we can unseal it.'

'Really?' Chard got up sharply, sending his chair crashing into the filing cabinet behind his desk. 'I suppose I'll have to come with you.'

'Thank you, Sir.'

Chard was staring at the handle, waiting for Dixon to open the door. 'I expect DCS Potter will put me in charge of both cases, seeing as they're connected.'

Over my dead body.

Although, thinking about it, Dixon had seen enough of them lately.

◆ ◆ ◆

POLICE LINE DO NOT CROSS

Somebody had though. Either that or the wind had torn it down, the blue tape fluttering in the breeze, the end tangled around a small rose by the front porch of the mock-sandstone clad terraced house. The curtains in the living room window were drawn, as was the curtain behind the glazed front door; the bottom pane boarded up.

Were those footprints in the gravel underneath the window? If so, someone had been trying to peer through the gap in the curtains. A nosy neighbour, possibly.

'She didn't turn up for work one day, so we sent someone to have a look,' said Chard, pushing the key into the lock. 'She was in the Human Resources department; shift allocation, that sort of thing.' He waited while Dixon put on a pair of latex overshoes and gloves. 'Forensics have been over it, top to bottom, so we should be all right.'

Then Chard pushed open the door, the curtain swinging open with it.

'We got nothing from the neighbours. She'd not been here long and kept herself to herself.'

'How long?' asked Dixon.

'It's in the statements. Read them yourself.'

Stairs directly behind the front door; the living room open plan, if taking the kitchen door off counted as open plan. White tape marked out patches on the laminated pine floor, arrows pointing to more on the skirting board, although nothing was visible to the naked eye. The wall behind the brown leather sofa too, the tape fanning out. Spraying.

'You can see the blood with luminol,' said Chard. 'There was a rug here and the floor's been cleaned. And the sofa and the wall. The blood spatter's been looked at by a specialist.'

'What does the report say?'

'It's on the file.'

Counting to ten again. Dixon's anger management counsellor would be impressed. If he had one.

'There was a coffee table here. SOCO found wood splinters under the sofa, so she fell on it, maybe.'

Pictures on the wall by the kitchen door – few smiles to be seen; a boy in one of them.

'There's a son, Nathan,' continued Chard. 'Estranged. We've not been able to get hold of him yet. He's backpacking somewhere. Vietnam or somewhere like that.'

'How d'you know?'

'One of her colleagues in HR.'

'Where's her phone?'

'Never found it. There's an iPad though. The report's on the—'

Chard stopped mid-sentence when Dixon turned his back on him and walked into the kitchen. Someone had cleared the fridge, switched it off and left the door open. The heating was off too, and a kitchen knife missing from the block on the top.

He tapped the cat flap with his toe. Locked.

'The neighbour's feeding it,' said Chard.

'Which one?'

'That side,' with a wave of the arm to the right.

'Has Amy been here?' asked Dixon.

'No. She didn't want to.'

'You met her?'

'Yes. There's a statement from her on the file.'

Dixon stepped over the plastic covering the bottom three stairs and took the rest two at a time, stopping in the doorway of the master bedroom at the front of the house; small and almost filled by the king size bed. A built in wardrobe in the far corner, with sliding doors, and an en suite.

Family pictures covered the top of a bedside table. Babies – Amy and her brother, probably; another of the two of them building a sand-castle. The photographs were lined up diagonally, crammed on, leaving room only for a lamp and coaster. But there was a gap; space for one more in the middle. She wouldn't have wasted that, surely?

'One's missing,' he said.

'Bollocks.'

Dixon opened the top drawer and began flicking through the contents of a velvet box, moving the costume jewellery from side to side with his index finger, revealing a small wedding band in the bottom. Then he snapped the box shut.

Reading glasses, the cheap ones from Boots; tissues; a packet of jelly babies.

'Was she diabetic?'

Chard sighed. 'Read the report.'

No window in the bathroom on the landing and then a smaller bedroom at the back: Amy's.

A single bed against the wall, a pile of clothes on the floor. Make-up strewn across the top of a chest of drawers, a mirror on the wall above. Pictures mounted in frameless frames – no sign of Blu-Tack or Sellotape pulling paint off the wall.

'Is it rented?'

Chard nodded.

Snorkelling somewhere – he recognised Amy giving a thumbs-up to the camera, even behind the mask.

The wardrobe doors were open, several empty shoeboxes on the top shelf and a concertina file. Dixon lifted it down and placed it on the bed, then he began flicking through the compartments.

'It's empty,' said Chard, watching him through the open door. 'We've checked everything.'

Dixon picked it up and dropped it on the bed, allowing it to open naturally. 'There was something in it at some point,' he said.

'We think the killers took—'

'Killers?'

Chard smirked. 'Probably.'

Dixon had to agree, but he wasn't going to tell Chard that.

It had taken Louise over an hour and a whole packet of staples to sort out the documents, sitting at a vacant workstation, while Dixon had been to Yatton with DCI Chard: witness statements, forensic reports, post mortem. They had, at least, been provided with a bound photograph album.

She had been waiting for him, the box of papers on the bonnet of his Land Rover, when Chard dropped Dixon back to the visitors' car park at Portishead.

'Anything interesting?' he asked, as they sped south on the M5.

'One thing I don't quite understand, Sir,' replied Louise. 'When you look at the photographs, there's nothing out of place to the naked eye. Is there? You've been in.'

'They needed luminol to see the blood.'

'So, why did they break in? Uniform will only do that if they can see a problem, surely? A body lying on the floor, or the place looks like it's been burgled. Here, there was none of that. She might just have pulled a sickie and gone shopping for all they knew. And the statement from Amy is crap. It's a just a page and a half of Stella's normal routine and when Amy last saw her. There's not even anything about current relationships. Admittedly she was down at HPC but you'd get some background from her, surely?'

'You would. And I would. But Chard . . .' Dixon curled his lip. 'Is there a copy of the Policy Log?'

'No.'

'I'll look at it on the system.'

'It's weird.' Louise frowned. 'The neighbour heard nothing. She didn't see anything either.'

'Which one?'

'Number 16. And there's no statement at all from the people at number 20. Where are we going?' she asked, as Dixon flicked the indicator, turning on to the off slip at junction 21.

'Back to Yatton.'

Tall trees. Dixon hadn't noticed them on his visit earlier, but then having Chard breathing down his neck had been a trifle off-putting. Pine trees along the rear boundary of the terrace and more in front, planted by the developer, judging by the size. It was a dark and gloomy place, although it didn't help that they were investigating what would probably turn out to be a murder.

He flicked through the witness statement of the neighbour at number 16. 'Let's go and knock on the door,' he said, looking up.

A flash of grey hair in the kitchen window, then the front door opened, a figure dressed in yellow visible behind the glazed front door.

'Mrs Westmacott?' asked Dixon, holding up his warrant card.

'You were here earlier, dear, with that nice Mr Chard,' she said. 'You'd better come in.'

The layout of number 16 was identical to number 18, although there were more flowers – on the carpets, the wallpaper and the curtains.

'Would you like a cup of tea?'

'No, thank you.'

'Well then, what can I do for you?' asked Mrs Westmacott, gesturing to the sofa.

Dixon waited while Louise took out her notebook. 'You said in your statement that you hadn't known Stella that long?'

'Not really. She's been here a couple of years. Much nicer than the previous tenants. Noisy kids and motorcycles,' she said, rolling her eyes. 'Stella kept herself to herself.'

'How well did you know her though? Your statement's a bit sketchy on that point.'

'We used to chat from time to time. Amy was lovely too, but she was only home at weekends after she got the job at Hinkley Point. She drives one of the huge dumper trucks, you know.'

'We do,' said Dixon. 'Have you seen Amy since her mother disappeared?'

'She came home once a couple of weeks ago. It was late and she wasn't here long. Ten minutes, maybe.'

'Was she carrying anything when she left?'

'A bag; blue, I think,' replied Mrs Westmacott, sitting down in an armchair. 'A carrier bag.'

'Could you see what was in it?'

'It was dark, I'm afraid, and the streetlights aren't very good with all these trees. It wasn't clothes though. They'd bulge, wouldn't they?'

'What about before she disappeared, did you see any friends coming and going? Anyone?'

'There was a gentleman caller. I saw him a few times, late at night and never at weekends when Amy was home.'

'Would you recognise him if you saw him again?'

'No. It was none of my business, really. She was divorced and what she did was up to her.'

'What about noise from next door?'

'She was always very quiet. They're well insulated though, these properties.'

'How well d'you know the neighbours on the other side?'

'Not at all, really. They've just had a new baby.' Mrs Westmacott shrugged her shoulders. 'Gone to her parents', I think. Or his.'

'And you're looking after Stella's cat?'

'The police gave me the food from the cupboard.' Mrs Westmacott smiled. 'Just till she gets back, you know.'

Dixon slammed the door of the Land Rover. 'The local oracle and we've got a one page witness statement.'

'There's no mention of the gentleman caller.'

'No, there bloody well isn't.'

'No statement from her ex-husband either,' said Louise, putting on her seatbelt.

'There may be an explanation in the Policy Log, so we'll give him the benefit of the doubt on that for now.'

'Really?'

'No, not really,' muttered Dixon, watching Mrs Westmacott peering out of her kitchen window in his rear view mirror.

Yatton to Bridgwater in less than half an hour. The new Land Rover was certainly faster than the old one.

Dixon parked in the visitors' car park outside the Police Centre and checked his phone, which had been buzzing away in his pocket for most of the drive.

Three missed calls and two text messages, the first of which came from Roger Poland.

Definitely Steiner's handiwork between 8 and 10 last night. Report to follow

The second came from Dave Harding, who had also been responsible for two of the missed calls.

Nothing exciting in her belongings. Car found and on way to Scientific. No sign of Steiner yet

The other missed call had come from Deborah Potter, no doubt having her ear bent by Chard. She hadn't left a message and her car was in the car park, which was ominous.

'Find Stella's ex-husband, will you, Lou?' asked Dixon, when the lift doors closed behind them.

'Isn't that Chard's case?'

'He's Amy's stepfather, isn't he? Or was anyway. And you may find there's a first husband too, given that Amy has a different surname.'

'Hayward could be her maiden name.'

'Just check.'

'Won't we be treading on Chard's toes?'

'Stamping on them,' replied Dixon, stepping out of the lift.

Potter's team had started with the Agard employees, Amy's work colleagues, and Dixon spent the next half an hour scrolling through their handwritten witness statements which had already been scanned on to the system.

No one had seen or heard anything, nor had Amy mentioned anything unusual.

Brilliant.

Swabs were being taken for the DNA screening, looking for a match with the many samples of Steiner's DNA that were available, but that was now expected to take ninety-six hours, no doubt triggering more reminders from EDF that the shutdown was costing them millions. Still, that was Potter's problem.

An email from Scientific Services attached a selection of photographs of Amy's room in the accommodation block. It looked much like her room at home; a little more sparse, perhaps, and Blu-Tack was allowed: more snorkelling pictures and a couple of her brother on a beach somewhere, a surfboard tucked under his arm.

No pictures of her mother anywhere; or her father for that matter.

'There's nothing in her car, Sir,' said Pearce, his head popping up from behind the computer screen opposite. 'That's just a preliminary search, mind you.'

'What about her phone?'

'She's got a contract with EE but it's dead. No trace.'

'Anything on social media?'

'Not really. She posted the odd photo on Instagram, but that was work related stuff. Nothing on Facebook.'

'She was spotted leaving her mother's a couple of weeks ago with a blue carrier bag.' Dixon raised his eyebrows. 'The witness thinks it was blue anyway.'

'No sign of it, Sir.'

'What about the bitcoin?'

'Brick wall. There's a unique twelve word passphrase just to get to the pin number screen, then it's got two factor authentication, so they text you another code to enter. We'd need Steiner's mobile phone.'

The Incident Room upstairs was empty, the whiteboard still on the wall. It would make a poor substitute for a walk on the beach with Monty. That was usually when he did his best thinking, but it would have to do.

Dixon stuck a photofit of Steiner in the middle, the one with the beard and hair. Underneath it he wrote the word 'bitcoin' with a big red circle around it, and drew a line connecting the two, a large question mark either side of the line. Then a picture of Amy Crook, connected to Steiner with another red line. The word 'WHY?' next to it.

Finally, a photograph of her mother, Stella, connected to Amy with a solid red line, and then to Steiner with a dotted line.

'What *are* you doing?' asked Jane, appearing behind him.

'Trying to focus on what I do know, rather than what I don't.'

'Bugger all, by the looks of things.' She sat down on the edge of the table.

'Steiner's got bitcoin in that online wallet.' Dixon tapped the whiteboard with his marker pen. 'So, either he's been paid it, possibly for killing Amy, or he's using it to try to bribe his way out.'

'Or both.'

'Quite.'

'D'you think he killed Stella?'

'He was accessing the internet at Groom's Cottage the night she disappeared, so it's unlikely. What it does tell us is that Amy was targeted by Steiner. We can safely rule out anything random about her killing. That really would be too much of a coincidence. Mother and daughter within weeks of each other?'

'Where does that leave you with Chard?'

'Trying to fill in the gaps in his investigation.'

'I'm surprised you didn't swing for him.'

'You'd have been proud of me,' said Dixon, smiling. 'I spent most of the time counting to ten.'

Chapter Fourteen

Potter had finally caught up with Dixon in the canteen, the encounter going surprisingly well. First and foremost, she had agreed that there could be nothing random about the killing of Amy and the probable killing of her mother.

'Work around him,' she had said of Chard. 'He means well, he's just a bit . . .' Her voice had tailed off, leaving Dixon resisting the temptation to finish her sentence for her.

HPC was still off limits to him, and would remain so until Steiner was in custody. Movement on the roads was being monitored using HPC's delivery management system and the perimeter covered by CCTV twenty-four hours a day. All shipping had been stopped. It was just a matter of time; expensive time – Pickles rang again while Potter had been talking to Dixon.

There were even dog patrols on the beach. 'You could have been a dog handler,' Potter had said, spotting the look on Dixon's face.

'I don't think Monty's quite cut out for that,' had been his reply.

Resources were tight, the DNA screening accounting for a substantial portion of Charlesworth's budget. At best it would identify Steiner; at worst it would flush him out as the net closed around him. And doing so would lead them to whoever had been helping him.

In the meantime, surveillance on Steiner's sister would continue.

The meeting had only been interrupted by a call from the custody suite. Louise had come running in. A protestor had assaulted a police officer with his placard at the gates of HPC. He was down in the cells, asking to see Dixon.

All he would say was that his name was Ed.

'What did you want to talk to me about?' asked Dixon, pulling a chair out from under the table in the one interview room still sticking to the old layout. The rest left the interviewing officer sitting next to the interviewee, both of them opposite the tape machine; nice and cosy and all that, but a fat lot of good. Dixon avoided them like the plague.

'I got myself arrested deliberately,' replied Ed. 'I had to speak to you.'

'You called my colleague a fascist pig.'

'The group are watching me like a hawk and I'd never have got away otherwise. I had to make it look real, didn't I? Is he all right?'

'He'll live.'

'I need to stay overnight and then be let go in the morning, but I want the charges dropped.'

'What is it you want to tell me?'

'Oh no.' Ed folded his arms. 'Charges first.'

'Assaulting a police officer is a serious offence.' Dixon frowned. 'If your information is useful, I may be able to get that taken into account and a caution might be offered. Possibly. I'd need to speak to the arresting officer.' Dixon managed a pained expression, if only to stifle a smile. He'd already cleared it with the officer Ed had assaulted and the custody sergeant.

'That would do. A caution is fine.'

'Well?'

'Have you got the photofit?'

Dixon slid it out of his pocket and flattened it out on the table in front of Ed.

'The beard's shorter. He's shaving it under here,' said Ed, rubbing the underside of his chin with the backs of his fingers. 'There's more grey in it too.'

'You've seen him?'

'He walked into camp a couple of weeks ago and asked to join us. People had been drifting away since the build really got going, so Magnus said yes. We had no idea who he was then and they're shitting themselves now.'

'Who's Magnus?'

'The leader of the group, although I'm not sure how many are left now. It's been a real bad vibe since we found out about Steiner.'

'What's Magnus's surname?'

'No idea. I've only been there a few months, myself.' Ed was picking the dirt from under his fingernails and flicking it on the floor. 'I'd been over at the Arundel bypass on the A27, trying to save the trees. There's an ancient woodland there, but they announced the route and it's going north of it. Battle won, so I had to find something else to do. Hinkley seemed like a good cause. Free food too.'

'What name did he give?'

'Maggot.'

Gallows humour. Dixon had always hated it. 'That's it?'

Ed nodded. 'Nicknames only.'

'How long did he stay?'

'A few days, then he was gone.'

'Did he ever go protesting at the gates?'

'No. He kept saying he wasn't feeling well and stayed in the camp. He said he would, but never did. And then he was gone.'

'D'you know where?'

'You'd need to speak to Fly, but there's no way she'll talk to you. She saw him.'

Dixon waited.

'A man in a suit came across the cornfield. He spoke to Maggot. Ten minutes, maybe. Then a few days later he was gone.'

'What did this man look like?'

'A suit, that's what Fly said.'

'And that's all she said?'

'Suits all look the same.'

'Did he leave the camp at any time before he went for good?'

'A couple of hours the following evening, but he came back. Maybe the next day too, then he was gone the next.'

'All right, Ed,' said Dixon, standing up. 'I'm going to arrange for a colleague of mine to take a detailed statement from you. Then we'll see about that caution.'

Dixon had left Dave Harding trawling through the traffic cameras looking for the suit's car. He would almost certainly have avoided the delivery management route, so camera coverage would be limited to the outskirts of Bridgwater and Watchet; dashcam footage from patrol cars in the area at the relevant time too. If all else failed, then it would mean checking the delivery management system number plate records too, just in case.

'What do we know about Amy then?' asked Dixon, sitting down on the office chair next to Louise.

'She was born in 1995. Amy Louise Crook. Her mother we know about and her father killed himself a few weeks before she was born. I'm having trouble finding the inquest file, but the death certificate gives the cause of death as carbon monoxide poisoning.'

'And it records suicide, does it?'

'1(a) carbon monoxide poisoning; 1(b) suicide.'

'Have you googled him?'

'There's nothing going back that far. Mark found nothing on Amy's social media profiles either.'

'Keep digging,' said Dixon, standing up. 'I'd like to see that inquest file.'

'Yes, Sir.'

Peace and quiet in the corner of the canteen, a low murmur from those sitting on the other side, and the rattle of spoons in coffee cups. Dixon closed his eyes, forcing them open again when he felt himself drifting off to sleep. It wouldn't have taken much longer.

He looked down at Amy's personnel files and the bundle of documents from Chard's investigation into her mother's death on the table in front of him. Hardly light reading.

He drained his coffee, fumbling in his pocket for the money to buy another, the coins scattering across the floor, when he was distracted by his phone buzzing on the table in front of him.

He curled his lip, hating it when he didn't recognise the number.

'Nick Dixon.'

'Mr Dixon, my name's Danielle and I'm phoning from the diabetic unit at Musgrove Park. I'm ringing about your recent retinal screening appointment.'

'Er, yes.'

'The surgeon has looked at the results and there are some changes to the blood vessels at the back of your eye. I need to make an appointment for you to come in next week.'

'I'm right in the middle of something at the moment,' he said, grimacing.

'It *is* urgent. The ophthalmologist has said she could see you next Thursday afternoon.'

'Can I ring you back on Monday?' he asked, closing his eyes.

'I'll ring you then, if that's all right.'

If you must.

'Yes, that's fine, thank you.'

'Who was that?' asked Jane, peering around the door.

'Nobody,' he replied, forcing a smile. 'Just somebody trying to sell me something.'

'How much longer are you going to be?'

He shrugged his shoulders.

'I'll see you at Worle later then,' said Jane, turning on her heels.

Changes to the blood vessels at the back of your eye . . .

Dixon folded his arms tightly across his stomach, waiting for the cold sweat to pass. At least Jane hadn't hung around long enough to watch the blood drain from his face.

She didn't say which eye.

He looked up at the menu on the wall behind the counter and tried reading it with his hand over his left eye, then his right.

Get a grip! 'Some changes' could mean anything, and they can fix it with a laser anyway. It's just part and parcel of being diabetic.

He slid his phone into his pocket, resisting the temptation to open the web browser.

Whatever you do, don't google it.

The cleaners had finally booted him out of the canteen at 9 p.m. and he was now sitting at a workstation in the CID Area, the only light on the whole of the first floor coming from his desk lamp and the glow of his computer screen.

His emails didn't take long, the statements from Amy's work colleagues all expressing surprise that anyone would want to do her any harm at all. It had been a relief to have it confirmed that the injuries to her ears had been inflicted after death, but otherwise Davidson's post mortem report was not particularly enlightening either.

Her clothes had gone for forensic examination, more in hope than expectation of identifying where she might have been killed on the site before her body had been dumped in the silo.

Still no sign of Steiner, although day two of the DNA screening was due to start at 8 a.m. EDF were also coming to terms with a stoppage that might go into a fourth day. Potter had agreed that tunnelling operations could continue, which had sweetened the pill; all of those workers were on site and couldn't very well go anywhere.

According to her Policy Log, she was working on the assumption that Steiner knew the silo was to be filled with slag that morning, the search and DNA screening beginning with workers having any connection to the concrete batching plant. It seemed like a reasonable place to start.

Dixon leaned back against a printer on the side while he waited for the kettle to boil. He tried closing his eyes, but soon started to sway from side to side, a sure sign he was nodding off. An extra half spoonful of coffee and a few grains of sugar should fix that.

Then he sat down to update the Policy Log: Amy's mother was dead and her death was connected to Amy's own murder. Hardly rocket science, that one. And to assume otherwise meant entertaining the mother of all coincidences. Then he logged into Chard's Policy Log for the murder of Amy's mother, Stella. It hadn't been updated at all since the discovery of Amy's body. Having said that, she'd only been found that morning so maybe he'd give Chard the benefit of the doubt.

He curled his lip. Maybe not.

He opened the filing cabinet and took out the bundle of documents copied from Chard's investigation file, dropping the six inch thick wedge of paper on the workstation with a thud.

Another swig of coffee. Then he started with the witness statements.

Amy's was a page and a half long, reciting when she last saw her mother, her usual daily routine and giving a brief family history. Apparently, her mother hadn't seen her second husband for a couple of years. The divorce settlement had been amicable, though, neither having much to fight over anyway. Stella had no real friends either, her one close friend having died a couple of years before in a car accident.

And that was it.

Full of typing mistakes too.

The statements from Stella's work colleagues in the Human Resources team at Portishead were equally short, giving a brief account of what little they knew about her; not surprising, perhaps, when she'd only been there a year. There was no statement from the officer who first attended the scene in Yatton, which was odd, but then it was unlikely to be terribly enlightening either.

Missing appendices from the forensic report. He wondered who had done the photocopying.

The photograph album was more interesting – a darkened room, ultraviolet light illuminating the blood stains. Dixon counted three distinct spatter patterns on the walls: one starting at head height indicating that Stella had been standing up, then two lower down, presumably when further blows rained down on her after she had slumped on to the sofa, the final blows – a spatter pattern on the floor and another on the skirting board – then delivered when she had collapsed on the missing rug.

The blood spatter analysis confirmed it: five distinct blows. Cause of death would need to wait for the post mortem though, assuming Chard ever found her body.

Genial ineptitude. It was a phrase Dixon had heard used many times.

Chard was definitely not genial.

Dixon crawled into bed just before midnight. Monty grumbled at him when he pushed him on to the floor, but managed to jump back on the end of the single bed before Dixon got in.

Jane rolled over. 'What time is it?' she asked, rubbing her eyes.

'You don't want to know.'

She slid her hand across his chest. 'Push him on the floor.'

'I tried that.'

He turned on to his side and closed his eyes. It had been a long day and was going to be an even shorter night. And besides, Jane's parents were in the next room.

'You really are a little old fart sometimes,' she whispered, thinking he was already asleep.

Chapter Fifteen

'What the fuck are you doing here?'

Dixon stepped out of the lift, brushing past Chard. 'Doing your bloody job for you' was tempting, but instead he went for the matter of fact reply, 'Investigating the murder of Amy Crook.'

'Don't try to be clever with me.' Chard was following him along the corridor towards the Human Resources department at Portishead. 'What is it you want to know?'

'Anything they can tell me that's not in their witness statements.'

'There's nothing.'

'Then they can tell me that.'

'If there was, it would be in their bloody witness statements, wouldn't it?'

'Would it?'

Chard wrenched open the door at the top of the stairs. 'You haven't heard the last of this,' he snapped, letting it slam behind him.

Dixon peered through the small window in the door of the HR department. Eight workstations, all but two of them empty. Still, it was a Saturday.

'I'm looking for Linda Willetts,' he said, opening the door.

'That'll be me.' She was sitting next to the vacant desk, her long grey hair held back by a band, glasses on the end of her nose.

'This desk looks like it's been cleared. I'm guessing it was Stella's,' said Dixon, sitting down on the empty office chair and handing Linda his warrant card.

'Yes.' She frowned. 'What's going on?'

'Her daughter was found dead yesterday.'

'Not Amy?'

Dixon nodded. Slowly. 'I'm sorry. Did you know her?'

'Not really.' Linda sighed. 'How sad.'

'You said in your statement you didn't know Stella well,' continued Dixon, opening the drawers one by one.

'They're all empty,' said Linda, blowing her nose.

'You don't hot-desk then?'

'We're here all day, every day, so what would be the point?'

Dixon smiled. 'Quite.'

'No, I didn't know her that well, to be honest. She'd only been here a year and wasn't that talkative.'

'Tell me about the Friday, the last time you saw her, did she say anything unusual?'

'Not really.'

'It was the May bank holiday weekend. Did she say what she was doing?'

'Nope.'

'And what happened on the Monday morning?'

'We were supposed to be covering the bank holiday but she didn't turn up, so I tried ringing a couple of times and got nothing. Then I put a call out to Donna in Control to get someone to swing by and knock on her door, check she was all right.'

Dixon nodded. 'What did you know about her?'

'She was divorced from her second husband. Her first husband died. That's about it, really.'

'D'you know how he died?'

'No. She was estranged from her son too. He's gone off travelling.' She took a sip of Diet Coke from the can on her desk. 'Well, I say estranged, she did get a postcard from him once. She had it pinned to the partition there.' Linda was pointing to the blue screen behind Stella's computer.

'Where's all her stuff?'

'Boxed up. It'll be down in the evidence store, I expect. There wasn't a lot. The postcard, a mug, box of tissues, Cup-a-Soup, that sort of stuff.'

'Did she ever get any personal calls?'

'A couple from her daughter, maybe. On her mobile.'

'D'you remember anything she said?'

'Just that she couldn't talk, she was at work. She seemed quite conscientious, to be honest.'

'What did she do for lunch?'

'She brought her own. We all do. The canteen's crap and there's nothing else around here.'

'Was she in a relationship?'

'No.'

A loud cough came from behind the computer opposite Linda. Dixon glanced across just in time to see the top of his or her head duck down. He waited, the head reappearing slowly, green eyes fixed on Linda from behind a long fringe.

'Shut up, Siggy,' snapped Linda, her eyes wide.

'The damage is done,' said Dixon, leaning back in his chair.

Linda looked out of the window. 'There was a rumour she was in a relationship with somebody here.'

'Who?'

'No idea.'

'When did you first hear this rumour?'

'About six months ago,' replied Siggy. 'Sam told me in the kitchen.'

'Who's Sam?'

'One of the call handlers.'

'And who told her?'

'It's a him. No idea. Sorry.' Siggy jabbed her index finger at Linda. 'She already knew.'

'Someone told me at the Christmas party. It's a big place. There are hundreds of staff on the site and rumours are flying about all the time. You really can't—'

'And you've no idea who it might be?'

'No, sorry,' replied Siggy.

'Me neither,' said Linda. 'Hardly the end of the world, is it?'

A supplemental witness statement from Linda took no more than ten minutes. It would have to do. And he could always come back and get one from Siggy, if needs be.

Dixon was walking along the landing when a text arrived from Louise.

Potter and Lewis looking for u. All ships checked. No stowaways. 6 workers unaccounted for. Looking like Steiner poss got out before site locked down. Have u got body armour on?

Interesting. Maybe Steiner never intended to get away by sea? Maybe he never intended to get away at all. Dixon grimaced. If he had got away, he could be anywhere by now.

One more call to make then he'd head back to Express Park and face the music.

It was Dixon's first visit to Weston-super-Mare. Another new police station – lots of concrete and less glass this time. Not enough visitors' parking either, so he left his Land Rover across the bicycle racks. They obviously hadn't got round to painting the double yellow lines yet.

'I'm looking for PC Peter Bolt.'

'You can't leave that there,' said the receptionist, not even bothering to look up.

Dixon tried his warrant card.

'You still can't leave that there.'

'I'll take my chances, now where can I find PC Bolt? I checked and he's on duty today.'

The receptionist sighed, then he picked up the phone. 'Peter, there's a Bridgwater DI down here asking for you. Come and get rid of him, will you? He's parked across the front of the—Thanks.'

Dixon waited outside, keeping an eye on his car. 'Peter Bolt?' he asked, when a uniformed officer appeared.

'Yes, Sir.' Tall, with dark hair and a moustache; clipping on his tie as the front doors swung shut behind him.

'You were first into Stella Hayward's place over at Yatton?'

'Yes, Sir. I gave a statement.'

'Did you?'

'Yes, Sir. It should be on the file.'

'I'm investigating the murder of her daughter.'

'I heard about it,' replied Bolt, nodding.

'And what does your statement say?' asked Dixon.

'Not a lot, from memory. I looked through the letterbox, then broke in.'

'Why?'

Bolt tipped his head. 'What d'you mean?'

'Why did you break in? When I looked through the front window, there was nothing to indicate anything untoward at all. Yet you smashed the front door in.'

Bolt hesitated.

'The blood's only visible with UV light and luminol,' continued Dixon. 'The place had been cleaned. Even the leather sofa. As far as you knew, she could've pulled a sickie and gone shopping, surely?'

Bolt thrust his hands into his pockets, his eyes watching traffic passing by out on the main road. 'I seem to recall a neighbour . . . ?'

'The neighbours don't mention being there when you broke in.'

'I really don't remember, Sir.'

'I think you do.'

'I don't, Sir.'

'I think you remember exactly what happened.'

Dixon waited.

'Were you in a relationship with Stella Hayward?'

'No, Sir.'

'How else did you know the rug and coffee table were missing?'

'I honestly can't—'

'It took you over an hour from getting the shout to arriving at Hawthorn Crescent.'

'We got an urgent on the way. It was bank holiday Monday, I remember that.'

'Fine. So, was someone else there when you got there?'

'No, Sir.'

'What made you break in then?'

'No one had seen her for days.' Bolt slid his hands out of his pockets and folded his arms. 'She hadn't turned up for work and her mobile was switched off. It just seemed like the right thing to do at the time.'

'Really,' said Dixon, matter of fact. 'I hope to God you don't turn up at my house if I decide to bunk off for a couple of days.'

'What the hell d'you think you're doing?'

It made a change from the usual 'Where have you been?', the occasional expletive thrown in.

Potter was holding the lift doors open with her foot. 'There's me trying to keep Simon Chard out of your way,' she continued, 'and you're doing your best to rub him up the wrong way.'

'His investigation's full of holes,' replied Dixon, leaning back against the glass. 'And I need to fill them to find out why Amy was murdered.'

'Out.' Potter stepped to one side, allowing him out of the lift. 'What holes?'

'Stella failed to arrive at work on the Monday morning. So, PC Plod goes round there, looks through the letterbox and kicks in the door.'

'What's wrong with that?'

'The place had been cleaned and there was nothing to see. Not through the letterbox or the window. It only looked like an abattoir with luminol and a UV light, and he didn't have either of those.'

Potter was standing in front of the lift buttons, blocking them as the doors closed. 'Why did he kick in the door then?'

'He told me he couldn't remember. But the simple answer is that someone else was there. They either went with him or were at the house when he got there. Someone who knew the rug and coffee table were missing. The rumour mill at Portishead will tell you she was having a fling with someone.'

'Who?'

Dixon reached behind Potter and jabbed the lift button. 'No idea.'

'Does it matter?'

Mercifully, the lift was still on the first floor. 'Let's hope not,' said Dixon, stepping back in when the doors opened.

'And where are you going now?'

Spin.

Dixon wasn't a political animal, but he understood 'spin' and used it when he needed to. 'Going to interview Stella's ex-husband' would not have gone down well. Not with Potter, and certainly not with Chard. 'Going to interview Amy's stepfather', on the other hand, put a different spin on it. Same person; same questions. But no one, not even Chard, could argue with that.

Louise had the far more difficult job. Dixon had been quite specific: copies of the handwritten witness statements, which – for some reason – had not been scanned on to the system, and copies of the missing appendices from the forensic analysis report; and all of it to be done without alerting DCI Chard.

That left Dave and Mark following up Amy's friends.

Dixon glanced into the back of the Land Rover, at his body armour lying on the floor in the passenger footwell. It could stay there for the time being. Steiner was taunting him, that's all. And he didn't need body armour for that.

It hadn't taken long to find Neil Hayward. A quick glance at his Facebook profile – wearing a hard hat with the Amber Traffic Management logo on it – then a call to the company to find out that, yes, he worked for them and was currently supervising a set of temporary traffic lights at a burst water main on the A3052 near Newton Poppleford.

Dixon could have done without twenty minutes sitting in the traffic queue to get to the lights, but the East Devon countryside made up for it, two deer grazing on the edge of a copse across the field on the nearside; the moment of calm lost when a motorbike came screaming down the outside of the line of traffic. Then the lights changed, the traffic moved forward a hundred yards, and high hedges blocked the view. Typical.

He pulled into the roadworks behind an Amber Traffic van; no surprise that the logo was red, amber and green. Nobody seemed to be doing any work either – water still bubbling up from a hole in the road – except the man watching the lights. He hopped out of his van and walked back to Dixon's Land Rover.

'You can't stop there!' Arms waving.

'Neil Hayward?' asked Dixon, winding down the window and showing his warrant card.

'Yes.'

'Hop in.'

Hayward squeezed down the side of the Land Rover, opened the passenger door into the hedge and climbed in. 'What is it?' he asked.

'Working on a Saturday?'

'It's double-time and I need the money.'

'I wanted to ask you about your ex-wife, Stella.'

Hayward rolled his eyes. 'What's she done now?'

'Has no one been in touch with you?'

'Like who?' asked Hayward, sliding off his hard hat and putting it on the dashboard. He was tall and unshaven, with pockmarked skin. Dixon couldn't place the smell, until he saw the electronic cigarette sticking out of the top pocket of Hayward's overalls.

'Police.'

'No. Why? Should they have?'

'Yes, they should.' Dixon undid his seatbelt and shifted in his seat. 'I'm sorry to tell you that Stella has disappeared. She was last seen about three weeks ago.'

'Disappeared?' Hayward turned to face Dixon, his brow furrowed. 'What d'you mean "disappeared"?'

'She didn't turn up for work on the Monday morning. She was working for us at our HQ in Portishead—'

'I didn't know that.'

'An officer was sent to check on her and broke in. There was no sign of her, sadly, but a large quantity of blood was found at the scene.'

Hayward slumped back into the seat.

'I'm sorry to tell you that we're treating it as a murder investigation,' continued Dixon. 'And I'm also investigating the murder of her daughter, Amy.'

'Amy's dead?'

'Her body was found yesterday.'

'How was she . . . ?' His voice tailed off as he fumbled for his e-cigarette.

'Her neck was broken,' replied Dixon. 'When did you last see them?'

'I haven't seen them for two or three years. Amy kept in touch on WhatsApp, birthdays and Christmas, but that was it.' Hayward opened the passenger door, took a long drag on the e-cigarette and then blew the smoke out into the Devon countryside. 'It was never going to end well, but I never thought . . .'

Dixon waited. But not for long. 'Thought what?'

'That it was going to get her killed. She was obsessed. They both were. Nathan left and it drove me away in the end too. It was the reason we divorced, really. That and money worries, I suppose.' He wiped his nose on the back of his hand. 'What a fucking mess. And you're sure Stella's dead?'

'We haven't found her body yet, but we're treating it as murder.'

'And you've got no idea what it's about?'

'Not yet.'

Hayward's head was bowed, the only sound a soft click as he picked at dead skin on the palm of his hand with his fingernail. That and the traffic filing past the roadworks. 'It all started with her first husband, Liam. They had it good back then. Posh house in Blagdon. He ran his own company; remote access, that sort of stuff. Quite specialist, and they were doing very well. They had Nathan, and Amy was on the way. He bought Stella an MG Roadster and paid for it to be renovated. Then went and killed himself in it. Silly sod.'

'Why?'

'He got the contract for the platforms when they were fixing the monorail underneath the Second Severn Crossing.' Hayward glanced at Dixon, spotting his frown. 'There's a suspended monorail underneath the bridge. It runs right the way across, with stations and everything.

You can see it from Severn Beach. Anyway,' he continued, 'one of the platforms collapsed and three men fell into the water. One survived the fall and drowned, the other two were killed instantly. There was a health and safety investigation and Liam and his company were being prosecuted for corporate manslaughter.' Hayward took a deep breath through his nose. 'So, he killed himself the night before the trial. Gassed himself in the MG under the bridge.'

'Leaving Stella to clear up the mess.'

'A heavily pregnant Stella,' muttered Hayward. 'She was convinced that the platform had been sabotaged. That's what Liam always said, but he had no evidence. It was kill himself or go to prison, and he took the easy way out. Anyway, ever since then she's been trying to prove it was sabotage.'

'And did she?'

'Not that I know of. We had a good thing going and she threw it all away. Spent her life and what little money we had campaigning for this or that. The company was still prosecuted and then wound up, so she appealed that. That was before we met. Then she wanted a new inquest into the accident at the bridge. Campaigned for years for that – drove the local MP mad with it. She's been trying to get access to the files for years too, bombarding them with Freedom of Information requests. She even tried suing the Health and Safety Executive.'

'What for?'

'She claimed the decision to prosecute was flawed.' Hayward sighed. 'Cost thousands, that one.'

'What about Amy?' asked Dixon.

'I always felt sorry for her, to be honest. Poor kid. She never even met Liam and yet Stella sucked her into it all. Nathan wasn't having any of it and got out. Like me, I suppose. A waste of fucking time, all of it. She'll never find anything now.'

Dixon's eyes narrowed. 'I think she did, Mr Hayward,' he said, picking his words carefully. 'And I think someone killed them both for it.'

Chapter Sixteen

Dixon parked on the top floor of the car park at Express Park, the sound of Louise tapping on the glass just carrying above the ratchet of the handbrake.

'What is it?' he asked, winding down the window.

'You need to see this, Sir.' She handed him a plastic document wallet. 'Before you go in. And there's a welcoming committee in meeting room two.'

'Chard?'

'Potter, Charlesworth and Lewis.'

'What is it?' he asked.

'The missing stuff from the forensic report and the handwritten statements.'

'I've got a couple of calls to make. Best make them from here, I suppose.' He started winding up the window. 'You haven't seen me.'

'No, Sir.'

Fifteen minutes later Dixon walked slowly past meeting room 2, relying on his peripheral vision to see in. Charlesworth had his back to the glass, as did Lewis. Not so Chard, who pointed at him, Potter jumping up from her seat at the head of the table and opening the door. 'In here, Nick.'

Charlesworth took the lead. 'Chief Inspector Chard is complaining that you're undermining his investigation, re-interviewing his witnesses. Is that correct?'

'No, Sir,' replied Dixon, sitting down in between Potter and Lewis. 'They are not *his* witnesses and it is hardly surprising that the same people might have information relevant to both investigations. The neighbour, Mrs Westmacott, for example. She knew both Stella and Amy.'

'What about her ex-husband?' snapped Chard. 'I decided he wasn't relevant and that decision is recorded in my Policy Log.'

'I decided that he was and that decision is recorded in *my* Policy Log.' Dixon folded his arms.

'We need to clear this up once and for all,' said Charlesworth. 'It's clear to me we can't rely on you two to work together so we need to put one of you in overall charge.' He turned to Potter. 'I'm content to leave that decision to you, Deborah.'

'Thank you, Sir.'

'I'm the senior officer,' said Chard, staring at Potter.

'Let me have a word with Dixon,' she replied. 'I'll catch you up, Simon.'

Chard stood up and followed Charlesworth out of the room. Dixon watched them walking along the landing – Chard muttering away – Dave, Mark and Louise also watching from the CID Area on the other side of the atrium, the tops of their heads just visible over their computer screens.

'What the bloody hell's going on, Nick?' asked Potter, closing the meeting room door. 'I told you to keep out of Chard's way.'

Dixon glanced at Lewis.

'I'm your line manager,' said Lewis, leaning back in his chair. 'I'm staying.'

'All right.' Dixon was sucking his teeth. 'I'll give you the evidence. What you do with it is up to you.'

'What evidence?' demanded Potter.

He opened the plastic document wallet and took out a handwritten witness statement. 'This is a statement from Stella's neighbour, Mabel Westmacott. I just spoke to her on the phone and she confirms it is not an accurate contemporaneous record of what she said at the time, nor is it the statement she signed.'

'What?'

'It's been doctored. The last page has been rewritten and her signature on the bottom forged.'

'Why?'

'To remove reference to a gentleman caller. Stella was in a relationship with someone at Portishead – her work colleagues had heard rumours – and that someone is trying to see to it that it doesn't come out.'

'Rumours are no bloody good,' muttered Potter.

'That same someone was at the property when PC Bolt broke in,' continued Dixon. 'It explains Bolt's sudden loss of memory – he's covering for a fellow officer. How else would he have known the rug and coffee table had gone? And that Stella was possibly at risk?'

'At risk?' Potter raised her eyebrows.

'It's a long story.' Dixon sighed. 'Her first husband committed suicide the night before his trial for corporate manslaughter. There was an accident during the construction of the Second Severn Crossing and Stella was convinced it was sabotage. My guess is she found something and was killed for it.'

'You're not suggesting this officer is involved in her murder?'

'No. He was in a relationship with her and is trying to keep it quiet.' Dixon shrugged his shoulders. 'And let's face it, I can hardly criticise someone for having a relationship at work.'

'No, you can't.'

'You never doctored witness statements to cover it up,' said Lewis.

'No, I didn't. I never gave out confidential information either.'

'What?' Potter lobbed her reading glasses on to the table.

'The original corporate manslaughter file from 1995 is not in the archive. It was signed out a couple of months ago.'

'Long before Stella's murder,' said Lewis.

'Precisely.'

'Who to?' asked Potter. 'Do we know?'

Dixon nodded. 'The forensic report on Stella's house that's been scanned on to the system is incomplete. The appendix listing trace DNA and fingerprints from known sources is missing, although I can't tell whether it's been deleted or was just never uploaded. It documents PC Bolt's fingerprints on the door handles – front and back – the telephone handset, stuff like that. And a hair of his on the floor in the kitchen. Nothing unusual in that, you might think.'

'That's why we're on the database,' said Potter.

'It also lists DCI Chard,' continued Dixon. 'His DNA and fingerprints were found at the scene as well.'

'He's the investigating officer.' Lewis frowned.

'He is.' Dixon slid the missing appendix across the table. 'Louise got it direct from the lab.'

Potter snatched it off the table and began flicking through it. 'Oh shit,' she mumbled, her teeth gritted.

'What?' asked Lewis.

'His DNA was found on the bedhead.' She slid the report across the table to Lewis. 'Hair in the plughole. Fingerprints on the TV gizmo. He was the bloody gentleman caller, wasn't he?'

Lewis cleared his throat, trying to hide a nervous laugh. 'Either that or he watched a bit of telly, then had a shower and a lie down while he was investigating the crime scene.'

'It also explains why the second husband has never been interviewed,' said Dixon. 'The Severn Crossing investigation would've come out. Then the fact that Chard already had the file out of the archive. And I'm guessing that Amy's statement was doctored for the same reason.'

'Amy's statement has been doctored?' asked Potter.

'Have you read it?'

'How did he ever think he was going to get away with it?'

'The investigation was winding down already,' said Dixon. 'No body's been found. And if it wasn't for Amy's death the file would've been closed and that would've been that. After all, he hasn't got long to go now until he retires on a full pension.'

Potter grimaced. 'Well, he can bloody well kiss goodbye to that now, can't he?'

Dixon was leaning back against a filing cabinet waiting for the kettle to boil when Potter and Lewis finally emerged from meeting room 2, Chard striding along the landing on the other side of the atrium towards them.

He flicked off the kettle and listened, watching the blood drain from Chard's face as Potter spoke.

'Simon Chard, I am arresting you on suspicion of perverting the course of justice . . .'

Dixon had heard enough. He turned away and switched the kettle back on, turning back just in time to see Potter and Lewis leading Chard towards the lift. It was a short ride down to the custody suite.

Twat.

Twenty minutes later the lift doors opened and Lewis stepped out on to the first floor, Potter continuing up to the second floor and the Professional Standards Department, a plastic document wallet tucked under her arm.

'She's referring it to the PSD,' said Lewis, walking up behind Dixon's workstation in the window. 'You're taking over both investigations. The files'll be brought down overnight.'

'Yes, Sir.'

'What about Chard's team?' asked Lewis. 'There's four of them.'

'They'd better start by re-interviewing all of the witnesses.'

'I'll sort it out, although Professional Standards will need to speak to them first, so it's likely to be a few days.' Lewis shook his head. 'I just can't believe it.'

'We need to find out exactly what information he gave her, Sir.'

'Well, there's no way you can interview him. You'll have to give a statement to Professional Standards, so you can brief them then and they can ask him.'

'She finally gets access to that file via Chard and what she finds ends up getting her killed.'

'You don't know that.'

'Not yet.'

'He's going to pay a high price.' Lewis sighed. 'Should've kept it in his trousers. His wife'll divorce him too.'

'D'you know her?'

'We've met a couple of times.'

'As soon as Amy was murdered, he was stuffed,' said Dixon.

'I should imagine a case review would've picked it up,' replied Lewis, 'but he'd have been retired by then. Anyway, I thought you handled it very well. Most people would've confronted him in front of Charlesworth.'

'My job is to report to my line manager, Sir,' said Dixon. 'And I can't say I enjoyed it, in spite of everything.'

'Quite.'

Dixon spent the rest of the afternoon doing his witness statement for Professional Standards. Do the statement and email it to them – it was preferable to an invitation upstairs. He shuddered. His last visit to the Professional Standards Department had not ended well.

Chapter Seventeen

Footsteps running along the landing, the relative peace and quiet of the deserted canteen shattered before he had even taken his first sip of coffee. 'What is it, Lou?' Dixon asked, looking up to see her head peering around the door.

'There you are, Sir. Potter's doing her nut.'

'What now?'

'They've got Steiner cornered in Hinkley Point. He's up one of the tower cranes holding the crane operator hostage and they're saying he's got a sawn off shotgun.'

'How the hell did he get that in there?' Dixon jumped up, sending the plastic coffee cup flying.

'No idea, Sir.'

'Armed Response?' He snatched his Kit Kat off the table before the tide of spilt coffee reached it.

'They're arriving on scene now. Steiner's asking for you, though, Sir.' Louise grimaced. 'Says he'll release the crane operator when you get there.'

'Does he now,' muttered Dixon, dropping a handful of napkins on to the puddle of coffee.

'Can I tell DCS Potter where you are? Only she's giving me a hard time.'

'Tell her I'm leaving now and I'll get there as quick as I can.'

'Yes, Sir.'

The news vans had beaten him to it, the visitors' car park overflowing with them. So had the helicopters, the police helicopter hovering directly over the site, three others out to sea, their red tail lights visible through the drizzle.

It had taken him twenty minutes just to get through the queues on the outskirts of Bridgwater, even with the blue light on top of his Land Rover. Then he'd picked up a marked car, which escorted him the rest of the way – sirens wailing – through the roadblocks on the A39 at Cannington and into HPC.

Another shutdown. Pickles would be hopping.

Dixon left his Land Rover on the grass verge opposite the entrance to Hinkley and ran across to the turnstiles, Potter pacing up and down behind them with the head of security, Jim Crew.

'Here he is,' she said, clapping her hands. 'Let him in.'

Crew opened a security door to the side of the turnstiles. 'This way,' he said.

'Where the hell have you been?'

'I'm here now,' replied Dixon.

'We're in the Incident Room. Firearms are on scene.'

Dixon followed Potter across the concourse behind the turnstiles to Welfare Block East, and up to the first floor.

'You can see it from here.' She pointed at a yellow crane in the distance, surrounded by blue lights on the ground. 'We've got Armed

Response out there already. Four on the ground and one up each of the adjacent cranes. And we've evacuated all of the workers down there to Welfare Block West.'

'I thought the site was shut down?'

'We let some of them start again when they'd been interviewed,' replied Potter. 'And there's work going on seven days a week.'

'Steiner's in the cab with the operator and there's no clear shot,' said the Armed Response officer standing behind her. 'It's howling a gale too, so the cranes are moving.'

'You know Inspector Watts, I gather, Dixon?'

'We've met.'

'I don't want a repetition of last time either.' Watts folded his arms.

Chief Inspector Bateman walked over to the window, a mobile phone pressed to his right ear. 'Still no shot, Sir,' he said, his left hand across his forehead. 'Yes, of course, Sir.' He rang off and turned to Dixon. 'That was the ACC. He's given the order. If Steiner brings the gun up and they get a clear shot, they're to take it.'

Watts turned away, talking into his radio.

'Tell me about the crane operator,' said Dixon.

'His name's Alistair Curran,' replied Pickles, spinning round on an office chair, tapping the screen of his phone with his thumbs.

'Is he married?'

'Yes.'

Bateman frowned. 'Two kids . . .'

'Has anyone spoken to him?' asked Dixon.

'Not since Steiner first got up there. He smashed the radio, but we're in touch with him by mobile phone. He let us speak to Curran, just to confirm he's unharmed, and he's answered it when we've rung so far. Seemed quite calm, oddly enough.'

Dixon turned back to the window and looked at his watch. An hour of daylight at most; less with the cloud and rain. 'What's the weather forecast?' he asked.

147

'Rain until midnight, getting heavier,' replied Bateman. 'The wind is strengthening too, gusting up to fifty miles an hour.'

Vehicles on the service road were driving with headlights on. Dixon grimaced. Lights all around the site were already starting to twinkle in the gloom: Welfare Block West, a mile away at least; the cranes, with red and white lights on the jibs. And the police helicopter, the searchlight underneath dancing in the wind, trying to keep a fix on the cab of the tallest crane. Steiner had chosen well.

Dixon had never been a fan of sci-fi, but it reminded him of a scene from *Blade Runner*, or *The Terminator*, perhaps.

'They've got night vision scopes,' said Watts. 'But it's not easy to identify the target when the light goes. And they'll be trying to hit a moving target from a moving platform. Hardly ideal.'

'What's he said so far?' asked Dixon.

'Just that he wants you for the crane operator,' replied Potter.

'No demands?'

'Just you.'

'Talk him down,' snapped Bateman, a mobile phone in his outstretched hand.

'And if he won't come?'

'We wait him out.'

Dixon took the phone from Bateman and pressed the green button. Two rings. 'Steiner.'

'It's Nick Dixon. You wanted to speak to me.'

'I wanted to *see* you.'

'We can arrange that. Let Alistair go—'

'He prefers Al. Don't you, Al?'

'All right, let Al go, leave the gun and climb down. I'll meet you at the bottom. That's the only way this ends well, Tony.'

'For me or him?'

'Both of you.'

'Are you sure?' snapped Steiner. 'Because, let me tell you, he's not.'

'We found the business card. And you signed my name in the guest book at Groom's Cottage. What was that all about?'

'Kept you interested, didn't it?'

'You didn't seriously think I'd lose interest, did you?'

'Look, stop playing games. Are you coming up here, or not? I've got two cartridges, and they're both for Al, if you don't.'

'My superiors won't let me,' said Dixon, glancing at Potter, then Bateman. 'They seem to think I'm a target.'

'You have superiors?' The sarcasm was dripping from Steiner's voice. 'I doubt that very much. You've got ten minutes.'

Then the line went dead.

'How the hell did he get up there?' asked Dixon, handing the phone back to Bateman.

'God knows.' Potter rolled her eyes.

'How old is Al?'

'Twenty-seven,' replied Pickles.

'With two children? They must be young.' Dixon was watching the rain running down the window. 'I have to go up.'

'It's out of the question.' Bateman was shaking his head.

'And I have to go before it gets dark. It's the only way this ends well for Al Curran.'

'No.' Potter folded her arms.

'Can you get me out there?' asked Dixon, turning to Crew.

'Er, yes I can, but . . .'

'I've got body armour on.' He tapped his chest with his knuckles. 'And I can stay below the cab. He'll have to come out on to the jib if he wants to get a shot at me and then—'

'We've got him,' interrupted Watts.

'There's a trap door in the floor of the turntable,' said Crew. 'He'd have to open it but then he could fire straight down the ladder.'

'Is the turntable enclosed?' asked Watts.

'No.'

'Either way, he's going to have to leave the cab and then we've got him.' Dixon was rubbing his chin. 'Now, can we get on with it before I change my mind?'

◆　◆　◆

'Tell me about the crane,' said Dixon. He was sitting in the back of a minibus, pulling on the leg loops of a harness.

'It's the biggest on site,' replied Crew. 'It's been lifting the cooling water pipes into position. You'll be directly above the nuclear island and it's well over two hundred feet down to the bottom of the stressing gallery. Are you all right with heights?'

'What's a stressing gallery?'

'It's just a deep trench. The concrete of the reactor is placed under stress to strengthen it and that's where the steel cables are fixed. It's designed to withstand an impact from a 747.'

'I'll be sure to remember that the next time I get on a plane,' muttered Dixon.

'You climb up inside the mast. It's just a series of aluminium stepladders. It'll be wet, so be careful.'

Just like climbing in the slate quarries with Jake, thought Dixon, only back then they'd have bailed out when it rained and gone to the pub.

'There are landings every twenty feet,' continued Crew. 'Stay below the top one and it should give you some extra protection if he—'

'Thanks.'

'And be bloody careful,' said Bateman. 'I'll ring him and let him know you're on the way up.'

'Get the helicopter to back off as well, will you, Sir? I'll need to be able to shout to him.'

'Good thinking.'

'And tell Armed Response to be bloody sure they know who it is they're shooting at.'

Bateman grinned. 'I will.'

'I'll be the one wearing the helmet.' Dixon jumped out of the back of the minibus and ducked low into the rain as he ran across to the base of the crane, a man wearing orange overalls and a hi-vis jacket waiting for him by a steel gate.

'Are you the one going up?' the man asked.

'Yes.'

The man clipped a karabiner into the loop on Dixon's harness, then handed him the other end. 'This is your safety line. Clip into the safety rail if you go out on to the jib. It'll be windy up there, as well as wet. What are you like with heights?'

'Fine.'

'Up you go then.'

Dixon looked up at the first ladder, fixed inside the yellow frame of the mast and leading up to a steel landing, then another ladder above. He counted six in total, each of them twenty feet or so high. The helicopter had moved away, the noise of the engine just carrying over the wind whistling through the steel lattice frame of the crane. The searchlight was still trying to fix on the cabin above him, lighting it up and then plunging it into darkness as the helicopter swayed from side to side in the gusts of wind.

First ladder done; Dixon took a deep breath.

Laser eye surgery will be an effing doddle after this.

He glanced across at the nearest crane, the cab dark, the jib turning in the wind; no sign of the operator or the firearms officer, but he or she was there somewhere, keeping out of sight. Steiner would know, surely? He must have seen them climbing the mast, rifle slung over their shoulder.

Anyone with a half a brain would expect nothing less.

It may have been a golden rule, but Dixon had always ignored it. He looked down. When he had been sea cliff climbing, it had been waves crashing in at the base of the cliffs; now it was a circle of blue lights around the base of the crane. An ambulance was visible too, now that he'd climbed higher, waiting on the earthworks access road.

Rain was dripping off his Kevlar helmet and running down the back of his neck. He had been given it by Watts, the firearms officer, the radio activated, voices in an earpiece in his right ear.

'AR14, I have him in sight. Halfway up.'

Dixon froze to the ladder when a gust of wind ripped through the steel frame, the whole crane swaying from side to side. The jib was turning above him now too, the screech of the steel turntable adding to the whistle of the wind.

That was the sort of gust that would loosen roof tiles, he thought, remembering long dark nights listening to the old sash windows at home rattling and creaking in the wind. At least sea cliffs didn't move.

'Dixon?'

The shout came from above, while he was still below the last of the steel landings. He dialled Potter's number on his mobile phone and then dropped it back into his jacket pocket, a loud cough from him covering her voice when she answered the call.

'Is that you, Dixon?' A man's voice, shouting down from above.

'I'm on my own, Tony. All right?'

Potter got the message. Listen, don't speak.

Dixon stopped on the ladder just beneath the landing, the turntable directly above. The hatch in the floor was open, Steiner silhouetted in the beam of the helicopter's searchlight, the unmistakable outline of a twelve bore shotgun in hand.

'Keep coming,' said Steiner. 'And you can get rid of that helmet. I'm not stupid. It's got a microphone in it.'

'Where's Al?'

'You heard what I said?' Steiner scowled. 'Keep coming.'

Dixon stepped out on to the top landing.

'Now the helmet.' Steiner was lying flat on the turntable, his head screened from the crane opposite by the open steel hatch. 'Over the side,' he snarled, when Dixon placed the helmet at his feet.

He dropped it over the side and watched it fall away into the darkness.

'Now, keep coming.'

'Where's Al?'

'You'll see.'

Dixon climbed the ladder slowly, the crane swaying in a violent gust of wind as another squall tore across the site. The adjacent cranes were moving too; some turning, all of them swaying. He flinched. A shot from a moving platform? He wondered if he knew the officer with his or her finger on the trigger.

He stopped with his head just above the level of the turntable, Steiner having crawled backwards into the cab, keeping his head below the level of the steel kickplate. That explained that.

It took a moment for his eyes to adjust to the flickering light. The door of the cab was open, the searchlight streaming in from the helicopter hovering behind, the lights visible through the windscreen of the crane. The operator's chair was empty, a figure sitting hunched on the floor in the corner, his knees pulled up under his chin. He was staring at Dixon, his eyes wide.

'Al?'

'Yes, it's Al.' Steiner laughed. 'Who else is it going to be?'

'Are you all right?'

'Get up here,' snapped Steiner, both barrels pointed at Dixon's head.

He did as he was told. Slowly. Hoping that the firearms officer had seen him drop the helmet. Otherwise it was a clear shot at a head without a helmet on it . . .

'Where did you get the gun?' asked Dixon.

'Wouldn't you like to know.'

'Yes, I would.'

'It was thrown over the fence out near the bat house. All right?'

The photofit hadn't been far off. Six weeks' growth of beard, greyer than the artist's impression. The ponytail must be a hair extension. Horn-rimmed glasses were a nice touch. Steiner had clearly thought it through; there was even a new scar on his left cheek – self-inflicted, no doubt.

'You got me here,' said Dixon. 'So, what d'you want?'

'To explain.' Steiner lowered the gun, his back pressed to the steel side wall of the cab.

'Let Al go first.'

'No.'

'Can you climb down, Al?'

'Yes, I—' He tried to stand up.

'I said no.' Steiner lashed out at Al with his foot, kicking him in the side of the thigh.

'How d'you think this is going to end if you harm Al, Tony? Or me for that matter.'

'I know exactly how it's going to end.' Steiner stepped into the window of the cab, standing in front of the operator's chair, the shotgun down at his side. 'I bring the gun up and your boys on the crane over there earn their money.'

'Well, you don't need Al for that.' Dixon helped Al to his feet and pushed him towards the hatch in the floor of the turntable, shielding him from Steiner with his own body. 'Down you go,' he said. 'And keep going down. Someone will meet you.'

Steiner sighed as he watched Al disappear down the ladder. 'Just my fucking luck to run into you,' he said, kicking the chair in front of him. 'I've been running rings around plod for years and then you turn up.'

'Shit happens, Tony. But I'll take it as a compliment.'

'It was meant as one.'

'Tell me about your brother,' said Dixon, glancing across at the nearest crane.

'I haven't got a brother.'

'Paul.'

'Monique told you?'

Dixon nodded.

'I suffocated him. I never fitted in after he came along. I wasn't really their kid, was I?'

'What about Monique?'

'She was different.' Steiner glanced over his shoulder at the helicopter. 'And, besides, they never left me alone with her.'

'You got expelled from school too. What was that all about?'

'I used a bent coat hanger to burn some kid. Can't even remember why now.'

'Monique told me about your ears.'

'You got tinnitus?' he asked.

'Just diabetes,' replied Dixon. 'What was it you wanted to explain?'

'I was hiding with the hippies when a man came looking for me and said he wanted someone to go into Hinkley Point and cause a bit of trouble.'

'Why are you telling me this?'

'He double-crossed me.'

'Like Mrs Boswell?'

Steiner sneered. 'Daft old sod said I could stay in the barn, then a couple of days later I found her going off to call you lot. What else could I do? I was dragging her back and she just dropped dead on me.'

'Did you really have to leave her like that? Hanging.'

'No, not really.' Steiner grinned. 'I bet she was in a bit of a state when you found her.'

'You could say that.'

'She shouldn't have double-crossed me then, should she? That gets you killed. Plenty of people have found that out the hard way.'

'What sort of trouble did this man want you to cause?'

'He wanted me to sabotage the tarmac, for the roads like. There are piles of it in a compound. Something and nothing. He said he could get me in on a false ID and paid me five grand in bitcoin. Said he could get me out on a boat too. Then once I was in here he said he knew who I was and he'd turn me in unless I killed that girl, Amy. The dumper truck driver. Then he double-crossed me, didn't he?'

'What's his name?'

'I don't know,' replied Steiner. He wiped his nose on the back of his left sleeve, the shotgun in his right, still down by his side. 'He told me to dump her body in the silo; said it'd be filled the next morning and she'd never be found. Only it didn't quite work out like that, did it. They wouldn't let me on the boat at the jetty either. Said they knew nothing about it.'

'What did he look like, this man?'

'It was dark. Late fifties, maybe. He was wearing a suit and a coat with the hood up. When you're in my position, you don't ask too many questions. He was offering me a way out, for fuck's sake. And you were closing in.' He thrust his left hand into his coat pocket and pulled out a crumpled photograph. 'Here,' he said, throwing it to Dixon. 'He gave me this picture of her.'

The crane swayed again, the wind whistling through the rails on the jib. Steiner leaned forward and grabbed the arm of the operator's chair with his free hand, careful to keep the gun out of sight.

'You were just doing your job,' he said. 'But that bastard double-crossed me.'

'Well, you'll never get him if it ends here and now.'

'I won't,' replied Steiner, grinning. He slid his free hand into his inside pocket and took out his phone. Then he lobbed it to Dixon. 'You will. It's all on there.'

'Why don't you help me?'

'It was always going to end this way after the canal. And there's no way I'm going back to prison. Sitting in a cell listening to my ears?' Steiner cringed. 'No way. Not if I'm never getting out. And what would the chances of that be?'

'You never kn—'

'Bollocks.'

Another gust of wind, the crane swayed and Steiner stumbled on to the operator's chair. Dixon lurched forward to grab the gun – too slow. Steiner threw himself back against the windscreen of the cab and brought the shotgun up in his right hand, grinning at Dixon as he did so.

A muffled crack and the side window shattered, the glass flying across the cab in slow motion. Then the bullet hit Steiner.

Dixon turned away as blood and brain sprayed across his face. Steiner crumpled to the floor, oddly calm, a gaping hole where his forehead and left eye had been.

No longer troubled by the ringing in his ears.

A pool of blood began to seep across the steel floor of the cab, the crumpled photograph of Amy floating towards Dixon's feet. He stepped back out on to the turntable and slumped down against the railings, blood dripping on to his screen as he disconnected the call to Potter, her voice screaming down the phone: 'Nick? Are you all right, Nick?'

Chapter Eighteen

The crane was swaying more violently now, if anything, the wind stronger, and louder as it roared and whistled through the steel frame of the jib. Dixon was watching the lights along Burnham seafront twinkling in the distance across the Parrett Estuary, and the flashing lights on the Pavilion.

He slid his phone out of his pocket and tapped out a text message: *Steiner is dead*

Roger Poland's reply came in seconds.

Watching live on Sky News. Please tell me that's not you up the crane

Who else would it be, Roger? Who the bloody hell else?

Then he heard footsteps on the aluminium ladders below, and the next thing he knew Armed Response officers were standing in the doorway of the cab, their firearms pointing down at Steiner.

'He's dead.'

'Have you checked, Sir?' asked one, the other turning away and talking into his radio.

'No, I haven't checked. His brains are all over the floor.' Dixon stood up. 'And me.'

'Are you all right, Sir?'

'The blood's his.' He turned for the top of the ladder. 'Just make sure someone bags up that photo.'

'Yes, Sir.'

'And tell SOCO to keep an eye out for his ID.'

More Armed Response officers on the way up stepped to one side on the landing to allow Dixon past, two paramedics on the next landing. Another stopped in front of him and shone a torch in his face. 'Let's get you cleaned up,' she said.

Potter and Bateman were waiting for him when he finally stepped off the bottom rung of the last ladder.

'Are you all right, Nick?' asked Potter.

'Fine.' Dixon was undoing the buckle on his harness.

'Steiner's dead?' She was peering at the side of his face, lit up by the flickering blue lights.

'He got what he wanted.'

'So, what happens now?' asked Bateman.

'We find who killed Stella Hayward,' replied Dixon, sitting down on the bumper of the beat team Land Rover. 'And who paid Steiner to kill Amy. His phone needs to go to High Tech,' he said, handing it to Potter.

'What's the code?'

'He would've given that to me if—'

'It was the right call, Nick,' said Potter. 'We couldn't take any chances. For all we knew it was a ploy to get you up there.'

'You were listening?'

'We were.'

'Then you knew he wasn't going to kill me.'

'He said he wasn't. That doesn't mean he wasn't.'

'Here,' said the paramedic who had followed him down the ladders, handing him a bundle of medicated wet wipes. 'Use these.'

'Thanks.' Dixon stood up.

'Where are you off to?' asked Potter.

'Express Park to clean up. Then I'm going home.'

He had been sitting in the bottom of the shower for fifteen minutes before the pink water finally ran clear, the last of Steiner's blood washed down the plughole. He'd tried shampoo, but every time he closed his eyes he saw Steiner's forehead exploding right in front of him. Another memory etched on his mind that would take weeks to shift; another vision to add to the nightmares.

Not that he'd ever been troubled by many. A severed head in a golf course bunker; absolute darkness, the only sound water dripping; fire. That one had woken him up a few times.

'Level headed', the psychiatric report had said. Charlesworth had forced him into that after the factory fire. He'd told Jane it was just a meeting at Portishead, which was true. Technically.

'A remarkably relaxed attitude to near death experiences'. He shook his head. There'd been enough of them when he'd been rock climbing with Jake. 'Having an epic', they used to call it. An electric storm on the Matterhorn; falling off the crux of Poetry Pink – Jake jumping off the ledge to take up the slack rope – inches to spare that time; a hypo on Quiet Waters down in Huntsman's Leap; the knife edge ridge of Crib Goch on Snowdon at night in winter dressed in a dinner jacket and tie.

It was about adrenaline. The rush you get when you're still standing at the end of the day. Although Crib Goch had been more about beer, possibly.

A wry smile. Shit happens – no point in dwelling on it, Jake had said, the last time they spoke. The last time before he had been killed.

Dixon stepped out of the shower at Express Park and sat down on the bench, putting off what came next: get dressed, go home and face Jane. Now *that* he really was dreading. Louise knew, and had hit the nail on the head when she met him in the staff car park still drenched in Steiner's blood.

'You're going to wish he really had killed you when Jane's finished,' she had said, forcing a smile.

Louise had been trying to cheer him up, making light of it, of course she was. Always best, he thought. Shame it hadn't worked though.

He looked down at the black bin liner on the floor. His clothes could spend all night in the washing machine, but quite how he would explain the state of his jacket to the bloke at the dry cleaner's was beyond him. He had scrounged a T-shirt and an Avon and Somerset Police fleece top, which would do to get him home. Nothing for it. He had sat there so long he was dry now anyway.

He glanced at his phone. Six missed calls.

'Home to face the music it is then,' he muttered.

The back door of his cottage flew open, the burst of light catching Dixon still sitting in his Land Rover, staring at the stinging nettles in the flowerbed.

Jane opened the driver's door and leaned in, putting her arms around him and kissing him.

'You fucking idiot,' she whispered, holding his face in her hands, a smile of sorts on her lips.

He leaned forward, his forehead pressed to hers. 'How did you know?' he asked.

'I saw it on the telly. Then Lewis rang to let me know you were all right. He said Steiner was dead, so I thought it would be safe to come home.' She stepped back, letting him climb out of the Land Rover. 'What on earth were you thinking?'

'The crane operator was twenty-seven with two children. And Steiner said he just wanted a chat. What else could I do?'

'Lewis told me about Chard too. The bloody hypocrite; making your life a misery and all the time he was—'

'Let it go. He's not worth it.'

Then Monty was jumping up at him in the kitchen.

'I've lost count now,' said Jane.

'What of?'

'How many of your nine lives you've got left.' She smiled. 'C'mon, there's a beer in the fridge. No bloody milk, I expect.' She opened a bottle, sniffed it, shuddered, and then tipped it down the sink. 'We left in a bit of a hurry.'

Dixon was standing by the open back door, still holding the bin liner of clothes.

'That lot can go straight in the bin,' Jane said, running the tap. 'Are you seriously going to wear it again?'

'Good point,' replied Dixon, dropping the bag outside by the step.

'Your other stuff's upstairs on the bed, but I forgot your insulin. It's still in the fridge at Worle.' She lifted the lid on the bread bin and took out a bag, holding it at arm's length. Then she put her foot on the pedal and dropped it in the bin. 'I can pick it up in the week. I'll be popping over to see Mum and Dad, I expect. Will you be all right till then?'

'No idea,' said Dixon, turning for the bottom of the stairs. 'I'm just going to get out of this stuff.'

'Have you eaten?'

'I had something earlier.'

He sat down on the bed and allowed himself to slump back, watching the shadows and the headlights of passing cars on the ceiling.

'Nick!' Jane's voice, shouting from the yard at the back of the cottage. 'You'd better come and see this.'

'I'll be down in a minute.' Eyes closed, still lying on the bed.

'Now!' screamed Jane.

Dixon ran down the stairs to find her standing by the back door.

'Look at him,' she said. 'It's like he's drunk.'

Monty staggered over to Dixon's feet and slumped back on to his haunches, swaying from side to side. 'What's he eaten?'

'Just his biscuits. He was drinking from that thing over there, but I stopped him as soon as I—'

'Has he been sick?'

'No.'

Dixon ran over to the far side of the yard and picked up a small terracotta dish, the dregs of a pink liquid in the bottom. He sniffed it. 'How much did he have?'

'Not a lot, I don't think. What is it?'

'Antifreeze,' replied Dixon, his face flushed, tears welling up.

'Is it serious?'

'Yes, it bloody well is.' He handed the dish to Jane. 'Take this, the vet will need to see it.' Then he slammed the back door of the cottage, before bending down and picking up Monty, the dog's head hanging over his arm like a rag doll's. 'My car keys are in my pocket. Quickly!'

Jane fished the keys out of Dixon's fleece pocket and opened the rear passenger door of the car. 'Get in the back with him,' he said, gently laying Monty down across the seat. 'Make sure he doesn't slide on the floor.'

'Someone put that there deliberately,' said Jane, tears streaming down her cheeks as Dixon accelerated away from the cottage. 'They must've done.'

Left at the end of Brent Street, Dixon was still accelerating when the Land Rover sailed over the railway bridge. 'Hold on to him!'

'I am!'

'Ring the vet and let them know we're on the way,' he said, passing his phone to Jane. 'It's in my contacts.'

Jane dialled the number and flicked on the speakerphone.

'Drakes emergency line. Tabi speaking.'

'This is Jane Winter. We're on our way with Monty. He's a large white Staffie and he's been drinking antifreeze.'

'I know Monty. Are you sure it's antifreeze?'

'Yes!' shouted Dixon from the driver's seat.

'We've got a sample,' said Jane.

'When was this?' asked Tabi.

'Five or ten minutes at most.'

'I'll wait for you by the back door. How far away are you?'

'Two minutes,' replied Jane, as Dixon accelerated along Berrow Road, flashing his headlights as he overtook a line of cars, hazard lights on, wiping the tears from his cheeks with the palm of his hand.

Jane leaned forward and peered at the speedometer over his shoulder: sixty-five. He slowed at the pedestrian crossing, then the metallic click of the accelerator pedal hitting the floor again.

'He's asleep, I think,' she said, looking down at Monty.

'Wake him up!'

'C'mon, boy, wake up.' Shaking him now.

Dixon glanced into the back to see his dog lift his head, his eyes rolling.

'He's not going to d—?'

'Don't say it,' he snapped, cutting Jane off mid-sentence.

Dixon screeched to a halt outside Drakes Veterinary Surgery and jumped out, leaving his Land Rover across the zig-zag lines on the zebra crossing, the yellow lights casting an eerie glow. He reached into the back and picked up Monty. 'Bring that dish,' he said, kicking the door shut.

Tabi was waiting for them at the back door when they ran around the corner, Monty's head hanging over Dixon's shoulder. 'Bring him straight in.'

Through a set of double doors and into a large room with shelves all around, medicine bottles lined up along them.

'You're sure it's antifreeze?' she asked, running across to an operating table. 'Put him here.'

'Yes,' replied Dixon. 'Where's the dish?'

Jane handed it to the vet.

'Ten minutes ago, you say?' Tabi was sniffing the pink liquid.

'Yes, no more than that.' Dixon was looking up at the ceiling. 'We came straight here.'

'Has he eaten?'

'Dry biscuits, a whole bowl of them just before that,' replied Jane.

'Has he been sick?'

'No,' replied Dixon.

'All right, I'm going to make him vomit,' said Tabi, filling a syringe. 'A bit of diluted hydrogen peroxide should do the trick. You may want to wait outside?'

'No bloody fear.'

'Can you hold his head?'

Tabi emptied the syringe down Monty's throat and began rubbing him under his chin. Then he lurched to his feet and vomited over the side of the operating table, his sides heaving with the strain.

Pink dog biscuits, the fluid dark pink too.

'Looks like they've absorbed some of it, at least,' said Tabi. 'We'll give him a minute and then do it again.'

Jane leaned over Monty, his head in her hands, and pressed her forehead to his. 'It's going to be all right.'

Tabi refilled the syringe. 'Let's make him vomit again.'

More pink biscuits, the fluid clearer this time.

'Once more should do it.'

'Is he going to die?' asked Dixon, holding back the tears. Just.

'Ethylene glycol poisoning is usually fatal,' replied Tabi, with a grimace. 'But you got here quickly and the biscuits have absorbed a lot of it, so there's a good chance.'

'It's my fault,' gasped Jane. 'I didn't see him quick enough.'

'It's not your fault,' said Dixon. 'You weren't to know.'

'Let's make him vomit again.' Tabi was flicking the syringe. 'Last time, all right?'

Two pink biscuits this time, the fluid clear. Monty collapsed on the table, panting.

'I'm going to need to keep him in. I'll put him on a drip to keep him hydrated and there's some stuff I can give him to support his kidneys. That's the risk in these cases, kidney failure, but we should know within forty-eight hours.'

'Can we stay with him?' asked Jane.

'Let me get him settled. I need to get a catheter in his front leg and take some blood.'

Dixon was scratching Monty behind his ears. 'How long?'

'Give me half an hour or so.'

Dixon sat down on a bench in one of the shelters on the seafront and looked across at Hinkley Point, blue lights still flickering away in the middle of the site, just visible through the drizzle across the estuary.

The streetlights had gone off, making it well after midnight.

'You've had a helluva day,' said Jane, taking his hand.

'I've had better.'

'He's going to be fine, I know he is.'

'You heard what she said.'

'Tabi wanted to know if he's insured.'

Dixon swallowed hard. 'That dog is going to the beach one last time, even if I have to carry him all the way.'

'What about the money?' asked Jane.

'Fuck the money.'

Chapter Nineteen

A short walk down through the churchyard, using the torches on their phones; the back door of the surgery was standing open when they got back twenty minutes later. It was a small waiting area, separate from the main surgery – Dixon hadn't really noticed it on the way in. A few posters on the walls and a box of tissues on the windowsill.

'Ah, there you are,' said Tabi, opening the inner door. 'It's just a question of how much he's ingested. The blood results are normal, as far as I can see, but I'll do some more in the morning and send them off to the lab. Our machine's pretty basic, I'm afraid. He's on a drip and I'm giving him fomepizole for his kidneys. He's had a light sedative too.'

'Will he live?' asked Dixon.

'I really don't . . .' Tabi's voice tailed off.

'I don't want him to suffer.'

Tabi nodded.

'If a decision needs to be taken,' mumbled Dixon, 'I want to know straightaway. I don't care what time of the day or night it is.'

'I'm on duty and will be keeping an eye on him all night. Don't worry.'

'I just want to be here if . . . if you have to . . .' Dixon could feel his eyes welling up again. He squinted, trying to hold back the tears, but it just made it worse.

'He's not showing any signs of distress at the moment,' said Tabi, putting her hand on his arm. 'I will tell you if I think he is.'

'Thank you.'

'Go in and see him.' She opened the door. 'It'll do him good to hear your voice.'

The back wall of the recovery room was lined with cages, a chihuahua sitting in the cage to Monty's left wearing a surgical collar and looking none too chuffed about it. A black and white cat too, in a cage above.

Monty hadn't noticed.

Dixon squatted down in front of the cage, reached in and stroked his dog behind the ears. Monty was lying on his side, his eyes closed. He opened them, stood up slowly and tottered to the front of the cage, trailing a saline tube behind his bandaged front leg, the bag hanging from the rungs above his head.

'Don't come out,' said Dixon, gently pushing him back in. 'C'mon, lie down, old son.'

Monty slumped down on to the blanket and rolled on to his side as Jane knelt down in front of the cage.

'I'll try him with some food later,' said Tabi. 'If there's any change, I'll let you know, I promise.'

'We'll go,' said Dixon. 'Let him sleep.'

'And ring me if you're worried.' Tabi smiled. 'Any time.'

A patrol car was parked behind the Land Rover on the zig-zag lines, the only light in the road the flashing yellow beacon on the zebra crossing.

'We'd better not be getting a ticket,' snapped Jane.

'I thought it was you,' said PC Cole, appearing around the side of the Land Rover. 'I recognised the—' His grin quickly faded. 'Is everything all right?'

'Monty's been poisoned,' said Jane.

'Is he going to be OK?'

Dixon kicked the front tyre. 'We won't know for a couple of days.'

'Poisoned deliberately?'

'Antifreeze in the yard behind the cottage,' replied Jane. 'Someone had put out a saucer of it. One of those terracotta plant pot dish things.'

'When?'

'Today. A couple of hours ago, maybe.'

'Leave it with me,' said Cole. 'I'll make some enquiries. A bit of house to house. See if anyone saw anything.'

Dixon's eyes narrowed. 'If you find anything, you tell me, all right?'

It felt odd, sleeping without a large dog on the end of his bed, grumbling at him every time he moved. Dixon woke early and spent another half an hour sitting cross-legged in the bottom of the shower; too busy worrying about Monty now to feel sorry for himself. Monty was different. Whether he lived or died was out of Dixon's hands. A puddle of antifreeze under the Land Rover he could understand and he'd never have forgiven himself. Or the person who sold it to him. But a saucer of it? He grimaced.

If Monty dies, someone will pay for that. Dearly.

'The vet's on the phone,' said Jane, sliding open the shower door a crack.

'Is he all right?' asked Dixon, scrambling to his feet.

'She wants to speak to you. Shall I flip it to speakerphone?'

He nodded. 'Hello,' he said, his eyes wide, the water still running.

'Hi, it's Tabi. I thought you might like to know I've just fed Monty some fish and vegetables.'

'I thought you were ringing to tell me he was—'

'No, no. He's doing OK so far. I liquidised it and fed it to him through a syringe. Nice and bland. He's kept it down and now he's nodded off again.'

Dixon puffed out his cheeks. 'Can I come and see him?'

'*We,*' said Jane impatiently.

'When d'you want to come?' asked Tabi.

'Now.'

'You do know what time it is?'

'Yes.'

'Er, yes, of course then. I'm here all weekend.'

Monty was covered in a blanket, the clear plastic tube still attached to his foreleg. He slept through their visit after the initial excitement when they walked into the recovery room. And so did Dixon, sitting on the floor, leaning back against the wall opposite the cage. It was enough that they each knew the other was there, thought Jane.

By rights they should be out on the beach. Sunday had dawned clear, a full moon still up, the tide out. Perfect.

'I'll take some more blood and check his kidney function later,' whispered Tabi. 'If he can come home, you'll need to get a liquidiser. They're twenty quid in Tesco's. Or you can borrow mine.'

'I'll get one later,' replied Jane.

'Plain fish and vegetables or rice, something bland like that. Every four hours or so. I'll give you some big syringes.'

'Thanks.'

'It said on the news you've got Steiner,' said Tabi. 'There's a telly upstairs in the staffroom. You could hear the shots on the TV coverage, even over the helicopter.'

'He was the one who went up the crane,' whispered Jane, pointing at Dixon. 'They got the operator out then a firearms officer got Steiner.'

'I wondered if it was him. Bloody hell, he's had a belly full of it, hasn't he.' Tabi frowned. 'Is he all right?'

'Fine, I think. You never quite know, really.' Jane shrugged her shoulders. 'He bottles things up.'

◆ ◆ ◆

The CID Area was deserted when Dixon stepped out of the lift on the first floor of Express Park just before 9 a.m. He'd spent several hours at the vet's, most of them asleep on the floor of the recovery room, but he had held Monty while Tabi took some more blood before he left.

'Are you all right with blood?' she had asked.

Dixon had smiled.

The door of meeting room 2 flew open and DCI Lewis shouted across the atrium as he walked along the landing. 'What are you doing here? You're supposed to be taking a few days off.'

'Bollocks.'

'What about your dog?'

'The vet's going to text me the blood results. There's nothing I can do except wait and I'd rather keep busy if it's all the same to you.'

'They're using the Incident Room upstairs, if you're sure.' Lewis stepped back into the meeting room. 'Deborah Potter's taken over the investigation.'

'Ma'am,' said Louise, nodding towards the stairs when Dixon appeared at the top.

'What are you doing here?' asked Potter.

'Keeping busy.'

The Incident Room on the top floor still hadn't been dismantled after the investigation into the missing girls had been wound down, over forty workstations still in situ, only four of them occupied: Dave, Mark, Louise and Potter.

'Chard has been released for the time being,' said Potter, gesturing to the vacant workstation opposite her. 'The files on Stella Hayward's murder are downstairs and you'll get his team when they've been interviewed by Professional Standards. Until then it's just you, but if you need help I can send someone down from Portishead.'

'I thought you were taking over the investigation?'

'Not now you're here.'

'Thank you, Ma'am.'

'We're closing down the Incident Room at Hinkley, but they've said we can use the beat team office as and when.'

'When.'

'Really?'

'You heard what Steiner said before he had his brains blown out,' said Dixon. 'Someone got him into Hinkley on a false ID. And threw the shotgun over the fence.'

Potter sighed. 'It was empty.'

Dixon stared at her, his expression blank. He rubbed his cheek, convinced he could feel Steiner's blood trickling down it. Again.

'Did you hear what I said?' she asked. 'His gun was empty.'

'Does Bateman know?'

'No.'

'What about the AR officer who pulled the trigger?'

'Not yet.'

Dixon had his elbows on the table, his forehead resting on his hands. 'He gave me no indication that the gun was otherwise than fully loaded and his finger was on the trigger the whole time.' He looked up. 'You were listening to the conversation. If he had then—'

'They'll be pleased to know you'll say that.'

'It's the truth. You heard what he said. There was no way he was going back to prison.' Dixon shook his head. 'I had him though. He lost his balance when the crane moved and—'

'He brought the gun up,' said Potter.

172

Dixon nodded. 'Yes, he did.'

'That was the order, "if he brings the gun up", and that's what it looked like from the other crane. You can't blame them.'

'I don't.'

'Some shot though,' muttered Pearce. 'From a moving crane, at a moving crane.'

'Good. Then we'll say no more about it,' said Potter. 'The Independent Office for Police Conduct will go over the whole thing anyway. Focus on Amy and her mother.'

'What about Steiner's fake ID?'

'Scientific recovered it from his body,' replied Potter. 'It shows him as an employee of Agard – the same company Amy worked for – but they've never heard of him.'

Dixon curled his lip. 'What about the Severn Crossing prosecution file?'

'Professional Standards have got it. It was recovered from Chard's house.'

'I'll need to see it.'

'Leave it with me.' Potter stood up. 'You'll get a transcript of Chard's interview when they've finished with him as well.'

'I need to speak to him.'

'No chance.' She picked up her handbag and headed for the top of the stairs. 'And I hope your dog's OK.'

'Thank you, Ma'am.'

'How *is* Monty, Sir?' asked Louise, when Potter's grey streaks had disappeared from view down the stairs.

'We won't know for a couple of days.'

'I hope it works out.'

'Thanks.'

'Good news about that git Chard, hey, Sir?' Pearce grinned. 'He really had it in for you, didn't he? And all the time he was knocking . . .'

His voice tailed off when Dixon glared at him. 'All right, maybe it's not good news,' mumbled Pearce.

'It's just going to be us for the time being,' said Dixon. 'So, we need to focus. Let's start with what we know.'

'Steiner was paid in bitcoin to murder Amy,' said Louise. 'By person or persons unknown.'

'We don't *know* that, do we?'

'He must've been. And it must be related to what Stella was investigating, Sir,' said Harding. 'It can't be a coincidence that she'd just got access to the old file. She must've found something, confronted someone with what she'd found out, maybe, and paid the price for it.'

'We're assuming she's dead then?'

'Yes,' replied Harding. 'She must be. Otherwise she'd have come out of the woodwork when Amy was killed.'

'Have High Tech cracked Steiner's phone?' asked Dixon.

'His passcode was his date of birth,' replied Louise. 'But there's nothing in there, really. Two unregistered mobile numbers and that's it.'

'What about his bitcoin wallet?'

'We'll never get into that. There's the twelve word passphrase to get to the login screen, then a four digit pin number.'

'Even if we get in, it won't tell us much, Sir,' said Harding. 'Every transaction may be identifiable, but all you get is a random string of letters and numbers. It doesn't tell you where the money has come from.'

'And there's no way of finding that out?'

'We're on to Bitfly, but I wouldn't hold your breath.' Louise folded her arms.

'There isn't,' said Harding. 'That's the whole point of bitcoin, the anonymity. More so if you're doing it over the dark net.'

'And was he?'

'Yes, Sir,' replied Louise. 'He'd got the TOR app installed on his iPhone.'

'What have you found out about Amy then?' asked Dixon, looking at his phone.

Creatinine and urea levels higher but still within normal range. Just fed him again. Jane here. Tabi

'She'd been at HPC six months,' replied Pearce. 'Bit of a star, apparently. Her best friend was Michelle. She's training to be a pharmacist at Frenchay Hospital.'

'Have you spoken to Michelle?' asked Dixon.

'Only on the phone. She got too upset to talk properly.'

'So, we don't know whether Amy was actively participating in her mother's investigation?'

'No, Sir.'

'Still no sign of her phone?'

'No, Sir.'

'What about Stella's iPad?'

'There's a report from High Tech on the system,' replied Harding. 'Not a lot, is the short answer. Plenty of photos and lots of FaceTime calls to and from Amy's phone, as you would expect. Emails too, but there's nothing exciting.'

'Speak to Michelle again,' said Dixon. 'We need to know whether it's just a coincidence that Amy was working at HPC. After all, it's the biggest construction project in this part of the country since the Second Severn Crossing.'

'Shall we go and see her?'

'Yes.' Dixon turned to Louise. 'We'll come at it from the other end. I want to know everything about the first husband's company.'

'Crook Engineering.' Louise flipped open her notebook. 'It was wound up after his death though.'

'Employees?'

'The witness statements will be on the prosecution file.'

'Have you tried the Inland Revenue?'

'There are a couple on the books.' Louise closed her notebook. 'But he did a lot of cash in hand and they weren't so hot on it back then.'

A small team; a large investigation. Sometimes as Senior Investigating Officer you just have to stick your neck out and pursue a line of enquiry, thought Dixon, although this time it wasn't unreasonable to pursue the same one that Stella had died for. 'All right, let's assume Stella found out the platform had been sabotaged – or at least got close, close enough to get her killed. Who stood to gain from that?'

'Centrix Platforms,' said Louise. 'They took over the contract for the platforms to complete the monorail.'

Dixon smiled. 'You know what to do.'

Bateman had at least had the wit to record Dixon's confrontation with Steiner, holding his phone next to Potter's, and a transcript was already on the system when he logged in. Dixon sighed as he scrolled down. How much more would Steiner have given him if he'd taken him alive? Still, no point crying over spilt milk. Or blood. Or antifreeze for that matter.

He slid his phone out of his pocket and tapped out a text message. *Where are u? Nx*

Jane's reply came before he had finished typing the first paragraph of his witness statement.

Tesco's getting a liquidiser fish and veg. He can come home later :-) Can you pick Lucy up at Highbridge train stn 1852 she's coming down to help Jx

He snatched his phone off the desk and dialled her number.

'I'm at the checkout.'

'What did Tabi say?'

'There's no change, I'm afraid, so try not to get your hopes up. She just thinks he'll be better off at home. We've got to take him back in the morning for more blood tests. He's still got the catheter in his leg but he'll be off the drip. How do I get pills into him?'

'Sliced turkey.'

'Now you tell me.' Muffled voices. 'Sorry, I've got to get some sliced turkey. Over there?' Jane came back on the line. 'If there's any change, I'll let you know.'

'What time are you picking him up?'

'Four.'

Jane rang off, leaving Dixon staring at the picture of Monty on the beach that he used as the wallpaper on his phone.

'Sir?'

He looked up, careful not to blink in case it released the tears that had welled up.

'Centrix Platforms was wound up in 2005. Voluntary liquidation,' continued Louise. 'Raymond Harper was the owner, but he died in 2004. There's a widow though. Anne. She lives over at Bleadon.'

'Give her a ring and see if she'll speak to us this afternoon.'

'Yes, Sir.'

'Who have we got from Crook?'

'There's the operations manager,' replied Pearce. 'He must have retired by now, but he's on the electoral roll at an address in Frome.'

'We'll go and see him as well then.'

The next two hours were spent writing his witness statement, reliving the events of the night before on the crane. Not that they hadn't been going round and round in his head on a loop ever since, albeit a short one: the spray hitting his face, blood, brains, the crane swaying and the wind whistling. Within ten minutes of emailing his statement to Potter, Dixon was on his way to Frome. Out and about, doing what he did best. He glanced into the back of the Land Rover at Monty's empty bed.

'He's going to be fine, Sir,' said Louise. She was sitting in the passenger seat, looking over her shoulder at the same empty dog bed. 'Before you know it, he'll be—'

'I shouldn't have googled it.'

'Tell me about Colin Rowland,' said Louise, changing the subject.

'He was the operations manager at Crook Engineering, Liam Crook's right hand man working on the bridge platforms. I'm assuming he wasn't prosecuted because he wasn't a director of the company. That's about it, really. Until we get the prosecution file.'

An hour later Dixon turned into Trinity Street, Frome, a row of small terraced sandstone cottages on his left, each with white cornicing around the windows and doors; some with dormer windows, most without.

'It's that one,' said Louise. 'With the olive green door.'

There were no double yellow lines to park on – Dixon was in that sort of mood; his dog was dying and someone was going to pay for that, even if it was just a traffic warden.

He checked his watch when Rowland answered the door, a glass of red wine in his hand.

'It's past the yardarm, Inspector,' said Rowland, peering at their warrant cards. 'You'd better come in.'

The carpet in the living room was cream with several red stains, wine rather than blood. Probably. A rug in front of the red brick fireplace was also stained, the edge singed where logs had rolled out of the grate. Dixon opted for a wooden chair rather than the sofa.

'What can I do for you?' Glaswegian, definitely; Rowland was small, stocky, with short grey hair. Good at darts too, judging by the trophies on the otherwise bare shelves.

'You used to work for Crook Engineering, Mr Rowland?'

'Is that what this is about?' Rowland was rubbing the back of his neck. 'Fuck me.'

Dixon waited. He glanced across at Louise, perched on the edge of the sofa with her notebook on her knee.

'I never thought . . .' Rowland's voice tailed off.

'What?'

'Has Stella found something?'

'Stella Hayward is missing, Sir,' replied Dixon. 'I'm investigating her disappearance and the murder of her daughter, Amy.'

'Och, fuck, no.' Rowland drained the wine glass. Stood up and walked towards the half empty bottle on the mantelpiece.

'Would you mind leaving that until we've finished, Sir?'

'Of course, sorry.'

'Tell me about the manslaughter prosecution.' Dixon hesitated, watching Rowland's eyes fixed on the wine bottle. 'You weren't prosecuted?'

'They were going to. Manslaughter, for fuck's sake. They said they wouldn't if I cooperated and Liam told me it was all right. "Do what you have to do, Colin," he said. So, I told them what they wanted to hear and left out the bits they didnae want me to say.' Rowland sneered. 'Bastards.'

'I haven't seen your witness statement yet, Sir,' said Dixon.

'It's a crock o' shite. I'd have said it in the witness box though, but it never came to that. Hostile witness? I'd have given them fucking hostile witness.'

'What were you going to say?' asked Dixon.

'The platform was sabotaged. There's no two ways about it. One whole end of it collapsed. That's four bolts, including the safety rail. The tossers from the HSE reckoned they'd sheared off. They found one in the mud and said it was all rusted up. It'd been in the water for three months before they found it. What the hell did they expect?'

'What about the safety ropes?'

'The lads were harnessed up, just as they should've been, but whoever sabotaged it took out the safety rail they were tied to as well. The ropes slipped off the end and doon they went.'

'What about risk assessments?' asked Dixon.

'You're sounding a bit too much like that Health and Safety bastard,' snarled Rowland. 'They were done. And I don't care what they say. I did 'em myself.'

'It's my belief the platform was sabotaged, Mr Rowland,' said Dixon. 'Stella got too close to proving it and—'

Rowland wiped away tears with his sleeve, his face contorted and flushed. 'After all this fucking time.'

'I believe it to be the motive behind her disappearance, and the murder of her daughter.'

'Work was stopped for six weeks.' Rowland was picking at loose threads on the arm of the sofa, where a cat had been sharpening its claws. 'It took that long to recover the bodies. Then the funerals.' Rowland took a deep breath, exhaling through his nose. 'Another company went in and finished the job after the bridge opened. There's a monorail under the road, suspended like, with the track above the carriages. You can see it from the beach. I still go down there sometimes.'

'What for?'

'They were good lads.' Rowland's eyes glazed over.

'What can you tell me about the company that took on the contract?'

'Nothing, really.' Rowland hesitated. 'Centrax Platforms or Centrix, something like that. I'd not come across them before.'

'Did you think they had anything to do with the sabotaged platform?'

'Liam thought so. They'd tried to buy him out and he'd told them to go to hell. I never knew any of this at the time. Stella told me years later.'

'When did you last see her?'

'Three year ago, maybe. Longer.'

'Who d'you think sabotaged the platform?'

'Fuck knows. We had a team of regulars, but for a job like that we had a load of cash in hand lads. Climbers, some of them. We used them for window cleaning jobs too. High rise blocks, offices, stuff like that. They'd abseil in, that sort of thing. Cheaper than platforms every time.' Rowland smiled. 'Cannae do it nowadays, mind.'

'Did Stella ever tell you who she thought was behind it?'

'She always thought there must have been a middle man, but she didnae know who it was. Theories, she had, but that was it. She thought the investigator from Health and Safety was bent too. She had no real idea, to be honest. Last time I saw her anyway.'

Chapter Twenty

A blue rinse and a Siamese cat, the patio door ajar, a rope scratching post on the dining table saving the arms of the sofa and chairs. Just like his late grandmother, thought Dixon, standing in the large windows at the back of the bungalow.

Hinkley Point was hidden by the haze miles away across the Parrett Estuary, the tide in, but Dixon could make out the lighthouse and the churches at Burnham and Berrow. It was an unusual view of Brean Down, for him, but not for the residents of Bleadon, perhaps. Almost an island – it wouldn't take much of a rise in sea levels.

Mrs Harper liked pink. And she had kept her late husband's collection of military figurines, a whole display cabinet given over to them by the fireplace. The odd Beswick figurine had crept in and seemed out of place in amongst the Paras and Royal Marines; Jemima Puddle-Duck, Benjamin Bunny and a few shire horses.

Louise was peering at the photographs on the mantelpiece when Dixon turned back to the view from the window, across a manicured lawn and flowerbeds full of roses and hydrangeas, the garden sloping away down to a drystone wall, with cows in the field beyond. He was thinking back to the last time he walked out to the fort at the end of Brean Down with Monty.

The last time? Think positive; the previous time.

'Do you take sugar?'

The shrill voice shouting from the kitchen was not enough to bring him back to the present.

'No, thank you,' replied Louise.

Cups and saucers rattling on a tray heralded Mrs Harper's arrival in the living room, a nudge from Louise dragging Dixon away from the window.

'It's a grandstand view you have,' he said, spinning round.

'It's why we built the bungalow. 1972, that was. Been here ever since,' replied Mrs Harper, pouring the tea.

Definitely a hint of blue. Smartly dressed too. Either she had made the effort or she had been out for Sunday lunch. No one wears a three strand pearl necklace for a visit from the police, do they?

'Now, what was it you wanted to talk to me about?'

'Your late husband's company, Centrix Platforms,' replied Dixon.

'We sold that when he died. Our accountant was the executor of the estate and he managed to sell it as a going concern, I think that's the phrase. Another company bought it, took on the staff and contracts and then wound it up.'

'When was that?'

'Ray died in 2004. On his sixtieth birthday.' Mrs Harper stood up and walked over to the mantelpiece, handing Dixon a photograph that had been hidden behind a council tax bill. 'That's us at a Rotary do.'

Black tie and a big smile for the camera, an arm around his wife.

'Was it sudden, his death?'

'We had time,' replied Mrs Harper, a hint of a tremble in her voice. 'He had a heart bypass, which bought him a year or so. We managed a cruise before the end.'

'How long had he been running Centrix?'

'He started it from scratch in the early eighties, hiring out hydraulic platforms. Then it went from there, really.'

'Where was he based?'

Mrs Harper smiled. 'We started out in a barn on a farm over at Puxton. It was cheap, and got us going, but then the farmer built a golf course and we had to move. Ended up in a unit over at Walrow, the industrial estate at Highbridge. It had plenty of yard space for the platforms, tow trucks and what have you.'

'You expanded rapidly?' asked Dixon, watching Louise scribbling in her notepad.

'We did. It was a competitive market, and there were lots of fly-by-night companies setting up using climbers on ropes, so hiring platforms was never going to last. That's when we got into the bigger construction contracts, fixed platforms, that sort of stuff. Window cleaning firms won't bother hiring a platform when they can send a couple of lads down on the end of ropes, a bucket hanging on their harness.' She put a plate of biscuits on the coffee table in front of Louise. 'Having said that, it was the best thing that ever happened to us.'

Dixon raised his eyebrows. If someone wants to talk, let them.

'Ray put a lot of effort into growing the business,' continued Mrs Harper. 'Lots of entertaining and corporate hospitality. It's not what you know, it's who you know. We grew by acquisition too. He bought a small company in Bristol, which gave us the contract for the Clifton Suspension Bridge and the old Severn Crossing. We had nearly fifty staff at one point.'

'Have you heard of a company called Crook Engineering?'

Mrs Harper took a swig of tea. 'They were becoming our main competitors in this area. An aggressive young man he was. Liam somebody. Ray suggested a merger at one point, but he said no. Then he undercut us on the Second Severn Crossing contract. We had to lay a few men off when that happened, but he took them on, so it wasn't the end of the world. It's quite specialist work.'

Dixon nodded. And waited.

'One of our lads died.' She shook her head. 'I'm sorry, I can't remember his name. Ray went to the funeral though, I remember that much. It was after that we got the contract. It was for the monorail under the bridge. We had to drop everything and get it done. I think it shook Ray.'

'Why?'

'Well, because it could just as easily have happened to us.'

'What did your husband say about the accident?'

Mrs Harper hesitated. 'Three men died, Inspector. It shook him up. I know it did.'

'But what did he say to you about it?'

'Nothing. Just that the bolts sheared off. I remember he went out and replaced every single one on all our platforms. And the safety harnesses too. Health and Safety were all over us. Everything had to be done properly.'

'Liam Crook alleged that the nuts and bolts had been tampered with. Sabotaged. Did your husband ever mention that?'

'Not to me.' Mrs Harper sat up. 'I know Crook tried to say that, but it never went to trial because he . . .' Her voice tailed off.

'Do you know who he alleged was behind it?'

'He tried to make out it was us, because we got the contract. Look, it was nonsense. We got the contract because there was no one else who could do it in the time allowed. And even then the Prince of Wales opened the bridge with us still underneath fixing new platforms. The monorail wasn't finished for another six months.'

'How much was the contract worth?'

'I don't remember that sort of detail, I'm afraid. In fact, I'm not sure I ever knew.'

'A six month expedited contract on the Second Severn Crossing?' Dixon stood up and walked over to the mantelpiece, picking up another photograph of Ray Harper, this time in hi-vis jacket and white hard hat. He was standing on a platform holding a clipboard, the old Severn Bridge in the background.

'It would've run into the millions, I can say that much,' said Mrs Harper. 'That one was taken under the viaduct the day the monorail was finished.'

'And your husband had nothing to do with the monorail?'

'No. Another company did that, using our platforms.'

'Did he give a statement to the police?'

'No. Why would he?'

'In response to the allegations made by Liam Crook.'

'Nobody took them seriously, Inspector. He was cutting corners, using cash in hand staff and old equipment. It was the only way he could undercut us. Then he made up those lies to try to wriggle out of it.'

Dixon was sitting in the driver's seat of his Land Rover, staring at the telegraph pole outside Mrs Harper's bungalow. Louise was talking into her mobile phone, but he wasn't listening.

The phone in the bungalow had been on the sideboard in the living room, so no amount of loitering on the doorstep would allow him to eavesdrop on Mrs Harper's conversation. And there would be a conversation, with someone, even if it was just her sister – assuming she had one, of course. It was probably going on already, he thought, watching a starling land on the telephone cable.

'That was Dave,' said Louise. 'They've got Amy's friend, Michelle, at Express Park and he thinks you need to hear it yourself.'

'Hear what?'

'What she's got to say.' Louise frowned.

The southbound on-slip at junction 22 on the M5 always brought back memories. A school bus going over on two wheels, cricket bats and pads flying everywhere. The huge loop had caught out other drivers too, shiny new sections of Armco barrier testament to that.

'If you think about it, we know no more than Stella at the moment. A rusty bolt fished from the sea and allegations made by her husband, Liam, in his defence.'

'And look where it got her,' said Louise, under her breath.

Dixon ignored her. 'We need to know what it was that she found out. And it must be on the prosecution file Chard gave her access to.'

'You said all the papers had gone from her house?'

'There was an empty concertina file and shoeboxes.'

'Cleared out by her killer or killers?' asked Louise.

'Either that or by Chard trying to cover his tracks.'

'Bit late for that.'

A bit late indeed. Dixon accelerated into the outside lane, wondering how long Chard's relationship with Stella had been going on. It would be interesting to know if it had started before or after he had reported Dixon for failing to disclose his personal relationship with a murder victim. Not that it made a difference. Dixon hadn't disclosed it, and so he had been guilty of misconduct. Not that he had ever had any intention of doing so. A chance to catch Fran's killer would have been worth it, even if 'it' had been a career in supermarket security, or worse still, a return to the legal profession.

He wondered whether Chard would feel the same.

And what was it on that file that had got Stella killed? Chard's statement would make interesting reading.

He parked on the top floor of the staff car park and followed Louise through the security door.

'You haven't swiped your—' She thought better of it.

'Dave's checking the traffic cameras again,' said Pearce, when Dixon sat down at a workstation opposite him. 'He's doing number plate recognition in Yatton for the weekend of Stella's disappearance. Chard's team are redoing the witness statements too. Potter is keeping an eye on them.'

'Good.'

'I left Michelle sitting in reception. She was happy to wait for you.'

Louise ran along the landing and looked over into the atrium below. 'Leggings and a red top?' she asked, reappearing next to Pearce's desk.

'That's her.'

'What's she said so far?' asked Dixon.

'Just that she was happy to come in, but owed it to Amy to speak to the top man. We figured that was you.'

Dixon took the lift and was sitting in a ground floor meeting room when Louise opened the door for Michelle.

'This is Michelle Croxton, Sir,' said Louise.

'Has someone offered you a drink?' he asked, gesturing to a chair.

'I'm fine, thank you,' she mumbled, glancing around the room. Mousey brown hair down her back, black leggings and a red sweatshirt, the logo hidden behind folded arms. She placed her phone on the table in front of her face down.

'We wanted to ask you about Amy,' said Dixon, as Louise sat down next to Michelle. 'You're not under arrest or anything like that.'

'I know.' She was running her fingers through the ends of her hair, pulling out knots.

'How long had you known her?'

'We were at school together. Then we went to the same uni. I studied psychology and she did engineering.'

'An odd choice, engineering.'

'It was because of her father. Everything was because of her father.'

'When did you see her last?'

'About a month ago. We went for a night out in Weston.'

'You knew she was working at Hinkley Point?'

'She was watching someone,' replied Michelle. 'It was as close as she could get, she said.'

Dixon waited.

'I don't know the bloke's name, but they'd found out the man responsible for awarding the bridge contracts was working at Hinkley. He'd been in the . . .' – she looked blankly at Dixon – '. . . procurement, is it?'

He nodded.

'That's it, the procurement department at the company that built the Second Severn Crossing. And now, here he was, working at Hinkley Point. It was too good a chance to miss, apparently, so Amy got herself a job there.'

'Do you know which company he's working for at Hinkley?'

'No, sorry. Amy never said. It wasn't EDF though, I know that much.'

'Did she mention Tier 1 or Tier 2, perhaps?'

'Not that I remember.'

'And you've got no idea of his name?'

'No.'

'Nor the company he works for?'

'Nope.'

'When did they find out about him?'

'About six months ago. Stella, that's her mum, found out where he was and it seemed too much of a coincidence.'

'And what was her plan?'

'Just to keep watch. It was a good job anyway, but she wanted to see if any contracts were sabotaged. You know they always thought her father was innocent?'

'Yes.'

'They reckoned this bloke had something to do with it. He was the one who took the contract away from her father's company and gave it to someone else.' Michelle took a deep breath. 'Then Stella got access to a file or something. Amy said she didn't want to know how, but I

188

got the impression her mum was shagging someone. That was the last time I heard from her.'

◆ ◆ ◆

'Maybe he's the suit Ed was talking about?' asked Louise, watching Dixon slump down on to a swivel chair in the CID Area.

He sighed. 'Let's assume he works for a Tier 1 contractor. D'you know how many of them there are?'

Louise shrugged her shoulders. 'Ten?'

'Ninety. And each of them has multiple Tier 2 companies beneath them, each contract worth millions.' Dixon leaned back in his chair. 'We'll have to come at it from the other end. See if you can find out who was in the procurement team for the bridge. There was a joint venture set up to build it, but God knows where the records will be.'

'The bloke who told Stella might be Chard?' Louise raised her eyebrows.

'He might. So we need access to that bloody prosecution file.'

Chapter Twenty-One

'Consultant, non-prac.' It was a crafty way of keeping a retired solicitor's name on the letter paper, as if that would fool anyone. Maybe he was being a bit harsh. Robert Jackman & Co Solicitors would look a bit odd without Robert Jackman's name on the letterhead somewhere, even with his son, Cris, one of the remaining two partners.

Dixon had never worked in a small firm and wondered whether he might feel differently about the legal profession if he had done so. He had trained in a large firm, 'factory' he used to call it, hot-desking in an open plan office, nine chargeable hours a day his target. Not easy when he spent most of his time photocopying, such was the life of a trainee solicitor.

He had left the day his training contract finished, starting his police training at Hendon the following Monday. A day off a couple of months later to attend the ceremony at Chancery Lane and he had been admitted to the Roll of Solicitors; a shake of the Law Society president's hand and Dixon had never looked back.

He was still on the Roll, which made him a solicitor (non-prac.) too. Maybe when he retired from the police he'd go back to it. That had been the only reason he kept his name on the Roll; keeping his options open. If nothing else, it was better paid than supermarket security. Just.

'Robert Jackman & Co, can I help you?'

Dixon snatched the phone off the desk, disconnecting the loudspeaker.

'I'm trying to track down Robert Jackman. I'm assuming he's retired?'

'Can you phone the office tomorrow? This is the out-of-hours emergency line.'

Dixon rattled off his name and rank.

'I'll try to connect you with his son, Crispin,' replied the operator. 'You've come through to a call answering service.'

Barber's *Adagio*. Dixon cringed, hoping he wouldn't be on hold too long.

'It's enough to make you slit your wrists,' he said – under his breath, he thought, but loud enough for Louise to hear.

'What is, Sir?' she asked, her head popping up from behind the computer on the other side of the partition.

'Listen.' He flicked on the loudspeaker.

'Inspector Dixon? You wanted to speak to my fa—'

He cut it off again, watching Louise shaking her head.

'Yes, please, Sir. I'm assuming he's retired now.'

'He is. What's it about?'

'Liam Crook.'

'Now there's a blast from the past. How come you're involved, can I ask?'

'Stella Hayward is missing, Sir, and I'm investigating her disappearance.'

'Oh, good God. How . . . was she . . . You can't tell me, of course you can't.' A long sigh. 'Yes, my father would be happy to speak to you, of course he would. He knew the family well. I can't believe—'

'Where does he live, Sir?' asked Dixon.

'Over at Burrington, do you know it?'

'"Rock of Ages" and all that.'

'That's it. Rickford Lane, number 5. It's the turning opposite the pub; a little white cottage a hundred yards or so on the left. He may be in the pub though. Look for a man with a French bulldog.'

Dixon made a note of the old man's mobile number, despite being warned that it would probably be switched off. Either at home or in the pub, so they couldn't go far wrong, Crispin had said. Although, as it turned out, Robert Jackman was midway between the two and heading home, walking in the middle of the road with a newspaper tucked under his arm and his dog on the end of a long lead.

'D'you think he's deaf?' asked Louise, frowning as they followed them along the lane.

The old man turned and watched Dixon park his Land Rover across the drive, blocking in an old BMW, an older Morris Minor rusting away in the carport behind it.

A brown check shirt full of holes, the sleeves rolled up, black corduroys and wellies covered in mud, a pair of reading glasses on top of his head holding back long, straggly grey hair. He let the dog off the lead and then dropped the newspaper in the bin.

'You found me then?' asked Jackman, walking over to Dixon's Land Rover. 'My son rang the pub. You'd better come in.'

Dixon and Louise followed Jackman round the back of the cottage and in the back door, squeezing past the piles of magazines stacked just inside.

'You'll have to forgive the mess. The place was spotless when my wife was alive. Rather gone to pot since then.' Jackman slid off his wellington boots and flicked them across the kitchen floor. 'Have a seat,' he said, gesturing to the kitchen table. 'So, what's Stella been up to then?'

'Stella is missing, I'm afraid, Sir. And her daughter, Amy, was found dead in an empty silo at Hinkley Point.'

'Oh, God. When was this? The poor bug—'

'You acted for Stella's husband, Liam, when he was prosecuted, is that right?'

Jackman sighed. 'Cris said Stella had disappeared but he never mentioned Amy was dead as well.' He began flicking crumbs off the table. 'Stella never could let go. I felt sorry for her in the end. Stopped charging her too.'

'Tell me about Liam.'

'I'd done all sorts for him. He was one of my first clients when I set up on my own. Employment stuff mainly, and a bit of debt collection to begin with. He was a good client; always paid his bills. Sailed a bit close to the wind at times, cut the odd corner here and there. Then he got the contract for the Second Severn Crossing.'

'What sort of corners?'

'Nothing drastic. It was mainly cash in hand in the early days, and he was a bit more relaxed than I'd have liked towards training and manual handling.' Jackman leaned over and picked up his dog, sitting him on his lap. 'He had climbers on and off the payroll, using their own equipment, that sort of stuff.'

'What about on the bridge?'

'That was later and he'd had to sharpen his act up by then. It'd gone from swinging about on the end of ropes cleaning windows to industrial platforms. He got the ISO 9002 accreditation and used a Health and Safety consultant for his risk assessments. He was doing things properly by then. He had to for the bidding process. There was a Scottish bloke working for him who was quite sharp too, I remember.'

'What went wrong?'

'Nothing as such.' Jackman slid his glasses down on to the end of his nose and peered at Dixon over them. 'The platform was sabotaged.'

'You believed that?'

'He was my client and that was his case. Of course I believed him.'

193

Dixon hesitated. 'I'm a solicitor, too, Sir,' he said. 'And of course we always believe our clients. It's our job.' He took a deep breath. 'But what did you really think? Off the record, if needs be.'

Jackman smiled. 'I see what you're getting at,' he said, nodding. 'Four bolts failed and they produced one nut with a rusted thread they said they'd found in the mud underneath the bridge. They tried to say it had sheared off but it was impossible to tell either way, if you ask me. Look, the platform was less than a year old. I know because I advised him on the bank guarantee he signed when he borrowed the money to buy them. So, yes, I believed him. And I thought there was a reasonable prospect of an acquittal at trial.'

'Did you tell him that?'

'Time and again. He rang me the day he died – the day he killed himself – and we had the same conversation. Again. The risk assessments had been done, the staff had been trained. Yes, some of them were cash in hand, but that was hardly relevant. There was no negligence. It was sabotage.'

'Did you have an expert's report?'

'We did. He said the bolts must have failed, all of them, at the same time, for the platform to have collapsed in the way it did. I even got a metallurgist to look at the nut the prosecution found and he estimated it had been in water for longer than a year. Odd when you think that the platform was less than a year old. The case should never have been brought, but they needed a scapegoat.'

'But the company was convicted?'

'Without Liam there to give evidence, it was inevitable, really.' Jackman leaned back in his chair with his hands behind his head. 'Stella appealed, but that was thrown out and the company wound up when it couldn't pay the fine. Then she tried a judicial review of the decision to prosecute him, claiming it drove him to commit suicide.'

Jackman spotted Louise's frown. 'When a public body, such as the Health and Safety Executive, take a decision you don't agree with, you can challenge it through the courts and it's called a "judicial review". They're expensive and rarely succeed, at least back then anyway.'

'When did you last see Stella?' asked Dixon.

'Three years ago, perhaps. It was when I was still working as a consultant. I drafted some Freedom of Information requests for her.' He let out a long sigh. 'She was still after that file.'

'What might have been on it that would've helped her?'

'Did she get access to it?' asked Jackman, his brow furrowed.

'She did,' replied Dixon, nodding. 'I can't say how, but she did get to see it, or parts of it anyway. And a few weeks later she's disappeared and her daughter is dead.'

'Everything the Crown disclosed was on my file and she saw it and had copies of it. She was the executor of Liam's estate so she was entitled to it.' Jackman was watching his dog licking the remaining crumbs off the kitchen table. 'The only thing it can be is witness statements and reports not disclosed by the Crown. That was what she was after with all the FOI requests. Have you seen the prosecution file?'

'Not yet, Sir,' replied Dixon.

'Nowadays, the CPS are supposed to disclose everything, whether it's helpful to the defence or not. Back then they buried it if it was helpful to the defence.'

'What about your own files?' asked Dixon.

'There'll be one for the FOI requests. That was only a few years ago. The rest will have been destroyed by now, once any original documents had been returned to the client.'

'Stella's place had been cleared out.'

'You need to get hold of that prosecution file then,' said Jackman. 'And the Health and Safety Executive file, if you can.'

'Did Liam ever say who he thought was behind it, Sir?' asked Dixon. 'If he was alleging the platform had been sabotaged, who did he think had done it?'

Jackman was breathing deeply through his nose, his eyes fixed on an empty salt cellar, a few grains of rice sitting in the bottom. 'Let's just say he always thought it odd that Centrix were able to take on the contract at such short notice.' He clenched his fist. 'You can't slander the dead, so I'll just say it. Centrix bloody well knew and were prepared for it. Does the name Ray Harper mean anything to you, Inspector?'

'I spoke to his widow earlier today.'

'Look, we had no evidence,' mumbled Jackman. Backpedalling, thought Dixon. 'But there were ex-Centrix staff up there that day, working cash in hand for Liam, so you work it out.'

'I intend to, Sir.'

Jackman was closing the front door behind them when he hesitated, stepping out into the porch and taking hold of Dixon's elbow. 'You asked me if I really believed the platform had been sabotaged.'

'I did.'

'Do you?'

'Yes, Sir, I do.'

'Perhaps they'll get justice after all then. It's just a shame they didn't live to see it.'

'I don't think he likes fish and vegetables,' said Dixon, peering through the kitchen window.

Lucy chuckled. 'Most of it's in Jane's hair.'

Lucy was turning out to be a handful, not that Jane would admit it. She was just grateful that Dixon had spotted her sitting at the back of their mother's funeral with her foster parents. Not that he could have missed her, with her hair dyed jet black, nose studs and earrings.

He had picked her up from Highbridge railway station, as instructed, although a bit late, hooting the horn on his Land Rover several times to no avail. Lucy had been sitting on a bench outside the station, eyes closed, head nodding to loud music pumping through her earphones.

The nose studs had gone, and most of the earrings too; testament to her new ambition to become a police officer, he assumed.

Jane had been adopted not long after she had been born and certainly got the better deal, Lucy having painted a grim picture of life with their drug addict mother, Sonia: in and out of foster homes; some good, some bad. No, Jane had landed on her feet with Rod and Sue. She knew that. What she didn't know was that they could have had children of their own, but chose her. They had confided in him when he went to see them about marrying her. Or rather Sue had blurted it out, through the tears.

'Jane needs to know that,' he had said.

'In our own time, Nick,' Rod had replied.

Fair enough. It was not his place to tell her. But he would, one day, if Rod and Sue left it too late.

Lucy was going to be Jane's bridesmaid too. Dixon smiled. She was a good kid, even hitch-hiking down from Manchester during the hunt for the two girls. She'd used the money they gave her for food to pay for a taxi over to Catcott, so she could join in the search.

Jane was sitting cross-legged on the floor in front of Monty, the dog's head bowed, a liquidised green mulch dripping from his jowls. She inserted the end of the syringe in the corner of his mouth and pushed the plunger with the base of her thumb; Monty swallowed some of it, the rest dripping on to the soggy kitchen roll on the floor. Then he shook his head, sending a spray of green sludge across the units.

It makes a change from blood spatter, I suppose, thought Dixon, watching Jane picking lumps of it out of her hair.

Monty wagged his tail when Dixon opened the back door. Not much, just the tip, but that was enough to bring a smile to his face.

Jane stood up. 'He's had some of it. Here, you try,' she said, handing Dixon the syringe.

'What is it?'

'Cod and mixed veg, just like Tabi said.' She shrugged her shoulders. 'I can't get his tablets into him either. He won't touch the turkey.'

'The old fashioned way it is then,' said Dixon. 'Where are they?'

'Here.'

Two: one white, one pink. 'Now?'

'With food,' replied Jane.

Dixon stood over Monty and raised his index finger. 'Sit.'

Nothing.

'Trained him yourself, did you?' asked Lucy. She was leaning on the door frame, the black and white film behind her on the TV paused.

'Thanks for coming,' said Jane, Lucy backing away when she tried to give her a hug.

'You're covered in food!'

'Look, old son, it's for your own good.' Dixon took hold of Monty by the muzzle and pushed the fingers of his left hand in between his teeth, opening his mouth. Then he rammed the tablets down his throat with his right hand, before clamping the dog's mouth shut and rubbing his throat. 'Swallow, you little dev— That's it, they've gone.'

Jane raised her eyebrows. 'I dread to think what would've happened if he'd bitten you.'

'Not a chance.'

He sat down on a clean bit of floor and filled the syringe from the Pyrex jug. 'C'mon then,' he said, patting the floor in front of him.

'Just a bit at a time,' said Jane. 'You need to be careful it doesn't go into his lungs.'

Dixon pushed the tip of the syringe into the corner of Monty's mouth. Then he pressed the plunger. Half an inch would do, all of it swallowed in one go.

'He's doing it for you,' muttered Jane, wiping the kitchen units with a cloth.

The catheter was still on Monty's front leg, wrapped in a bright pink bandage.

'We're due back at eleven tomorrow, after morning surgery. Tabi's going to run the blood tests again.'

'What did she say?'

'It's still too early to tell.'

'More?' asked Dixon, holding up the empty syringe.

'That makes four, which'll do for now.' Jane looked at her watch. 'We've got to do it again at ten o'clock.'

'I've got to go back to Express Park, but I can come back if you're—'

'I'll let you know.'

'What about the pills?'

'That's it till the morning.'

'Have you eaten?'

Jane dropped the cloth in the sink. 'I went in Tesco's and came out without anything for us. Lots of fish and veg, but—'

'The pub does takeaway.' Dixon picked up Monty in both arms and carried him into the living room, placing him gently on his blanket on the sofa.

'I'll go,' said Lucy.

'Just ring me if he—'

'Of course we will.'

The canteen was closed when Dixon arrived back at Express Park just after 8 p.m. Not that he was after food; it was more about spreading the files out across the empty tables.

It took him twenty minutes to flick through those parts of Chard's file that he hadn't already seen; no mention anywhere of the most likely motive for Stella's disappearance, although the reason for that was now, mercifully, common knowledge.

Chard had at least made extensive proof of life enquiries and found none; her phone hadn't been used, nor had her bank account been touched. There were no social media or email logins and her car hadn't moved, or if it had, it hadn't been caught on any traffic cameras, which was unlikely. No, Stella was dead. Dixon knew that. But where was her body?

The inquest files had arrived: four of them. One each for the three men killed when the platform collapsed underneath the Second Severn Crossing, the verdicts accidental death; and one for Liam Crook, much thinner, the verdict suicide.

Still no prosecution file though, so he would have to make do with the witness statements given at the inquests. And Liam's suicide note – the nearest Dixon was going to get to his witness statement.

Dave and Mark had been busy interviewing Amy's work colleagues too, and there was a pile of statements from each, laid out on separate tables.

'You swiped in,' said Lewis, peering around the door.

Dixon ignored the jibe.

'Potter's coming down in the morning to interview Chard with a superintendent from Professional Standards,' continued Lewis. 'We can watch it on a monitor.'

'We?'

'She thought I ought to be there.'

'Fine with me,' replied Dixon. 'What time?'

'Nine.' Lewis smiled. 'How's your dog?'

'Still alive. What about the prosecution file?'

'You'll get it tomorrow.' Lewis waved his hand. 'I'll see you in the morning.' Then he was gone.

Dixon shook his head, then turned to the inquest statements, such as they were. An inquiry into the facts of who they were and how they died – it was all well and good, but he was more concerned with whose fault it was, and he wouldn't know that until he saw the prosecution file.

Seven surviving employees had given statements. They had been moving the platforms, one either side of the monorail, ready for employees of another company to fix the next section of track, when one of the platforms collapsed. Three witnesses on the platform opposite remembered a distinct 'ping', which they thought was a bolt shearing off, and then they saw it go, watching their three colleagues fall to their deaths.

Dixon frowned. He wasn't learning much that was new; and certainly nothing that might be relevant to the who and why Stella and Amy had been murdered.

Stella had been to the inquests and seen all of these witness statements and it had not got her killed. But seeing the prosecution file had. Yes, that was where the answer would be. If it was anywhere.

Got three syringes into him. He's fine. Jx

Was it ten o'clock already? He had learned only one thing of any use from Amy's work colleagues: she always ate lunch in the canteen in Welfare Block East, no matter where she was on site. Interesting. Perhaps the focus of her attention worked in Welfare Block East? It was where the beat team office was too. And from tomorrow, was where Dixon and his team would be.

Liam's suicide note made grim reading, a copy on the file, the original having been returned to Stella after his inquest. Apologies, denials, pleas for forgiveness, professions of undying love. Dixon winced. 'Undying' was the wrong word. Then came the last line, which hit him in the pit of the stomach when he read it out loud.

'"Tell our daughter I loved her with all my heart, even though we never got to meet. I will be her guardian angel, watching over her every step of the way. I know she hasn't got a name yet, but I like Amy, if you don't mind."'

Chapter Twenty-Two

He parked at the end of Allandale Road, the streetlights already off to save electricity. After midnight then, but the moon made up for it, lighting up the beach.

Dixon opened the back door of the Land Rover and waited for Monty to jump out.

'For fuck's sake,' he snarled, slamming the door. Then he set off down the steps to the beach.

The channels in between the sandbanks shimmered in the moonlight, the water draining out of them, catching up with the tide on its way out; the wet sand dotted with worm casts.

A good night for star gazing too, the only light pollution coming from Hinkley Point, across the estuary, and Wales in the far distance.

Not that he was in the mood.

He could pick out the tower cranes and wondered whether the cleaner had a head for heights. Not a job for the unwary; he didn't envy them that one. The welfare blocks were lit up too, the accommodation block hidden by the turbine halls of Hinkley Point A – somebody somewhere wondering how close he was getting. The answer was 'not close enough'.

Yet.

A ship was leaving the jetty on the outgoing tide; it would be back again in a few days, with another load of aggregate, or blast furnace slag from Port Talbot, probably.

It was a perfect night for a walk on the beach. Dixon stopped, picked up a stone and sent it skimming across the muddy water of a shallow channel.

A walk, without his dog?

What the bloody hell was the point of that? he thought, turning back towards the steps.

The cottage was dark, so he parked out in the street and peered through the front window. Jane was asleep on the sofa, with Monty curled up next to her, his bandaged leg hanging over the edge.

It would be a challenge getting in without waking them both up.

'How is he today, Sir?' asked Louise, when Dixon appeared in the CID Area just before 9 a.m. the following morning.

'He's back to the vet at eleven. So, we'll know more after that.'

'Chard's here. Surrendered about an hour ago.'

'He's got a solicitor with him,' said Pearce.

'Lewis was looking for you too.' Louise pointed to meeting room 2 on the other side of the atrium. 'He was in there. I told him you were on your way.'

'Let's see if we can get a transcript of the 1995 trial, Lou,' said Dixon. 'When Crook Engineering was prosecuted for corporate manslaughter.'

'Yes, Sir.'

'And chase up a list of the employees on the Severn Crossing so we can cross-reference it with everyone inside Hinkley. Let's have another go at getting hold of the son too. He's in the Far East, not on the bloody moon.' Dixon turned to Harding. 'Dave, can you go over the proof of life stuff done by Chard's lot? See if they've missed anything.'

'Yes, Sir.'

'Get ready to move too. We're setting up an Incident Room back at Hinkley. We can use the beat team office this time.'

'They won't like that,' muttered Pearce.

'Tough.'

'Where will you be, Sir?' asked Louise.

'Watching Chard's interview. DCI Lewis is going to be holding my hand, apparently.'

'What for?'

'God knows.'

'Ah, there you are,' said Lewis when Dixon stepped out of the lift on the lower ground floor. 'He's in interview room four with his brief. Potter's on her way down.' He opened the door behind him. 'We're in here.'

Dixon sat down in front of the monitor, a frown etched across his forehead. Chard was visible, sitting next to his solicitor, the seats opposite them still empty. Chard was staring at the table in front of him, aware of the cameras and keen to avoid them.

'Dixon, you're here,' said Potter, shutting the door behind her. 'We'll be going in shortly. I just wanted to remind you that it's being taken care of.'

'What is, Ma'am?'

'Chard. You're a professional, so I expect you to behave like one.'

'What's that supposed to mean?'

'Just watch the interview. And stay calm.'

Dixon folded his arms and leaned against the table behind him. He glanced up at Lewis, standing with his back to the door like a nightclub bouncer.

'Detective Chief Inspector Simon Chard.'

Dixon turned back to the monitor. It was comforting to be watching in black and white; all the best films were in black and white.

'My name is Superintendent James of Professional Standards and sitting to my right is Detective Chief Superintendent Potter, whom you know. This interview is being recorded and you remain under caution. Do you understand?'

'Yes.' Chard's arms were folded tightly across his chest, pulling the knot of his tie.

'You have a solicitor present. Please identify yourself for the tape.'

'Rebecca Parkman of Boyce Allen and Co.'

'Simon, you've been arrested on suspicion of perverting the course of justice and this is your chance to tell us what happened.'

'You know what happened.'

'I want you to tell me,' replied James. 'Start by telling me when and how you met Stella Hayward.'

'It was at the Christmas party. One of them anyway. We'd met before that in the canteen at Portishead. It was just flirting, really.'

'Who initiated the relationship?'

'She did.'

'And it was sexual?'

Chard nodded.

'You know the drill, Simon. For the tape, please.'

'Yes.'

'How often did you see her?'

'A couple of times a week. It was always at her place in Yatton. My wife can't know about this.'

'That's out of my hands,' replied James, looking back down at his notes. 'When did she tell you who she was?'

'Easter time, maybe. I'd heard of the Crook case, of course I had, but I never realised it was her.'

'What was your relationship like at that time?'

'It was getting serious. I was even thinking of telling my wife, but hadn't got round to it.'

'And what happened?'

'She asked me if I could get her access to the old file. I said no, at first, but she was very persuasive.'

Potter was fidgeting in her seat, Dixon could see that on the monitor.

'And did you?' asked James.

'In the end. I got it out of the archive and took it to her place. Just overnight so she could have a look. I thought, what harm could it do?'

'I think we know the answer to that one now, Simon.'

No reply.

'Why didn't you take it back the next day?' continued James.

'I was going to. I just never got round to it, that's all.'

'So you kept it at home?'

'In a filing cabinet.' Chard sighed. 'And now you've got it.'

'What did she find on the file?'

'I don't know, I never looked at it myself. And I hardly saw her after that. She'd got what she wanted and dropped me like a stone. I didn't think anything of it; decided I was well out of it, to be honest, before my wife found out. Then I saw in the call logs that she hadn't turned up for work and they wanted a welfare check. I got there just as uniform turned up.'

James waited.

'Look, I'm not proud of what I did. Twenty-nine years. Twenty-nine fucking years and there was no way I was getting drummed out because of this. And besides, what were the chances it had anything to do with her disappearance? It was a load of bollocks.'

'So, you doctored the statements?'

Chard looked up at the ceiling. His solicitor leaned across and whispered in his ear. 'No, I'm not . . .' He turned back to Superintendent James. 'Yes, I did. Just to remove the . . .' His voice tailed off.

'Just to remove what?'

'Reference to me and the past. It was a good investigation apart from that. We made extensive proof of life enquiries. Interviewed everyone, I just edited out reference to me or anything that might lead back to me. It was hardly relevant, was it?'

Dixon sneered. Talk about digging yourself a hole.

'You edited out reference to the Severn Crossing strand of enquiry, which now appears to have been the motive, Simon.'

'It wasn't at the time. That only came to light when Amy was killed, and by then it was too late. Then that tosser Dixon turns up . . .'

'Tell us about your interview with her daughter, Amy.'

'She didn't know who I was. We'd never met. So it was just a routine witness interview. She said her mother had got access to the prosecution file and found some new evidence. And, yes, I changed her statement to take that bit out.'

'Why didn't they go to the police when they found this new evidence?'

'They didn't trust us. Amy said her mother wanted to try to find out more about the people identified, then they'd hand it all over to their solicitor.'

'And Amy didn't say what this new evidence was?'

'No, and I didn't ask.'

James glanced across at Potter, who was shuffling the papers on the table in front of her.

'Simon,' she said, looking up. 'You've been arrested on suspicion of perverting the course of justice, but we're also investigating other matters and have a number of things we wish to put to you, which may or may not result in additional charges.'

'What other matters?' asked his solicitor.

'You weren't involved in the hunt for Steiner, Simon,' said Potter, turning back to Chard. 'So you could not have known that he made veiled threats against Detective Inspector Dixon. As a consequence of those threats, Dixon vacated his home in Brent Knoll and we placed it under round the clock surveillance. Even he didn't know that.'

Dixon spun round and glared at Lewis, still standing with his back to the door.

Potter opened the file in front of her, slid out a photograph and handed it to Chard. 'This is a photograph taken by Detective Sergeant Black from the upstairs window of the Red Cow public house in Brent Knoll, opposite Dixon's cottage. Can you identify for me, please, the car seen parked outside the cottage?'

Chard hesitated.

'It's your car, isn't it, Simon?'

'Yes.'

'When was it taken, for the tape, please? Look at the time stamp.'

'The day before yesterday at 1.32 p.m.'

'And in this photograph,' said Potter, sliding another across the table, 'a figure can be seen walking down the side of the cottage. Can you identify that person for me, please?'

Chard glanced up at the camera and smirked. 'It's me.'

'What is that in your right hand?' asked Potter.

'A bottle of antifreeze.'

'This bottle?' asked Potter, sliding a third photograph across the table. 'This bottle was recovered from your car.'

'Yes.'

'What did you do behind the cottage?'

'Him and his fucking dog,' sneered Chard. 'I've been on the job since before he was born and—'

'I'd like to take a break at this point,' interrupted his solicitor. 'There are various matters I'd like to discuss with my client in private.'

Dixon spun round, his face flushed, nostrils flaring. 'You knew?'

'Potter warned me yesterday. I'm just here to see you don't do anything stupid.'

'In the light of your admission, Simon,' said Potter, 'you will face additional charges of criminal damage and administering a poison contrary to section 8(b) of the Animals Act 1911. Is that clear?'

Dixon turned back to the screen, watching Chard crumple before his eyes.

'Look, I . . .' Chard wiped his cheeks with his sleeves, his body rocking backwards and forwards in his chair.

'I'd go no comment, if I were you,' said Dixon.

'No comment,' mumbled Chard.

'Maybe I'll visit him in prison.' Dixon switched off the monitor. 'Sooner, if Monty dies.'

Twat.

◆　◆　◆

'You had my place under surveillance?'

Potter was rubbing the back of her neck. She glanced at Lewis.

'He's fine,' he said.

'We thought there was a chance Steiner might turn up there. He made a point of letting you know he knew where you lived.' She shrugged her shoulders. 'Only we got more than we bargained for.'

Dixon shook his head. 'I knew he had it in for me, but poisoning my bloody dog?'

'He was jealous,' said Lewis.

'It's just a shame we didn't appreciate the significance before the damage was done,' said Potter. 'I'm sorry.'

'You couldn't have known.'

'How is he?'

'He'll be at the vet now,' replied Dixon, looking at his watch. 'He's having more blood tests. Jane's been feeding him through a syringe every four hours to keep him going.'

'She's a star, that girl,' said Potter, smiling.

'I know.'

'I've looked at the prosecution file from 1995.' Potter grimaced. 'The index refers to a bundle of statements not disclosed to the defence, but it's missing. It looks like she kept it and Chard didn't notice.'

'Dozy pillock was too busy getting his leg over,' Lewis perched on the corner of the table and folded his arms.

'And all of the documents had been cleared out of her place, hadn't they?' asked Potter, shooting a sideways glance at Lewis.

Dixon nodded. 'What about the Health and Safety Executive file?' he asked.

'Missing.'

'Well, that's that then,' muttered Lewis.

'Not necessarily. Stella's neighbour told me she saw Amy leaving the house with a blue carrier bag. This was after Stella disappeared and the bag was flat, not bulging, which tends to suggest it was papers rather than anything else. It could be the missing statements.'

'You'd better find it, Nick,' said Potter. 'Otherwise we're back to square one. We don't really know any more than Stella did at the moment.'

'Yes, we do. We know there's something out there to be found and someone prepared to kill to keep it hidden. The tragedy is they both had to die for it.'

'Chard's going to be charged and then released on bail later today. You won't do anything stupid, will you?'

'He won't,' said Lewis.

Bloods show kidney function still within normal range. Tabi thinks we're winning! Getting the hang of the syringe too. Home to feed him now. Jx

The text arrived while Dixon was standing in the queue to sign in at Hinkley Point. Thirty or so babbling teenagers in front of him, all of them wearing police uniform; it could only be the police cadets on a guided tour of the site. The beat team sergeant, Martha Sparks, was there too, meeting the cadets, he assumed. Either that, or she had been tipped off Dixon was in reception and was waiting to intercept him.

Dave Harding and Mark Pearce had been despatched to the Health and Safety Executive office in Bristol to find out how and why their file was listed as 'missing'. Louise was still at Express Park, going through the prosecution file while she waited for calls to be returned: the Crown Prosecution Service and the British Consulate in Laos.

The security guards recognised him, but didn't seem able to work out whether he was with the police cadets or not, although they must have rung the head of security, Jim Crew, anyway, given that he appeared behind the counter, watching Dixon's every move. Crew waved him to a vacant window and switched on the microphone.

'Are you with the police cadets today, Sir?'

'No.'

'Who are you visiting?'

Dixon leaned forward and spoke quietly into the microphone. 'No one. I am investigating the murder of—'

Crew held up his hand, then slid a clipboard under the security glass. 'Just put my name, Inspector. Will this be a regular occurrence?'

'It will.'

'I'll give you a seven day pass, then you can come in via the turnstiles instead of through here.'

'We're going to be setting up an Incident Room in the beat team office.'

'Have you cleared that with Mr Pickles?'

'I haven't told him yet, no.'

Dixon needn't have worried. Pickles was waiting for him when he filed out of reception behind the now silent teenagers. Brown leather brogues and a Rupert Bear waistcoat under his tweed jacket, but Pickles seemed to get away with it. He was still hopping from one foot to the other too.

'An Incident Room, Inspector, is that right?'

'Yes, Sir.'

'But you've caught Steiner, surely?'

'We did, Sir, but he got in here – let me rephrase that – someone got him in here and I intend to find out who that was.'

'And why presumably?' asked Crew, now standing behind Pickles.

'I know why, Sir.' Dixon smiled, waiting for the obvious question. Pickles had stopped fidgeting, although Crew had started, his eyes fixed on Pickles as he rubbed his chin.

Pickles beat Crew to it, but only just. 'Are you going to tell us then, Inspector?'

'No, Sir.'

'It looks like Martha's going with the police cadets,' said Crew, 'so I'll show you up to the beat team office. What about the rest of your colleagues?'

'They'll be over later, Sir.'

'Better give them seven day passes too, Jim,' said Pickles. 'You will need to be accompanied when you're on site, Inspector.'

'I understand that,' replied Dixon.

'I can do it,' said Crew.

'There we are then.' Pickles forced a smile. 'You'll keep me posted, Inspector?' He hesitated. 'Although, thinking about it, I hope I'm not the first to know when you make an arrest; then it would be me being arrested, wouldn't it?'

'Quite so, Sir.'

Six workstations in the beat team office, and a lock on the door. Dixon wondered who had the keys. Lockable filing cabinets too. There was even a whiteboard on the wall, with this week's shift rota on it, by the looks of things. It would have to do.

Martha Sparks burst in, breathing hard. 'David Pickles rang me,' she gasped. 'Nobody told me you were coming in, Sir.'

'Shouldn't you be with the police cadets?'

'There's no need. They're being shown round by someone from the communications team. And they can't get off the minibus anyway.'

'Who has keys to this office?' Dixon was looking out of the window at the accommodation block in the distance.

'We've got keys to all of the rooms,' replied Crew. 'And the facilities manager has some.'

'Can we get the locks changed?' Matter of fact. 'It's not going to be much good as a police Incident Room if it's not secure.'

It was a tight squeeze in Amy's room in the accommodation block. Martha Sparks was watching Dixon from just inside the door, their every move being followed by Jim Crew peering over her shoulder from the corridor.

The room was small, with a low ceiling, and the mattress had gone from the fixed single bed, revealing pine slats. Dixon leaned over. Nothing underneath. A small dressing table was fixed to the wall on the left, next to a wardrobe, which had been cleared, the doors standing open, the shelves empty.

'It's been checked,' said Martha. 'SOCO were in here for ages.'

A grey powder had been dusted on the drawer handles, photographs taken of any fingerprints that showed up.

'Her stuff went back to Express Park,' continued Martha. 'There wasn't a lot though.'

'I've seen it,' said Dixon.

He sat down on the edge of the bed and began flicking at the carpet tiles on the floor with the edge of his shoe. Glued down, probably. Then he stood up and lifted the slats on the bed, checking the tiles below.

Nothing.

Then he replaced the slats and sat back down again.

A box of tissues had been left on the window sill, the only trace of Amy. Dixon picked it up and shook it, before ripping the last of the tissues out.

'Empty,' he said, stuffing them back in.

He slid the drawers out and placed them on the bed, checking the back of each and inside the dressing table.

'What about her car?' he asked.

'Last I heard it went off to Scientific,' replied Martha.

Dixon slid his phone out of his pocket and tapped out a text message to Louise.

Is the report on Amy's car available yet? Find out if there was any civil litigation arising out of the accident at the bridge pls

'Are you going to be much longer?' asked Crew, pushing past Martha in the doorway.

Dixon ignored him, got up and looked out of the window, watching a line of lorries queueing to get into the site.

'There's a floor above us?' he asked, pointing at the ceiling.

'Yes,' replied Crew. Impatient now.

'Have you got the police in there, Jim?' The voice came from behind Crew, the owner dwarfed by his frame.

'This is Aziz, Inspector. The facilities manager.'

Aziz squeezed past Crew. 'We wanted to know when we can put someone else in here, please?'

'Not yet, Sir. We'll let you know when you can,' replied Martha.

Aziz sighed. 'It's a waste of a room.'

'Where's her dumper truck?' asked Dixon, turning to Crew.

'It'll be out on site.'

'I'd like to see it, please.'

'You're joking?'

'The cab is her place of work.'

214

'Give me a minute.' Crew stepped back into the corridor, dialling a number on his phone.

'Has someone checked it?' asked Dixon, turning to Martha.

'No, Sir. Not that I know of anyway.'

'What about the ceiling tiles?' he asked, looking up.

'They're fixed,' replied Aziz.

Dixon reached up and prodded the corner of one with his finger. Glued, just like the carpet tiles. Each tile was square and held in place by a steel frame; seriously low budget stuff, but then it was temporary accommodation.

'Let's try them all,' he said, prodding the next one.

'Surely, SOCO will have—?'

'I don't know what SOCO have done, Sergeant. Only what I've done.'

Crew reappeared in the doorway, a large frown etched on his forehead as he watched the prodding of the ceiling tiles, Martha using the edge of her mobile phone.

Aziz looked at Crew and shrugged his shoulders. 'I told them they're fixed.'

'Her truck is over at the Agard compound, Inspector. It hasn't been touched since she parked it there herself. They haven't got anyone else to drive it yet, so it's just sitting there.'

Dixon allowed the silence to hang in the air, while he and Martha checked the last of the ceiling tiles.

'Right then,' he said. 'Can you take me over there?'

Chapter Twenty-Three

Dixon tightened the hard hat, trying to stop it flopping about every time he turned his head. It would make it awkward climbing the ladder too.

The yellow dumper truck towered over him; he counted twelve rungs on the ladder just to get access to the cab.

'It'll take a hundred tons at a time,' said the man in the Agard hi-vis jacket, the company logo emblazoned across his back. 'Surprisingly easy to drive though.'

He waited for Dixon to adjust his hat.

'Well, up you go.'

'I'll wait down here, Sir,' said Martha, standing at the bottom.

Crew was watching him through the windscreen of the EDF Energy Land Rover, a red flag mounted on a long pole on the roof fluttering in the breeze.

Dixon was halfway up the ladder before he was level with the tops of the tyres. He looked down; first floor window height, maybe. Certainly in his little cottage.

'Big, innit?' said the Agard man on the ladder below him.

Dixon stepped across on to the metal landing at the top of the ladder and looked around at the almost lunar landscape, bare earth as far as the eye could see.

'We've shifted four million tons of earth so far and it's all here,' said the man, stepping off the top rung. 'It'll be landscaped and grassed over. Never know it was here in a couple of years.'

Dixon peered into the cab. It was mounted in the middle of the truck, with two black leather seats inside, one for the driver, the other set back behind.

'It's got all mod cons.' The man unlocked the door. 'Air conditioning, power steering, obviously, and—'

'Nobody's been in since Amy parked it here?'

'No.'

'May I?'

The man stepped back, allowing Dixon into the cab.

'And only she drove it?'

'That's right. Next year when the site is working twenty-four-seven we'll have another driver at night. We're training them at the moment, but for the time being it was just Amy.'

Dixon sat down in the driver's seat and pulled down the sun visors, half expecting a set of keys to drop down.

'You've been watching too many American films.'

Hardly.

Then he felt around under the seats, and behind them.

'What are you looking for?' asked the man.

'No idea.'

'There's a pocket in the back of the seats.'

Dixon slid his hand into both. Empty.

Bollocks.

'D'you drive one of these?' he asked.

'Can do.'

'Let's say you wanted to hide a file. Thin, maybe half an inch thick. Where would you put it?'

'In here?' The man pursed his lips. 'Under the floor mats. Either that or the carpet above your head. There's nowhere else, really.'

Five minutes later Dixon climbed down the ladder empty handed.

'No luck, Sir?' asked Martha, as he stepped off the bottom rung.

He shook his head. 'We'll have to find another way.'

◆   ◆   ◆

'Stop the car,' said Dixon, spinning around in the passenger seat of the EDF Land Rover, his hard hat on his knee.

'I'll pull in here.' Crew turned into a car park on the left and stopped next to two minibuses, a line of police cadets leaning over the railings, listening to their tour guide. The Viewing Gallery was a raised platform with a grandstand view overlooking the nuclear islands, the reactor on the right starting to take shape, the new sea wall beyond them, the concrete batching plant a mile or so away to the left and Welfare Block East half a mile off to the right. Tiny fluorescent dots, each a hi-vis jacket, moving about amongst the concrete and machines like ants.

'You get a better view from—' Dixon left Crew talking to himself as he walked over to the railings and set off back out to the road, crossing between two slow moving lorries and walking along the front of Welfare Block North; workmen still inside fitting it out: more changing rooms and another canteen, by the looks of things.

Footsteps behind him; Crew running to catch up.

'You're not supposed to be out here,' he said, standing with his back to a steel fence to allow the line of lorries to crawl past.

Dixon had stopped at the corner of a fenced off compound, several diggers and a road tarmac machine standing idle on the far side, behind a Portakabin and a van. And three huge piles of steaming tarmac, just tipped off the back of a dumper truck.

'Who are Hardman Tarmacadam?' he asked, reading the sign on the side of the van.

'Highways, Tier 2, road surfacing,' replied Crew. 'This road we're on now has been moved twice already and it'll move again when Welfare Block North is finished. There's an office block going here, from memory.'

'Who's the Tier 1?'

'Myles Construction is the Tier 1 for associated developments. Then you've got Tier 2s for the tarmac, line painting, drainage, traffic lights, bridges, stuff like that. You can check the supply chain. It's online.'

'Where's the Myles office?'

'Welfare Block East.'

The beat team office was empty, apart from Louise, sitting at one of the workstations.

'Dave rang, Sir. He said the HSE file was never archived as it should've been. They've hunted high and low.' She stood up, picking up her mug. 'They said it should be identical to the police file anyway. Dave and Mark are on their way back now. And the CPS are sending over the trial transcript. I asked them about witness statements not disclosed and got the usual flannel.'

'Blaming it on the investigating officers, I suppose,' said Dixon. 'What about damages claims?'

'The widows of the three men who died sued and the claims were settled by Crook's insurers. They got the fixed sum for bereavement damages and future loss of earnings. Not sure how much they got in all. D'you want me to find out?'

'Don't bother.'

Louise picked up the milk carton and shook it. 'Did you find the missing blue file?' she asked, filling the kettle.

'No. If Amy still had it then it's gone. Unless it's in her car?'

'Nope. There's an email from Scientific.'

Dixon tipped his head, a loud click coming from his neck.

'We're still floundering in the dark then?' asked Louise.

'You're forgetting what Steiner said.' He was waiting for a computer to start up. 'You've seen the transcript from the crane?'

'Yes, but—'

'Tarmac.'

'Eh?'

'Steiner said he'd been paid to come in here and sabotage the tarmac. That means somebody wants Hardman Tarmacadam's contract. Money is changing hands too, if some of it was given to him to do the deed. Hardman are a Tier 2 company laying the internal roads. They were awarded the contract by Myles Construction, the Tier 1 company with the contract for associated developments.' He opened a web browser. 'It's a bit like when Crook Engineering were awarded the contract for the platforms under the Second Severn Crossing.'

Louise nodded.

'We know – believe, I should say – that the platforms were sabotaged and the contract was then taken away from Crook and given to Centrix,' continued Dixon, gathering momentum. 'On the back of that, we suspect Centrix was behind the sabotage. But in order for the sabotage to have had the desired effect, the person whose job it was to award the contracts must have been in on it, surely? Ray Harper of Centrix is hardly going to go to the risk of sabotaging Crook's platforms unless he knows he's going to get the contract, is he?'

'No, Sir.'

'Remember it was worth millions.'

'So, the person in charge of the contracts was on the take?'

'He must've been. The plan doesn't work otherwise. "Give me a hundred grand and you can have the contract." I can hear them saying it now. And that same person must be here, inside Hinkley, which explains why Amy came here.'

'And whatever Stella found in the files confirmed it?'

'I'm guessing she confronted him and paid the price. It was Amy's death warrant too, they just had to find her. Remember that article in the HPC newspaper?'

'*The Point.*'

'She was here, so they got Steiner to do the job with the promise of passage on a boat, and then hung him out to dry when her body was found. We were supposed to assume he'd got in here, she'd recognised him and—'

'She was killed a couple of days after that article was published.' Louise was opening the drawers in turn. 'There's no bloody sugar.' Then the cupboard underneath. 'We can't prove any of this at the moment, though, can we, Sir?'

'Not yet.'

Updating the Policy Log was a pain in the arse sometimes. No doubt Potter would be checking it from time to time too. Dixon frowned. Give it twenty minutes and she'd be on the phone. Either her or Lewis anyway. Documenting his decision making process; otherwise known as giving them a stick to beat him with if it all went wrong.

It seemed logical though, not that logic had ever played much of a part before. He'd just followed his nose, and it had worked up to now.

'Floundering in the dark' was the phrase Louise had used, and Dixon hated it. The investigation needed a clear direction and this was it; whether it was right or wrong would come out in the wash.

Twenty minutes? It took ten, his phone buzzing on the desk in front of him.

'Yes, Ma'am.'

'There's a lot of guesswork in there.'

'There is.'

'You've got no evidence.'

And this week's prize for stating the bleedin' obvious goes to—

'Not yet, Ma'am. But there's the statement from Amy's friend that she came to Hinkley to watch someone connected to the SSC.'

'What does that prove?'

'The answer is here, Ma'am. Amy came here, someone paid Steiner to get in here and sabotage the tarmac, then to kill Amy. It all points to Hinkley.'

'Charlesworth's had the Home Office on the phone. EDF are going along with it at the moment, but their patience is running out. There have been rumblings at board level and the Home Secretary has already had the Energy Minister on the phone twice.'

Dixon knew the signs. 'How long have I got?'

'Seventy-two hours.'

'This is the list he asked for.' Crew handed Louise a sealed envelope when she opened the door. 'It was locked,' he said, gesturing to the handle with a frown.

'This is an Incident Room and it's a murder investigation.' Dixon spoke without looking up from his computer.

Crew hesitated.

'Is that everything?' asked Louise.

'Er, yes.'

Dixon waited until she locked the door again. 'Let's have it then.'

'What is it?'

'A list of all the Myles employees with security clearance.' Dixon unfolded the pieces of paper. 'One hundred and seventy-seven.'

'Not many then,' said Louise, rolling her eyes.

'We just have to cross-reference it with the SSC employees. How far have you got with a list of their—'

'Nowhere, I'm afraid. I've tried the three companies that formed the joint venture and none of them have kept any records going that far back. Two of them have merged since then as well, which makes it worse.'

'Typical.'

Dixon glanced down the list. If he was right, then the person he was looking for was a decision maker. He snatched a highlighter pen off the desk and began working down the job titles.

Interesting, some of them. He wondered what a 'director of strategic engagement' was. Whatever it was, a director was worth following up, as were the managing director, chief executive, chairman, finance director, operations manager – the list ran to seventeen in total, each with the word 'director' or 'manager' in the title. It was as good a place as any to start.

'We need the security files for this lot,' said Dixon, handing the list to Louise.

'Personnel files too?'

'No. I don't want to let them know we're looking at them yet.'

'Leave it with me,' she replied. 'Crew gave me his extension number somewhere.'

In the meantime, Google would have to do. The Myles Construction website wasn't particularly illuminating, the information for shareholders giving the names of the board members, but that was it. Dixon downloaded the company annual report, soon deleting it. He tried Companies House, which gave much the same information. Then he googled each of the directors in turn, scrolling through pages of press releases and LinkedIn profiles.

'I never got the hang of LinkedIn,' he said under his breath; louder than he thought, obviously.

'It's like Facebook but for business people, that's all,' said Louise, her head popping up from behind her computer. 'Instead of connecting with friends and family you connect with other business people. It's an online networking thing.'

Dixon curled his lip. He remembered an email coming round when he was training to be a solicitor, quickly consigned to the trash folder. Networking – standing around with a glass of wine in his hand in a room full of people who were equally disinterested, making small talk, before the obligatory exchange of business cards. He'd been once, to some lunch club or other, before he'd wised up to it.

He clicked on the LinkedIn profile for the managing director. 'You've got to sign up to view their profiles,' he said, clicking the Back button.

'I'm a member, Sir,' said Louise. 'If you want me to do it.'

'Try the managing director first.' Dixon was standing behind her, watching her log in. 'You haven't completed your profile,' he said.

'Not yet.' She typed in the name and hit Enter. 'There he is, Sir. John Hart, managing director, Myles Construction Plc.'

He took pride in his profile, more so than Louise anyway.

'Can you print it off?' asked Dixon.

'I can save it as a PDF file and then print it.'

'Do that for each of them then, and we'll see what we get.'

He was listening to the whirr of the printer, reading the transcript of Liam Crook's interview, when Louise appeared next to his work-station and dropped a bundle of paper on to his keyboard. 'I haven't stapled them,' she said.

'What is it with people putting their CV online for the whole world to see?'

'It'll only be the bits they want people to see,' replied Louise.

'Even so.' Dixon was flicking through the pages.

'What's a CIMA?' she asked.

Dixon hesitated. 'Chartered Institute of Management Accountants.'

'What's a management accountant?'

'They do company accounts, that sort of stuff.' The finance director, Philip Scanlon CIMA. 'He's "results driven, self-motivated and resourceful", it says here. Who wrote that, I wonder?'

'He did.'

Dixon glanced down the page. Educated at Bristol Grammar School and Staffordshire University. 'What d'you notice about his work experience?' he asked, handing the page to Louise. He watched her eyes scanning the page.

She grinned. 'Really?'

'Vanity,' muttered Dixon, shaking his head.

Scanlon had worked for three companies, each listed with dates and job title. Myles Construction as finance director since 2015; for twenty years before that he was finance director with an engineering firm in Bristol, and before that procurement manager 1992 to 1995, Danson SSC Plc.

Idiot.

Chapter Twenty-Four

Steiner's dirty work.

That was one way of looking at it; one way of spinning it. Dixon preferred Jackman's take on it though, even if he had been Stella's solicitor. The fact that the same people had crossed Steiner was his problem.

It was an uncomfortable feeling all the same.

'This is about justice for Stella and Amy. All right?'

Louise, Dave and Mark frowned at him in unison, their 'who are you trying to convince?' unspoken.

They hadn't been there. In the crane. Had they?

'And Liam, Sir,' said Louise, filling in the gaps.

'Are you all right, Sir?' Dave asked, looking puzzled. He turned to Mark and raised his eyebrows.

Dixon wiped his forehead with the palm of his hand and looked at the clear fluid, glinting in the strip light directly above his workstation.

See, it's just sweat. What did you think it was?

He took a deep breath.

Shit happens. Get over it.

'The Home Secretary doesn't want us upsetting EDF for any longer than we have to, so she's given us seventy-two hours. After that we have to clear out.'

'What are they trying to hide?' asked Mark.

'It's the adverse publicity. Making investors nervous, I expect.' Dixon shrugged his shoulders. 'Politics.'

'Gits.'

'We do, at least, have a focus now.'

'Even if it's the wrong one,' muttered Dave.

'That's my decision, Dave. All right?'

'Yes, Sir.'

'And if you've got any other lines of enquiry, please tell us.'

He shook his head. 'No, Sir.'

'Philip Scanlon it is then,' said Dixon. 'Dave, I want you to see if you can place his car in and around Yatton at the time we think Stella disappeared. Check his mobile phone positioning too. Mark, I want to know everything about him. Usual stuff.'

'Yes, Sir.'

'Lou, see if you can find anything to connect Scanlon with Centrix or Raymond Harper.'

'What about the other enquiries?' she asked.

'The floundering about in the dark?'

'Er, yes.'

'Drop it.'

'You wanted to see me, Inspector?' Pickles was standing in the doorway of the beat team office on the first floor of Welfare Block East. No tweed jacket over the Rupert Bear waistcoat this time.

'I was told you were in a meeting, Sir,' replied Dixon.

Pickles was shifting from one foot to another. 'Look, we're anxious to get this sorted out as quickly as we can, as you might imagine.'

'Thank you.' Dixon gestured to a vacant chair. 'I wanted to understand the contract bidding process.'

'Oh, good God, don't tell me that's what this is all about.'

Dixon raised his eyebrows.

'Of course you can't, sorry.' Pickles sighed. 'We have a contracts team based at our head office in Bristol,' he said, sitting down on a swivel chair opposite Dixon and turning to face him. 'They award and manage the Tier 1 contracts. They've all been awarded now, as you might imagine. Each Tier 1 company is then responsible for awarding the Tier 2 contracts in their particular sector.'

'And do they choose who to award the Tier 2 contracts to?'

'Yes, within some constraints. The bidding process is restricted to companies that have pre-qualified. They have to demonstrate—'

'Who to?'

'Us. They have to demonstrate that they have the necessary resources in place to deliver. And a robust and resilient business plan. They'll then be issued with an invitation to tender for the relevant contracts.'

'And the tender process?'

'It's quite laborious – this is a multi-billion pound project, after all.' Pickles was looking out of the corners of his eyes at the whiteboard on the wall behind Dixon. 'There's a professional services group, which consists of advisors we've approved to assist companies with their bids. Accountants, lawyers, project managers, people like that.'

'But once a company has been pre-approved and issued with an invitation to tender, is it up to the Tier 1 contractor who wins the bid?'

'Subject to our approval, yes.'

'Have you withheld it?'

'Once.' Pickles folded his arms. 'It was for the canteen and the bid was so low as to be unsustainable. They could never have done it at that price, not with a sensible number of staff.'

'Any others?'

'Not that I'm aware of, no.'

'Has any contract been taken away from a Tier 1 or 2 company after it's been awarded?'

'Not a Tier 1, no. And only one Tier 2. That was for the materials testing.'

'And what's that when it's at home?'

'Road surface testing. We don't want them subsiding and they have to be able to take the weight of the lorries. There's some testing gauge they use. It wasn't a huge contract. No big deal, mercifully.'

'When was this?'

'Early on. It covers the roads across the site; it'll be miles by the time we've finished.'

'Who lost the contract?'

'I really can't remember.'

'Can you find out, please?'

Pickles nodded.

'Who got the contract in their place?' continued Dixon.

'Tyrer Materials Testing. You may see the van around the site, I'm not sure if he's here at the moment.' Pickles glanced out of the window. 'It really was one of the smaller contracts.'

'Part of the associated developments sector?'

'Yes. Myles are the Tier 1.'

'Can you let me have a list of the companies pre-approved to apply for the Tier 2 tarmac contract?'

'Myles should be able to let you have that,' replied Pickles.

'I don't want to ask them, Sir, if you don't mind.'

'Er . . .' Pickles shook his head. 'Yes, I can organise that. I'll get someone from our contracts team to drop it over.'

'Thank you.'

Louise waited until Dixon closed the door behind Pickles.

'One of the companies unsuccessful first time must have paid Scanlon to set this up, so they can have the tarmac contract when it's taken away from Hardman,' she said.

'It would be interesting to talk to someone at the firm that lost the original materials testing contract too.'

'Wouldn't it.'

Monkton Heathfield on the northern outskirts of Taunton was only half an hour away; thousands of new houses and more in the planning. New roads too, and pavements; more than enough to keep a materials tester busy.

It had been easy to find the grey van, South West Density Testing written on both sides in bright blue. A man in equally bright blue overalls was setting up what looked like a steel tripod on the road surface.

'Mr McConachie?' asked Dixon, winding down the window of his Land Rover.

'Aye.'

'Detective Inspector Dixon. We spoke on the phone.'

'Aye.'

'What's this?'

'This is a dynamic cone penetrometer. The weight slides down this pole and drives a cone into the ground; how far gives you a measurement of the density of the subsoil. It needs to be even along the whole road, else it collapses.'

'And if it's not?'

'They shore it up with aggregate and we test it again. Then they lay the road surface when we give them the green light.'

'This is what you were going to be doing at Hinkley?'

'Started doing it, aye. I was using the plate bearing test over there though, and taking core samples to test at the lab. Measuring the bearing capacity where they wanted to put the roads.'

'And you lost the contract.'

'Nope. It was taken away from me. Not that I'm that bothered, to be honest. There aren't enough hours in the day to do the work I've got.'

'Why did you bid for it then?'

'It seemed like a good idea at the time. I was looking to expand, so I put in a bid and got it. Then that bastard Scanlon . . .' His voice tailed off. 'Like I say, I'm not that bothered.'

'What happened?'

'Someone was playing silly buggers with my core samples. The measurements were all over the place. Then the next thing I know Scanlon pulls the plug on me.'

'He gave the contract to—'

'Tyrer.'

'Do you know Tyrer?' asked Dixon.

'Know him? I trained the little shit, didn't I? Then he gets his own machine and sets up in competition with me.' McConachie was clenching his fists. 'I should've known, but like I say, I'm not that bothered and I sure as hell can't prove anything.'

'How do you know they'd been tampering with your samples?'

'They took them and sent them to me.'

'Who did?'

'The operations manager at Myles. I reckon they came from somewhere else on the site, so it gave the wrong readings. You can imagine what happened when the first lorry went along the road. The surface was all over the place.' McConachie lobbed a spanner into the back of his van. 'Easy enough when you think about it.'

'So, you think the operations manager was behind it?'

231

'Either that or someone was tampering with my reports. I emailed them in. What happened to them after that is anyone's guess.' McConachie sneered. 'Scanlon giveth and Scanlon taketh away.'

A thin wisp of smoke was rising from the middle of the Great Plantation when Dixon parked across the gate behind Kilverton House.

'Someone's still at home,' he said, opening the driver's door into the hedge and squeezing down the side of Land Rover.

Wading through the long grass had soaked their trousers up to their knees by the time they reached the gate into the wood.

'Not nearly so glamorous when it's pissing down with rain, is it, Sir,' said Louise.

One of the tents had gone, but otherwise the camp was unchanged, although it was saturated, rain dripping off the trees long after it had stopped raining.

'Ed's gone.' A woman's voice, shrill, and coming from the partially completed roundhouse in the middle of the camp, the smoke rising from a hole in the middle of the roof.

'I'm looking for Fly,' said Dixon, more in hope than expectation.

'She's done nothing wrong,' came the reply.

'I need her help.'

Silence.

'Bollocks to this,' muttered Dixon. He stepped forward and held back the tarpaulin, peering into the darkness. A familiar waft of sweet smelling tobacco hit him.

'Shit!'

The man burned his fingers snatching open the door of the wood burning stove, before throwing a hand rolled cigarette into the flames.

'Two people are dead,' said Dixon, sighing loudly. 'I'm really not interested in a bit of bloody cannabis. Now will you get out here so we can talk.'

Dreadlocks, sleeveless T-shirts; and bare feet – Dixon shuddered.

'You're Fly?' he asked, turning to the woman.

She nodded, her beads jangling.

'And you'll be Magnus?'

The grunt sounded positive, rather than negative.

'This is a photo of Amy. She was twenty-four years old.' Dixon handed Fly a picture of Amy, in a bar somewhere, smiling at the camera. 'She had her neck snapped at C3, right about here,' he said, pointing to the back of his own neck. 'I'm trying to catch the man who did it.'

'We thought that was Steiner,' said Magnus.

'Someone paid him. Someone you saw, Fly.'

'The suit?'

A LinkedIn profile picture, printed off in colour, a few years old, perhaps. It would have to do for the time being, until the identity parade, at least. 'Is this him?' he asked, the photograph in his outstretched hand.

Fly hesitated.

'This is a photograph of Amy's mother,' said Dixon. He had come prepared. 'She's missing. There was blood all over her house.' Matter of fact. 'Amy's brother still doesn't know.'

'It was getting dimpsy,' said Fly. 'And he had his hood up. I really don't . . .'

'What about his car?'

'It was parked over where your Land Rover is.'

'Was it like this?' asked Dixon, handing her another photograph.

'No, it was blue, I think. Like I said, the light was going.'

'Like this?' A photograph of the same type of car, in blue.

'Yes, that's it. What is it?'

'A Maserati.'

'Let me see his photograph again.' Fly shuffled the photographs, bringing Scanlon's picture to the top. 'It could be him. The glasses were the same, and he had a moustache.'

'I'm going to need your real name, Fly. And an address. Mobile phone number too, if you've got one.' Dixon tried his best disarming smile. 'Would you be willing to attend an ID parade too?'

'Must I?'

He handed the picture of Amy back to her.

Fly stared at the picture, watching the raindrops smudging Amy's smile. 'All right,' she said.

◆ ◆ ◆

'Back again, Inspector,' said Manners, striding across the field. 'I was cutting the leylandii and saw you going into the plantation.'

'Yes, Sir,' replied Dixon.

'There's only a couple of them left now. Magnus, Fly and one other, I think. The rest've done a bunk.'

'Do you know where they've gone?'

'Sizewell C, I think. Hinkley's a done deal, but there's still a chance to stop that one. It's at the planning stage now.'

'Where's Sizewell C?' asked Louise.

'Suffolk,' replied Manners. 'There's a much bigger camp and I reckon you'll find them there.'

'Thank you, Sir.'

'You got him then?' asked Manners.

'Steiner, yes, Sir. Not before he—'

'I know.' Manners cleared his throat. 'I'm sorry, I had no idea he'd been staying in the plantation. I would've said if I'd—'

'Of course you would, Sir.'

'It was a transient population, people coming and going all the time, nicknames only, and I tended to leave them to it.'

'It's fine, Sir,' said Dixon, turning towards the gate. 'You couldn't have known.'

And at least Manners wouldn't have to explain it to Amy's mother.

Chapter Twenty-Five

What time you home? Monty needs his tablets. Jx

The text had arrived just as Dixon was dropping Louise back to her car at Hinkley Point. There was a missed call too – an 01823 number – the diabetic centre again.

'What time in the morning?'

Louise waited, but not for long.

'What time d'you want me in the morning, Sir?'

Dixon took a sharp intake of breath as he turned to Louise. 'Seven, in the beat team office,' he replied.

'I'll let Dave and Mark know.'

'They're still here, by the looks of things,' he said, gesturing to their cars parked on the other side of the car park.

'Shall I go in?'

'Send them a text.'

Louise smiled. 'Yes, Sir.'

Three hundred and seventy-five lorries a day through Bridgwater, but the road was quiet on Dixon's drive home, the only sound the clunk of the windscreen wipers and the rumble of his diesel engine.

Walking his dog was out – for the time being, God willing – so he'd have to do his thinking behind the wheel of his Land Rover. Hardly peace and quiet, but it was the next best thing.

A Tier 1 finance director on the fiddle. That would go down well with EDF. And killing to cover his tracks. If Stella had found something to connect him with Centrix, then it was certainly motive enough. More than enough.

He could prove Scanlon's presence at the SSC, but nothing more. Stella had spent years trying to clear her husband's name, to prove the platform had been sabotaged, so had her solicitor, but they'd never got close. Best not to try. Instead, focus on Scanlon's involvement in Stella's murder on the basis that SSC was the motive.

After all, if Stella was right and Scanlon had been instrumental in the sabotaging of the platform, then he was responsible for the deaths of three men. Four, if you include Liam.

Dixon was biting at the dry skin on his lips.

But you've got no evidence of that either.

He could just imagine the look on Charlesworth's face.

It was true though. The best Dixon could say was that Scanlon was a 'person of interest', and that wasn't going to get him far. There was fraud, possibly, if he could prove McConachie's allegations about the materials testing contract. Obtaining a pecuniary advantage by deception. It was like nicking Al Capone for tax evasion. Now there was an American film worth watching; not in black and white either, although quite why they picked a Scottish actor to play an Irishman was beyond him.

Hypertension. It was a serious condition. He wondered whether Pickles had ever been formally diagnosed – all that fidgeting and hopping about from one foot to another. Maybe he was just 'highly-strung'? Strung out, more like. Director of Communications; he's going to have some serious communicating to do when all this comes out, thought Dixon.

Random thoughts popping into his head, gone again with the flash of another set of headlights coming towards him. He wondered whether he would see flashing lights when the laser zapped whatever was going on at the back of his eye. And whether it would hurt. He flinched. Maybe he would google it, after all?

Chard was out of his hair at last, but at what price? It wasn't often Dixon took an instant dislike to someone, but he had to Chard. And he'd been proven right time and time again. Chard would get three years for perverting the course of justice – more, possibly, given that he was a police officer – and a couple of months for the criminal damage, the Animals Act offence dropped if he pleaded guilty to the other charges. That was the way these things usually went. No doubt the sentences would run concurrently too, so he wouldn't actually serve any time for Monty's poisoning.

Sentencing was a joke sometimes. But then, in the eyes of the law, Monty was just an item of personal property that Chard had damaged.

Damage. Dixon sneered. Chard would learn about that if Monty died.

He parked out in the road and looked through the living room window. The lights were on and the curtains open, Lucy sitting on the kitchen floor, syringe in hand; Monty sitting in front of her.

Jane was asleep on the sofa, head back, mouth open. Every four hours throughout the night she'd been up feeding Monty.

The television was on. Dixon recognised the voices. Alec Guinness and Julie Christie.

Doctor Zhivago again.

Monty turned and spotted Dixon in the window, trotting over and standing with his paws up on the window seat, tail wagging. Lucy was not far behind him with a handful of kitchen roll to catch the fish and veg dripping from his jowls.

'Nick's here,' she said, looking up.

Jane yawned her way to the front door, opening it as Dixon appeared around the corner.

'How's he doing?' he asked.

'He's taking the mickey now, if you ask me. He ate a whole tin of tuna at lunchtime, from his bowl, and now he won't touch food again unless it's from the syringe.'

'He's got you two wrapped around his little finger, hasn't he?'

'Tell me about it.'

'Has he been out?'

'Not yet,' replied Lucy.

Jane and Lucy watched from the open back door while Dixon followed his dog around the field behind the cottage, lighting the way with the torch on his phone, checking everything the dog looked at, let alone sniffed.

'What time's he due back at the vet?' he asked.

'After morning surgery again,' replied Jane. 'Eleven.'

'These are his tablets,' said Lucy, pointing to them on the worktop as Dixon closed the kitchen door behind them.

'Brace yourself, old son.' He clamped his fingers around Monty's muzzle.

'He wriggles like an eel when I try it.' Jane sighed.

'They've gone,' said Dixon, standing up.

'I'll finish giving him this.' Lucy sat down cross-legged on the kitchen floor, so Dixon and Jane left her to it, slumping down side by side on the sofa.

'I really can't begin to—'

'Then don't,' interrupted Jane, taking his hand.

'It was Chard.'

'What was?'

'Potter had the cottage under surveillance – they thought Steiner might turn up here – and caught our poisoner instead.'

Jane sat up sharply. 'Chard poisoned Monty?'

'There's a photograph of him walking round the back with a bottle of antifreeze in his hand. And he's admitted it.'

'The utter fucking—'

'We'll be in court to watch him get sent down, don't you worry. And if Monty dies—'

'He won't.' Jane squeezed Dixon's hand. 'How's the investigation?' she asked, changing the subject before he could dwell on it.

'We have a person of interest,' he replied. 'Dave and Mark are checking cars and phones to see if we can place him at the scene.'

'Who is it?'

'The finance director of one of the companies at Hinkley. He was at the Severn Bridge thing too.'

'When will you know?'

'Tomorrow.'

'I'll text you when I know the blood results,' said Jane. 'I'll feed him later, if you like.'

'You get some sleep. I'm doing the midnight one and Lucy's setting her alarm for four in the morning. We've got it covered.'

'What would I do without you?' Dixon leaned back and closed his eyes.

'You're not seriously planning to arrest the finance director of a public limited company at Hinkley Point, the largest construction site in Europe.' Charlesworth folded his arms. 'The press will have a field day. And we'll have the bloody Home Secretary on the phone again before you can say nuclear meltdown.'

Dixon was sitting in meeting room 2 at Express Park, having been ambushed by Charlesworth before he had a chance to make the arrest. Potter was there, DCI Lewis and the press officer, Vicky Thomas.

He slid his phone out of his jacket pocket and looked at the screen, the buzz attracting Charlesworth's attention.

'Something more important to attend to, is it, Dixon?'

'Yes, Sir. It is actually.'

Bloods normal. Taking him home :-) Jx

'Share it with us, do.'

Dixon ignored him, instead tapping out a reply to Jane.

Thank you! Nx

'Let's hear it, Nick,' said Lewis. 'Why Scanlon?'

'You'll need more than the fact he worked at Danson SSC,' said Potter.

'I've got more than that,' replied Dixon, sliding his phone back into this pocket. 'You've read the statement from Hamish McConachie?'

'We have,' replied Potter.

'It doesn't prove he killed anyone, does it?' snapped Charlesworth.

'It does prove he's fiddling the contracts. And if he was doing that at the Severn Bridge—'

'Is there any connection to Centrix?' asked Potter.

'Scanlon's LinkedIn profile says that he was educated at Staffordshire University, although it was called the North Staffordshire Polytechnic when he was there. 1975 to 1978. The same time as Raymond Harper.'

'Did they know each other?'

'We don't know. Harper was studying civil engineering. I don't know about Scanlon.'

'Meaningless,' muttered Charlesworth.

'Is that it?' asked Lewis, his eyes bulging.

'Dave Harding and Mark Pearce have been on it all night, Sir,' replied Dixon. 'Stella was last seen leaving Portishead after her shift finished on the Friday and it wasn't until the Monday morning that PC Bolt kicked the door in.'

'And?'

'Scanlon's car is picked up on the traffic cameras at junction 21 on the M5 and then again on the A370 at Yatton. This is just after nine thirty. Then again just after midnight, going in the opposite direction.'

'Where does he live?' asked Charlesworth.

'Clevedon, Sir.'

'We need to get Scientific to check his car,' said Potter.

'Then there's the statement from Miriam Hackeson, otherwise known as "Fly",' continued Dixon. 'She thinks it might have been him she saw in the Great Plantation talking to Steiner. She identified his car, but that was across a field, at dusk, with no street lighting, so I'm not holding my breath. I'd like to try an ID parade though. Once I've arrested him, it'll be over to Scientific – his car and his house.'

'Once you've arrested him, the clock starts ticking, Dixon,' said Charlesworth. 'You've got ninety-six hours max.'

'That's an improvement then, Sir,' replied Dixon, smiling. 'It was only seventy-two hours yesterday.'

Chapter Twenty-Six

Dixon turned into the park and ride on his way back to Hinkley, spotting the Scientific Services van and the flatbed lorry waiting at the bus stop before he had passed the entrance.

It looked odd, stuck in the middle of rolling fields, a brand new car park, packed with cars and motorcycles. Temporary, EDF had said when they got planning permission; just to accommodate the workforce during construction, it would be returned to fields once the power station was complete. The tarmac ripped up, the area landscaped and grassed over. Still, it was too far from anywhere to be much use for anything else.

'Have you got the keys?' shouted Donald Watson, leaning on his car while he pulled a set of overalls over his shoes.

'Not yet,' replied Dixon. 'Which one is it?' he asked, leaving his engine running.

'That powder blue Maserati over there.' Watson was pointing towards the middle of the car park. 'We'll have to do it the old-fashioned way then,' he said, rolling his eyes. 'Just tip us the wink when you've nicked him.'

Dixon glanced at the crane on the back of the flatbed lorry, big enough to lift the Maserati clean out of its parking space, although it might scratch the shiny new Land Rover parked next to it.

'Better wait until we've got the keys,' he said.

'We haven't got all day.'

Martha Sparks and two other officers from the beat team were waiting for him when Dixon arrived at Hinkley Point. Straight through the turnstiles with his seven day pass, he managed to get in without being spotted by Jim Crew hovering in the reception area.

'Where are Dave and Mark?' he asked, as Martha shut the door of the beat team office behind him.

'They went home,' said Louise. 'They'd been here all night. I've briefed Martha and her team.'

'Anything else?'

'The son's on his way back. He was backpacking in Laos. The consulate have broken the news to him and he gets into Heathrow tomorrow.'

Another difficult conversation to look forward to.

'Where's Scanlon's office then?' asked Dixon, turning to Martha.

'Upstairs,' she replied. 'At the far end of the building.'

'D'you know him?'

'No, Sir.'

Dixon hesitated. It was an uncomfortable feeling, making a speculative arrest. Still, Potter had approved it. Finding the evidence to charge Scanlon was stage two, with EDF, the Home Secretary and Charlesworth all breathing down his neck. Of the three, Charlesworth had the ability to cause him more immediate problems, perhaps.

The clock would start ticking the moment he nicked Scanlon too, as Charlesworth had been at pains to point out.

'Have we checked where he is?'

'Yes, Sir,' replied Louise. 'He's at a meeting over at Welfare Block West.'

'Do we wait until he gets back?' asked Martha.

'No. We get him now.'

The ride over to Welfare Block West took ten minutes, two officers following the minibus in the site patrol car, the red flag on the roof fluttering in the breeze. Dixon knew the way now: past the Viewing Gallery and the highways compound, then fork right before you get to the concrete batching plant.

'They're still excavating the second nuclear island,' said Martha, leaning across Dixon and pointing out of the window of the minibus. 'See that digger over there? Thirty tons of earth in one scoop. They arrived in bits and were assembled on site.'

Dixon frowned. What was it about Hinkley Point that turned everyone into a tour guide?

'The sea wall's nearly finished,' continued Martha. 'It's built to withstand sea level rises or even a tsunami.'

'What about sea level rises *and* a tsunami?'

The minibus stopped at a set of traffic lights before the bridge over the earthworks access, the construction site on their right, the bare earth towering over them on their left. Dixon looked down into the bottom of the chasm under the bridge at the huge dumper trucks following the dirt track up to the dump, their hoppers full to the brim with mud.

Everywhere mud.

It reminded him of old photographs of the Somme.

'The meeting's on the first floor,' said Louise, as the minibus pulled up outside the welfare block. Prefabricated units piled on top of each other to produce a three-storey office block, EDF's own office occupying the whole of the first and second floors. 'It's a monthly Tier 1 review with all the finance directors.'

Dixon was first through the double doors at the top of the flight of stairs.

'We're looking for Philip Scanlon,' he said. 'He's finance director for Myles Construction.'

'Shall I let him know you're here?' asked the receptionist.

'No. Thank you.'

'He's in the boardroom.' The receptionist pointed. 'Along the corridor, first door on the left.'

Dixon stopped outside the boardroom and peered through the window in the door. A long table littered with paper and empty cups and saucers, he counted sixteen men and women sitting either side, with one vacant chair at the far end. Scanlon must be sitting with his back to the door.

'There's a door at the far end.'

'I'll get it,' said Martha, tapping a uniformed colleague on the shoulder. They set off along the corridor, heads at the conference table turning to watch them through the glass partitioning.

Soundproofed in a temporary office block. Why couldn't they have done that at Express Park? thought Dixon.

David Pickles spotted him looking through the window and jumped up from his seat, so Dixon opened the door and stepped forward into the boardroom before Pickles could come out, Louise and a uniformed officer right behind him.

'Can I help you, Inspector?' asked Pickles, raising his eyebrows.

'I'm looking for Mr Scanlon, Sir,' replied Dixon, glancing around the table; all of the heads now turned towards him, a moustache at the far end.

'Philip?' Pickles was looking to the far end of the conference table, his head tipped to one side.

Scanlon glanced at the door to his right just as it opened, revealing Martha Sparks and another beat team officer blocking his path to the back stairs. He sighed, then slumped back in his chair, arms folded.

'Stand up, please, Sir,' said Dixon, now waiting behind Scanlon's chair.

No response.

'We can do this the hard way, if you prefer.'

Scanlon stood up and turned to face him.

'Cuff him,' said Dixon, turning to Martha.

'Is this really necessary?' demanded Pickles from the far end of the table.

Dixon took a deep breath. 'Philip Scanlon, I am arresting you on suspicion of the murders of Stella Hayward and Amy Crook.' He paused, allowing the murmuring around the conference table to subside. Pickles sat down, his mouth gaping open. 'You do not have to say anything but it may harm your defence if you do not mention when questioned something that you later rely on in court.' Another pause, this time for the snap of the handcuffs. 'Anything you do say may be given in evidence.'

'Can you see Hinkley from here?' asked Louise, turning the telescope to look south along the coast.

'You can't see past Sand Point,' replied Dixon.

They were standing in the window of Scanlon's living room overlooking the Severn Estuary, with Cardiff in the distance, the sun streaming in through the huge windows. Even the balustrade on the balcony was glazed to preserve the view.

'From seven hundred and fifty-five thousand, it says on their website. There are still a couple available if you fancy it, Sir.'

Marine Place, Clevedon, was a terrace of new townhouses built on the clifftop above the old Victorian pier. It was a grandstand view, with a price tag to match.

'There's no garden and the beach is shingle,' muttered Dixon.

'You'd have thought he could afford some curtains, wouldn't you?' continued Louise.

All of the furniture was white, even the leather sofa; the tables stainless steel with frosted glass tops; the only splash of colour in the room coming from Union Jack cushions and a red rug on the light oak floor.

'I reckon he's bought the show home.'

'Find out when. And whether there's a mortgage on it.'

'Yes, Sir.'

Dixon turned round to watch a Scientific Services officer unplugging Scanlon's computer at the back of the open plan living space. He was lying on the floor, underneath a white desk, disconnecting cables that had been neatly hidden using cable ties.

The living room was on the top floor; 'reverse level' the architect had no doubt called it; upside down was a better description. And four floors without a lift.

Twit.

'It's going off to High Tech now, Sir,' said Louise. 'They found a couple of external hard drives in a drawer too.'

'What about his phones?' asked Dixon.

'The one in his pocket is personal and it's on the way to High Tech. The one on his desk was his work one.'

'And where are all his documents: papers, bank statements, stuff like that?'

'There's a scanner and a shredder, Sir, so maybe he scans everything, then shreds it. It might explain the external hard drives?'

'We'll soon see.'

The master bedroom on the second floor resembled a cell, were it not for the en suite and the curtains. Scanlon would be used to it then.

'They've got something in the utility room.' Louise was shouting from the top of the stairs. 'On the ground floor, Sir.'

'You'd have thought they'd have put a bloody lift in.'

The utility room was bigger than Dixon's kitchen, with a granite worktop and Belfast sink; washing machine and tumble dryer too, the doors of both open.

'Well?' asked Dixon.

'Blood on the laundry basket,' said the Scientific Services officer. 'Looks like he washed his clothes, but forgot to clean the laundry basket. Switch the light off and I'll show you.'

Louise flicked off the lights and they watched the officer wave an ultraviolet light over the washing machine. 'There's a smear here too, on the outside of the rubber seal, probably from when he was shoving the clothes in.'

It was a tiny smudge, appearing fluorescent violet in the UV light. But it was enough.

'And on the basket, here,' said the officer, illuminating more spots and a smear on the rim. 'Everybody's seen enough police dramas on the telly to wash their clothes, right? But how many forget to clean the laundry basket?'

'Will you be able to tell whose it is?'

'There's more than enough for that.'

'Looks like he's our man,' said Louise, as they walked across the car park behind Marine Place.

'One of them,' replied Dixon.

'Eh?' Louise frowned. 'Who else is there? Harper is dead, so that's Centrix accounted for. And we've got Scanlon, so that's Danson SSC, which is both ends of the Severn Crossing deal, isn't it?'

'We might as well call in at Portishead, seeing as we're up here,' he said, leaving Louise's question hanging. 'We can see what they've found in his car.'

Dixon pulled up outside the Scientific Services lab on the Avon and Somerset Police Headquarters complex half an hour later, Scanlon's powder blue Maserati sitting on the back of a flatbed lorry.

'Blood on the washing machine, I gather,' said Donald Watson, leaning in the passenger window of Dixon's Land Rover.

'And the laundry basket,' said Louise.

'Not as clever as he thinks then.' Watson grinned. 'He's replaced the carpet in his boot too. Missed a bit though.'

'Where?'

'Give me ten minutes to get it unloaded. There's a coffee machine in the office.'

Dixon and Louise were stirring their coffees with Bic biros when Watson tapped on the window, the empty lorry reversing out of the workshop behind him.

'There's nothing in the passenger compartment,' he said, popping the boot open with the remote control. 'See this carpet.' Watson pointed into the bottom of the boot. 'It's brand new.'

'How can you tell?' asked Louise.

'They checked with the Maserati garage, Lou.' Dixon had fallen for that one before. Never again.

'This bit too,' continued Watson, stifling a grin. He was stroking a piece of carpet on the underside of the boot lid with his latex gloved hand. 'Brand spanking new.'

'Have you looked under it?' asked Dixon.

'Not yet, but what's that you can smell?'

Dixon leaned over and sniffed inside the boot. 'Bleach.'

'It's the bit of carpet under here,' said Watson, reaching into the boot and pointing up under the chassis just behind the hinges. 'Just let me give it a spray of luminol.' Then he placed a UV light in the back of the boot pointing upwards. 'You'll need to lean in and look up under here. He probably couldn't see it against the dark carpet.'

'It looks like a handprint,' said Dixon, leaning over.

'There are a couple,' replied Watson.

Dixon sighed. 'Which means she was still alive when she was in here.'

'I'll map them out on a plan for you,' continued Watson, picking up the UV light. 'This should be enough to convict without the body, shouldn't it?'

Chapter Twenty-Seven

'Where is he?' asked Lewis, sitting down opposite Dixon in the canteen at Express Park.

'Downstairs,' replied Dixon, ripping open a packet of sandwiches. 'We're waiting for a DNA test before we interview him. His fingerprints match those found at the scene. We just want *her* blood in *his* car now, then we've got him.'

'Charlesworth wants to know if that's it. You've got enough to charge him, even if he goes no comment to everything. Harper is dead, which closes off the Centrix line of enquiry, and now you've got Scanlon.'

'I'm sure this is going somewhere,' said Dixon. 'D'you want to skip the flannel and get straight to the bad news?'

Lewis smiled. 'EDF have been on again. They're getting nervous about the publicity. There's some big visit next week, apparently. Chinese investors.'

'Who have they been on to?'

'The Energy Minister, who's been on to the Home Sec—'

'How long have I got?'

'Forty-eight hours,' replied Lewis. 'He's told them we'll pull the Incident Room off site the day after tomorrow.'

Louise poked her head around the door of the canteen. 'It's Stella's DNA in the boot, Sir,' she said, smiling.

'Right, well, let's see what he's got to say for himself then.'

Dixon's preferred room – the one with the table – was occupied, so he had been forced to use one of the new ones, designed by an idiot who had never conducted a police interview. A table between the interviewing officer and the suspect makes it too adversarial, or so he'd been told.

He glanced down at the monitor. Scanlon was sitting opposite the tape machine, his solicitor to his right, two vacant chairs to his left.

The suspect is more likely to engage with you, to trust you, if there's no barrier between you, or so they said.

Bollocks.

Dixon opened the interview room door and sat down next to Scanlon, who was cleaning his glasses on his shirt. Louise sat down on the vacant chair to Dixon's left. Then he switched on the tape.

'My name is Detective Inspector Nick Dixon; to my left is Detective Constable Louise Willmott. It is 4.42 p.m. on Tuesday 25th May. Interview with . . . State your full name for the tape, please.'

'Philip Robin Scanlon.'

'And to his right is his solicitor.'

'Madeleine Cooper – Miss – from Clarkes.'

'You have been arrested on suspicion of the murders of Stella Hayward and Amy Crook, Philip, and you are still under caution. Do you understand?'

'Yes.'

'I want to begin by taking you back to 1975.'

Scanlon frowned. 'Why?'

'You were studying at the North Staffordshire Polytechnic.'

'I prefer to call it Staffordshire University.'

'Why is that?'

'It sounds better.'

'Does that really matter now, after all this time?'

'To me it does.'

'What were you studying?'

'Business studies.'

'And how did you meet Raymond Harper?'

Scanlon tipped his head back, looking up at the ceiling. 'We . . .' He puffed out his cheeks, then began breathing heavily through his nose. 'The Real Ale Society. We both joined. It was just an excuse for a pub crawl, really.'

'Did you keep in touch?'

Scanlon nodded, still staring at the ceiling.

'For the tape, please.'

'Yes.'

'So, whose idea was it to sabotage the platform under the Severn Crossing?'

'My client has not been charged with any offence relating to that.'

'That's right, Miss Cooper.' Dixon smiled. 'At this stage we are looking at it purely as a motive for Mrs Hayward's murder.'

'I haven't seen any evidence that she has been murdered,' snapped Cooper. 'Have you found a body?'

'I'm hoping your client will be able to help us with that.'

She leaned over and whispered something in Scanlon's ear.

'Continue,' she said.

'We were both members of the local Rotary Club,' said Scanlon. 'He said his business was in trouble. He'd taken on staff in anticipation of getting the SSC contract, but then had been undercut. He'd even turned away work, he was that sure he'd get it.'

'I bet he was, with you on the procurement team.'

'I made sure he knew the bids that had come in, but then Crook got their bid in after his and it was lower. There was nothing I could do. It was the last phase and I was on my own after that, just managing the contracts. So I said to him, give me a reason to take the contract away from Crook and make it worth the risk. And he did.'

'How much?'

Scanlon closed his eyes. 'Two hundred and fifty thousand pounds.'

'That's a lot of money.'

'It was a multi-million pound contract.'

'Where's the money now?'

'Look, I'll tell you what I know, even admit my part in it, but don't ask me to tell you where my money is. I know you people, you'll confiscate the bloody lot.'

'Your house in Cleve—'

'It's not mine. It belongs to a trust. And it's offshore, so you can't touch it.'

Scanlon was an accountant, after all. 'Who sabotaged the platform?' asked Dixon, spelling it out.

'I don't know and I didn't ask. Before or after what happened. Ray arranged it. I just know that it wasn't supposed to go down like that. No one was supposed to die. He was devastated. We both were.'

'Didn't stop him taking the contract though, did it?'

Scanlon was staring at his shoes now, the laces missing. 'No.'

'And he let another man take the blame. So did you for that matter.'

'I know.'

'How did you feel when Liam Crook gassed himself in his car?'

'I—'

'Leaving a pregnant wife.'

'What could I do about it? I was in it up to my neck. Nobody was supposed to die.' He shook his head. 'The platform was supposed to have been empty.'

'Tell me about your relationship with Stella Crook, as she then was.'

Scanlon grimaced. 'She never gave up; became a thorn in my side. She appealed everything, wanted fresh inquests, a public inquiry, even sued the Health and Safety Executive. She could never let it rest. Living with it was bad enough, but with her pick, pick, picking, never knowing whether she'd find something, it was torture.'

'Would you have let it rest, in her position?' asked Dixon.

'I suppose not.' Scanlon folded his arms. 'You have to admire her, really.'

'Was that before or after you killed her?'

'What?'

'The admiration.'

Scanlon closed his eyes. 'Both.'

Cooper leaned across and whispered in Scanlon's ear. 'You don't have to—'

He waved her away. 'Yes, I killed her. She told me she'd got hold of the original prosecution file. God knows how, but she did, and there were photographs on it that had never been disclosed to the defence.'

'What photographs, Philip?'

He hesitated. 'No comment.'

'Did she show them to you?'

'No. Look, she said she could finally prove it was sabotage. So, I . . . You have to understand she'd been making my life a misery for over twenty years.'

'Your life? What about her life, Philip? And her children?'

'I know, I know.'

Dixon waited.

'I went to her house in Yatton. Tried to reason with her, but it was like trying to reason with a rabid dog. Then she came at me with a kitchen knife . . .' Scanlon's voice tailed off. Tears began to trickle down his cheeks. 'No, she didn't.' He sighed. 'She went into the kitchen and I followed her. She had a glass of wine on the side. She kept saying she knew and I was going to pay. So, I picked up a knife and . . .' He hesitated.

'And what, Philip?'

'Stabbed her.'

'How many times?'

'Three or four. She fell on the coffee table and the legs snapped off. I . . . I picked one up and hit her with it. Then I rolled her up in the rug. It was dark outside. I got her in the boot of my car, cleaned up her living room and buried her in the woods.'

'Where?'

'Up behind Cleeve.'

'And you can take us there, can you?'

'I'm not sure I . . . I don't know . . .' Scanlon was rubbing his chin. 'I don't think I could find it again. It was dark, there's no way I . . .'

'How tall was Stella?'

'Five-nine, maybe, I don't know.'

'And how much did she weigh?'

'I don't know, do I?'

'Fourteen stone, Philip. And you, you're what? Five-eleven and twelve stone?'

'Twelve and a half.'

'And you're seriously telling me that you carried her limp body – I won't say dead body because she was still alive at this point – wrapped in a rug out to your car and then—'

'Still alive?'

Dixon opened a folder on his knee and handed Scanlon a photograph. 'This is a photograph of a bloodied handprint left in the boot of your car. DNA testing confirms the blood is Stella's, but then we know that, don't we? Dead bodies don't leave handprints, Philip.'

'Oh, God. I thought she was dead. I thought I'd . . .'

'Were you on your own?'

Scanlon blinked, then swallowed hard. Too long, surely?

'Yes, of course I was.'

'And you're seriously telling me you can't remember where you buried her?'

'Please tell me she wasn't buried alive.'

'We can't, Philip, unless you tell me where she is.'

'I don't . . . I can't . . .'

'You washed your clothes?'

'Yes.'

'Forgot to clean the laundry basket though. This is a photograph of a smear of Stella's blood.' He handed another picture to Scanlon. 'Can you identify that item for me?'

'That looks like my laundry basket.'

'We've got your mobile phones and computer. Are you content to give me the login details, Philip?'

'No comment.'

Clearly, there was a limit to Scanlon's cooperation.

'We found three hard drives too.'

'Three?'

Dixon waited, watching Scanlon squirm. 'The two in the drawer of your desk, and another in an old briefcase in the loft,' he said, eventually.

Scanlon gritted his teeth.

Dixon opened the folder on his knee and shuffled the papers in it, not for any particular reason other than to make Scanlon wait for the next question, watching him out of the corner of his eye.

'How much did you pay Steiner to kill Amy?'

Scanlon shifted in his seat. He glanced at Cooper. 'One bitcoin. That's about five thousand pounds to you. That and passage on a boat was the price to . . .' He took a deep breath.

'Sabotage the tarmac?'

'How could you possibly know that?'

'He told me,' replied Dixon, spelling it out.

'That's right. Then once he was in there I told him to kill Amy. It was either that or I'd turn him in.'

'Dangerous business, double-crossing a man like Steiner,' said Dixon, shuffling the papers on his knee.

'I know that now.'

'Which boat was it?' he asked, fixing Scanlon with a cold stare.

'No comment.'

'He went to the jetty and the crew said they'd never heard of him.'

Scanlon smirked. 'Why would I let him get away after her body was found? He could take the fall for it and I'd be off the hook. I mean, who on earth would believe him?'

'I did, Philip.' Matter of fact. 'I looked him in the eyes and I believed him.'

'More fool you.'

Cooper looked up, expecting him to take the bait, but Dixon stifled the wry smile, keeping it to himself.

'And you made yourself scarce while all this was going on?' he asked.

'I was in head office for two days and at home that night.'

'Why kill her?'

'She was working with her mother. Always had been. I couldn't take the risk. Then I saw her in *The Point*. A big feature about the female dumper truck driver. Stella said they were keeping an eye on me.' He shrugged his shoulders. 'She was at Hinkley, for God's sake! What else could I do?'

Dixon reached down to the floor, picked up an evidence bag and handed it to Scanlon. 'Do you recognise this photograph?'

Crumpled and covered in blood.

'I took it from Stella's bedside table thinking we'd need it for . . .' His voice tailed off. 'I gave it to Steiner so he knew what Amy looked like.'

'And the shotgun?'

Arms folded tightly across his chest now. 'I threw it over the perimeter fence, into the bushes behind the bat house.'

'Where did you get it?'

'No comment.'

'How did you meet Steiner then?'

'He was in the Great Plantation. I went there to try to find someone to do the tarmac and . . .'

'One of the protestors?' Dixon looked up.

'Yes.'

'Not Steiner in particular?'

Another blink. 'No.'

'How did you know they'd be there?'

A frown this time. 'Everybody knew they were living in the woods.' Scanlon sneered. 'In a commune.'

'And did you recognise Steiner when you saw him?'

'Yes.'

'How did you get him into Hinkley?'

'As an employee of Agard. It was easy.'

Dixon raised his eyebrows. 'I thought there was an induction programme and security checks?'

'I faked his attendance at the induction programme and there are ways round the security checks.' Scanlon smirked. 'It's the same with all these places where the security is tight on the way in. Once you're in, no one will challenge you. 'Specially if you look the part – all it takes is a hi-vis jacket and a hard hat.'

'It's not what you know, it's who you know, eh, Philip?'

Silence.

'We may wish to interview your client again, Miss Cooper,' said Dixon, once Scanlon had been led back to the cells.

'You'll be charging him?'

'Not yet.'

'Releasing him on bail then?'

Dixon raised his eyebrows. 'A double murderer with known connections offshore—'

'I shall have to make a formal bail application.'

'You do that. It'll ramp up the chargeable hours, won't it?'

Dixon waited for the door to slam behind Cooper.

'We'll interview him again when we've cracked his phone and computer.' Dixon smiled. 'Did you see the look on his face when I mentioned the third hard drive?'

'Where's his money, d'you reckon?'

'The Cayman Islands, somewhere like that. Either that or he's got it all in bitcoin.'

'And you think he had an accomplice?' asked Louise.

'Do you?'

'Yes,' she replied, nodding.

'My guess is he killed her, then called for help to clear up the mess. He'd never have lifted her on his own.' Dixon was watching Louise sealing the interview tapes. 'Check his alibi for when Amy was killed, will you. Let's see if he really was at head office. If he was, then someone else searched her room in the accommodation block.'

'Really?'

'Found what they were looking for too.'

'The blue bag Amy took from Stella's house?'

'My guess is it was the photographs that Stella said proved everything.' Dixon stood up. 'Two of the ceiling tiles had been lifted and glued back down with the pattern the wrong way round. I got Martha to go back and break them but there was nothing up there. And he's confessed to her murder, which means there can be only one reason why he says he can't remember where Stella is buried.'

'He's protecting someone?'

'Exactly.' Dixon stood up. 'When will we get High Tech's report?'

'Should be available first thing in the morning, Sir.'

'In that case, he can sweat it out overnight. I'm going home, and I suggest you do the same.'

❖ ❖ ◆

Dixon sat down on the red leather sofa in the window of the Zalshah Tandoori Restaurant in Burnham-on-Sea, let his head tip back against the glass and closed his eyes, trying to escape the blood.

There was blood everywhere.

Blood red wallpaper; blood red tablecloths; the carpet a darker red – congealed blood; even the sofa was artery red.

The spray of Steiner's blood hit him again. He flinched, turning away sharply, beads of sweat trickling down his temples. He wiped his forehead with the palm of his hand and looked at it, expecting to see more blood seeping through his fingers.

Nothing.

A hand on his shoulder. 'Mr Nick, are you all right?'

He squinted, trying to focus on Ravi frowning at him.

'Cancel the takeaway, will you?' he mumbled, standing up.

'No worries,' said Ravi, smiling. 'I'll put the money on your account,' he shouted, as the door slammed behind Dixon.

Music was pumping out of the Railway Inn when Dixon stumbled past, heading for the seafront. He glanced in the window at the people shouting at each other, trying to make themselves heard over some pop song. Most of them smiling, laughing or watching the cricket on the big screen, not that they could hear the commentary.

He walked out to the end of the Pavilion, the bells and whistles of the fruit machines inside not quite drowning out the waves lapping at the base of the sea wall, the lights twinkling in the drizzle and reflecting off the water.

More lights in the distance, on the other side of the estuary. Red lights on the tower cranes, bright spotlights down by the sea wall, the third tunnel boring machine visible even from this distance, about to start its journey under the seabed.

'Are you all right, mate?' Two anglers fishing off the end of the Pavilion were staring at him.

'Never better,' he replied, with a wave of the hand.

He walked back along the seafront, down the steps and along the ramp below the wave return wall, the water lapping at his feet, the reek of fish and chips following him.

Would Stella think it had been worth it? Worth dying for? Possibly. He wondered whether she was resting in peace, wherever she was.

Maybe not.

She died knowing her whole family had been shattered and that Scanlon would get away with it. Again.

A funny thing, justice. What good would it do her now? Or Amy? Or Liam for that matter. But it was Dixon's job to give it to them all the same. Finding Stella, so she could be laid to rest with Liam and Amy, seemed more useful to them.

The rest was about punishment. Scanlon, and whoever he was covering for, had a price to pay. And it was Dixon's job to see that they paid it. Whether or not that resulted in more blood was up to them.

Dixon would dust himself down and, God willing, take his dog for a walk on the beach. And all would be well with the world. Until the next time he was drenched in blood.

'You're all wet,' said Jane, opening the back door of the cottage. 'And you've forgotten the food.'

'How is he?'

'Tabi took the catheter out of his leg, but he's back tomorrow for more blood tests.'

Maybe he'd stick to shoplifting cases in future? There's very little blood involved in most thefts. And Lewis had given him the chance when he'd threatened to take him off the hunt for Steiner. Dixon had seen enough blood to last a lifetime. He shuddered. 'Blood and death.'

'What about it?' asked Jane, putting her arms around him.

'I've seen enough. More than enough.' He sighed. 'I'm still washing Steiner's brains out of my hair.'

'I thought you'd had a shower.' She ran her fingers through his hair.

'Not literally.'

Jane kissed him. 'And what would you do instead?'

'God knows.'

'Did you get Scanlon?'

Dixon nodded.

'So, that's it then?'

'He's covering for someone. And I still have to find Stella.'

'Why don't you take some time off when this is over?' asked Jane. 'We haven't finished that holiday in the Lakes yet.'

'Not without him,' said Dixon. He was standing in front of the sofa, looking down at Monty. Sound asleep with his tongue hanging out.

'She gave him a mild sedative.'

'Has he had his tablets?'

'He took them in a bit of turkey,' replied Jane. 'His appetite's coming back, that's for sure.'

'Where's Lucy?'

'In the shower.'

'You two go over to the pub and get something to eat. I'll stay with him,' said Dixon, slumping down on to the sofa next to Monty. The dog woke up and lifted his head, resting it on Dixon's knee. 'When's he due his next feed?'

'Midnight, but he's eating from his bowl now.' Jane smiled. 'No syringe. There's some cooked fish and veg in the fridge. It just needs thirty seconds in the microwave. All right?'

❖   ❖   ❖

It was just before 11 p.m. when Jane and Lucy opened the back door of the cottage. The lights were off, the credits of an old black and white film paused on the TV screen.

They crept into the living room, finding Dixon fast asleep on the rug, his head resting on a cushion. Monty was curled up next to him, his eyes clamped tight shut.

'I think we ought to leave them where they are,' whispered Lucy.

Chapter Twenty-Eight

Dixon woke early and was sitting at a vacant workstation in the CID Area at Express Park by 7 a.m. scrolling through his emails, all of which he deleted apart from those from the High Tech Unit.

They had managed to crack Scanlon's iPhones, his passcode for both turning out to be his date of birth. Dixon shook his head. And who said accountants weren't imaginative?

His work phone contained nothing of interest whatsoever: several calls to and from colleagues, which was to be expected, perhaps; no internet search history and no photographs. A chess game had been installed, but never played.

His personal phone was a different matter entirely, the report extending to eleven pages, with appendices. Multiple unidentified mobile phone numbers, which would keep Mark Pearce busy, and an internet history that included the online bitcoin wallet, Bitfly.com.

Just like Steiner.

Dixon opened a web browser and typed in 'bitfly.com'. Then he clicked on 'Open an Existing Wallet', which took him to the login screen that asked for a twelve word passphrase – the digital equivalent of a brick wall.

'Morning, Sir,' said Louise. 'How's Monty today?'

'Back to the vet at eleven. She thinks we're winning though.'

'Are those the reports from High Tech?' she asked, nodding in the direction of the printer that was churning out page after page.

'That's just the one on his personal phone. There's bugger all on his work one.' Dixon stood up and flicked on the kettle, leaning back against the worktop, watching the paper piling up in the tray. 'Where's the one on his desktop computer?'

'They said that might take a few days. The hard drives were encrypted, apparently.'

'What about Bitfly? Did they come back to you with details of Steiner's account?'

'Not yet, Sir.'

'Chase them up again, will you? And make sure they know he's dead. They might be a bit more cooperative if they know he won't be suing them.'

'Yes, Sir.'

The pile of paper was nearly half an inch thick when the printer finally stopped. Dixon picked it up and began flicking through it, the top corner clamped in his right hand.

'The son's due in today, Sir,' continued Louise. 'He got in last night and is staying with a friend in Weston.'

'Is he coming here?'

'Didn't say. He's going to ring in when he wakes up.'

'Tell him I'll meet him wherever he is. There's no need to drag him all the way down here.'

'Yes, Sir.'

'What time are Dave and Mark due in?'

'Eight, I think. DCS Potter is coming down for a briefing at nine too.'

◆　◆　◆

Dixon parked on the beach at the northern end of Weston-super-Mare seafront and looked along Brean Down, jutting out into the Bristol Channel to the south. The tide was turning, just as it had been that day he had been plucked from the base of the cliffs by the lifeboat; a pair of binoculars and he might even have been able to see the fishing ledges he had climbed down from.

He glanced along the beach, spotting a figure in the distance walking towards him, hands thrust deep into coat pockets. No dog either.

'What is it, Lou?' he asked, putting his phone to his ear.

'Potter's here and she's not a happy bunny.'

'What about?'

'She was expecting a briefing, apparently.'

'Have you heard from Bitfly?'

'They're going to email the stuff over. It's the crack of dawn over there, but they promised to do it by lunchtime, our time.'

'Ask Potter to extend Scanlon's custody by twelve hours. I want to interview him again when we've got the bitcoin wallet stuff.'

'Yes, Sir.'

'What about Dave and Mark?'

'Dave's still looking at traffic cameras and Mark the phones. Nothing yet.'

'All right. Tell her I'm meeting the son and I'll be back as soon as I can.'

'I tried that.'

Dixon rang off and slid his phone back into his pocket; the figure walking towards him along the beach a little closer now. Straggly dark hair blowing in the wind, ripped blue jeans and a green coat. He was still too far away to see facial features, but he seemed to be walking towards Dixon's Land Rover with purpose. It must be Nathan, he thought, sliding out of the driver's seat.

'Are you the police?'

Bags under the eyes on one so young. Jet lag might explain that, or some chemical or other. Both, possibly. And a chipped front tooth, but then cosmetic dentistry was hardly going to be a priority when you're bumming around the world.

'You're going to tell me she was right all along, aren't you?' Nathan kicked a broken tennis ball along the sand.

'Let me start by saying how sorry I am, Nath—'

'How did she die?' Jaw clenched, fighting back the tears.

'I can't confirm that because we haven't found her body yet, I'm afraid. What we do have is a man in custody who has confessed to killing her.'

'Who is it?'

'Philip Scanlon. Does that name mean anything to you?'

Nathan sighed. 'The accountant bloke from the bridge. She always thought he must've been in on it.' He was staring out to sea. 'You didn't say what happened.'

'I can only tell you what Scanlon has told me. Are you sure you want to kn—?'

'Yes.'

'He says he used a knife and the leg of a coffee table. And that he buried her body. He hasn't told me where yet.'

'Will he tell you?' The tears were flowing freely now.

'I don't know.'

'I need to speak to Amy. Where is she? She's not answering her phone.'

Dixon cleared his throat. 'What exactly have you been told?'

'Just that my mother has been murdered,' replied Nathan. 'It was some bloke from the consulate. He didn't say how or why or anything like that.'

'Get in.' Dixon opened the passenger door of his Land Rover.

'Where are we going?'

'When did you last speak to your mother?'

'I don't know. Maybe a year ago. We didn't . . . I didn't . . .'

'And Amy?'

'A month, maybe. I'd Skype her when I got the chance.'

Dixon slammed the passenger door and then climbed in the driver's seat. 'Amy's dead, Nathan.' He was holding the steering wheel in his right hand and turned in his seat to face him. 'I'm sorry, there's really no easy way to—'

Nathan swallowed hard. 'Scanlon?' he asked.

'He's confessed to arranging it.'

'How did she . . . ?' His voice tailed off.

'Her neck was broken. It would've been instant, painless.'

'Have you got the man who did it?'

'He's dead; shot by a police marksman.'

Nathan was rocking backwards and forwards in the passenger seat, his arms folded tightly across his chest. 'I thought they were deluded,' he mumbled. 'And they were right all along.'

'Scanlon has made a full confession of his part in the Severn Bridge deal. The platform was sabotaged. A lot of money changed hands to see to it that the contract was taken away from your father.'

Nathan's eyes were clamped tight shut. 'He was innocent all along?'

'He was.'

'Why did he kill himself then?'

'He couldn't prove it.'

'Yeah, but—'

'Your mother found evidence: photographs – we don't know exactly what of yet – confronted Scanlon with it and he killed her. Then he arranged for Amy to be killed as well. Did you know she was working in Hinkley Point?'

'Yes.'

'She was there to keep an eye on Scanlon. He was working as finance director for a Tier 1 contractor.'

'She never told me that. They both stopped talking to me about it after I left.' Nathan's shoulders sagged, his head bowed. 'For years and years all Mum cared about was proving it wasn't Dad's fault. She was obsessed. It came first, all the time. She even sucked Amy into it.' He wiped his cheeks on the sleeve of his coat. 'There was a big bust-up one Christmas. I told her I'd had enough and left.'

'How old were you?'

'Eighteen. It was after she broke up with Neil.' Nathan looked at Dixon, his eyes glazed over. 'She'd said things would change after that, but they didn't.'

'Tell me about your father.'

'I was three when he died, so I've only got photos, and what my mother told me. She loved him, I know that much. She scattered his ashes at Severn Beach, down under the bridge.'

'What about aunts and uncles?'

'None. There's just me now.' The tears began to fall again. 'Can I see Amy?'

'Family Liaison can arrange that,' replied Dixon. 'There needs to be a formal identification anyway, if you feel up to it?'

'Mum always said she'd prove him innocent or die trying. And in the end she did both. Silly sod.' He forced a smile. 'It was a price she was prepared to pay though. I know that.'

'She loved him,' said Dixon.

'You will find her, won't you?'

Dixon dropped Nathan back at his friend's flat and was turning into the visitors' car park at Express Park when his phone buzzed in his pocket. He wrenched on the handbrake, sliding his phone out of his pocket with his other hand.

Made you an appointment with Tabi at 5 Jx

He tapped out a reply, before switching the engine off.

What for?

She wants to go over the blood results with you.

Potter was waiting for him at the top of the stairs. It was one disadvantage of the visitors' car park – you could be seen from the front windows; the only alternative was the staff car park and wait for someone else to open the door with their pass. Fine first thing in the morning, but he was in too much of a hurry.

'How was the son?' she asked, blocking the landing.

'He didn't know Amy was dead.'

'Really?'

'Someone at the consulate bottled it.'

'You've got an extra twelve hours to charge Scanlon,' said Potter. 'Will that be enough?'

'We've got enough to charge him now, even without a body. I just want to have another go at him. He's protecting someone.'

'We've got the stuff on Steiner's bitcoin wallet,' said Louise, when Dixon sat down at the workstation in front of her. 'I emailed it over to Donald Watson at Scientific. He's had a look at it and wants a word.'

'Donald?'

Louise shrugged her shoulders. 'Our resident expert, apparently.'

'How come you know so much about bitcoin then, Donald?' asked Dixon, the phone clamped between his shoulder and his ear.

'I bought ten back in 2011,' replied Watson. 'A pound each they were then.'

'Ten at five grand each . . .'

'Ah, but I haven't got them anymore,' said Watson. 'I sold them a couple of years ago.' He hesitated. 'Fifteen thousand each they were back then. Paid off my mortgage.'

'I'm in the wrong business,' said Dixon. 'I hope you paid your tax.'

'Louise sent me the stuff from Bitfly,' continued Watson, ignoring him. 'There's not a lot. He hadn't sold any, so there's just the one bitcoin sitting in there. What's interesting though is the last-sent-to address.'

'You mean the address it was received from, surely?'

'No, there's no such thing. All you can see is the address that particular bitcoin was last sent to.'

Dixon frowned. 'You've lost me.'

'It's incredibly complicated.' Watson cleared his throat. 'All you need to know is that all transactions are recorded in the blockchain – it's a computer program – and there are various explorers you can use to look at it. Now, you can't see a "from" address, because there's no such thing. Imagine it's like cash. You can't see where you received a five pound note from, can you?'

'No.'

'You might *know* where you got it from, but if you don't, you can't find out. And bitcoin is the same.'

'Why?'

'It's all about privacy, really. To stop the likes of you and me tracing it. Are you still with me?'

'Sort of.'

'OK, so we think we know the last-sent-to address for this particular transaction.'

'Think?'

'There are some situations when this might not work.'

'Do I need to know?' asked Dixon, turning to Louise and raising his eyebrows.

'Not really. Look, focus on the bitcoin address. It's a random string of letters and numbers – usually thirty-four. The address is only used once for a particular transaction and they're largely untraceable. What I can tell you though is that we can be reasonably sure the last-sent-to address for this bitcoin now sitting in Steiner's wallet was multi-signature.'

'How can you tell that?'

'It starts with a "3". It's to do with the address protocol. You don't need to know that either.'

'That's a relief.'

'Anyway, put it to him and see what he says.'

'I will.'

'A multi-signature wallet means that at least two people, each with a separate private key – think of that as a long password – control the bitcoin.'

'Two people.' Dixon smiled.

'I thought you'd like that,' said Watson. Then he rang off.

'He tried explaining it to me as well, Sir,' said Louise, dropping her chewing gum in the bin.

Dixon was jabbing the lift button with his finger. He had managed to grab a quick sandwich in the canteen, while they waited for Scanlon's solicitor to arrive. 'We're going to have to keep it simple and hope he doesn't understand the technology either. It'll be all about his reaction.'

At least they had the interview room with the table this time.

'You're still under caution, Philip. Do you understand?'

'Yes.'

'I've spent the morning with Stella's son, Nathan.'

Scanlon was looking around the room – the floor, ceiling, anywhere but at Dixon.

'You've taken his father, his mother and his sister. How do you feel about that?'

'Sorry,' replied Scanlon, his eyes coming to rest on the table in front of him.

'Do you want me to tell you how he feels about it?'

'No.'

'There's only one thing you can do for him now. One thing that might bring him some crumb of comfort. And that is to let him bury his mother.'

Dixon waited, watching Scanlon sitting motionless in front of him. The fidgeting had gone, and taken with it any hint of remorse, by the looks of things.

'Where is she?' he continued.

'No comment.'

Git.

'Moving on then. I wanted to ask you about your accomplice. According to Myles you were at head office in Bristol the day Amy was killed and the day after. Is that right?'

'Yes. It's called giving yourself an alibi. It was supposed to be anyway.'

'Who searched her room then?'

Scanlon frowned. 'I have no idea what you're talking about.'

'Yes, you do. The file of papers that Stella had – the photographs. You hunted high and low and didn't find it, did you?'

'No comment.'

'We have a witness who saw Amy leaving her mother's house in Yatton with it. So, let me ask you again, who searched Amy's room in the accommodation block? It couldn't have been you because you weren't there.'

'No comment.'

Scanlon was fidgeting again now, beads of sweat on his forehead glinting in the strip lights on the ceiling.

'We know someone did because two of the ceiling tiles had been glued back in position the wrong way round. Easy to spot that sort of thing when you live with someone with OCD.'

'I have no idea what you're talking about.'

'You have previously admitted sending Steiner one bitcoin. Is that right?'

'Yes. He gave me a bitcoin address and I made the transfer.'

'From your own bitcoin wallet?'

Scanlon was pulling at the skin on back of his hand, his brow furrowed. 'Yes.'

'Is that an online wallet or on your computer?'

'I have both.'

'Which did you make the payment from?'

'My online wallet.'

'And where had the bitcoin come from to make that payment?'

'No comment.'

'My guess is that it came from a tarmac company. The same one that you were going to give the contract to once you'd taken it away from Hardman Tarmacadam.'

'No comment.'

'That's fine.' Dixon curled his lip. 'I can work that one out for myself easily enough. There are only four companies pre-approved to bid.'

Scanlon closed his eyes.

'I'm more interested in the other signatory to your bitcoin wallet.'

Eyes wide open now, Scanlon stared at Dixon, his breathing shallow and speeding up.

'We've got access to Steiner's Bitfly wallet and we can see the last-sent-to address of the single bitcoin sitting in there.'

'No, you can't.'

'It's in the blockchain, Philip.'

Scanlon hesitated. 'What about it?'

'It starts with a "3". It's the address protocol, or so they tell me. Can't pretend to understand it myself. Odd that there are no "sent from" addresses too, so we have to make do with a last-sent-to, and this bitcoin was last sent to you, wasn't it?'

Scanlon leaned across and whispered in his solicitor's ear. She nodded.

'No comment,' he said.

'Last sent to you and your accomplice, A. N. Other. In your multi-signature online wallet starting with a "3".'

'No comment.'

'How about letting me have the login details? There's a twelve word passphrase and then a pin number. Then they text you a verification code. We've got your phones, so that's a start.' Dixon smiled.

'You don't stand a cat's chance in hell of getting in there. Do you have any idea of the level of encryption?' Scanlon smirked. 'Twelve random words from a list of two thousand and forty-eight. In the right order. Dream on. And they'll all still be there when I get out too, because you bastards can't confiscate them.'

Dixon shook his head. 'I've got more chance of cracking your twelve word passphrase, Philip, than you have of ever getting out of prison. And even if you do, bitcoin will probably be worth peanuts by then.' He turned to Scanlon's solicitor. 'Perhaps it's time you two had a conversation about sentencing. And don't forget, your client will be charged with five murders: the three workmen on the platform, Stella and Amy.'

Scanlon was shaking, his fists clenched.

'Is there anything else you'd like to say, Philip, before we wrap this up?' asked Dixon.

'Fuck you.'

Potter had been watching the interview on the monitor in the next room and was waiting for them in the corridor.

'We might as well charge him,' she said. 'You're not going to get any more out of him, are you?'

'It's unlikely,' said Dixon.

'So, what happens now?'

'We do it the hard way. If we can crack the bitcoin wallet, then the other signatory will get a text message alerting him we've logged in. Track that text and we're home and dry. Or, better still, be standing next to the bugger when his phone bleeps. Make a start, Lou, will you. I'll be back later.'

'Where are you going?' snapped Potter.

Dixon looked at his watch. 'The vet.'

'How do I make a start?' mumbled Louise, as the door slammed behind Dixon.

Chapter Twenty-Nine

Barking.

It had been a good sign, thought Dixon, as he carried Monty out to the Land Rover. No sign of Jane and Lucy either, although they had left a note:

Gone to parents. Back later. Let me know what Tabi says :) Jx

He parked in the car park behind the vet's and carried Monty into the crowded waiting room. It never ceased to amaze him how a dog of Monty's size could squeeze under an ordinary chair, his face peering out from behind Dixon's legs. He was shaking too; not even the sight and smell of the cats had distracted him.

'Monty?' Tabi smiled. 'I'm not sure who looks more scared, you or him,' she said, watching Dixon carry Monty into the consulting room and place him on the table.

'I had a shotgun pointed at me a few days ago.' Dixon hooked his fingers in Monty's collar. 'This is worse.'

'Well, it needn't be. I wanted to show you this.' She handed him a sheet of paper and traced the line of the graph with her finger. 'This is his blood urea levels, indicative of kidney function. That's the main risk with antifreeze poisoning. See the levels go up eight hours after he ingested it, just outside the normal range there though, and then they start to come back down. That's yesterday there. Well within the normal range and it'll all be out of his system now.'

'So, he's going to be fine?' mumbled Dixon.

'He's not going to be fine.' Tabi grinned. 'He *is* fine.'

A single tear landed on the piece of paper, smudging the end of the graph. 'I . . . er . . . don't know what . . .'

'Then don't say anything,' interrupted Tabi. 'He may be a bit wobbly for a while. Keep him on bland food and I've given Jane some metronidazole to support his digestion; half a tablet twice a day. All right?'

Dixon nodded, the teardrops landing on Monty this time. 'What about . . . ? Can he . . . ?' Eyes closed, deep breath. 'Go for a walk?'

'Yes, that's fine. Not too far to begin with. He's still recovering and it will have taken a lot out of him. I'd like to see him again in a week, just to see how he's getting on.'

'Thank you.'

'It was Jane who saved his life. And Lucy. I just followed the veterinary manual. They did the rest.'

Dixon lifted Monty off the table and put him on the floor. 'No more carrying you everywhere, you lazy little . . .' His voice tailed off.

'Remember, short walks for a few days. No tennis ball.'

His phone was buzzing in his pocket as he paid the bill, Monty pulling him towards the door.

'Do you want an itemised receipt?' asked the receptionist.

'No, thanks,' replied Dixon, fighting the urge to blink. Just one would send the tears cascading down his cheeks again.

'And another appointment in a week's time. D'you want to make it now?'

'Better had.'

'Morning or afternoon?'

'Either.'

He tucked the appointment card in his pocket and opened the door, his arm nearly ripped from its socket by Monty making his escape. 'And no needles this time,' said Dixon, squatting down and rubbing him behind the ears. 'We live to fight another day, old son.'

'Well?' asked Jane, when Dixon finally answered his phone. 'How is he?'

'He's fine. Thanks to you.'

'What did she say?'

'Kidney function is normal. Short walks for a while. She wants to see him again in a week.'

'So, that's it?'

'It is.'

'Where are you going now?'

'To the beach.' Dixon smiled. 'Where else?'

'It's a beach, but not as we know it,' said Dixon, lifting Monty out of the back door of the Land Rover and clipping on his lead. He had parked at the end of the lane, tight to the hedge, the huge viaduct of the Second Severn Crossing towering over them.

The tide was in, lapping at the lichen covered rubble along the shoreline, two dog walkers in the distance upstream on the concrete path that followed the base of the sea wall; railings along the top and a tarmac road behind it.

Dixon followed the track down to the water's edge underneath the bridge, eerily quiet, despite the traffic above, the only sound the water lapping at the concrete slipway. Above him the viaduct curved away into the distance, the bridge towers in the middle at least a mile away.

'You can have a potter about,' he said, a text message arriving just as he was unclipping Monty's lead.

We're on Berrow Beach. Where are you? Jx

Severn Beach. Sorry! Nx

He didn't have to wait long for Jane's reply.

Doh! :-(

He looked up at the green monorail track on the underside of the viaduct, imagining workmen on suspended platforms either side bolting it in place. Not difficult here, he thought, only fifty feet or so above the ground, but out there in the middle, several hundred feet above the raging River Severn? That must have been a different matter altogether.

The maintenance compound behind the sea wall was all that was left of the original construction site, probably. Vast once, it now covered an area the size of a couple of tennis courts, with two prefabricated units, a container and four vans behind high security fencing. Several stacks of traffic cones too.

Steel steps rose up to platforms either side of the monorail track, a yellow boxcar sitting in the station. It looked more a like a steel container with windows than a train carriage.

'I bet there's no buffet car either,' muttered Dixon.

He followed Monty back up to the concrete track, heading upstream towards the old Severn Bridge, just visible in the distance. Oddly enough he could hear the traffic now and looked back to the viaduct, following several lorries as they crossed into Wales.

Somewhere near where Liam had parked that night in 1995 too. Poor sod. And he had been innocent all along.

A bunch of flowers was fixed to the railings with cable ties. Ages old, by the looks of things, the colour gone, the plastic shredded, most of the petals ripped away by the wind. He reached up and pulled out the card, wedged between the stems. Smudged by the rain, but he could still make out the message. Just.

Liam, still fighting, love you always, Stella xx

He swallowed hard, dropping the card into his pocket and turning into the wind. Still fighting?

You won, Stella.

A twelve word passphrase. He had pretended not to have heard Louise when he left Express Park, but she was right. How on earth do you make a start? 'Aardvark', perhaps? He wondered if that really was the first word in the dictionary.

In the right order too. He remembered Scanlon's sneer. Twelve words from a list of two thousand and forty-eight. What list? It narrowed it down a bit, but . . .

Maybe he'd buy a lottery ticket on the way home? He had more chance of winning that. Although perhaps he had used up his slice of luck lately, he thought, watching Monty sniffing a piece of driftwood.

It was an unusual view of Steep Holm out in the Bristol Channel framed by the huge concrete pillars of the viaduct, so he slid his iPhone out of his pocket and took a photograph of the island, just visible through the haze. And a picture of Monty, which he sent to Jane.

A few more photographs under the viaduct, and some of the monorail. He checked the zoom on his camera. It was impossible to get a sense of the scale of the thing, even with his dog in the foreground.

He began scrolling through the photographs he had taken, deleting two that had come out blurred, and one more of the view towards Avonmouth – hardly picturesque.

That left eight, making a total of five hundred and twelve. He'd have to watch the memory on his phone.

Five hundred and twelve photographs. And most of them of Jane or Monty on a beach somewhere.

He sighed.

For fuck's sake.

An hour later Dixon was running along the landing at Express Park with Monty trotting along behind him. He jerked open a filing cabinet and pulled out the report on Scanlon's personal mobile phone.

'Look at you!'

He spun round to see Louise leaning forward on her swivel chair, both hands rubbing Monty's back.

'You got on all right at the vet then?' she asked.

'He's got the all-clear.' Dixon was flicking through the photographs in the appendices. All of them had been printed off, so he tore them out of the report.

All twelve of them.

'I spoke to Donald Watson about the twelve word passphrase,' said Louise. 'He says it's a mnemonic seed phrase. You're supposed to commit them to memory and the twelve words come from a . . . Hang on.' She glanced down at her notebook. 'BIP39 word list. It's something to do with their conversion to binary code, but it's seriously secure. He said you'll never get in.'

'Have you got the list?'

'I can print it off.'

'Thanks.' Dixon headed for the stairs up to the old Incident Room on the second floor. 'Where are Dave and Mark?' he asked.

'They nipped to the pub, I think.'

'See if they'll come back. Otherwise, it's just you and me.'

Dixon had sellotaped the photographs in a row along the top of the large whiteboard on the wall and was sitting back on a workstation staring at them when Louise arrived at the top of the stairs with a copy of the list.

'I was right,' she said. 'They were in the pub. They'll be here in ten minutes.'

Dixon gestured to the photographs. 'Each one of these is a reminder for Scanlon, a trigger, for the twelve word passphrase.'

'Shit,' muttered Louise. 'They were on his phone.'

'They were.' Dixon reached down and clicked his fingers. Just once was all it took and Monty was sitting on the floor next to him. 'The first thing we've got to do is check that this is the exact order they appeared in the photo album on the phone.'

'Here's the list,' said Louise, handing Dixon a copy. Then she picked up a phone off a vacant workstation. 'I'll ring High Tech.'

'What we don't know is how cryptic he was being,' he said, picking up a marker pen.

The first photograph was a simple picture of a large diamond, so he began flicking through the word list, writing the words 'diamond', 'jewel' and 'panther' underneath it.

'Panther?' asked Louise, frowning.

'Surely you've seen *The Pink Panther*?'

'Yeah, I have. It's the one with Steve—'

'Peter Sellers, Lou. It's the one with Peter Sellers and the Pink Panther was a diamond. Anyway, you see if you can find any others you think might be it and I'll move on to the next one. What did they say about the order?'

'It's correct.'

A picture of a lettuce; and oddly enough 'lettuce' wasn't on the list. 'Diet' was though, and 'salad', so he wrote them on the board underneath the photograph and moved on to the next.

The Incredible Hulk. Dixon hated cryptic crosswords at the best of times.

'Let me have a look, Sir.' Pearce snatched the list from his hand, the waft of beer unmistakable.

Dixon waited, puzzlement etched across his forehead.

'This is fun,' said Pearce. 'Give me the pen.' Then he wrote the word 'banner' underneath the photograph.

'Banner?' demanded Louise.

'Bruce Banner.' Pearce grinned. 'He's the character who becomes the Incredible Hulk when he gets angry. You must've seen the film?'

'No, I haven't.' Dixon stood up. 'Right, that's it. I'm going to drop Monty home and get something to eat. I'll be back later.'

'Even if we get past this, we've still got to find his pin number,' said Pearce.

'Let's hope it's his date of birth,' replied Dixon. 'He used it for his phone passcode. And he clearly thinks the passphrase is uncrackable. Maybe he was more relaxed about the pin number.'

'What do we do if not?'

'Let's worry about that if and when we get there. All right?'

Chapter Thirty

Once through the door of the Red Cow, Dixon dropped Monty's lead and watched the dog make a beeline for their usual table in the corner by the fire.

'A pint for me, please, Rob, and whatever they're having.'

'They've got fish and chips on order too?'

'Yes, please.'

'Nice to see His Lordship out and about.' The barman smiled. 'We had your lot upstairs for three days on the lookout for Steiner.' He looked up as he was pulling Dixon's pint. 'Caught your poisoner instead.'

Dixon fished his wallet out of his back pocket.

'I would have told you, only they said not to,' continued Rob.

'Don't worry about it.'

A drink in each hand and another trapped between his fingertips. 'He's given you a Diet Coke, Lucy. Is that all right?' asked Dixon, placing the drinks on the table.

'Fine, thanks.'

'Is this by way of an apology?' Jane frowned.

'What for?'

'Severn Beach indeed. What the bloody hell's at Severn Beach? We raced back from Worle expecting to find you on Berrow—'

'She's winding you up,' said Lucy, grinning.

Dixon sighed.

'He smiled then,' said Jane, turning to her sister. 'I'm sure he did.'

'I've been smiling since I came out of the vet's, thanks to you,' he said, wrapping his arms around Jane and kissing her. 'And you.' He leaned over and hugged Lucy, sitting in the corner.

Jane looked down at Monty stretched out on the floor in front of the fire. 'Has he had his tablet?'

'And his supper.'

'We just need to find a way of getting rid of that green stain around his muzzle.'

'It'll soon go.'

'Looks like he's thrown up,' muttered Lucy.

'I'll have your mushy peas then?' Dixon laughed.

'Shut up!'

'What's happened to Chard?' asked Jane.

'He's been released pending investigation. Potter said he'll be charged with criminal damage on top of whatever else; perverting the course of justice, probably.'

'He'll go down for that lot.'

'A couple of years, I expect.'

'Tosser,' said Lucy.

'She's a good judge of character, your sister.' Dixon took a swig of beer.

'What did you find at Severn Beach?'

'A cryptic crossword. Twelve photos on his iPhone and a twelve word passphrase to crack his bitcoin wallet.'

'I'm good at crosswords,' said Lucy.

Dixon slid his phone out of his pocket and opened the word list. 'Find a word in that list that matches a picture of the Incredible Hulk then, clever clogs.' He watched her scrolling down through the list. 'That'll keep her busy for a—'

'Banner!'

Dixon rolled his eyes. 'Bruce,' he said.

'Give me another one,' said Lucy.

'There's a picture of a small river with the sun shining through the trees beyond it.'

'Give me a minute.' Lucy grinned. 'Any flowers?'

'No.'

'Not "blossom" then. It could be "meadow".' More scrolling and sighing. '"River" . . . or "tree". Next.'

'Who's having tartare sauce?' asked Rob, standing over them with a plate of fish and chips in each hand.

'Saved by the bell,' muttered Dixon.

It was just before 10 p.m. when Dixon arrived back at Express Park. Louise, Dave and Mark had been joined by DCI Lewis, who was sitting on the corner of a workstation frowning at the whiteboard.

'Ah, there you are,' he said, when Dixon appeared at the top of the stairs.

'How's it going?'

'We've got something credible for most of them. We don't like this one though,' replied Lewis, pointing to the ninth photograph along. 'All we can find is "flight" and it doesn't seem close enough.'

'Why a Spitfire?' asked Pearce, shrugging his shoulders.

'Let me have a look at the list,' said Dixon, sitting down on a swivel chair in front of the whiteboard. He began flicking through the pages.

'It can't really be "airport" either,' said Louise.

Dixon dropped the list on to the workstation behind him. 'Pen,' he said, holding out his hand.

'What is it?' asked Lewis, handing him his marker pen.

'Never in the field of human conflict has so much been owed by so many to so . . .' His voice tailed off as he wrote the word 'FEW' in block capitals underneath the photograph of the Spitfire.

'Few,' said Lewis, through a long sigh.

'For fuck's sake,' muttered Harding.

'You really are a bunch of—'

'It's nice to have you back, Sir.' Pearce grinned.

'Shut up, Mark.'

'Yes, Sir.'

'What do we do now?' asked Louise.

'We try every combination until we get through to the login screen,' replied Dixon.

'I'll leave you to it,' said Lewis. 'I haven't seen my wife for a week. She's probably run off with the milkman.'

Dixon looked along the line of photographs as Louise powered up a computer. Lucy had been spot on, the words 'meadow', 'river' and 'tree' scribbled underneath that photograph.

Several only had one word underneath – the photograph of the 'bullet', for example. And the 'can'. He stared at the photograph of the Second Severn Crossing, the word 'bridge' scribbled underneath. Surely it meant more to Scanlon than that?

'We think that last one's "advance",' said Harding, pointing to a black and white photograph of troops advancing across no man's land.

'It's a still from the original version of *All Quiet on the Western Front*,' said Dixon.

'Bollocks,' muttered Pearce. 'Front's on the list so we'd best add it.'

'Quiet isn't.' Dixon dropped the list on to the vacant chair.

'What do I do then?' asked Louise, gesturing to the screen in front of her.

'Try the top one of each and see what happens.'

'Trouble is, Sir,' said Harding, frowning, 'if it doesn't work, we won't know which answer is wrong, will we?'

'So we keep trying until we get in.'

'We could be here all bloody night!'

Dixon smiled. 'Well?' he asked, turning to Louise.

'Error, invalid passphrase,' she said. 'The words are still there though, so I don't have to retype them every time.'

'I'd stick them on the clipboard, just to be on the safe side,' said Pearce.

'Change "diamond" to "jewel" and see what happens,' said Dixon.

'Same again,' said Louise, glaring at the screen in front of her.

'All right, all right. Let's start with the words we think it's most likely to be and see where that gets us. So, "jewel".'

'Not "diamond"?' asked Pearce.

'Too obvious. Then "diet", "banner", "loan", then—'

'What about "borrow"?'

'It's a "loan shark", Dave. Not a "borrow shark",' said Pearce.

'I just thought it was too obvious, that's all.'

Dixon rolled his eyes. 'What's next: "three", "code", "bullet", "meadow", "few", "can", "bridge" and lastly "advance".'

Louise sighed. 'Error, invalid passphrase. And I'm locked out for an hour now.'

'That'll be done by the IP address,' said Pearce. 'Give High Tech a call and they can assign you a new one.'

'They'll need to keep doing it,' muttered Louise. 'We really are going to be here all night.'

'We need to do this methodically,' said Dixon, sitting down behind a vacant computer and switching it on. 'If we each try different combinations, we should get there in the end.'

By 4 a.m. Dave Harding and Mark Pearce had gone home, leaving Dixon and Louise sitting at workstations covered in plastic coffee cups. Someone had switched off the coffee machine at midnight, but the kettle in the CID Area came to their rescue.

Dixon stacked his coffee cups and dropped them in the recycling bin. 'One of them must be wrong,' he said, turning back to the whiteboard.

'Just one?' asked Louise, stifling a yawn.

'Did you ring your husband?'

'He's fine. He understands.'

'Where's the word list?' asked Dixon, spinning round. He snatched a copy off Louise's workstation and began looking down the words. 'Go through the combinations again, but instead of "bridge" try "accident".'

'OK,' said Louise.

He was flicking through the pages, listening to Louise talking to herself behind him while he scanned down the list: 'now', 'nuclear', 'number', 'nurse', 'nut'.

He froze.

'Stop what you're doing.'

'What is it?' asked Louise, looking up from behind her computer.

'Change "accident" to "nut" and try again.'

'Nut?'

'How was the platform sabotaged?'

'The nuts and bolts were . . .' Louise's voice tailed off.

'You can just imagine the tosser each time he logged in.' Dixon sneered. 'A private joke.'

'It isn't private anymore.'

'No, it bloody well isn't.'

Dixon was standing in the window watching the sun come up when Louise screamed.

'I'm through to the next screen. It says "Enter Your Pin"!'

'What were the words?' he asked, running over to the whiteboard.

Louise waited until Dixon had cleaned it and picked up a pen. 'They're "jewel", "diet", "banner", "borrow", "three", "code", "bullet", "meadow", "few", "can", "nut", "front".'

'That's a good night's work, Lou,' he said. 'You go home, get some sleep. And don't set your alarm.'

A few hours' sleep on the sofa, the sun just coming up as he had closed his eyes. It would have to do.

Now he was standing on platform 1 at Highbridge railway station with Lucy, waiting for the 0912 to Bristol Temple Meads.

'Thank you for helping with Monty.'

'It's fine. I'm just glad he's going to be OK.'

'Me too.'

'I *am* coming to the Lakes with you when you go?'

'Yes, of course. We'll pick you up on the way. All right?'

Lucy smiled. 'Your phone's buzzing.'

An 01823 number. 'Not the bloody hospital again,' he said under his breath, frowning at the screen before holding it to his ear. 'Nick Dixon.'

'Mr Dixon, it's Danielle at the diabetic centre, Musgrove Park Hospital. I rang you a few days ago about your retinopathy results. You were going to ring me back on Monday and never did.'

'Yes, sorry. I'm right in the middle of—'

'I don't want to worry you, but it is very urgent and we need to get you in sooner rather than later.'

Dixon turned away when Lucy crept up behind him. 'Can I call you back?'

'We can do next Friday now, there's an appointment at four o'clock with the ophthalmologist, Mrs Jobson. That's a week tomorrow. Is that any good for you?'

'I haven't got my diary in front of me, I'm afraid.'

'Well, let's put you in for that and you ring me if you can't come. How does that suit?'

'Er,' Dixon sighed, 'fine, I suppose.'

'I'll write to confirm it. Thank you.'

Dixon rang off.

'Who was that?' asked Lucy, frowning.

'Just somebody trying to sell me something.'

'No, it wasn't.'

'Your train's coming,' said Dixon, picking up her bag and trying to change the subject at the same time.

'There's a problem with your eyes, isn't there? What's retinopathy?'

The train stopped and he opened the doors, throwing Lucy's bag into the carriage.

She held the doors open with her hand and leaned out, scowling at him. 'It's serious, isn't it? You're going blind!'

'I am not going blind.'

'If you don't tell her, I will.'

'All right, all right.'

Lucy grinned. 'And for fuck's sake, ask her to marry you.'

Twenty minutes later, Dixon was sitting at a workstation in the CID Area at Express Park, Jane perched on the corner.

'You cracked it then?' she asked.

'Louise did the hard work,' replied Dixon.

'Did Lucy get her train?'

'Yes. I promised her we'd pick her up on the way to the Lakes.'

'You've got to finish this first, haven't you?' Jane was looking at the papers spread out across the workstation in front of Dixon. 'What's all this?'

'The 1995 prosecution file. There's just something bugging me. I can't believe I missed it, to be honest.' He leaned back in his chair and folded his arms. 'Think about it. Four bolts are tampered with and the platform collapses. They're either undone or cut with a hacksaw, I expect we'll never know, but only one is found when the seabed is searched. A nut that's sheared off.'

'You think it was planted?'

'It must have been. The others are probably still down there. And there's no statement anywhere from the diver who found it. Or any photographs.'

'It would've been a police diver, surely?'

'Exactly. I'm guessing his statement wasn't disclosed so it was in the folder that Stella got hold of. Perhaps it exhibited a set of photographs? She must've recognised the name, put two and two together somehow and got killed for her trouble.' Hands behind his head now. 'Whoever it is, there must be a connection with Scanlon.'

'Maybe they're both working at Hinkley?' Jane leaned over and kissed Dixon on the cheek. 'You need a shave,' she said, rubbing his chin.

'Thank you, Sergeant.'

It was moments like this that made it all worthwhile, thought Dixon, as he waited for the barrier to open at the Avon and Somerset Police Headquarters at Portishead. He was watching the officer on duty in the guardhouse, phone to his ear. Then he lifted the barrier and waved the car in front of Dixon through.

That feeling of being on the right track, knowing that it was just a matter of time. Usually he didn't have long enough to savour it. This time was different.

He wondered whether Stella was watching, wherever she was. He hoped so.

'Name?'

'Dixon,' he replied, presenting his warrant card.

'Visiting?'

'The archive.'

'I'll ring them and let them know you're coming.'

'No need,' he replied, smiling.

The guardhouse officer's medals were still jangling as Dixon accelerated under the barrier and followed the service road around to the archive unit in the basement of the admin block.

'You look like shit,' said the clerical officer behind the counter, a pair of reading glasses balanced on top of his head.

Dixon had been warned about the banter. 'It's been a long night,' he said, forcing a smile.

'What can I do you for?'

'Dive team records. I'm told they're here.'

'We've only got pre-2002.'

'1995. There was a search of the seabed under the Second Severn Crossing.'

'What d'you want?'

'Everything you've got.'

'Give me a minute.'

Dixon sat down on a split plastic chair, leaned back against the wall and closed his eyes. But there was no chance of going to sleep. Not now.

He checked his phone. No signal. It was one advantage of working in a basement, perhaps. But then he would miss the sunrise. Maybe Express Park wasn't all bad.

'It's weird,' said the clerical officer, reappearing at the counter, his reading glasses on the end of his nose. 'There's nothing. No statements or photos, so I'm guessing they didn't find anything?'

'Is there a log or anything like that?'

'There'll be the dive team supervisor's logbook, but that's just dates, places and personnel.'

'That'll do,' said Dixon. He could feel a bead of sweat running down the small of his back. His breathing quickening too. Definitely not a hypo. He'd had breakfast in the canteen at Express Park as soon as it opened and done his jab.

'Here it is,' said the officer, placing a large green book on the counter. He opened it to reveal handwritten entries; different pens, different handwriting. 'When was it?'

'May I,' said Dixon, turning the book around and ignoring the frown. At least the officer had realised it wasn't a question.

Dixon began flicking back through the pages, each listing searches here, there and everywhere: Bristol Harbour, the River Avon underneath Clifton Suspension Bridge, Bridgwater Docks, drains under Weston-super-Mare.

Yes, he'd definitely complain a bit less about Express Park in future.

Then came the entry he had been looking for: 23 to 29 March 1995; River Severn beneath SSC viaduct. It even gave the latitude and longitude: 51° 34' 40.3608" N and 2° 42' 55.6884" W. Dixon glanced down the list of personnel taking part. He didn't recognise any of the names.

Except one.

Getting out of Portishead with the original logbook tucked under his arm had been a bit of a struggle. Several forms had had to be signed and the clerical officer had insisted on authorisation from someone higher up the food chain.

DCS Potter had come to Dixon's rescue. After all, she was sitting in meeting room 2 at Express Park waiting for him.

She was still there when he walked past the glass partition an hour later.

'Well?' she shouted through the open door.

Dixon glanced across the atrium to the CID Area, where Louise was sitting behind a computer. He raised his eyebrows and she gave a thumbs-up in reply.

Dixon opened the logbook at the relevant entry and slid it across the table to Potter.

She shook her head. 'How did you—?'

'Excuse me, Ma'am,' said Louise, poking her head around the door.

'Come in.'

'What've you got, Lou?' asked Dixon.

'Ex-Royal Navy. He was one of our dive team officers for five years between 1992 and 1997, then he left to go on the oil rigs. More money, I expect.'

'What d'you want me to do?' asked Potter.

Dixon smiled. 'Nothing, Ma'am.'

'I'd better let David Charlesworth know.'

'Will he tell anyone at EDF?'

Potter frowned. 'We'll tell him afterwards,' she said. 'Just to be on the safe side.'

Chapter Thirty-One

Dixon waited while Louise, Dave and Mark filed through the turnstiles. Their Hinkley Point passes still worked, which was a bonus, but for how much longer?

'Find out where he is, will you, Lou?' he asked, watching through the window as PC Cole and PCSO Sharon Cox signed in at reception. He had bumped into them in the staff car park on the way out of Express Park and brought them along for the ride. And the backup. It seemed fitting somehow that Sharon should be in at the death too, although that was an unfortunate choice of words.

He could think of few people he'd rather have watching his back than PC Cole too.

'He's at the Viewing Gallery,' said Louise, jogging back from the security office with a smirk on her face. 'The Assistant Chief Constable is there too. Routine visit, apparently.'

There were four Assistants, but Dixon knew which one it would be before he asked the question. 'Not—?'

'Yes, Sir.'

Two beat team officers pulled up in a patrol car.

'Where's Martha?' asked Dixon, leaning in the passenger window.

'She's gone to check the bat house, then she's got a meeting in Welfare Block West,' replied the driver. 'We've lined up a minibus to get you out to the Viewing Gallery. We'll be following you, Sir.'

'Thank you.'

The ride out to the Viewing Gallery took ten minutes, mainly due to the queue of lorries at the entrance to the Welfare Block North construction site. A couple of cranes had moved, perhaps, and the last tunnelling machine had gone; it was easy to guess where. Otherwise it was difficult to see much of a difference, but then it had been only two days since his last visit.

At least they were spared the tour guide this time.

Dixon spotted Charlesworth standing at the railings looking out across the site, as the minibus turned into the car park. He was flanked by hi-vis jackets, all three of them wearing white plastic hard hats.

The patrol car parked alongside them, Charlesworth spotting the familiar vehicle markings, and then Dixon as he climbed out of the minibus.

'What the hell's going on?' he snapped, striding towards them, the hi-vis jackets close behind him.

'We're looking for your head of security, Jim Crew,' said Dixon, turning to David Pickles.

'Why?' asked Charlesworth.

'I really don't have time—'

'He had to leave,' said Pickles.

Dixon grimaced. 'When was this?'

'About five minutes ago. He had a call from the security office.'

'On his mobile?'

'Yes. Then he went in the Portakabin,' replied Pickles, gesturing to the unit behind him, the door standing open and blowing in the wind. 'He just said "OK, I'm needed elsewhere", made his apologies and left.'

'Which way did he go?'

'He got in a maintenance van and went that way.' Pickles was waving in the direction of Welfare Block West and the concrete batching plant.

'It's a white Ford Fiesta with an orange light on top,' said a beat team officer. 'I've told them before about leaving the keys in their vans.'

Dixon looked west along the service road, the van sandwiched between two lorries waiting at the traffic lights on the small bridge. He sprinted across to the minibus. 'Follow that van,' he yelled, jumping in the passenger seat. Dave Harding slid open the side door behind him and he and Mark Pearce scrambled in as the minibus driver accelerated away, the patrol car right behind them with Cole and Sharon Cox squeezed in the back.

The van was two hundred yards ahead. It pulled out and raced across the bridge, jumping a red light and sending a lorry swerving into the Armco barrier on the nearside. Workmen in fluorescent overalls working on an aggregate conveyor belt turned at the sound of racing engines as the minibus tore after it along the service road.

A line of lorries was coming towards them, a Land Rover with a blue light flashing and a flag on the roof overtaking them on a head-on collision course with Crew's van, its headlights flashing at him.

'Who the hell is that?' demanded Dixon.

'That'll be Martha,' said the minibus driver.

'What's she playing at?'

'She must be trying to stop him.'

'Playing chicken, more like.'

Dixon watched the van and Land Rover racing towards each other, the Land Rover sounding its horn. At the last second Crew's van veered off the road and down the ramp to the construction site, dirt flying up as it hit the bottom and sped off along the groundworks access road, overtaking a dumper truck heading back towards the excavations at the second nuclear island, its hopper empty.

'Where does he think he's going?' asked Dixon.

The small van was sliding on the dirt track, Crew fighting the steering wheel to control the skid.

'There's no way out,' said the minibus driver.

Martha sped down the ramp, following the van.

'Can you get hold of Martha and tell her to call off her pursuit?'

'No, Sir.'

'Follow them.' Dixon tapped the driver on the shoulder.

'I can't. I'm not allowed down there. We ain't got no flag on the roof.'

'Neither has the van. Just do it.'

Crew, with Martha's Land Rover behind him, sped out of sight around the corner as the minibus accelerated down the ramp.

'I'll get the bloody sack for this,' muttered the driver.

'No, you won't,' said Dixon.

The minibus slowed as it turned the corner, all but the two blue turbine halls of Hinkley Point A on the skyline obscured by a cloud of dust, a blue light flickering in the maelstrom of grit and mud flying through the air. An empty dumper truck was stationary on the nearside, the driver out of his cabin and standing on the platform at the front peering down as the dust began to settle.

The minibus stopped, all of them waiting in silence for the dust to clear.

Martha's Land Rover was first to loom out of the cloud, parked sideways on in front of a heavily laden dumper truck, the orange light still flashing on the roof. The dumper was heading towards the earthworks, a pile of mud visible above the cabin, the driver in his fluorescent jacket leaning over the wheel, his forehead resting on his hands.

'Where's the van?' asked Pearce.

Dixon sighed. 'Under the truck.'

The yellow metal steps at the front of the dumper were visible now, the mangled roof of the white van embedded in them, the orange light still on top. The rest of the van was wedged under the engine compartment of the truck, dwarfed by the huge tyres.

'Call it in, Dave,' said Dixon, jumping out of the minibus.

Martha was standing behind the Land Rover, talking into her mobile phone. 'Yes, and an ambulance. We're down on the earthworks road, not far from the access ramp. We're going to have to close it off, so tell Sam to stop the diggers and hold all the dumpers where they are. Yes. Until I say so.' She rang off.

'Is he dead?' asked Dixon.

Martha grimaced. 'I was on my way over to the bat house when I got the call. I was trying to stop him.'

'And what call did you get?'

'Just that he'd stolen a van.'

Dixon peered in under the offside rear tyre of the dumper truck at the bonnet of the van wedged under the hopper lift. Both front tyres had blown out and there was a small gap between the driver's door and the sump, enough to look in if he tipped his head to one side and used the torch on his phone. There was even a chance Crew might be alive if he'd thrown himself across the passenger seat. Dixon winced.

Perhaps not.

'Is there a chance the casualty is alive?' asked Harding, appearing next to Dixon, still with his phone clamped to his right ear.

'He's been decapitated,' said Dixon, taking a deep breath. 'So, the answer to that one is no.'

'I never stood a chance. He just came belting round the corner and went straight under me.'

'It's all right, Sir.' Dixon looked up at the dumper driver, now standing on the metal landing outside his cab, the blood leaching from his knuckles as he gripped the railings. 'Stay in your cab and we'll get a ladder to get you down. OK?'

'Is he dead?' he asked, looking down at the back of the van.

'I'm afraid he is, Sir.'

'Oh, God.'

'Let's get a ladder down here as quick as we can,' said Dixon.

Martha stepped back, speaking into her radio.

Orange lights flashing now, alternating with the blue, reflecting off the puddle under the van – Dixon hoped it was oil; sirens in the distance too. He turned to see a patrol car pull up next to the minibus, Louise in the passenger seat.

'Is he dead?' she asked, when Dixon walked over and opened the door.

'He is.'

'The call came from the security office.' Louise dropped her phone into her handbag. 'They were just letting him know we were looking for him.'

'Go with Dave, Lou. Search his desk in the security office. And get Scientific to lift his car. Not his house until we get there. All right?'

'Did he have a wife and kids?' she asked.

'He did.' Dixon slammed the car door. He was watching the dumper truck driver climbing down a ladder. The driver tried to look under his truck, but turned away, before the man holding the ladder led him to a pick-up truck and sat him in the back.

'We'll need a statement from him,' said Dixon.

'I'm sure that'll be fine,' replied Martha. 'I know him.'

'We'll need one from you too.'

'It wasn't the truck driver's fault. Like he said, he never stood a chance.'

'How fast was Crew going?'

'At least fifty, and accelerating hard. He was pulling away from me.'

'And why did you pursue?'

'I wasn't pursuing him.' Martha frowned. 'I was just following him. Keeping him in sight; trying to anyway. He braked, though. Hard.'

'Not suicide then,' said Dixon. He was watching a line of blue lights approaching along the service road from the main entrance: two ambulances and three police cars, two of them estates from the traffic division.

'How long is this going to take?' asked Martha, holding her radio to her shoulder.

'The rest of the day, probably,' replied Dixon, 'but you'd better check that with the road accident investigators. They're here now.'

'Do we have any witnesses?' asked a uniformed police sergeant, climbing out of a marked Volvo estate.

'Three,' replied Martha. 'Me, and the dumper truck drivers. He was overtaking one and went under the other.'

'Let's get these vehicles out of the way so we can measure his skid before it rains.'

'How will you get the van out from under it?' asked Dixon.

'Back the truck off, I expect. We may have to let the tyres down on the van.' The police sergeant was peering in under the dumper truck with a torch. 'What happened?'

'He was a murder suspect fleeing arrest.'

'How on earth—?'

'He knew we were coming.'

'Well, he's not going to tell you much now, is he, Sir?' The traffic sergeant shook his head. 'Police Complaints will want to have a look at it too.'

Louise was leaning back against the front wing of Martha's Land Rover, watching the pool of blood under the van getting larger.

'Can you remember the twelve words, Lou?' asked Dixon.

'Etched on my memory,' she replied, shrugging her shoulders.

'And you've got Scanlon's phone with you?'

'Yes, Sir.'

'Log into the bitcoin wallet then. His phone passcode was twenty-five, ten, fifty-six.'

'What's she do—?'

'Logging into the bitcoin wallet,' said Dixon, cutting Mark Pearce off mid-sentence. 'If she gets in, Crew will get an alert via text message.'

'Well, the pin number's not twenty-five, ten.' Louise sighed. 'I'll try ten, fifty-six.'

Dave Harding and Mark Pearce took up position either side of the nearside rear wheel of the dumper truck, Dixon by the offside.

'I've got the verification code and I'm entering it now,' said Louise. 'That's it, I'm in.'

Dixon leaned over, listening for the text message arriving on Crew's phone somewhere in the carnage under the dumper truck.

A muffled 'bleep, bleep' just carried over the sirens wailing in the distance.

'Did you hear that, Sir?' asked Harding, straightening up.

'You might as well go and leave this to us now, Sir,' said the traffic sergeant.

'Not until I've got his mobile phone.'

Chapter Thirty-Two

'The curtain definitely moved,' said Louise, looking up at the first floor window.

Dixon pressed the doorbell again.

The upstairs curtains were drawn behind leaded windows, a magpie picking at the new ridge on the thatched roof.

'It must be rented,' said Dixon, watching a small plume of smoke rising from the chimney. 'Nobody would be daft enough to light a fire in a thatched cottage if they owned it, surely? I wouldn't.'

'You'd be surprised,' said Louise.

'Cottage' was a bit of a stretch too. At least four bedrooms, thought Dixon, counting the dormer windows.

'How much d'you reckon it would cost to re-thatch?' asked Louise.

'More than you and I earn in a year,' replied Dixon, ringing the doorbell again. 'Put together.'

'I can hear footsteps,' whispered Louise, her ear to the front door.

Fully clothed under that dressing gown, and the hair's dry under that towel, thought Dixon when the front door opened. 'Mrs Crew?'

'Yes.'

'Mrs Angela Crew?'

'Yes.' She frowned, the lines on her forehead masked by the layer of make-up.

'May we come in, please?' asked Dixon, handing her his warrant card.

He waited. She could've read the small print as well by the time she handed it back.

'Is he dead?' she asked, oddly matter of fact.

'It would be better to do this inside, if you don't—'

'Is. He. Dead?'

'Yes.'

She retreated into the hall with a loud sigh. 'The kitchen's through here. I was just going to have a coffee.'

A faint smell of alcohol, although it was difficult to tell over the perfume.

'After you,' said Dixon, watching her unwrap the towel and drop it on the bottom of the stairs. She shook her head, but her hair hardly moved; testament to the power of hair spray, probably.

'I'm sorry,' she said, draping the dressing gown over the banister. 'I thought you were bailiffs.'

Dixon wondered in what world two police officers delivering her husband's death message was preferable to bailiffs. No doubt he would find out.

'Was it a car accident?' asked Angela, sliding a wine bottle behind the microwave, the tremble in her voice conspicuous by its absence.

'Is there someone who could come and sit with you, perhaps?' Dixon tried a disarming smile. Not every marriage is a happy one, he knew that well enough, but he would tread carefully – for the time being.

'Round here?' Angela sneered. 'You've got to be kidding.'

'A solicitor then?'

She frowned. 'Why do I need a solicitor?'

'Mrs Crew, your husband was under investigation for murder and—'

'Murder?' Angela was filling the kettle. 'You've got that wrong. He never killed anyone.'

'I should tell you that we have a warrant to search these premises. There are officers outside and . . .'

Louise stepped forward and took the kettle from Angela when it started overflowing. 'Here, let me,' she said, turning off the tap and emptying some of the water down the sink.

The first tear appeared, smudging Angela's mascara. 'How did he die?'

'It was a traffic accident at Hinkley Point. He was in a van that was in a head-on collision with a dumper truck.'

'There's a speed limit, isn't there?'

'He was trying to escape arrest, Mrs Crew.'

She took a deep breath through her nose, exhaling as she slumped on to a kitchen stool. 'I warned him. Time and again. I said you'd catch up with him. Begged him to leave, but he wouldn't.'

'Leave and go where?'

'We have a house on Antigua. Well, I say "we", it's owned by a trust. Our house in Driffield is too.' She closed her eyes. 'That's Driffield near Cirencester.'

I bet it is.

'And this is rented?' asked Dixon.

'He had a relocation allowance.' Angela shrugged her shoulders. 'It pays the rent. Who the bloody hell would want to live in this dump? It's like something out of *The Wicker Man*.'

Dixon slid the search warrant across the kitchen table. 'I'm going to get the team in and start the search now. Is there really no one we can ring for you? What about your children?'

'They've got lives of their own.'

'We'll also need to speak to you, as you might imagine. At the moment you're a witness and not under arrest. I have to warn you that may change though, so you may wish to have a solicitor present. It's entirely a matter for you.'

'Let's just get it over with.'

They sat down in the living room, Angela on the sofa with her back to the door, resisting the temptation to turn round and watch the uniformed officers filing past the door.

'We'll need the keys to your car too, please, Angela.'

'My handbag's on the side in the hall.'

Louise fetched it, waiting while Angela fished out a Jaguar key fob and handed it to her. 'It's on tick. Everything is. That's what the bailiffs are coming for.'

'Can you tell us where your husband was on the evening of Friday, May the first?' asked Dixon, when Louise had sat down, pen at the ready. 'If it helps, it was the Friday of the bank holiday weekend.'

'He went out about ten or so. Didn't say where he was going. I tried ringing him, but he'd left his phone on the hall table. I remember it because we were supposed to be going away the following morning.'

'What time did he get back?'

'No, idea, sorry. I was asleep.'

'All right, let's start at the beginning. When did the two of you meet?' asked Dixon.

'At a friend's wedding in 1991. We got married the following year.'

'So, you were married throughout his time in the Avon and Somerset Police?'

'Yes.'

'And when he worked on the Second Severn Crossing accident?'

'How could you possibly know about that?' Angela was rummaging in her handbag for a packet of cigarettes. 'Yes,' she said, lighting up and blowing the smoke out through her nose.

'What happened?' asked Dixon.

'It was a friend of his, someone he knew from before. They went climbing together. And scuba diving. I really have no idea who. He fiddled with some bolts and the platform collapsed. Three men died, as you know.' She picked up an ashtray off the coffee table and held it in her hand. 'Next thing he's asking Jim to see to it the bolts aren't found. He gave him a rusty one to bring up instead. It was a dangerous job as it was. There were only a couple of hours a day when it was safe to search – you know what the tides are like down there. Anyway, some money changed hands. It was all offshore and he used it to buy the house at Driffield.'

'What's the address?'

'Driffield Lodge. It's on the edge of the park. It's got tenants in it at the moment.'

'And you knew about this?'

'He told me after he left the police. When he bought the Lodge.'

'What about the house in Antigua?'

'We've only had that a year or so. He's been on the fiddle at Hink . . . ley . . .' Her voice tailed off when she stubbed out her cigarette.

Dixon waited.

'Philip got in touch. He said there was billions sloshing about and did Jim want a piece of it,' continued Angela, lighting another. 'That's Philip Scanlon. D'you know him?'

'We've met.'

'He was up to his old tricks at Hinkley and needed Jim's help. Just like the old days, he said. So, he got the job there and I ended up in this godforsaken hole. I blame myself, I suppose.' She was staring into the bottom of the ashtray. 'I've got expensive tastes and he tried to keep up.'

'You knew?'

'Yes, I did.'

'Mrs Crew, we're going to need to finish this at Bridgwater Police Centre.' He stood up. 'I am arresting you on suspicion of money laundering. You do not have to say anything but it may harm your defence if you do not mention when questioned something that you later rely on in court.'

The tears were flowing freely now.

'Anything you do say may be given in evidence.'

Dixon watched Louise lead her out to a waiting patrol car and then turned back to the living room, starting with the photographs on the mantelpiece. None of them were recent, that much was evident from the smiles and the hair colour; at a wedding – not their own; at the races – Dixon recognised Taunton Racecourse; with a horse in the winners' enclosure.

Expensive tastes indeed.

'Is there an office?' he asked, stepping out into the corridor.

'They're using a spare bedroom, Sir,' replied a uniformed officer carrying a computer. 'Upstairs at the back of the house.'

Definitely his rather than hers, thought Dixon, pulling on a pair of latex gloves. He sat down on the office chair, the dust free patch on the desk in front of him evidence of where the computer had been until a few moments ago, the lead from the keyboard trailing on the floor.

Scuba diving pictures on the wall, the water clear blue – the Red Sea, maybe – and an underwater camera sitting on the DVD shelf behind the desk. Dixon glanced along the film collection, a mixture of his and hers – mostly American; there were one or two he might have given houseroom to. At a push.

Somebody liked jigsaw puzzles too. Angela, probably. She was going to have plenty of time for them now.

Dixon flicked open an old briefcase on the floor and began rummaging through the papers: mostly old copies of Crew's CV and copies of letters applying for jobs. He hadn't kept the rejections.

Box files full of old private pension statements. Dixon shook his head. Fifty pounds a month would hardly have covered the weekly fuel bill for the Jag, let alone the lease payments.

The filing cabinet was empty. Either that or an officer had beaten him to it and bagged up the contents. The drawers in the desk had been cleared out too. All except a stapler, a Bluetooth speaker, Sellotape, a pair of headphones, a packet of envelopes and a small rectangular box, blue with a white lid. Dixon was old enough to recognise photographic slides. Just.

He held them up to the light in turn, careful to touch only the white plastic frame. Scuba diving again, this time the water murky green rather than clear blue. Warships on the sea bed, a diver sitting astride a large gun on the deck, the barrel covered in barnacles, seaweed trailing in the current.

'You're wanted back at Express Park, Sir,' said a uniformed officer poking his head around the door. 'Mr Charlesworth is there and—'

'I'm on my way,' he replied, dropping the box of slides into an evidence bag.

'That's it then?' asked Charlesworth, his eyebrows disappearing up under his hat. 'We can close down the Incident Room at Hinkley?'

'Yes, Sir.' Dixon was standing on the steps outside Express Park, with Charlesworth, Potter, Lewis, and the press officer, Vicky Thomas, all staring at him.

Lesson learned. Use the staff car park in future.

'What about Crew's wife?'

'She's been arrested for money laundering and I'll be interviewing her shortly.'

'EDF will be relieved.'

'They shouldn't be,' replied Dixon. 'There's still the tarmac contract and who paid for it to be sabotaged. Others, possibly. We'll see what Crew's wife says.'

'Refer it to the Serious Fraud Office,' said Charlesworth, turning to Deborah Potter. 'They can foot the bloody bill.'

'Yes, Sir.'

'What else, Dixon?'

'Finding Stella.'

'There's no need, surely? Scanlon has confessed and we've got her blood in his car. That's enough for a conviction without the body.'

Deep breath – count to ten.

'If you say so, Sir,' replied Dixon, smiling.

'We certainly shouldn't be committing a lot of resources to it.'

'We're saving money now that we've pulled the surveillance on Steiner's sister.'

'Not nearly enough. What else?'

'That just leaves whoever tampered with the bolts on the platform underneath the Severn Crossing.'

Charlesworth turned to Lewis. 'We haven't got the budget for that, have we?' He frowned at Dixon. 'You're joking? You don't seriously expect to find them after all this time?'

Chapter Thirty-Three

The lift doors opened on the lower ground floor, Dixon and Louise on their way down to the custody suite to interview Angela Crew.

'Oh, shit!' Louise jabbed the button, closing the lift doors.

'What is it, Lou?' asked Dixon, looking up from the papers in his hand.

'Nothing, Sir.'

He leaned forward, forcing open the doors. Then he stepped out into the corridor, directly into the path of DCI Chard and his solicitor, Rebecca Parkman.

'Back so soon,' he said, glaring at Chard.

'Another interview with Professional Standards,' came the mumbled reply.

Louise ran out of the lift and stood in between them, her back to Dixon.

'How is your dog, Inspector?' asked Parkman, her arm across Chard's chest.

'Fine, as it happens.'

Chard sneered. 'He can't be.'

'We went to the beach yesterday.' Dixon's smile morphed into a cold stare. 'We'll be going again tomorrow, Simon. And we'll be going again the day your cell door slams shut. You just remember that.'

'I will.' Chard's eyes narrowed.

'My client would like to make it clear that he regrets—'

'I doubt that very much,' interrupted Dixon.

'My client regrets getting caught,' muttered Louise.

'Will you be seeking a compensation order?' asked Parkman.

Dixon nodded. Slowly. 'The vet's bills are nearly two thousand pounds so far.'

'You won't see a penny,' said Chard.

'I'll let Monty's insurers know, Simon.'

'My wife's divorcing me.'

'I don't blame her,' replied Dixon, pushing past him and striding along the corridor.

A sharp suit. Pinstripe. Reading glasses on the table in front of her; arms folded, notebook closed.

Dixon recognised the signs straightaway before he had even closed the interview room door behind him, and the handwritten statement on the table in front of Angela Crew confirmed it.

'You are still under caution, Angela. Do you understand?' he asked, when Louise flicked on the tape machine.

'My name is Amanda Laycock, Inspector. I am a partner in Tice and Co Solicitors, acting for Mrs Crew.'

'Tice and Co?'

'Cirencester.'

That explained that.

'My client will be reading from a prepared statement.'

Dixon sighed. 'Go ahead, Angela,' he said.

She picked up the piece of paper, a hint of a tremble in her hands. 'My name is Angela Crew. I currently reside at Manor Cottage, Fiddington, and my husband, James Alexander Crew, otherwise known as Jim, was the head of security at the Hinkley Point C construction site. I have been advised that my husband is dead.'

She must have read the lesson in church as a child, or something, thought Dixon. Either that or she was involved in amateur dramatics and it was all just an act. A convincing one, all the same.

'I make this statement setting out the extent of my knowledge of my husband's affairs, but wish to make it clear at the outset that it was an abusive relationship. I was not at any time a willing participant in my husband's criminality and was subjected to prolonged coercion and control throughout our marriage. The abuse, lasting many years, was physical, sexual and emotional and my solicitors hold a file detailing two attempts to divorce, both withdrawn by me due to very genuine fears for my personal safety. There will also be records at the hospital in Cirencester of three visits made by me for physical injuries arising from assaults by my husband, although I did not give the real cause of the injuries when asked. My doctor can also confirm a prescription of anti-depressant medication and the reasons for it.'

'What about the local police, Angela?' asked Dixon.

She looked at her solicitor, who nodded.

'I called them twice. Once about three years ago. The time before that was millennium night. He got drunk at a party and said I'd been talking to another man. It wasn't a happy new year.'

'And the police attended?'

'Yes.' Angela frowned. 'Shall I continue with my statement?'

'Go ahead,' replied Laycock.

'I first became aware of my husband's involvement in criminal—'

'I'm sorry to interrupt,' said Dixon. 'I would just like to ask a couple of questions about what you've already told us, Angela. Is that all right?' he asked, turning to her solicitor. 'Purely about the domestic abuse.'

'It's up to you,' said Laycock, smiling at Angela.

Angela nodded.

'How far did you get with the divorce proceedings?' Dixon leaned forward, his elbows on the table in front of him.

'You can see the file, if you like. They can see the file, can't they, Amanda?'

'If you consent.'

'Then I consent.' Angela took a deep breath. 'The first time it was just the first letter from Tice and Co. He went berserk, saying it'd all come out.'

'What would?'

'Where the money had come from. He was terrified. Threw me down a set of stone steps and cracked my head open. There's still a scar under there somewhere.' Angela ran her fingers through her hair. 'I told the hospital a ladder fell on me in the orchard.'

'What about the second time?'

'He was served with a petition that time, but then he found me at my sister's house. That'll be the hospital in Brighton. My sister saw what happened too, so she can confirm everything.'

'Have you spoken to specialist domestic abuse officers?' Dixon smiled. 'They can help with counselling and—'

'It's fine.' Angela shook her head. 'Now.'

Today was a day of lessons, thought Dixon. Use the staff entrance, for one. And you're not *always* right about people. Most of the time, possibly; just not always.

'Shall I carry on with my statement?'

'Yes, please do, Angela.'

'I first became aware of my husband's involvement in criminal activity in 1998 when he bought Driffield Lodge. We had been living in rented accommodation up to that point. He told me the money was offshore and the property would be owned by a trust, but we could live in it rent free. When I asked him where it came from, he got aggressive.

All he would say was that he helped get a friend out of trouble when he was a police diver, switching some bolts during a search under the Second Severn Crossing. Then a few years later—'

'Sorry, can I just ask about this friend?'

'It was someone he knew before we got married,' replied Angela. 'He never said a name. A young lad he used to go climbing and scuba diving with, I think.'

'What sort of climbing?'

'They went to the Alps a few times, I think. He showed me some old photos once. Slides. He always used to take slides.'

'What about Philip Scanlon?' asked Dixon.

'I'm coming to that.'

'Carry on with your statement,' said Laycock.

'Where was I?' Angela's eyes scanned down the page. 'A few years later, here we are. He got a new Range Rover. Then a share in a race-horse. Every time I asked him where the money had come from, he got aggressive, and sometimes violent. So, I stopped asking and started spending. Shopping became a sort of refuge. It was during this period that I met Philip Scanlon. He was "the money" and I got the impression that Jim was doing work for him, but I am not sure what type of work it was or how he got paid. I had learned the hard way not to ask. Then he got the job at Hinkley Point.'

'When was that?' asked Dixon.

'Three years ago, maybe.' Angela turned back to her written statement, her brow furrowed, the make-up long gone. 'Jim did say once it was easy money to begin with, taking bribes to place contracts. Then when all contracts had been awarded, it got more difficult. They had to become more inventive, he said. I don't know what he meant by that.'

'OK, Angela, I'm going to stop you there,' said Dixon. 'Your late husband's involvement in contracts at HPC will be the subject of an investigation by the Serious Fraud Office and no doubt they will wish to speak to you about what you know. As far as I am concerned, your involvement is limited to that of a witness. I am now terminating this interview and you're free to go.'

Louise switched off the tape.

'I would still like to see your medical records,' said Dixon. 'And the divorce file you mentioned.'

'Fine with me,' replied Angela.

'You'll remain an important witness too, so do let us know where you're—'

'I'll be at my sister's in Brighton.'

'You're releasing my client without charge?' asked Laycock, frowning. 'Surely that's a decision for a senior officer?'

'Only if I ask them.'

Jane had been fast asleep on the sofa when Dixon arrived home, not even the ping of the microwave waking her up. Monty hadn't barked when he'd heard the diesel engine either, which was odd, but he'd jumped off the sofa quick enough when he smelled the masala sauce.

'Not a chance, matey,' Dixon had said, stirring it with a spoon. 'Fish and veg for you, just like the vet said.'

He sat down on the edge of the sofa just as the streetlights went off, plunging the cottage into darkness, eating his Slimming World curry by the light of his phone.

'What time is it?' asked Jane, yawning.

'Half past midnight.'

'Where've you been?'

'Going through the statements again. And Crew's photos.'

'Look, unless Scanlon tells you where she is, the chances of finding her are virtually nil. We'll probably get a call in a year or so from a dog walker who's stumbled on her in a ditch somewhere.'

'Unless they buried her,' mumbled Dixon, through a mouthful of curry.

'That's worse, not better.'

'There's still whoever tampered with the bolts on the platform.'

'After all this time? You've got to be kidding.'

'Has Monty been out?' asked Dixon. He got up and wandered into the kitchen, flicking the living room light on.

'No.'

He dropped his plastic curry tray into the sink, the fork clattering on the plates piled up in the washing up bowl. 'I'm going to take him down the lane. Won't be long.'

Odd that Crew had been a climber, thought Dixon, following Monty along the narrow lane towards Brent Knoll, the moonlight just enough to avoid the potholes. He'd spent several hours flicking through the slides retrieved from Manor Cottage, scuba diving ones mixed in with the climbing.

Either Crew had been using old equipment or his ice axe dated it by twenty years or so. He'd have been about thirty then. All except one of the photographs was of him too, so he and his mystery partner must have used the same system as Dixon and Jake: take photos of each other and then swap.

It probably worked the same with scuba divers too, although Dixon hadn't really been able to identify Crew in the photographs, let alone anyone else, behind the masks and breathing apparatus.

There was one climbing photograph that wasn't Crew though – that much was clear from the clothes and the build – but whoever it was had left their balaclava on for the summit pose. It couldn't have been deliberate. Not back then, surely?

The reality was that Jane was right. He had Stella's body to find and no idea where to start looking. And a killer answering 'no comment' to every question he was asked, his accomplice dead.

And what about Angela? She was as much a victim as Stella and Amy. Well, maybe not quite as much, perhaps. He wouldn't make the same mistake again though. Not that anyone had known, mind you.

'Have you had enough already, old son?' asked Dixon, looking down at Monty. The dog had stopped in a field gateway and was staring up at him, panting.

Shame, that. Dixon had been avoiding sleep whenever possible, the vision of Steiner's head . . .

Enough of that. Shit happens.

Ten minutes later he crawled into bed and put his arm around Jane.

'Are you awake?' he whispered.

'No.'

'Let's go back to the Lakes next week. I've got a tent somewhere if we can't find a cottage.'

'I'll find a cottage, don't worry.' Jane yawned. 'Now get some sleep.'

Dixon had missed three calls from Louise by the time he parked on the top floor of the staff car park at Express Park the following morning. She must have been watching from the windows in the CID Area too, because she was holding the staff door open in one hand, her phone in the other.

'What is it?' he asked.

'Scientific have got Crew's DNA in Scanlon's car,' she replied, smiling. 'A hair on the passenger headrest.'

'An accessory before or after the fact. It hardly matters now. What's Dave come up with on the cameras?'

'Nothing.' She let the door slam behind Dixon. 'Wherever they took her, they stayed off main roads and the motorway.'

'What about Mark?'

'He was waiting to hear from Vodafone but he was grinning like a Cheshire cat when I saw him in the canteen.'

'When was that?'

'Twenty minutes ago.'

They were walking along the landing when Pearce leaned over the balustrade from the floor above. 'Up here, Sir, if you've got a minute.'

He was standing back admiring a large map stuck to the whiteboard when Dixon and Louise reached the top of the stairs. Dave Harding was sitting on a swivel chair, his eyes closed.

'Nothing on the cameras, Sir,' said Dave, sitting up.

'What've you got, Mark?'

'Mobile phone masts, Sir.' Pearce puffed out his chest. 'Stella was last seen leaving Portishead just after 5.20 p.m. on the Friday. We've got nothing on the cameras and Scanlon's mobile phone is pinging the masts in Clevedon all night, telling us he's at home.'

'Not necessarily. He may just have left his phone at home. And he had two anyway.'

'Exactly.' Pearce grinned. 'It's his work phone. Either he forgot it was in the car or maybe he didn't think we'd check it. Either way, it pops up in Kilve in the early hours of Saturday.'

'Kilve?'

'There's a weak signal from the EE mast at Hinkley Point. That's what put me on to it. Weak on the Vodafone mast at Nether Stowey and then Orange on the A39 west of East Quantoxhead. That makes an almost perfect triangle.'

Pearce was pointing at the map, but Dixon wasn't watching.

'A perfect triangle with Kilve right in the middle. And that mast is giving a strong signal.'

'What about Crew's phone?' asked Louise.

'That's hitting the Nether Stowey and Cannington masts, so it looks like Crew's at home in Fiddington. His phone is anyway – Scanlon left his personal mobile at home, so he probably told Crew to do the same. Or vice versa.'

'Angela said he went out and left his phone on the hall table.' Dixon walked over to the map on the wall and stood in front of it, his arms folded.

'Here, Sir,' said Pearce, marking out the triangle with the tip of his pen.

It didn't happen often, that feeling when it all drops into place – like a line of dominos going over, or admiring the last piece of a huge jigsaw puzzle. 'We'll need a full search team and Scientific Services.' Dixon allowed himself a sly smile as he turned back towards the stairs. 'I want the ground penetrating radar too.'

Chapter Thirty-Four

Twenty-four acres, not including the Great Plantation. It would take the ground penetrating radar most of the day just to cover the open fields. And woods were always slower due to false readings from tree roots. Let's hope they buried her in the open, thought Dixon, watching the operator pushing the radar along a line marked out with string, the small wheels bouncing over the clumps of grass. It looked more like he was painting the boundary on a cricket pitch.

'Don't forget under the solar panels,' Dixon had said, leaving them to it.

And that was always assuming they hadn't fed Stella to the pigs.

The piggery was on the eastern side of Kilverton House, the prevailing wind taking the smell away from the property more often than not. Dixon wiped the raindrops from the end of his nose as he watched two Scientific Services officers wearing white overalls and masks collecting samples from the feeding trough. That would be the easy bit. Collecting and testing the dung would be an entirely different matter.

A vet had arrived to shut the pigs in. 'Grim business,' he muttered.

'How long would it take them to . . . ?' Dixon's voice tailed off.

'A couple of days. Lactating sows have a big appetite and there are four of them.'

'And what's going to be left?'

'Hair, teeth. Bone fragments, I expect. If they had any sense they'll have cut her up before—'

'I get it.' Dixon rolled his eyes.

'The teeth will be the best bet for DNA,' said the vet. 'Less chance of the stomach acid getting at the pulp.'

The solid oak front door of Kilverton House had been opened with battering rams; it had taken two, and the door frame would be expensive to repair, the original cast iron lock buckled. The burglar alarm had gone off too, confirming that Hugh Manners and his family really were out.

Shame.

'The Great Plantation's clear, Sir,' said PC Cole, appearing by Dixon standing in the porch. 'The protestors have all gone.'

'Let's get the Suffolk lot to check the camp at Sizewell. We still need Fly as a witness.'

'Yes, Sir.'

Then Louise appeared in the hall, holding her mobile to her shoulder. 'They've picked him up at Heathrow, Sir,' she said, smiling. 'He was in the Plaza lounge at Terminal 4 with his wife and kids, waiting for a plane to Houston. He said he was going to visit her parents.'

'I bet he did.'

'They're bringing him down now.'

The fireplace in the living room was large enough to stand in, the mantelpiece covered in highly polished silver frames; the photographs of children, mainly.

'It's Lewis.' Dixon was frowning at his phone. 'Yes, Sir,' he said, looking up at the ornate carved wooden ceiling.

'I've had Charlesworth on the phone again.'

'One day he's going to piss off and let me get on with my job.'

'I'll ignore that.'

'Yes, Sir.'

'You do know Hugh Manners is a baronet?'

'Does that make a difference?' Dixon sighed. 'He's a suspect in a murder investigation.'

'You've arrested a peer of the realm.'

'A baronet is not a peer, Sir.'

'Don't split hairs with me.'

'No, Sir.'

'Look, Charlesworth bends my ear and I bend yours. That's the way it works. I just hope to God you know what you're doing.'

'She's here, Sir.'

'Well, you'd better find her then.'

Lewis rang off, leaving Dixon admiring the oil paintings on the wall, his phone still to his right ear. Gilt frames with small brass name-plates on each identifying the subject of the portrait, all of them bearing the name 'Manners', the oldest – John Manners, 1st Bt. – dated 1531 to 1587.

'He's a baronet?' asked Louise.

'Apparently so,' replied Dixon, sliding a copy of *Burke's Peerage* off a bookshelf. He tipped his head. 'Look, the twit's marked his own entry with a yellow sticky. He's the twelfth baronet, which makes that one his father,' he said, pointing to a painting in between the front windows.

'It's like something out of the National Trust,' said Louise.

'It'll probably end up *in* the National Trust if he goes down.'

'I wonder if you can have the title withdrawn?'

'No idea,' replied Dixon, staring at the Manners family coat of arms on the wall above the door: a red shield with a crown above and a large snarling dog either side rearing up at it.

'It's another world, isn't it?'

'They're human beings, Lou, just like you and me. I'm more interested in what he's done than who he is.'

'With Stella, you mean?'

Four floors, twelve bedrooms, an annexe; it was going to take some searching. Then there were the outbuildings, stables and the barn. Dixon glanced out of the window just in time to see a Range Rover Evoque being loaded on to a flatbed lorry.

'His Discovery was in the short stay car park at Terminal 4,' said Louise.

'Were their tickets single or return?'

'I'll find out.'

Dave Harding poked his head around the door. 'They think there are secret passages upstairs, Sir,' he said, 'but we can't find the door.'

'There may be some plans somewhere. Where's his office?'

'We haven't found it yet, Sir.'

'Let's get a surveyor out here then,' said Dixon. 'Before anyone starts knocking down walls.'

'Shall I ask DCI Lewis to authorise the fee?'

'No.'

'The radar's done the back field and they've found nothing,' continued Harding. 'They're going to do the walled garden next.'

'Tell them to do the fields at the front next, Dave. No one's going to bury a body under their own vegetable patch unless they absolutely have to, are they?'

'It's enough to put you off your asparagus,' muttered Pearce, his voice carrying from the corridor.

'Wouldn't it be fun if these bookshelves hid a door.' Louise was smiling as she tugged at each in turn.

'You've been watching too much telly,' said Dixon, stepping back out into the hall.

'The office is in the corner of the library, Sir.' PC Cole was standing at the bottom of the stairs, gesturing to the door opposite. 'In the far corner. The door looks like bookshelves but it isn't.'

'Any plans?'

'No.'

The books were painted on the door, so it was just for effect. Dixon puffed out his cheeks. The shelves were full height, perhaps fifteen feet from floor to ceiling, with a ladder on wheels. He ducked under it and stepped into the office.

Another fireplace, modern shelving this time, two filing cabinets, computers, and a single photograph on the wall, blown up and mounted in a thin chrome frame. A dark picture with a burst of sunlight reflecting off rippled snowfields – a mountainside definitely, tiny figures on a ridge in the foreground, well above the photographer. The sun low in the sky. Dawn, maybe? Were the climbers going up or down?

The photograph might have been blown up from a slide, possibly. It was tenuous at best. The real search was taking place outside. Without Stella he had nothing and he knew it.

'Look for photographs,' Dixon said, still staring at the photograph on the wall when a Scientific Services officer walked in. 'Climbing or scuba diving. Anything with other people in.'

Jim Crew, preferably.

'Yes, Sir.'

Dixon tore off his latex gloves as he walked out through the kitchen and into the rain, heading for the outbuildings. A double garage on the right, the doors open, a climbing rope and an old style harness hanging on a hook just inside the door.

'They've got something in the field behind the pig pen,' said Louise, running around the corner of the house. 'This way, Sir.'

He followed her around the front of the house, across the gravel drive and along the track towards a group of officers staring at the ground in front of them. They were in the corner of the field, screened from the house by the piggery and a line of trees along the boundary of a tennis court.

'What is it?' asked Dixon, climbing over the fence.

'Here,' said the radar operator, rain dripping off his wide-brimmed hat. He was pointing at a black and white screen. 'The waves penetrate the ground and bounce back. You see them as horizontal lines on the screen. Anything down there creates a wave in the returning signal. 'See, these are pipes, a small one and a bigger one there. This wave here. It's much bigger. That's something else.'

'What?'

'It could be a body. It's consistent with what we've seen before, but we won't know for sure until we dig it up.'

'How deep is it?'

'Three feet or so. The ground's wet, and it's clay soil, so the waves can't penetrate much deeper than that anyway.'

Dixon sat in the driver's seat of his Land Rover and watched the Scientific Services officers setting up a large tent over the scene of the dig, the radar operator continuing his search of the rest of the field, the radar in one hand and an umbrella in the other.

The search of the piggery had been abandoned in favour of the dig, the officers taking advantage of some respite from the smell. And if the signal in the ground proved to be Stella, then further examination of the piggery would be a waste of time anyway. It made sense.

Dixon recognised the Volvo estate parking behind his Land Rover and watched in his rear view mirror as Roger Poland got out, waving at him when he spotted him watching. Dixon leaned over and opened the passenger door.

'How's it going?' asked Poland, climbing in the passenger seat.

'They've got a signal. They're just starting to dig now.'

'I had a call to say there might be a body.' Poland opened his bag and took out a Thermos flask, handing Dixon a steaming cup of coffee. 'Here,' he said, 'this'll warm you up. I bet you haven't eaten either, have you?'

'No.'

'It'll have to be chocolate. Will a Kit Kat do?'

'Thanks.'

'What happens if it's not the victim?' asked Poland.

'We keep looking. There's still fifteen acres to search and the pig shit to—'

'He'd have had to chop her up for that.'

'So I'm told.'

Poland smirked. 'You do know he's a baronet?'

'I'm sure there's a reason people keep mentioning that, but I can't think what it might be.'

'I'll shut up,' said Poland, smiling.

Donald Watson had arrived to take control of the dig and it wasn't long before he was poking his head around the side of the tent and waving at Dixon.

'You're not going to like it,' he said, shaking his head.

'What is it?'

'See for yourself.'

Dixon looked into the bottom of the shallow grave. And it was a grave. Just not Stella's.

'Fuck it,' he muttered. 'Is the vet still here?'

'My guess is it's swine flu,' said Watson, the light from the arc lamps reflecting off the pale skin of a dead pig, the earth brushed back to reveal its front legs and head. 'Either that or foot and mouth. Months ago too.' He pinched his nose. 'Not weeks.'

'Are you a vet as well?' asked Dixon.

'It'll be something notifiable to the Min of Ag, that's why he buried her.'

'Her?'

'It's definitely female.' Watson shrugged his shoulders. 'You could nick him for that, at least. It's illegal to bury dead farm animals.'

'I had bacon for breakfast.' Poland was rubbing his stomach.

'We'll fill the hole in and finish on the piggery,' said Watson. 'If we get the samples off to the lab tonight, you should get the results in the morning.'

'Thanks.'

Dixon stepped back out into the rain and watched the radar operator walking along the far hedge line.

'What if she's not here?' asked Poland.

'Then I haven't got a leg to stand on and Charlesworth will have a field day. Everything else is circumstantial.'

'And you're sure she's here?'

Dixon nodded.

'Well, as far as I'm concerned, if you say she's here, then she's here. You're never wrong.' Poland turned up the collar on his coat. 'And I should know.'

'She's here,' said Dixon. 'Somewhere. Just waiting for us to find her.'

Chapter Thirty-Five

'Hugh—'

'Inspector, my client is the 12th Baronet Kilverton and if you are intent on putting him through this farce, at least have the decency to address him correctly.'

Dixon had been warned. Three piece grey pinstripe suit, gold pocket watch, thinning grey hair swept back. And a real knighthood of his own. It wasn't often the senior partner of a law firm turned out for a police interview, let alone came all the way down from London for one. But Sir Malcolm Guttridge QC had. A Queen's Counsel too; unusual that, for a solicitor.

Charlesworth had been climbing the walls; still no body, the evidence circumstantial at best and Guttridge's threats of suing Avon and Somerset Police for wrongful arrest ringing in his ears. Dixon resisted the temptation to look up at the camera on the wall just under the ceiling, but he could feel Charlesworth's eyes fixed on him, burning through the lens. Potter's too. They were watching on the monitor in the adjacent room.

'My apologies. Sir Hugh.'

Manners was leaning back in his chair, arms folded. There was a word for the look on his face, but Dixon couldn't quite find it. Bored, possibly. Condescending, certainly. Supercilious even. Like he had a bad smell under his nose.

Dixon could sympathise with that. He still hadn't shifted the smell of rotting pig.

'You are still under caution.'

Guttridge coughed. 'I have explained that to my client.'

'I'm sure you have, Sir,' said Dixon, matter of fact. 'But you will appreciate that I also have to explain it to him for the tape.'

'Proceed,' snapped Guttridge.

'Is this going to take long?' asked Manners, looking at his watch. 'There's another flight just before midnight.'

'You left university in 1994, Sir Hugh. Is that right?' asked Dixon.

'Dropped out, as you well know.' He folded his arms. 'There seemed little point at the time. My father was ill and I'd be taking over running Kilverton when he died. I hardly needed a degree for that.'

'What were you studying?'

'Archaeology.'

'And your father died in 1997?'

'That's right. September 1997.'

'What did you do for those three years?'

'Travelled, mainly. I did a bit of scuba diving here and overseas. Worked my way across America. A lot of it was cash in hand.'

'Window cleaning?'

Manners frowned. 'Yes, some.'

'A lot of climbers used to do that, I gather,' said Dixon. 'Abseiling in.'

'I didn't climb.'

'Really? You've still got your old harness and rope in the garage. Use that for cutting the leylandii, I suppose? You'd need a head for heights to do that.'

'I've never had a problem with heights, but that doesn't make me a climber.'

'Tell me about the photograph on the wall in your office.'

'I was given it.'

'Who by?'

'I don't remember. It's a print anyway, I think.'

'Were you there when it was taken?'

'Where is this going, Inspector?' asked Guttridge.

'It looks like the summit ridge of Mont Blanc to me.'

'I've got no idea where it was taken,' said Manners, looking away.

'Move on, Inspector,' demanded Guttridge.

'Did you do any work for Crook Engineering, Sir Hugh?' he asked.

'I don't remember. The work was piecemeal, a bit here and a bit there, wherever and whenever I could get it. Summer months usually, then I'd bugger off abroad for the winter.'

'What about Centrix Platforms?'

'No.'

'Do you recall working on the Second Severn Crossing?'

'I have advised my client not to answer any questions concerning the Second Severn Crossing.' Guttridge was peering over a pair of reading glasses that were perched on the end of his nose. 'If you have any evidence he was there and working on the project, I suggest you put it to him. Otherwise, kindly move on.'

'You see, I don't believe you intended to kill anyone, Sir Hugh,' continued Dixon. 'The platform was just supposed to collapse and the workers would be fine, swinging about on their safety harnesses. Or maybe it was supposed to be empty? That's what Philip Scanlon said.'

Guttridge sighed. He leaned across and whispered in Manners's ear.

'No comment.'

Sort of inevitable, thought Dixon. 'But you tampered with the wrong bolts and the safety rail failed.'

'No comment.'

'Three men died.'

Manners was looking around the room, his eyes settling first on the door, then his fingernails; his hands flat on the table. To stop them shaking, no doubt.

'A simple accident would have been enough for Crook Engineering to have lost the contract,' continued Dixon. 'Wouldn't it?'

'No comment.' Face flushed now.

'How much did they pay you?'

'Enough, Inspector,' snapped Guttridge. 'If you have evidence, please put it to my client. If not, please move on.'

'You flew to Thailand the day after the accident,' said Dixon. 'Why?'

'No comment.'

'Do you have evidence of that?' asked Guttridge.

'The passenger manifest from British Airways flight BA215, departing London Heathrow for Bangkok.'

Guttridge looked at Manners and nodded.

'It was a holiday,' said Manners. 'Scuba diving.'

Time to make him sweat a little. 'Does the name James Crew mean anything to you?'

'No comment.'

'He was on the dive team that recovered the single rusting nut from underneath the Second Severn Crossing. Friend of yours, was he?'

'No comment.'

Dixon was sure he could see beads of sweat.

'Climbing partner, perhaps? Maybe he took that photograph on the wall in your office?'

'No comment.'

'We know he took this one. It was in his slide collection,' said Dixon, handing a copy of the picture of the unknown climber to Manners. 'Is that you?'

'No.'

'What about Philip Scanlon then? When did you meet him?'

'Who is this Scanlon?' Guttridge was peering over his reading glasses.

'He was the money,' replied Dixon, turning to Manners.

'No comment.'

Dixon slid the photograph of a scuba diver sitting astride a gun on the deck of a sunken warship across the table, both Manners and Guttridge leaning forward to examine it.

'That's the 88mm gun on the deck of the SMS *Cöln*. It was scuttled in Scapa Flow,' said Manners. 'I've dived it several times.'

'So has Mr Crew,' replied Dixon. 'We found a similar photograph—'

'That's hardly surprising if he was a scuba diver, Inspector,' interrupted Guttridge. 'You really are going to have to do better than that.'

'Everyone diving Scapa Flow goes down there,' said Manners, shrugging his shoulders. 'It's the most intact of the wrecks.'

Dixon took a deep breath, the vision of Charlesworth sharpening a knife flashing across his mind. 'You said you didn't know Steiner was hiding in the Great Plantation. Why?'

Manners hesitated, thrown momentarily by Dixon's sudden change of tack. 'Because I didn't.'

'But you told Scanlon he was there?'

'I'm assuming you have evidence of that,' demanded Guttridge.

'I don't know this Scanlon person,' mumbled Manners. 'Or Jim Crew. And I told you, I didn't know Steiner was in the Great Plantation.'

'How else did he know Steiner was there then, I wonder?' asked Dixon.

'You need to ask him that,' said Guttridge.

'Unless he saw him when they came to Kilverton House to dispose of Stella Hayward's body?'

'Who came to Kilverton House?' asked Guttridge, snatching his reading glasses off the end of his nose.

'Scanlon and Crew,' replied Dixon. 'Returning the favour, was it? Crew had got you out of trouble at the SSC and now it was your turn to return the compliment.'

'No comment.'

'I'm assuming you have found Mrs Hayward's body, Inspector,' said Guttridge, his voice loaded with sarcasm.

'We have several digs at Kilverton House ongoing, Mr Guttridge. Thus far we have found a dead pig.'

Manners bowed his head. 'Esmeralda,' he said. 'Cressida was heart-broken when Esme died.'

'My client will admit a single offence contrary to the Animal By-Products Regulations,' said Guttridge. 'Sir Hugh accepts that he should not have buried her in the field. But that is hardly an arrestable offence, so unless you have anything else, I imagine you'll be releasing him?'

'Sir Hugh, there's a son – not much older than you were in 1995 – who's lost his father, sister and mother thanks to you. Now, I say again, I do not believe that you intended for those men to die on that platform, nor for Liam Crook to take his own life, but the least you can do is let that boy bury his mother.'

Dixon was sure he saw a single tear. A blink and it was gone. 'No comment.'

Fuck it.

Guttridge slid the lid on to his fountain pen. 'When will you be releasing my client?'

'The search is ongoing, Sir. There is also DNA testing of various samples taken from the piggery—'

'You're not seriously suggesting my client fed her body to his pigs?'

'I don't know whether he did, or whether he didn't, Sir,' replied Dixon. 'But he will remain here, in custody, until the search is complete and we get the DNA results.'

'And when is that likely to be?'

'Tomorrow morning.'

'That went well.' Charlesworth was sitting on the edge of the table in the adjacent room, his arms folded.

Potter leaned forward and switched off the monitor.

'Guttridge is right, Dixon,' continued Charlesworth. 'You've arrested a baronet without a shred of bloody evidence.' He shook his head. 'We're going to be sued for wrongful arrest. I know we are.'

'They'd need to prove that no reasonable officer would have made an arrest in the same situation, Sir.'

'I know the law.'

'It was also *necessary* to make the arrest because he presented an immediate flight risk.'

'He was at the airport, I know that.'

'Have you got anybody who can place him at the Second Severn Crossing?' asked Potter.

'Not yet, Ma'am. Dave and Mark are working on it now.'

'And you've got no evidence he contacted, or even knew, Crew or Scanlon?'

'We're waiting for the phone records, but he knew James Crew was known as "Jim".'

'I imagine Guttridge would tell you that was a slip of the tongue,' said Potter.

'He even denied being a bloody climber, didn't he.' Charlesworth shook his head. 'So, apart from a few scuba diving photographs – that could have been taken years apart anyway – you've got no connection with Crew whatsoever.'

Dixon forced a smile. 'Look at the transcript of my conversation with Steiner on the crane again, Sir. He was quite specific in the words he used: "Scanlon came looking for me," he said.'

'Anybody could have told him that though, Nick,' said Potter. 'One of the protestors, Lady Manners even.'

'You've well and truly dropped the ball, Dixon,' snarled Charlesworth. 'People keep telling me you're the best we've got. If that's right, then God help us.'

'Let's see what we can find overnight,' said Potter. 'There are still two digs ongoing. We'll have the DNA results then too, and we can review it properly.'

'Yes, Ma'am,' said Dixon, opening the door.

'You'd better hope you find some—'

Dixon slammed the door, cutting Charlesworth off mid-sentence. *Dickhead.*

The dig in the walled garden had finished by the time Dixon arrived back at Kilverton House, the tent gone, a gap in the lines of asparagus apparent from the turned over soil. And the hole.

'It's a kiddie's time capsule,' muttered Donald Watson, standing next to Dixon. Both of them were staring at a pipe, sealed at one end, the other broken open to reveal various documents and photographs sealed in plastic envelopes. 'Copies of birth certificates and stuff like that. Recent too.'

'What about the other one?'

'It's over near the wood.'

'The Great Plantation?'

'It's a bit deeper. Out through that door and it's on the other side of the leylandii. Don't hold your breath though.'

It was more of a gazebo with side walls than a tent, bright arc lamps inside; shadows moving – digging – the earth piling up either side of the hole.

'You still here, Roger?' asked Dixon, when Poland emerged from the tent.

'I'd got the afternoon off anyway,' he replied.

'Where's the radar?'

'On the other side of the wood now. He's done pretty much everything else.'

'What's this then?' Dixon was standing on tiptoe, trying to look over Poland's shoulder.

'A dog.' Poland shrugged his shoulders. 'There's a line of them. Labradors mostly, I think, although this one's bigger, possibly a Newfoundland, according to the vet. He's gone now though. When they cut back the vegetation you can see little gravestones for each of them.'

Dixon gritted his teeth.

'They're digging them up anyway, just in case,' continued Poland. 'Charlesworth giving you a hard time?'

'You could say that.'

'Do you want me to ring him? I could remind him what you did for—'

'Forget it. He took great delight in telling me I'd got no real evidence. And I haven't. Tenuous connections and a leap of faith.'

'Maybe you should try the wizard again?' asked Poland, his eyebrows raised.

'Him?' Dixon turned away. 'I need more than a dope smoking clairvoyant this time.'

'You're still convinced she's here?'

'I am.'

'If you have to release him, then he'll either flee or come here and move the body, then flee.'

'I know, Roger,' said Dixon, kicking the wet seeds off a dandelion stalk – some floated away on the breeze, the rest splattered across the toe of his shoe. 'And we'll have let her down again.'

Chapter Thirty-Six

It was just after midnight when Dixon slid his feet in either side of Monty, curled up on the end of the bed. Jane rolled over and put her arm across his chest. Her eyes opened, although not quite enough to part her tangled eyelashes.

'Any luck?' she mumbled.

'No.' Dixon was lying on his back, staring at the ceiling. 'No one can place him at the Severn Crossing. Revenue and Customs have got nothing because it was all cash in hand. Nothing on the phones and we can't find a thing at Kilverton. They probably just turned up with Stella's body in the boot and told him he owed them a favour.'

Jane raised herself up on one elbow. 'Have you considered the possibility he's got nothing to do with it?'

'No. And besides, it's more about finding Stella now anyway. Manners I can worry about later. He denied being a climber and yet he's got a rope and an old harness he uses to cut his own trees. I spent an hour scrolling through the climbing logbook online to see if he'd ever done any new routes.' He curled his lip. 'Nothing.'

'They get to name it?'

'Always. That's the convention. You climb a new route, you get to name it.'

'Have you done any?'

'Jake did a few at Pembroke and Cheddar before he was killed.'

'He was hardly going to do them after, was he?' Jane smiled.

'I suppose not.'

'Maybe Manners used a different name back then, so people wouldn't know who he was?' Jane frowned. 'If he was bumming around, doing cash in hand jobs, he wouldn't want people to know he was a baronet.'

'He didn't inherit the title until his father died.'

'Well, there's a first time for everything,' said Jane, kissing him on the shoulder.

'A first time for what?'

'Being wrong.'

'You know just what to say.' Dixon flicked on the bedside light. 'I haven't done my bloody jab,' he muttered. 'Sorry.'

Jane pulled the duvet up over her head.

'Anyway, I'm not wrong,' continued Dixon, pushing the needle into his bicep.

'He may have fed her to the pigs.'

'He hasn't got the stomach for that. He's way out of his depth. And I'd like to have interviewed him without Guttridge there. There was the odd flicker in amongst the no comments.' Dixon flinched when he pulled out the needle. 'He knows I know what happened.'

'He also knows you'll never prove any of it without Stella's body.'

'He was just a lad, earning a bit of cash to pay for his climbing and scuba diving.' He dropped his insulin pen into the drawer of his bedside table. 'And three men died because he undid the wrong bolts.' Dixon slumped back on to his pillow. 'Is my insulin still in the fridge at your parents'?'

Jane sighed. 'Forgot it, sorry.'

'I'll have to get it tomorrow. I need a new night cartridge.'

'You'd better put your prescription in too.'

'Yes, doctor.'

'What happened after the platform collapsed then?' asked Jane.

'He gets his old diving partner to bail him out and switch the bolts on the seabed.' He turned off the light. 'Once they were found, the investigation focused on Liam, with Manners safely out of the way in Thailand.'

'And your evidence?'

Dixon closed his eyes. 'I can place Scanlon's work mobile in Kilve the night we think Stella went missing. And then there's Scanlon looking for Steiner in the Great Plantation. How did he know he was there, I wonder? The connection with Crew—'

'What connection?'

'They were old climbing and scuba diving partners.'

Jane rolled over. 'So, basically, what you're telling me is you haven't got any evidence.'

'I suppose I am.'

'That's never stopped you before,' replied Jane, yawning.

Rod answered the door in his dressing gown the following morning, watching Jane run past him and into the kitchen, her shout of 'Nick's insulin' just carrying over the rumble of the diesel engine.

Dixon was parked on the pavement. He wound down the window and shouted over to Rod. 'We didn't get you up, did we?'

'No.'

'What's all that?' he asked, gesturing to a large pile of mud in the front garden.

'Water leak.' Rod shrugged his shoulders. 'And because it's on our property the bloody water board won't pay.'

'Have you found it?'

'Not yet. I've got a horrible feeling it's under the path.'

'Thanks, Dad,' said Jane, kissing Rod on the cheek as she ran past clutching a box of insulin cartridges in her hand. 'See you tomorrow.'

'What's tomorrow?' Dixon was watching her climb in the passenger seat.

'Mum's doing a Sunday roast, pork, if you can . . .' Her voice tailed off. 'Your phone's buzzing.'

Dixon frowned at the screen. 'It's Louise.'

'You'd better answer it.'

'What is it, Lou?' He switched the engine off.

'It's not good, Sir,' she replied. 'The DNA results are negative. Potter's here and she's going to release Manners. Guttridge is here too. Stayed in a hotel last night, apparently.'

Dixon closed his eyes.

'She was asking me what time you're due in. Charlesworth's on his way down too.'

'What did you say?'

'I said I didn't know.'

'Thanks.'

Dixon rang off and slid his phone back into his pocket.

'The DNA results?' asked Jane.

'Negative.'

'What happens now?'

Dixon glanced back down at the pile of mud in the front garden. He took a deep breath through his nose. 'What are you doing today?'

'It's Saturday, so Tesco's, probably,' replied Jane.

'Want to help me find Stella instead?'

Dixon spotted Charlesworth and Potter watching from the huge floor to ceiling windows on the first floor of the Police Centre at Express Park when Jane turned into the visitors' car park. Roger Poland was already there, leaning on the bonnet of his Volvo estate. He was talking to Dave and Mark. Louise was sitting in the driver's seat of her car talking on her mobile phone. Parked behind her was a patrol car with PC Cole, Sharon Cox and another PCSO Dixon didn't recognise.

'Who are we waiting for?' he asked, sliding out of the passenger seat of his Land Rover. He resisted the temptation to wave at Charlesworth and Potter.

'Donald Watson's on his way,' replied Louise. 'Said he'd be here in ten minutes.'

'Tell him to meet us there.'

He glanced back up at the windows above, where Lewis had now joined Charlesworth and Potter. Charlesworth was waving his arms, Lewis shaking his head; Potter's arms were folded. He could imagine the discussion taking place: Charlesworth wanting whatever it was he was up to stopped; Lewis telling him to let Dixon play it out; Potter sitting on the fence.

Then Charlesworth pointed at Jane sitting in the Land Rover. 'And what the hell's she doing here?' Dixon sighed. You didn't need to be a lip reader to understand that one.

'Are you sure you don't want me to speak to him?' asked Poland, looking up.

'If I'm right, I won't need it, Roger. If I'm wrong, it won't help.'

Dixon slid Stella's card out of his coat pocket; her message smudged, but every bit as powerful as the day she had fixed the flowers to the railings under the Second Severn Crossing.

Still fighting . . .

'Let's go before Charlesworth comes down,' he said.

Donald Watson was waiting for them in a lay-by on the A39 and pulled out behind the line of vehicles, two other Scientific Services officers sitting with him in the front of the van. Three should be enough, thought Dixon, as they turned into Kilve.

'This is nice,' said Jane, as they drove down through the village.

No smoke coming from the Great Plantation this time, but then the protestors had moved on.

'The entrance is on the left,' said Dixon when he noticed the brick wall on the nearside. The lane opened out on a bend beyond the field, the wall on the left curving away to ornate steel gates that were standing open, the pillars of red brick each with a stone orb on top.

'Bit posh, isn't it,' muttered Jane.

'Must've got a taxi home,' said Dixon, when Jane parked outside Kilverton House, the front door of the house swinging open before she had switched the engine off.

Manners was pacing up and down in the porch with his solicitor, Guttridge, who was dialling a number on his mobile phone.

Dixon waited until the line of police vehicles had parked behind his Land Rover and then climbed out of the passenger seat.

'What the bloody hell is going on, Inspector?' shouted Guttridge, sliding his phone back into his pocket as he strode across the gravel turning area in front of Kilverton House.

'Where are your wife and children?' asked Dixon, turning to Manners.

'Staying with friends.' Manners stepped back behind Guttridge. 'They'll be back later today. We've got no cars, in case you hadn't noticed.'

'My client has been released. So, unless you have another search warrant—?'

Dixon looked at Louise and raised his eyebrows. She stepped forward.

'Sir Hugh Manners, I am arresting you on suspicion of assisting an offender.' Her voice was loud and slow, but Dixon wasn't listening, instead watching Manners. And the blood drain from his face.

Manners turned to stare at Dixon when Louise's lips stopped moving.

'You still have not got a single piece of evidence. Your search found nothing,' said Guttridge, breaking the silence Dixon had left hanging.

'Wait here,' he said, striding off in the direction of the barn, painfully aware of the umpteen pairs of eyes watching him, the only sound the crunching of the gravel beneath his feet. Looking like an idiot he could live with; Manners getting away with it would be tough; not finding Stella? That was the stuff of sleepless nights.

Dixon stood in the doorway of the barn, looking up at the climbing harness hanging on a nail. An old chest harness, simple faded red and yellow nylon webbing, with no padding on the belt. It was the type climbers used forty or fifty years ago, maybe, and the type companies still gave out as safety equipment to staff. Uncomfortable, but cheap.

He unhooked it and looked at the label. Nothing.

Then the webbing belt. A single word written on the inside in black marker pen; faded, but still visible. Just.

CENTRIX

Manners was whispering in Guttridge's ear, his back to Dixon as he walked over from the barn.

'Bag it up,' he said, handing the harness to Louise in front of Kilverton House.

'My client believes he may have done some work for Centrix in the past,' said Guttridge. 'That still doesn't prove anything.'

Dixon took a deep breath, then turned to the Scientific Services officers waiting by their van. 'Dig up the pig. Then keep digging.'

Manners spun round, his eyes wide.

'She's buried under Esmeralda. Isn't she, *Sir* Hugh?'

Chapter Thirty-Seven

The hole was deep. Deeper than Dixon had expected. Moving Esmeralda had not been easy either, the job finally done by his Land Rover, two planks and a rope tied to his tow bar.

Now he was standing in the wet grass with Jane, his feet soaked through, watching Donald Watson kneeling in Esmeralda's grave, scraping the foul smelling earth away with a hand trowel.

Was it Stella's grave too?

They'd find out soon enough.

'My feet are soaking wet,' whispered Jane.

'Mine too.'

Manners was standing by the pig pen, flanked by PC Cole and PCSO Sharon Cox, his hands cuffed behind him. Guttridge was pacing up and down, talking into his mobile phone.

'Charlesworth's here,' said Poland, glancing over Dixon's shoulder at the sound of wheels crunching the gravel in front of Kilverton House. 'The harness should be enough to keep him happy, surely?'

'She's here, Roger,' replied Dixon.

'We've got something,' said Watson, his arm outstretched. 'It's a rug. Let me have a brush, someone.'

'Is it her?' asked Charlesworth, looking down into the hole with his hands on his hips.

'There's a body,' continued Watson. 'We'd better have the tent and lamps.'

'You were right.' Manners sighed. 'They wanted me to feed her to the pigs, but I—'

'I'll call you back.' Guttridge spun round, hastily disconnecting his call. 'You don't have to say anything, Hugh.'

'Yes, I do. I should've said something long before now.'

Dixon glanced at Louise, but she already had her notebook out, ready to go.

'I couldn't do it,' continued Manners, his head bowed, the long hair almost hiding his face. 'So, I buried her under Esmeralda.' He took a deep breath through his nose. 'You were right about the Severn Crossing too.' Looking at Dixon now. 'I was working at Centrix at the time and Ray Harper told me to get a job on the bridge with Crook Engineering. He told me which bolts to undo. I was in Thailand when I found out men had been killed. That I'd—' He slumped back against the wall of the pig pen.

'Just to be clear, it was an accident,' said Guttridge. 'My client did not intend—'

'I put Harper in touch with Jim and he got me off the hook,' continued Manners, stepping forward and looking down into the grave. 'I never saw either of them again after that. I tried to forget about it and move on but *she* made that impossible.'

Guttridge cleared his throat. 'You've said enough, Hugh.'

'She got hold of a photo album.'

'What—?'

Dixon raised his hand, silencing Charlesworth.

'Jim found it in the daughter's room at Hinkley and burned it. They were pictures of the search for the bolts under the viaduct. He'd taken them and they had his name on the label.' Manners shook his head. 'It meant Stella made the connection between Jim and Philip Scanlon; they were both involved in the Severn Crossing thing and now here they were, together again at Hinkley Point. Scanlon had no choice, he said. He had to kill her.'

'My client was not involved in the murder of Stella Hayward. I just want to make that absolutely—'

Manners dropped to his knees in the wet grass. 'They just turned up with the body and wanted me to . . .' His voice tailed off.

Dixon waited.

'I'd never even met Scanlon before,' continued Manners, tears trickling down his cheeks just visible through the straggly hair. 'The next thing I know, they've found Stella's daughter working in Hinkley and they needed to get rid of her too. So, I told them about Steiner in the Great Plantation.'

'Right, that's enough,' said Guttridge.

Dixon stood over Manners, the significance of what he had just said not lost on him either. 'Hugh Manners, I am arresting you on suspicion of conspiracy to murder Amy Crook. You do not have to say anything but it may harm your defence if you do not mention when questioned something you later rely on in court.'

Cole and Sharon Cox dragged Manners to his feet.

'Anything you do say may be given in evidence,' continued Dixon. 'Did you get all of that?' he asked, turning to Louise.

She grinned, snapping her notebook shut.

'Get him out of here then, before his family turns up.'

'It seems you were right all along, Dixon,' muttered Charlesworth.

'Yes, Sir.' He was watching Manners being led through the long, wet grass towards the patrol car.

'Well done.'

'Thank you, Sir.'

'The CPS may want to charge him with murder.' Charlesworth turned back to his car. 'But we'll see what it looks like after you've interviewed him.'

Jane took Dixon's hand and squeezed it. 'It's over.'

'I'd like to have met her,' he said, staring down into the grave. 'She was a fighter and she never gave up.'

'A bit like someone else I know.'

Stella's face had been revealed now that Watson had pulled back the rug and scraped away the mud. Her eyes were open, rolled back into their sockets; her hair thick with mud and congealed blood; her right hand visible, the skin yellow and black, the fist clenched.

Defiant to the last.

Chapter Thirty-Eight

It had been Jane's idea to park on the beach. Another few weeks and the council would be closing the gate and charging six quid for the privilege, so why not make the most of it while we can, she had said.

It was a special moment too, thought Dixon, opening the back of the Land Rover and watching Monty tear off after his tennis ball, kicking up the wet sand behind him. A few short days ago his dog had been at death's door and now here he was, running along the beach. Thanks to Jane.

'Tabi said no tennis ball.' She scowled.

'Just a couple of goes.'

The tide was going out, leaving behind it lines of seaweed and foam. Above that, dry sand was being whipped along at ankle height by the wind.

'Which way?' asked Jane, watching the sandstorm at her feet.

Dixon slid his hand into his coat pocket. It was still there, the small black velvet jewellery box. And now was as good a time as any, surely? Before he found himself going blind.

Yes, he would tell her. And give her the chance to walk away.

'Let's go that way,' he said, nodding towards Burnham and a huge tree stump that had been washed up on the tide months before. They would sit on that for a few minutes – they always did – and that would be his chance.

'Your folks didn't mind me skipping lunch, did they?' Dixon kicked Monty's ball along the beach. 'I just didn't fancy roast pork, somehow.'

'They were fine,' replied Jane. She sat down on the tree stump, right on cue. Not that she was a creature of habit, or anything. Apart from the mild obsessive compulsive disorder, of course, but Dixon had learned to live with that.

'Have you dropped something?' she asked, frowning at him.

He smiled. 'Try to think of another reason why I might be down on one knee.'

'Oh, shit!'

'Not quite the reaction I was hoping for.'

Jane tipped her head. 'Did you have something you wanted to ask me?'

'I've been carrying this around for weeks,' he said, taking the jewellery box out of his pocket.

'Weeks?'

'Just waiting for the right moment.'

'And this is the right moment?'

'On a deserted beach, with *our* dog.' Dixon opened the box. 'It's perfect.' He took her hand and looked into her eyes – just a moment's hesitation: 'Jane, will you marry me?'

She leaned forward and kissed him on the lips. 'Yes,' she whispered. 'Of course I'll marry you.'

They kissed, ignoring the raindrops that were running down their noses.

'Now what's he doing?' Jane looked down at Monty digging right next to her, slowly covering her shoes with clumps of sand. 'Why doesn't he just pick the ball out of the hole?' She laughed. 'Stupid dog.'

Both front paws scrabbling for all they were worth, sand spraying out behind him; it was usually his ball, sometimes a stick. Sometimes nothing at all. Dixon smiled to himself as he watched Jane laughing at Monty.

All was well with the world.

Almost.

Then he slid the ring on to her finger.

'It's beautiful,' she mumbled, waggling the fingers on her left hand, watching the diamond glinting through the raindrops.

Dixon reached behind her head, pulled up the hood on her coat and kissed her again, the rain heavier now, if anything.

'Your phone's buzzing.' Jane sighed. 'I can feel it in your coat pocket.'

'That's my heart fluttering.'

'You're taking the piss now, aren't you?'

Author's Note

A great many people have offered their assistance with *Beyond the Point* and it would be wrong not to acknowledge that while I have the chance, particularly when I have been almost entirely dependent on others for much of my research.

Firstly, I should like to express my sincere thanks to my friend and former professional colleague, Tony Steiner, for lending his name to my arch-villain. For the record, Tony is not a serial killer (just in case there should be any doubt about that!).

I should also like to thank EDF Energy Plc for their kind permission to feature Hinkley Point C and for granting me access to the site. It was a leap of faith on their part, for which I am most grateful.

And to David Hall and Clare Paul, without whom this novel would not have been written. Their invaluable assistance at every stage of development has been pure gold, not only in arranging a guided tour of HPC, but also for sharing their local knowledge and then acting as unpaid editors.

My sincere thanks must also go to my wife, Shelley, and my unpaid editor-in-chief, Rod Glanville, for reading the first draft on an almost daily basis over a long and hot summer.

To my professional editors at Thomas & Mercer: Laura Deacon, Hatty Stiles and, as ever, Katie Green (who interrupted her maternity leave especially for me). Thank you.

And last, but most certainly not least, I should like to thank you, the reader. I do hope you enjoyed reading *Beyond the Point* as much as I enjoyed writing it!

Damien Boyd
Devon, UK
December 2018

About the Author

Damien Boyd is a solicitor by training and draws on his extensive experience of criminal law, along with a spell in the Crown Prosecution Service, to write fast-paced crime thrillers featuring Detective Inspector Nick Dixon.

Printed in Great Britain
by Amazon